P

'Obedience is of par

she stood before me

not tolerate objections, protests or any hesitation when I tell you what to do. You will comply instantly with my commands, no matter what they are.'

Slippng my blouse over my shoulders, she unhooked my bra, exposing my naked breasts to the men. 'Remove your skirt and panties.'

Tugging my skirt down, I slipped my thumbs between my panties and my hips, watching the men as their eyes widened with expectation. My embarrassment rising, my fear soaring, I stepped out of my skirt and pulled my panties down . . . there was no escape.

Also by Ray Gordon in New English Library

Arousal
House of Lust
The Uninhibited
Submission!
Haunting Lust
Depravicus
The Splits
The Degenerates
Enslaved
Girl School
Sextro
Sex Practice
Hot Sheets
Addicted
Red Hot
Doctor Sex
Naked Lies

Sextortion

Ray Gordon

nel

NEW ENGLISH LIBRARY
Hodder & Stoughton

First published in Great Britain in 1999
by Hodder and Stoughton
A division of Hodder Headline
First published in paperback in 1999
by Hodder and Stoughton

A New English Library Paperback

10 9 8 7 6 5 4 3

A CIP catalogue record for this title
is available from the British Library.

ISBN 0 340 74815 X

Typeset by Hewer Text Ltd, Edinburgh
Printed and bound by
Mackays of Chatham plc, Chatham, Kent

Hodder and Stoughton
A division of Hodder Headline
338 Euston Road
London NW1 3BH

Chapter One

There are two sides to every coin. Good and bad, love and hate – sex with love, sex with lust. Money can incite generosity or greed; success, praise or jealousy.

It was only when I'd found success that I discovered the world to be full of greed and jealousy. I'd set my sights on my goal and worked hard to achieve it. But the covetousness of others loomed in the sky like a dark cloud rolling in over the sea, ultimately and inevitably engulfing me.

Looking back over the few short weeks of my nemesis, I see myself. My naked body sprawled over the dining room table, my hands and wrists tied with rope, my thighs spread to the extreme, my sexual centre is obscenely bared. As burning sensations permeate my buttocks from the merciless thrashing wreaked upon me, I feel the wet female tongue exploring between my sex lips, snaking around the silken entrance to my sacrosanct vagina, teasing my clitoris.

Steel rings are clamped tightly around my ballooning breasts, studded leather straps biting into my thighs. I wince as my abuser plunges her potent fingers into my sperm-drenched, fleshy cavern, stretching the satiny walls of my sex canal, massaging deep inside my vagina before sucking my clitoris into her hot mouth.

Humiliation and degradation besiege me as my naked audience look eagerly on. I am, therefore I think. What further horrendously perverted acts will I be forced to endure before the night of debasement is out? Whatever follows, I can sink no deeper into the viscous pool of depravity! Dragged across the perilous threshold of debauched sex, there is no longer a woman in me. My femininity has been pillaged, robbed, as my naked body has been used to satisfy the shameful cravings of my mistress.

An ardent finger searches the valley between my tensed buttocks, seeking entrance to my private duct. As I whimper and beg for my freedom, I try to block out the repugnant reality by squeezing my eyes shut. But the poacher finds my secret rosebud, penetrates me, delves deep into my private hole as I am forced to suck on an erect penis.

The stark reality of my plight grips me as the penis swells and twitches, its salty sperm suddenly flooding my mouth, bathing my tongue. I cough and splutter as the man drives his huge glans to the back of my throat. Gulping hard as two hot mouths close over my sore nipples and a second digit enters my anal canal, I pray for the degradation to end.

Gushing sperm fills my cheeks. How much more can I endure – the ruthless whippings, the crude sex? But I know there is no escape, that I'll be forced into obscene sexual acts again and again. My body, my temple, is nothing more than an object to gratify the carnal desires of my perverted abusers. I am their slave, I belong to them, I am theirs to do with as they wish, when they wish.

I wonder now whether I could have avoided the horrors, the degrading sexual abuse. I wonder now if I would have chosen to avoid them. For hasn't the coin always two sides? Love and hate, good and bad, repugnance . . . and desire! If I'd known then what I know now . . . But I was naive, trusting, innocent, oblivious to the wicked plans that had been drawn against me. I'd been led unsuspectingly down a blind alley to a world of debasement, a domain where evil reigned – beckoned.

* * *

My journey down the road to defilement had begun after enjoying lunch with my editor. Discussing the huge success of my first novel, I had felt elated, heady more with excitement than with the flow of sparkling wine. With a second blockbuster in the offing, my future looked brighter than ever. It seemed that I couldn't put a foot wrong.

I drifted home from the metropolis on my euphoria, desperately excited, to tell my husband the wonderful news. Bursting through the front door, I found *he* had some news for *me*. My gaze locked to his pallid countenance, I couldn't believe that my world had been turned upside down and inside out. His lips were moving, his dark eyes transfixed on mine, but the sinister words barely registered in my swirling mind. I felt dizzy, confused, as if caught in the ethereal web of a dream.

'Blackmail?' I finally gasped, disbelievingly. 'Danny, that's ridiculous!'

'Ridiculous or not, it's true,' he sighed, his expression tormented.

'You *are* joking, aren't you?'

Wringing my hands as I waited in anticipation for him to laugh and tell me that he was having me on, I watched him mooch across the lounge and gaze out of the window. His expression pained, his forehead lined, he looked tired and drawn, mentally anguished.

My mind was a whirlpool of devastation as I recalled leaving for London that morning. I had been bubbling with excitement and enthusiasm, and Danny had told me how proud he was of me. But now? A million thoughts raced through my head, hurting me. I couldn't think straight, my mind blurring as he finally turned to face me.

'Selina, I'd hardly joke about a thing like this,' he scolded me with a severity I'd not known before.

'A girl turned up on the doorstep and demanded money for keeping quiet?' I asked incredulously, shaking my head.

'Yes.'

'Keeping quiet about what?'

'She knows about the insurance fiddle.'

I stared at him, wondering what on earth he was talking about. Insurance fiddle? Blackmail? He was more than partial to a few glasses of scotch and, for a moment, I thought he'd been drinking. But no, he hadn't been on the alcohol. His expression couldn't have been more sober!

'*What* insurance fiddle?' I asked pathetically.

'The kitchen ceiling, remember?'

'The kitchen— That was years ago, Danny! Besides, it was only a few hundred pounds.'

'It was almost a grand.'

'Whatever it was . . . How does this girl know about it?'

'It doesn't matter how. The point is, she knows.'

Now he came to mention it, I remembered the scam only too well. Desperate for pennies at the time, inventing an insurance claim had helped us through our impoverishment. Danny'd been a struggling writer, a failed writer, while I worked part-time at the library for a meagre wage. Only too well aware that it was wrong, illegal, I'd filled in and dispatched the claim form. Although perfectly feasible that a burst pipe in the bathroom could have flooded the kitchen ceiling, I'd been riddled with guilt, my heart missing a beat every time the front doorbell rang. Thankfully, the man from the Pru hadn't appeared in person to check the non-existent damage and a cheque for nine hundred-odd pounds had duly arrived, saving us from financial disaster. We'd thought that was that.

'There's no way she could know about it,' I reasoned, trying to understand what was happening. 'Unless she works for the insurance company and . . .'

'I'm sure she doesn't work for them,' he murmured.

'You should have told her where to go, Danny! Anyway, making a false insurance claim is hardly blackmail material! Had you told her in no uncertain terms . . .'

'Initially, I did tell her where to go. But then she . . .' He winced and bit his lip. 'Selina, there's more.'

'More?'

'She also knows about the affair you had with Barry.'

My thoughts drifting back eight years, surfacing from the recesses of my racked mind, I wondered how Barry could have led me down the garden path as he had. He'd stolen my love and my virginity, promised me the stars . . . before I'd discovered he was married with three children. I'd been rocked by devastation, shaken to the very core by his fantastic web of lies. But what had Barry got to do with this strange girl?

'Danny, that was before I met *you*!' I exclaimed, confusion spreading through my mind like toadstool spores.

'Selina, you were screwing a man who was married with three kids! You're a celebrity now, in the public eye. If the tabloids get hold of this, what the hell's going to happen to your squeaky-clean image?'

'I didn't know he was married!' I countered. 'The minute I found out, I ditched him.'

'You know that and I know that, but the media . . .'

'This is a dream, Danny – tell me it's a dream.'

'It's a nightmare, Selina.'

It *was* a nightmare, and I longed to wake up and find myself in bed with the morning sun streaming through the window, its warmth bathing my body. But only cold darkness engulfed me. Blackmail? Who was the girl? How did she know so much about me? My mind was a lake with a thousand questions riding on ripples of confusion.

'How much money?' I asked resignedly.

'Five grand.'

'*What?* No, I'm not going to . . .'

'Selina, we have no choice. You've been portrayed as Miss Perfect, happily married, squeaky-clean . . . Can you imagine the headlines? Miss Goody-two-shoes screws insurance company.'

'No one's going to bother about that!' I returned angrily. 'It's hardly a juicy story! Good God, thousands of people must have fiddled their . . .'

'Top author in sex romps with married man.'

I knew he was right. Once the tabloids had got their sharpened teeth into me, they wouldn't let go. They'd find Barry, talk to his wife, his children would discover their father's dark secret and . . . Squeaky-clean image? That's how the media had portrayed me. Radiant housewife and part-time librarian shoots to overnight stardom. TV chat shows had embraced me, expounding on my first novel, my love of cooking, gardening, homemaking . . . Lovemaking with married men wouldn't exactly fit the image!

Trying to compose myself, I walked to the kitchen and filled the kettle. I didn't want tea or coffee but I had to do something, occupy myself, hold my head above the turbulent waters threatening to suck me under. Danny followed me and leaned against the worktop, torment mirrored in his deep-set eyes. This was what success had brought me. Fame, fortune – and blackmail!

'Where are we supposed to leave the money?' I asked nonchalantly, as if suddenly resigned to the fact that I had to pay up.

'She's calling tomorrow,' he sighed.

'She's coming *here* to collect the money?'

'Yes.'

'Then let's call the police.'

'Selina, we can't involve the law.'

'Why not? Good God, there's a girl coming here, blackmailing me, demanding money and . . .'

'If we call the police, she'll be arrested.'

'Exactly!'

'And she'll sell her story.'

Nonchalance succumbing to fear, I couldn't believe that someone could glibly come to my house and demand thousands of pounds – and there was nothing at all I could do about it. It was like having a thief enter my home and steal my treasured belongings from under my nose. The situation was incredible, like something out of a horror movie. I couldn't just hand over five thousand pounds to a stranger! Besides, she'd be back for more and . . .

'Follow her and find out where she lives,' I proffered, pouring two cups of coffee.

'D'you think I hadn't thought of that?' Danny snapped. 'While I was waiting for you to come home I did nothing other than think of all the bloody possibilities! There's no way out of it, we have to pay her.'

'What time is she coming?'

'Three o'clock.'

'I'll be at the TV studio.'

'Yes, I know. Look, get the money first thing in the morning. I'll make it clear that it's a one-off payment, threaten her and . . . Oh, I don't know. All we can do is hope that she grabs the money and runs.'

I tried to convince myself that she *would* grab the money and run. She'd be taking quite a risk by coming back for more and I could only pray that we'd never see the treacherous tart again once we'd paid her off. It was a glimmer of hope glowing in the gloom, I knew. But it was all the hope I had, and I wasn't going to let it go.

Walking into the garden, I breathed in the heady fragrance of the night-scented stock, the freshly mown grass. The evening sun warming me, I wandered across the lawn and sat on the bench beneath the beech tree, trying to fathom what had happened to my world, my life. The advance for my first book had paid off the mortgage, bought us a new BMW, given us a romantic holiday . . .

My dreams shattered, my hopes destroyed, I didn't see how I could write a second book. My heart wouldn't be in it and my mind wouldn't be on it, and besides, *she*'d demand more money. What was the point? I asked myself. God knew, the Inland Revenue had taken a big enough chunk of my first advance, and were demanding more. What with the Revenue and the blackmailing tart . . . What was the point?

'Selina, I've been thinking,' Danny said pensively as he ambled across the lawn with his coffee. 'This girl must know someone who knows you.'

'Not necessarily. She might know someone who knows someone . . .'

'Yes, but let's assume that she knows someone who directly knows you. Who did you tell about the ceiling?'

'I can't remember, it was a long time ago.'

'You told Chrissy, right?'

'Yes, but I've known her since I was eight years old. She wouldn't . . .'

'No, no, I'm not saying that she's involved. What I'm getting at is that Chrissy might have told this girl and, if that's the case, she obviously knows her. The girl's in her mid-twenties, not much younger than you – or Chrissy, for that matter.'

'So?'

'So, let's make a few assumptions. You've lived in this town all your life, and I reckon she lives here, too. She probably went to the same pubs and clubs as you, she probably knew the people you knew. She might even have known Barry.'

'Yes, but how does that help us? We can easily find out where she lives and who she is by following her tomorrow afternoon.'

'I don't think it's a good idea to follow her.'

'Why not?'

'She might spot us, and she might not be working alone.'

'Danny, I haven't robbed a bank or murdered someone – all I did was . . .'

'We can't be too careful, love.'

'Don't tell me she's part of a gangland . . .'

'I'm not suggesting that. I just think we should try and find out as much as we can about her without her knowing.'

'Shall I ask Chrissy who she told about the ceiling?'

'No, let's not say anything yet. Try to think of all the people you told about it. I realize that it was a long time ago, but try. Look, I need to clear my mind and think constructively. I'm going for a walk, I'll see you later.'

Danny was right, I ruminated, watching him mooch across the lawn with his hands in his pockets. It was best not to tell Chrissy, or anyone else. If I thought back to all the people I knew at the time, the few I might have mentioned the scam to, it should be possible to determine the girl's identity. But, even if we knew who she was, what could we do?

I couldn't help but feel sorry for Danny. He'd tried so hard with his writing, and failed so miserably. He'd put his all into his latest book, spending months and months writing and rewriting, only to receive rejection after rejection from literary agents and publishers.

The sad truth of the matter was that he couldn't write, I conceded glumly. He hadn't got a clue! And now, just when I was being wooed by my publisher to put the icing on my success with another book, a menacing shadow hovered. What was the point? I asked myself again as I wandered into the house. I had to be strong, I knew. I had to fight this whippet, bring her down and . . . And what? Making my plans, I climbed the stairs to my den and took a new exercise book from the desk drawer. I couldn't fight an unknown quantity, someone I didn't know, someone I'd never seen. It would be like sparring with a shadow.

The first thing to discover was the girl's name and address. Making notes in the book, trying to recall the people I'd known at the time, those I might have mentioned the ceiling to, I was determined not to let her ruin me. It was her against me, one to one. I had to think positively, put things into perspective. The scam couldn't be proved and was in any case insignificant – but Barry was another matter. I could always deny the affair, but people would only think there's no smoke without fire. And the tabloids were pretty adept at making their own bonfires!

I dragged my mind back to Barry. Our relationship had been no secret. Everyone had known about it – except his wife. Any one of twenty or thirty people could now be pulling the plug on the affair. *Barry?* Could *he* be working with the opportunist hussy? I pondered. The very idea was ludicrous.

The trip to the TV studio could wait, I decided. It was only to run through one or two things in connection with a chat show I was to appear on the following week. First things first, I told myself pragmatically. Despite Danny's warning, I decided to hide in the street and follow the girl once he'd given her the money. It wasn't much of a plan – if she was driving, I might lose her, and if she was walking, she might hop onto a bus. A weak strategy, I conceded, but better than nothing.

I didn't sleep that night. Tossing and turning, my mind racked with worry and anger, I finally left Danny to his snoring and went downstairs to make some tea. I'd planned to start my second book that morning, but my plans had been shattered. I could think of nothing but the unknown girl, the bitch. No doubt she was sleeping, dreaming of collecting five thousand pounds, while I drowned in my anguish.

Watching the sun climb above the trees at the end of the garden, my thoughts became clearer. Knowing that I had no choice other than to pay her, and that she'd be back for more, I came to a rash decision. I wouldn't write the second novel. We owned the house and had a new car, and the royalties from the first book would keep us going for quite some time. Another one hundred thousand pounds would have been great, but with the Revenue and the bitch both taking their chunks, the effort seemed pointless.

We could live quite happily, I convinced myself. Although my heart had been set on writing novels, I could turn my hand to short stories and not only bring in a little money but satisfy my creative yearning. If the bitch turned up demanding more money, Danny could tell her that there was no more – and that there'd be no more books.

No more money? There was about ten thousand left in my bank account. I'd give the bitch half and we'd survive on the rest until the next royalty cheque arrived. I'd made my plan and was going to stick to it, no matter what.

'You're up early,' Danny remarked, wandering into the kitchen in his boxer shorts.

'I couldn't sleep,' I sighed, wishing he'd left me alone with my thoughts for a while longer. 'Want some tea?'

'Thanks.'

'Danny, I've decided not to write the second book,' I enlightened him as he sat at the table.

'*What?* Selina, are you mad?'

'Far from it. I'm not going to be blackmailed, Danny. This is my life, and no one's going to intrude like this. She'll be back for more, and if there *is* no more . . .'

'Christ! It's insane to turn down a hundred grand!'

'Insane or not, I've made my mind up.'

Shaking his head as I poured him a cup of tea, Danny was obviously stunned. Maybe insanity *had* touched me, perhaps I *was* mad, but it would solve the problem. And besides, I knew I couldn't write another book with heavy clouds of anxiety hanging over me.

'You'll change your mind,' he asserted. 'It's just that all this has thrown you.'

'Thrown me? It's done more than throw me,' I snapped, passing him his tea. 'For Christ's sake, it's turned my life upside down!'

'Have you remembered who you told about the ceiling?'

'No, it's impossible to think back. I could have mentioned it to anyone and . . . Danny, this is ridiculous.'

'How do you mean?'

'All this nonsense about the bloody ceiling.'

'It's not so much the ceiling, it's Barry.'

'OK, so I was going out with a man who was married with kids.'

'Selina, you know how the tabloids love digging up stuff on people in the public eye.'

'Yes, but . . .'

'And we don't know what else they'll discover about you.'

'There *is* nothing else!'

'Isn't there?'

'No!'

'I wasn't going to tell you, but . . . The girl said that she has more on you.'

'Such as?'

'I don't know, she wouldn't tell me.'

'Look, she's coming here this afternoon. All we have to do is drag her into the house and . . .'

'And what? Beat her up? Bash her around a bit and get ourselves arrested for assault?'

'I don't know. This is crazy, Danny. A girl comes here and demands money, and there's nothing we can do about it?'

'We'll pay her off and that will be that.'

'Yeah, and pigs might . . .'

'I'm going up to take a shower.'

Pacing the kitchen floor, I was in two minds as to whether to call the police or not. Although I had Danny I felt so alone in the battle, as if the world was against me. But what could the police do? Hide in the house and arrest her when she turned up? As Danny had said, she'd sell her story and that would be that – my ruination. The bitch had wrecked my evening, and my night, and was now destroying my day – and I hadn't even met her!

I realized how vulnerable I was, the vulnerability of all people with skeletons in their cupboards. But what were my feeble skeletons? Ripping an insurance company off and being conned and used by a married man? I was hardly a criminal! Had it not been for my success, no one would have bothered about me, taken the slightest interest in boring Selina Goodman. But I *had* been successful, and I was to pay dearly for that success.

I rang the TV studio with my excuses and then walked into town to draw the cash out of the bank. Five thousand pounds of my hard-earned money going to a complete stranger . . . It had to be done, there was no choice. But, as I walked home clutching my bag, I sensed that I was making the biggest mistake of my life. *Don't do it!* my thoughts told me. *You're digging a hole that you'll never be able to climb out of!* I should have listened to my thoughts.

Dressed in my blue jacket and matching skirt, I lied to Danny, telling him that I was going to the studio. Had I said that I was going to follow the girl he'd have tried to talk me out of it, and I didn't want that. I'd made my plan and was going to stick to it.

I gave him the money, one hundred crisp fifty-pound notes, and left the house at eleven. With four hours to kill, I walked into town, had lunch at a small restaurant, and then wandered aimlessly around the common. What was I doing? Normally, I'd have been in my den, my fingers bashing away at the keyboard. What the hell was I doing wandering aimlessly around the common?

By two-forty-five I was lurking in the street, waiting for the girl to arrive. Even if I failed to discover where she lived, I had to see her. What did she look like? Was she fat or thin, tall or short – plain or attractive? My heart in my mouth, I watched a young woman walking along the street, wondering whether it was her. Another woman stopped outside my house and rummaged through her bag, but then walked on. Did she have skeletons in her cupboard? By three-fifteen there was no sign of the bitch, so I went home. For a moment I wondered whether the whole thing had been a hoax. But I was very wrong.

'Where did she get to?' I asked as I burst into the kitchen to find Danny gazing out of the window. 'I've been waiting in the street for ages.'

'I thought we'd agreed . . .'

'I know, but I decided to follow the bitch.'

'She turned up at two o'clock.'

'*Two?* But she said . . .'

'She's obviously not stupid, Selina. She must have thought that we might try something and decided to arrive an hour early.'

'You gave her the money?'

'Yes, I did. It was strange. She took the cash, gave me a kiss and grabbed my crotch.'

'Grabbed your— Why would she do that? Did she say anything?'

'Nothing. I came back inside and spied through the letterbox. The minute she'd gone I dashed down the path into the street, but there was no sign of her.'

'She couldn't have walked to the corner that quickly. Perhaps she was in a car.'

'When I came back to the house, I heard a car drive off. She must have leaped into her car and hidden on the floor, knowing that I'd probably try to follow her.'

'You're right, she's not stupid. She's a bitch, but not stupid.'

'If you didn't go to the studio, where have you been all this time?' he asked accusingly.

'Walking, having lunch, thinking . . . Anyway, let's hope that's the end of the matter. Not that I believe for one minute that it is.'

The following morning, a hand-delivered envelope lay on the doormat. Ripping it open, I was shocked to discover a photograph of the girl clutching a wad of notes as she kissed Danny. Another showed her grinning as she groped his crotch. Scrawled on the back of one of the photos was a note demanding another five thousand pounds. *Or the newspapers will receive the pictures of your husband paying a prostitute for her services.*

I couldn't believe it. My husband paying a prostitute? Now she really did have something on us! She was clever, very clever. Having an accomplice hiding somewhere in the bushes to take photographs, she'd obviously planned the whole thing meticulously.

Danny went wild, swearing and cursing as he looked at the photos and read the note. 'She's really got us now!' he sighed. 'If the bloody papers . . .'

'There's nothing to prove that you were paying a prostitute,' I interrupted him, wondering where the hell this would all end.

'No, but if she says that she's a prostitute, they'll believe her. We can't prove otherwise, can we?'

Foolishly, we paid her another five thousand. She turned up at the house two hours early, again catching Danny by surprise. I was at the studio, but he followed her this time, keeping his distance as she rounded corner after corner, before seemingly disappearing into thin air. Ten thousand pounds. The nightmare had begun, but it was only the beginning. The beginning of a living nightmare that was to plunge me mercilessly into the murky depths of depravity.

A week later, as I was sitting at my desk thinking about a short story, the phone rang. My heart almost stopped as the girl's giggles resounded through my head. How she had the audacity to ring me, I had no idea.

'I like your husband,' she said huskily. 'He's very good-looking.'

'What do you want?' I hissed through gritted teeth, my heart racing as my anger soared.

'When did he last fuck you?'

'*What?*'

I hung up, her obscene words reverberating through my racked mind. What sort of person was she? A blackmailer, yes, but . . . I dialled one four seven one and a mechanical voice told me that the caller had withheld their number. 'Shit!' I cursed as the phone rang again. Ignoring it, I let it ring until it was driving me mad like a relentlessly dripping tap in the middle of the night.

'Don't hang up, it's not nice,' the voice said impishly as I finally grabbed the receiver.

'Look, if it's more money you want, there is none!' I returned firmly.

'I want your husband.'

'What do you mean?'

'I want him to fuck me.'

'Good God, I have never . . .'

'Selina, I have to tell you that I'm working for someone. He specializes in digging up dirt on celebrities and . . .'

'Go to hell!'

Banging the phone down, I lurched to the window. Seething with anger, my breathing unsteady, my heart banging hard against my chest, I knew I had to calm down. It was raining, the droplets of water running down the glass like tears – my tears. *I want him to fuck me.* Her filthy words wouldn't leave my mind, echoing through my aching head, driving me insane.

I wasn't going to say anything to Danny but when he walked into my den and asked who had phoned, I broke down and told him exactly what the girl had said. He stood there staring at me, obviously stunned. For a moment, I wondered whether he thought me mad. *I* wondered whether I was mad!

'She really said that?' he finally asked, frowning at me.

'I'm not making it up!' I snapped.

'OK, OK, calm down.'

'Calm down? She's had ten thousand pounds, and now she wants . . .'

'Look, I'll have our phone number changed.'

'That won't do any good,' I sighed despondently.

'Yes, it will. We'll go ex-directory and . . .'

'She'll come here, Danny! She won't give up simply because the bloody phone number's changed!'

This wasn't so much a nightmare as a horror story! *I want him to fuck me.* My mind numb as Danny rambled on, I gazed out of the window again. His words fluttering around the room, drifting past me, I wondered whether the bitch had just been having a laugh, winding me up. She'd hardly come to the house and . . . She was winding me up, there was no doubt in my mind.

Obviously noticing that I wasn't listening, Danny left the room and closed the door. Images of my husband having sex with another woman filling my mind, I realized that truth really *was* stranger than fiction. What a story this would make! What a book! Shaking my head as stark reality hit me, I sat at my desk. I felt tired with worry, sick with anxiety. I couldn't even think about a short story, let alone write one!

Whether I'd fallen asleep or into a state of shock, I didn't know. When I finally came to my senses and looked around me in the falling dusk, I wandered downstairs. Danny had left a note on the kitchen table telling me that he'd gone to see a private detective. I *had* fallen asleep, I reflected. He must have looked in on me before going out and decided that I needed the rest.

A private detective? I pondered as I filled the kettle for coffee. At least Danny was doing something constructive, unlike me. But what could a private detective do? If he discovered who the girl was and where she lived, there'd be little we could do about her – apart from have her bumped off. And if she really was working for someone . . .

Answering the front door, I found myself staring at an attractive young blonde – and instinctively knew that it was the bitch. Her deep blue eyes smiling at me, she wasn't at all what I'd expected. I don't know what I'd expected, but it wasn't this! She was stylishly dressed in a white blouse and turquoise miniskirt with matching stilettos and, for a moment, I thought I must be wrong.

'I've come to introduce myself,' she said, pushing past me and stepping into the hall. 'I'm your friendly blackmailer.'

'You're crazy!' I hissed. 'How the hell you have the nerve to . . .'

'Mmm, a nice house,' she murmured, walking through the hall to the lounge.

'Get out!' I screamed, chasing after her. 'How dare you . . .'

'My boss is waiting down the road so I wouldn't do anything rash if I were you,' she warned me, impertinently plonking herself in an armchair. 'You're going to be seeing quite a lot of me so I thought we'd better get to know each other.'

'Get to know each other? Christ, you've got a nerve!'

'Selina, we don't have to fight. Just calm down and hear what I have to say.'

'Calm down?'

'I want your husband.'

'My God, you really are insane!'

'I'm the sort of girl who gets what she wants, and I want sex with your husband.'

Leaning against the piano to support my sagging body, I stared at the bitch, unable to believe what she was saying. I could understand blackmail, demanding money – but sex with Danny? For one terrible moment, in my confused thinking, I wondered whether Danny was working with her. But no, he'd been doing everything possible to help me. Had he wanted money, all he had to do was ask. Besides, it was *our* money, not mine, and he knew I looked at it that way.

As she stood up and marched to the door, my mind was in turmoil. She was well-dressed, well-spoken and . . . Blackmailers weren't necessarily common, scruffy people, I reflected. And besides, she *should* have been well dressed, seeing as I'd given her ten thousand pounds!

'I'll be back tomorrow,' she purred, strutting into the hall.

'You will *not*!' I spat.

'Tomorrow evening, to have sex with your husband – while you watch.'

As she slammed the front door shut, I broke down, sobbing uncontrollably. What the hell had happened to my life? I wondered. What had I done to deserve this? Again,

I thought of Danny. *Was* he working with the girl? Of course he wasn't, but there was that niggling doubt at the back of my mind. In some respects, it made sense. He could have told her about the ceiling, about Barry and . . . No, my thinking was going way off course!

'Are you OK?' Danny asked as he opened the front door, finding me sitting on the hall floor in tears. 'Hey, what's happened?'

'She came here!' I snivelled, climbing to my feet. 'She wants me to watch you having sex with her!'

'She *what*? Selina, you need a rest, a break from it all.'

'You don't believe me, do you?'

'I'm not saying that, it's just . . .'

'She wants you to fuck her, as she put it.'

'This is complete and utter madness! For Christ's sake . . .'

'Would you have sex with her?'

'Of course I wouldn't! What sort of question is that?'

'Danny, do you know this girl?'

'Know her? I've only met her twice.'

'I mean, are you in this with her?'

'*What?* Fucking hell, I can't believe this!'

'I'm sorry, but I had to ask.'

'As if I'd . . . Look, this may sound cold and callous, but you're the one she's blackmailing, not me.'

'What do you mean by that?'

'I mean, I'm not going to get involved. Taking your money's one thing, but *I'm* not going to have anything to do with her.'

'If it came to the crunch, you wouldn't help me?' I found myself asking.

'I *am* helping you, I've been to see a private dick.'

'But if she insisted that . . .'

'I have to say this, Selina. I'd do anything for you, and you know that, but I will not sell my body for sex. There's no way

I'm even going to entertain the idea. And as for you thinking that I'm in it with her . . .'

As he stomped up the stairs, a tear ran down my cheek. I must have been mad to think that he could be involved. Insane! I'd upset him, I knew, but I'd had to ask him, had to tell him what was on my mind. I'd been feeling so alone, so desperate with worry that I wasn't thinking properly. To suggest that Danny . . . Guilt swamped me as I went into the lounge and flopped onto the sofa. He'd been trying to help, and I hadn't even asked him what the private detective had said.

If the bitch came round the following evening, I wouldn't answer the door. She could go to hell as far as I was concerned. Whether she sold her pathetic story to the tabloids or not, I was beyond caring. No one was going to rule my life, dictate to me like this!

The phone ringing, I was about to grab the receiver but thought better of it. The last thing I wanted was to hear her voice again. Danny had obviously taken the call upstairs and, if it was the bitch, I knew he'd tell her where to go. Gazing at the phone, curiosity getting the better of me, I pressed the secrecy button and carefully lifted the receiver.

'Yes, I came round this evening,' the bitch was saying.

'I don't want you coming here.'

'Danny, Danny, you don't seem to understand.'

'I understand only too well! You're a blackmailing cow!'

'I want you to fuck me, Danny.'

'There's no more money, my wife's not going to write any more books, and I'm not going to have anything to do with you.'

'You're going to have a lot to do with me. I'll be round tomorrow evening and, unless you fuck me, the papers will have my story. I'll tell them that we've been having an affair for a year, that you long for my hot, wet cunt and . . .'

As Danny hung up, I gently replaced the receiver. That's what I'd wanted to hear, my husband telling her where to go, putting the phone down on her. Again, I felt extreme guilt for even thinking that he could be involved with her, let alone asking him if he was. I felt as if I'd betrayed him.

Curling up on the sofa, I cried myself to sleep and dreamed of Danny having sex with the bitch, her beautiful naked body sprawled out on the lounge floor as he drove his penis deep into her treacherous vagina. My mind whispered dreadful things to me in my sleep. I wanted to die.

Chapter Two

Obviously needing my sleep, I didn't wake until ten the following morning. My back aching, the horrendous events of the previous evening slowly filtering into my mind like sand flowing through an hourglass, I clambered off the sofa and searched for Danny. There was no sign of him. He'd probably gone for a walk, I ruminated, slipping out of my crumpled skirt and blouse.

After taking a shower, I dressed and went downstairs to make some tea. The note was propped up against the vase of red carnations on the kitchen table. 'Gone to see the private dick.' No *dear Selina*, no *love from Danny*, no kisses . . . He was obviously still upset with me, but I could hardly blame him.

To my horror, I found another envelope on the doormat, this time containing a photograph of the grinning girl entering my house. The shot had been taken from such an angle that I wasn't in the frame. This was obviously another act in the prostitute scam, the damning evidence building quickly. Put it all together, the girl kissing Danny, taking a wad of money, holding his crotch, entering the house . . .

Everything was happening so rapidly. I felt as if I was in a fast-flowing river, unable to reach the bank and stop myself from going over the weir. What would she do next? What should *I* do next? I had no idea. I kept wondering how the hell all this had started, how it was escalating at such a frightening rate. We should never have paid her the first five thousand, I chastised myself. Had Danny not answered the door, she'd not have had the photographs. That had been our first mistake.

'Hi,' Danny smiled as he walked into the kitchen. 'Sorry I've been so long.'

'Danny, last night – I didn't mean to . . .'

'It's all right, I understand.'

'It was just that . . .'

'It's OK, Selina.'

'When she rang, I listened on the phone in the lounge.'

'She's got a bloody nerve, she *really* has! Anyway, I've been to see the private dick again. It'll cost us, but he's going to park in the street this evening. He reckons that . . .'

'Don't answer the door, Danny. I don't want her here again.'

'No, listen. He's hoping to see her park her car. He wants us to let her in to give him time to call a copper he knows. From the registration number, he can get her name and address.'

'How will that help?'

'He's going to put the frighteners on her. I dread to think how, but . . .'

'She's working for a man who dishes the dirt on celebrities and . . .'

'Shit! Why didn't you tell me?'

'She mentioned it last night. I forgot . . .'

'What else did she say?'

'Her name's Diana.'

'I'd better ring the dick and let him know. I wish you'd told me earlier, Selina.'

'I'm sorry.'

'It's OK, I'll go and ring him now.'

I spent the rest of the morning sitting at my desk, staring at the computer screen while Danny persevered with his own writing. Although I'd decided never to write another book, I tried to think about my second novel. I'd written the synopsis and my head had been brimming with ideas, but now? Talk about writer's block: I couldn't construct one sentence! All I could think about was the girl coming round that evening, having to let her in and listen to her crude demands for sex.

'How the hell did I get into this?' I muttered, finally giving up all hope of writing and switching the computer off. But at least we had help now, the private detective. He'd find out about the girl and . . . No doubt he was used to this sort of thing and knew how to deal with blackmailers.

Danny returned to his scribbling after a ham-salad lunch, while I sat in the garden. Checking my watch every five minutes, the afternoon dragged on as the evening drew closer. Finally, I went up to the bedroom and changed. For some reason I felt in competition with the girl – as if I had to out-dress her. Perhaps, subconsciously, I was afraid that Danny might fancy her. She was extremely attractive and . . . but I was sure I had no worries on that front.

Donning a red miniskirt and white silk blouse, I brushed my chestnut hair and applied my make-up meticulously. I knew I looked good – far better than that tramp! But, more importantly, I *felt* good.

By seven o'clock, I was feeling far from good – I was a nervous wreck! Pacing the lounge floor, wringing my hands and knocking back glasses of wine like there was no tomorrow, I almost jumped out of my skin when the doorbell rang. Praying for the detective to be in the street, I flashed Danny an anxious look. What was he thinking? I wondered as he brushed his hair away from his dark eyes. Smiling reassuringly, he took a deep breath and went to answer the door.

Gulping down my wine, I refilled the glass for the umpteenth time, my hands shaking uncontrollably as I heard the door close. Following Danny into the lounge, wearing a gabardine coat, the bitch grinned at me. I felt a mixture of hatred and anger, frustration and defeat as Danny offered her a drink. Watching him pour her a glass of Chablis, I realized how ridiculous the situation was. Our blackmailer was standing in our lounge ordering white wine! I could have wrung her bloody neck!

'This is cosy,' she smiled smugly, sipping her drink and placing her glass on the mantelpiece. 'Do you mind if I take my coat off?'

'No, of course not,' Danny simpered, a little too friendly for my liking.

As she took her coat off and tossed it over the armchair, I gasped with horror. Underneath that one outer garment she was completely naked! Standing with her back to the mantelpiece, her face beaming as she proudly displayed her firm young breasts, her well-trimmed blonde pubic thatch, she watched for my reaction. All I could do was stand there, unable to speak, unable to believe what I was seeing. The audacity, the gall . . . And I'd thought I'd out-dress her!

I turned and looked at Danny, wondering what he was thinking as he stared at her curvaceous young body. A thousand demented thoughts tumbled through my aching head. Did he fancy her? Did she turn him on? Did he want to fuck her? Still speechless, my eyes darting between him and the naked girl, I was absolutely stunned.

'We might as well get down to business,' she said huskily, cupping her breasts in her hands and flicking her erect nipples. 'Come on, Danny – come over here and finger my cunt.'

'You dirty bitch!' I finally managed to spit. 'You filthy, dirty little . . .'

My words tailed off as Danny walked across the room and stood before her. I thought he was going to slap her face as he placed his glass on the mantelpiece and raised his hand, but he held his head, obviously shocked by her impertinence. Moving forward, I was about to dowse her in wine when a succession of flashes lit up the room like lightning. Turning, I looked through the window just in time to see someone dashing down the front path. Danny rushed out of the room in pursuit of the bitch's accomplice, the front door slamming shut as he raced into the street.

'Just a little more evidence,' the girl smirked. 'The three of us in your lounge enjoying a cosy drink will make quite a nice shot. What with me naked, I don't think there'll be any doubt as to what we were up to, do you?'

I was still too dazed, too numb with shock to speak. This was incredible! I didn't know whether to smash her in the face or . . . All I could do was stand there, open-mouthed, my hands trembling, my heart racing wildly as adrenalin coursed through my veins.

Why blackmail *me*? I wondered. There were plenty of people who had far more money than I had. Although I'd thought the girl insane, she was far from it – she was clever, devious beyond belief. But, apart from building evidence against me, taking my money, what was her ultimate aim? To take my husband?

'I was too bloody late,' Danny panted, scowling at the girl as he returned to the lounge.

'Too late to halt the proceedings,' she grinned, parting her vaginal lips with her slender fingers and displaying the most intimate part of her young body. 'Come on, Danny – kneel down and finger my cunt.'

He looked at me like a child, as if asking what he should do. How the hell did I know? What with the tart's latest photographs, the evidence was more than damning. It was blatant proof that my husband and I had an illicit relationship with a whore!

'Danny, I need to speak to you,' I gulped, leaving the

room. As he followed me into the kitchen, I closed the door. 'What the hell do we do?' I whispered urgently.

'I don't bloody know!' he returned angrily. 'She's got more bloody photographs now. I'll tell you one thing, I'm not going to touch the filthy tart!'

'But, the evidence she's got . . .'

'I know, I know! Do you think I'm fucking stupid? I'm sorry, I didn't mean to have a go at you. Christ, this is getting worse by the bloody minute.'

'There's only one way out of it,' I sighed resignedly.

'No way! I'm not going to . . .'

'Do as she asks, just this once, and the next time we'll . . .'

'Selina, I am *not* going to . . .'

'Christ, Danny! She's got so much on me now that she could ruin me! You said yourself about the tabloids. Pictures of you and me in the lounge with a naked tart . . . What will my publisher think, let alone our friends and neighbours?'

'Fuck the neighbours!'

'Just finger the bitch and then tell her to bugger off. We'll never let her in again, we won't answer the door or . . .'

'And she'll go to the papers, Selina.'

'Yes, but it'll give us time. We need time to think, to plan our next move. Besides, the private detective might have . . .'

'You do realize what you're asking me to do, don't you?' he interrupted me. 'Adultery, Selina – I'd be committing adultery while you watch.'

'You don't have to go all the way, just . . . just finger her.'

'How are you going to feel, watching me do that? What's this going to do to our relationship?'

'Nothing, it's just a cold, clinical act.'

'All right, but I'm not at all happy about this.'

'*You*'re not happy? How the hell do you think *I* feel?'

We returned to the lounge to find the girl sitting with her thighs spread, her legs over the arms of the chair, her glistening vaginal entrance clearly displayed between her yawning sex lips. Massaging her clitoris with her fingertips, her eyes partially closed, she was obviously delighting in my plight as she let out little gasps of pleasure.

Truth stranger than fiction. The words haunted me. I could never have dreamed up a story like this! I had a damned good imagination, but this was beyond imagination, it was . . . I didn't know what is was. To call it a nightmare would be an understatement. It was a living hell!

As Danny knelt on the floor and flashed me an accusing look, his hand tentatively moving towards the young tart's bared femininity, I gazed at the lewd scene in bewilderment. Stretching her fleshy sex lips wide apart, fully exposing her clitoris, she ordered him to finger her. I moved closer, standing by the side of the chair and focusing on her pink inner lips, her gaping vaginal entrance. I'd never seen another woman's vulva, let alone one displayed so blatantly, so crudely – still less one on offer to my husband!

Again, I found myself wondering whether Danny fancied her, whether the lewd sight turned him on. The girl looked as if she was posing for a dirty men's magazine. Danny was a normal red-blooded male – so why shouldn't he become aroused? But this was different, I tried to convince myself – she was blackmailing us.

Parting her pussy lips further, the slut again repeated her vile demand. As Danny's finger entered her, she gasped and moved forward in the chair until her buttocks were over the edge of the cushion, his finger now fully inserted into her luscious vagina. Massaging her exposed clitoris, she looked up at me through her eyelashes and offered me a salacious grin.

'That's nice,' she murmured dreamily. 'But I want more fingers up my cunt.' Complying, Danny slipped another two fingers into her lubricating vagina, looking up at me every now and then, no doubt wondering what I was thinking. But I wasn't thinking anything. My mind blank, I felt numb, as if I'd been anaesthetized. My husband fingering a naked young girl while I watched . . .

'Now you've juiced my cunt, I want you to fuck me,' she breathed in her crudity.

'No!' I cried as another series of flashes illuminated the room.

'More evidence,' she purred. 'It's no good chasing my friend, he'll be well away by now.'

'You're a fucking bitch!' Danny hissed, yanking his wet fingers out of her glistening honeypot. 'If you think I'm going to . . .'

'I don't think, I *know*!' she giggled. 'Come on, get your stiff cock out and fuck my hot cunt. Fuck me really hard – and then spunk up my cunt.'

Frowning, his expression anguished, Danny looked up at me again. Stiff cock? *Did* he have an erection? I wondered. His words teased me. *What's this going to do to our relationship?* I didn't know what it would do. The normal reaction to infidelity was devastation, anger, hatred – and, almost invariably, divorce. But this situation was hardly normal and I felt no such emotions towards Danny. I hated the girl, but . . .

'I'm waiting for you to fuck me,' she grinned.

'No!' Danny returned firmly.

'I now have photographs of you fingering my cunt with your wife watching you. Selina Goodman, best-selling novelist, a household name . . .'

'Look, we might be able to raise a little more cash,' Danny said sullenly.

'I want you to raise your *cock*!' she giggled.

Her filthy words grating on my mind, I watched Danny tug his zip down. A tear ran down my cheek as I drew the curtains and he pulled his penis out. If we had to go through with this, I wasn't going to have any photographs taken of the vile scene. We were giving the detective time, I had to remember that. Danny fucking the girl was simply a means to an end. Checking for chinks in the curtains, I took a deep breath and stood by the chair, mesmerized by his penis – stiff, erect and ready for vaginal penetration.

He must have been aroused, I mused as he moved nearer, his swollen glans hovering close to the tart's gaping vaginal entrance. Would any man be able get an erection in this situation? What was he thinking? His penis wouldn't stiffen unless . . . I tried to steer my thoughts away from lovemaking and look upon the imminent act as cold and clinical, vile and filthy.

'Shove it right up my wet cunt,' the slut breathed in her vulgarity as she eyed his solid penis. 'Come on, fuck my beautiful cunt.' What would his thoughts be were the roles reversed? I found myself wondering. Were I to be reclined in the chair with my vagina on offer to another man, a stranger, what thoughts would fill his mind? Would he cry rivers of tears from the devastation? Would his heart break?

As I watched his purple glans slip between her wet inner lips, sexual contact made, adultery committed, my faith, my very being, crumbled. My thoughts screamed at me. *No!* Marriage vows had been broken, torn asunder, and I wondered how many times I'd be forced to watch the illicit coupling. This was only the beginning, I knew instinctively as his shaft entered her, gliding deep into her pleasure hole as she gasped and writhed in the chair. This was only the beginning.

'Mmm, you've got a big cock,' she murmured appreciatively, her head thrown back, her eyes closed. Danny didn't look up at me as he withdrew his glistening penis and thrust into her again. How did I feel? I didn't know, all reality, all perception paralysed. It was as if, in my dreams, I was watching a blue movie.

'Spunk up my cunt!' she cried, her long blonde hair veiling her flushed face as Danny thrust into her again and again. Thoughts bobbed in the wash of my mind. She obviously had no regard for her body, no respect for her femininity, no morals. Her essence was that of a filthy, stinking swamp. She was the devil's daughter incarnate.

The squelching sounds of sex filling my aching head as Danny repeatedly withdrew his wet penis and drove into her trembling body, I prayed for the vile act to finish, for the girl to leave us to pick up the pieces of our broken marriage. Marriage? What sort of marriage would I have after watching my husband screw a young girl? I'd always thought our lovemaking to be sacred, an act so private, so intimate, creating a spiritual bond between us. Never had I even dreamed of giving myself to another man, and Danny's trustworthiness had been rock-solid. We'd built our marriage on the granite foundations of faith, trust and loyalty, and now . . .

My tortured thoughts drifted. *Do you, Danny Goodman, take this woman . . . ?* Our vows had been tossed into the gutter, washed down the drain into the sewer to be devoured by rats. But, although technically he'd committed adultery, he hadn't been unfaithful – had he? *We are gathered here in the eyes of God . . .* He was having sexual intercourse with another woman, but we were in this together, we had no choice. Despite my desperate rationalization, I knew that the next time we made love it would be no good. Relentless images of him screwing the girl would flood my mind, drowning my arousal, my emotions, mocking our lovemaking.

'Coming!' the bitch screamed, her naked body shaking violently as she rocked her hips to meet his thrusts. My legs sagging as I watched Danny's glistening penis slide in and out of her vagina, I turned away as he grunted in his sordid release. His sperm pumping into the girl, the act was complete – fidelity broken. The rats had feasted.

Lurching across the room as he made his last thrusts, I flopped onto the sofa, the girl's orgasmic whimperings and my husband's low moans reverberating around the ruins of my mind. *Ten thousand pounds, and now this*, I reflected numbly. What would she demand of us next? More money? More sex? Undoubtedly!

Where to go from here? I pondered. What choice did we have? Carry on with the debauchery, move house . . . Like a feckless butterfly my thoughts fluttered, alighted on the private detective. He was our only hope. But, even if he put the frighteners on the girl, as he'd put it, it was too late – the damage had been done. We might be able to rebuild our marriage but, in my heart of hearts, I knew that I could never forget, never erase the vile scene from my mind.

'You're a good fuck,' the girl breathed as Danny withdrew his penis and stood up. She turned her head and looked directly, mockingly at me. 'He's a good *fuck*, Selina. I'm looking forward to another *fuck* tomorrow night. ' She stressed the hurtful obscenity. I didn't return her cruel gaze as Danny zipped his trousers. I couldn't bear to see the flagrant pleasure on her face, the blatant delight reflected in her bright eyes. As Danny disappeared upstairs, I watched her rise to her feet, sperm dripping from her treacherous vaginal crack and running down her inner thighs. She'd done it – she'd taken my husband. She'd won.

'I'll see you tomorrow evening,' she grinned, grabbing her coat and covering her naked body. 'Another evening, another fuck.'

'You'll never see me again!' I hissed, leaping to my feet as she neared the door.

'Now, now, Selina – don't be nasty.'

'Yes, turn up tomorrow evening,' I smiled. 'Turn up and you'll see what I have in store for you.'

'Threats won't get you anywhere,' she returned, buttoning her coat. 'I have enough evidence now to . . .'

'Whatever evidence you have, it won't do you any good if you're— No, I won't say anything now. You turn up tomorrow and you'll discover your fate.'

'My boss will be waiting outside, Selina.'

'Yes, and *I'll* be waiting inside. I'll look forward to seeing you again – for the last time.'

As she tossed her golden tresses over her shoulder, I thought for a moment that I detected fear in her expression. She knew as well as I that, even if she did have someone waiting outside, it wouldn't do her any good if she was locked in the house. But without plans my threats were empty, futile.

Leaving the house, her stilettos clicked as she strutted down the drive to the street. I was going to follow her, but I knew there was no point. She wasn't stupid. I heard a car speed off, the engine racing as she made her escape into the dark of the night. Gazing at the armchair, the white stains on the cushion stark evidence of the evening's debauchery, I poured myself another glass of wine.

'Has she gone?' Danny asked as he finally joined me.

'Yes, she has,' I murmured, not catching his gaze. 'Did you enjoy it?'

'Selina!'

'I'm sorry, I . . . It's just that you came. I didn't think you'd be able to get an erection, let alone . . .'

'That's because I closed my eyes and imagined that I was with you. While I was upstairs, I came to a decision. What I did, I did for you, Selina – but I'm not going to do it again. You remember I used the words "cold" and "callous"?'

'Yes.'

'Well, no doubt they'll come to your mind when I tell you

that *I*'m not the one she's blackmailing, and I'm not going to have any more to do with her. I'm sorry, love, but . . . She's blackmailing *you* and you'll have to pay her. I'm not paying her with sex, you'll have to pay her with money.'

'Danny, there *is* no more money!'

'I've been thinking about that, too. You've been offered another one hundred thousand advance for your second novel. You'll have to take it.'

'No, I made up my mind not to . . .'

'OK, so she gets no more sex and no more money. On your head be it.'

'Danny!'

'If you won't pay her, then she'll go to the papers. I'm not going to spend the rest of my life screwing another woman to save your career, your face. Yes, it is cold and callous, but . . . As I said earlier, what's this going to do to our relationship? You watching me screw another woman night after night . . . We won't *have* a bloody relationship if I do that! The choice is yours, Selina – your marriage *and* your career – or nothing at all.'

Watching him leave the room as I gulped down my wine, I pondered on his words. The choice was mine? I now had two people forcing my hand! I could see Danny's point, and I was pleased that he wanted nothing more to do with the girl, but I'd have to spend the rest of my life writing novels to pay her off. The continuation of my marriage and my career – or the end of both? Never would I have believed that I'd have to make such a choice! Money or sex? Talk about between the devil and the deep blue sea.

I *wouldn't* write another book, I decided. If I did, with every sentence I wrote I'd be thinking of the bitch. I couldn't do it. Without more books, it wouldn't really matter if sordid stories of my relationship with the girl surfaced. I'd no longer have a career for her to destroy. What people thought didn't matter, either. I'd move house, live somewhere in the country away from prying eyes, lewd comments – and the filthy bitch.

Again, I didn't sleep well. Nightmares chased me like monsters through dark corridors, pursued me through rooms where vulgar orgies were enacted. Sex loomed in my dreams, obscene sex, adultery, infidelity. Images of my husband's erect penis driving into the girl's vagina haunted me until I finally woke in a cold sweat.

Danny was still sleeping when the post arrived. I recognized the envelope from the publisher and hesitated before opening it. At some stage I'd have to tell them that my writing career was over, but what could I say? What possible reason could I give for forgoing another one hundred thousand pound advance – another blockbuster?

The royalty cheque was for just over eight thousand pounds. In a flash of inspiration it occurred to me that only the publisher and I knew about it. There was no way the bitch could find out, unless she had a friend at the bank who was in a position to check my account. I'd open another account with a different bank, I decided as I wandered up to my den. I wouldn't tell anyone, not even Chrissy, my best friend – not even Danny.

Secrets from Danny? The thought sent a shiver up my spine. It wasn't that I didn't trust him – just that I knew I had to hold on to this money. If he didn't know about it, he couldn't talk me into paying the bitch – which I was sure he'd try and do. He had no idea about the book sales, or the royalty payments. If I put each cheque into another account, I'd build up a nice little sum for . . . for what? For a rainy day. A tearful day.

'You're writing!' Danny gasped as he entered my den and discovered me bashing away at the keyboard.

'Only a short story,' I replied without looking up.

'Selina, I really think you should give your next book some serious thought.'

'I have, and I'm not doing it.'

'I've got an idea,' he smiled, perching himself on the edge of my desk. 'After last night . . . Well, what's done is done.'

'Yes, it is. What's your idea?'

'Take the advance and write the second book.'

'But . . .'

'Hang on, hang on. How long will it be before it's published? A year?'

'Maybe longer.'

'OK, so take the advance, start writing the book, and by the time . . .'

'By the time it's published we'll have spent it and the girl . . .'

'No, not spent it: *saved* it. The girl can do what she likes. You'll have your nest egg, even if she does succeed in ruining your career.'

'And in the meantime?'

'What do you mean?'

'I can't write a book all the time she's demanding sex with you. Anyway, before we make any plans you'd better ring the private detective and see how he got on.'

'Yes, I was about to do that.'

Pondering on Danny's idea as he punched the telephone buttons, I knew it was good. No one would know I'd taken the advance. But I couldn't write as long as the girl was threatening me, demanding to have sex with my husband. Maybe, if I gave her a couple of thousand pounds . . .

'Mr Wilkins? Hallo, it's Danny Goodman. Yes, we survived the evening – just! Were you able to follow her when she left? Yes, I know the pub. Past East Street and into Lennox Avenue, yes. You lost them on the motorway? I know, I've been caught in the traffic many times. What about the registration number? A hire car? I might have guessed. So, what now? Yes, this evening. No, she didn't say what time. OK, if I hear any more, I'll let you know.'

Danny knew he didn't have to tell me the bad news as he replaced the receiver and wandered across the room to the window. But I wasn't going to have the girl round again. Private detective or not, I couldn't endure another horrendous evening watching Danny screw her.

'You told me that you weren't going to have any more to do with her,' I said accusingly, turning to face him. 'If she's coming here . . .'

'I know, I know,' he sighed. 'We'll have to play it by ear.'

'*She* won't want to play it by ear, she'll want to play it by—'

'You're not going to pay her, and I'm not going to fuck her – excuse my French. All we can do is let her in, play for time, and then kick her out. The private dick's going to be ready this time.'

'He should have been ready last bloody time!'

'Yes, but he didn't know that . . . Have you got a better idea, Selina?'

'No, I suppose not.'

'Then that's what we'll do. About the book.'

'What about it?'

'No one will know that you've taken the advance.'

'That's true, because I'm not going to take it.'

'Well, at least give it some thought. It occurred to me that, if you took the money, we could move away, abroad, even. Anyway, think about it.'

'Yes, I will. Look, I want to get on with this short story.'

'OK. I'll be bashing out a load of bollocks, as is my wont. See you later.'

Move abroad? I pondered, gazing at my computer screen. It was a thought, but did I really want to leave my home, leave England? Why the hell should I have to leave? No, I wasn't going to run away! The plan would have to work. The bitch would turn up in the evening, we'd give her wine and, as Danny had said, play for time before kicking her out. The private detective had failed once – it was unlikely that he'd fail again.

I worked at the word processor for most of the day, somehow finding the inspiration to write. Danny went out for a walk around six, leaving me to get ready for the evening – not that I could out-dress the tart! But I felt positive this time, in control. The bitch wasn't going to have sex, or money, and I wondered what her reaction would be when we threw her out onto the street. I was almost relishing the prospect of the evening ahead!

Unfortunately, she arrived early, before Danny had returned from his walk. I showed her into the lounge and offered her a glass of wine, knowing full well that she was naked beneath her coat. Naked or not, she wasn't going to enjoy sex – or the evening!

'Where's my stud?' she asked impishly, sitting in the armchair.

'*My* stud is out,' I smiled. 'He's gone for a walk, giving us time for a chat.'

'I haven't come here to chat.'

'Tough, because that's what we're going to do. OK, I've come to some decisions. Number one, I'm not writing any more books so there'll be no more money. Number two, my husband won't be having sex with you again . . .'

'You've got it all wrong, Selina,' she grinned. 'Number one, unless you get an advance for another book I'll make sure that the newspapers pull you to pieces, ruin you. Number two, unless *you* have sex with me . . .'

'*Me?* Don't be ridiculous!'

'I'm serious.'

'My God, you're a filthy tart!'

'As I was saying, unless *you* have sex with me, you'll never see your husband again.'

'What do you mean by that?'

'My boss is . . . How shall I put it? He's looking after your husband.'

'You've been watching too much television!' I laughed.

'Have I?'

As she stood up and slipped her coat off, displaying her naked body, a bolt of fear rocked me. Where *was* Danny? What was taking him so long? I couldn't believe what was happening. Blackmail, sex with my husband, and now . . . My mind in turmoil, I leaned against the wall to steady myself. She wanted sex with *me?* No, never!

'OK, you can start by stripping off,' she smiled, sipping her wine as she relaxed in the armchair.

'If you think I'm going to—'

'Selina, if I leave here with bad news, then . . . My boss likes things to run smoothly, he detests problems. If anyone gets in his way he has a nasty habit of . . . Well, as I said, you'll never see your husband again.'

She was bluffing, I was sure as I scowled at her. Danny abducted? The idea was ludicrous! This was the sort of thing that happened in the movies, not in real life. Danny had gone out for a walk and she was just trying to frighten me, it was as simple as that. As the phone rang, she grinned knowingly.

'Ah, that's what I've been waiting for,' she purred. 'You'd better answer it, Selina.'

Lifting the phone, my heart racing, I was relieved to hear Danny's deep voice. 'Where the hell are you?' I asked angrily.

'Selina, I'm . . . I'm in a basement. Two thugs . . .'

'Thugs? Danny, are you OK?'

'Yes, but . . .'

The phone suddenly cut off. I replaced the receiver and

held my trembling hand to my mouth. My head spinning as I looked at the grinning girl, my stomach churning, I didn't know what to think, what to do. Where was the bloody private detective? Where the hell was Danny? What horrendous mess had we got ourselves into?

'OK, strip off,' the bitch ordered huskily. 'I want to have a look at your cunt.'

'Please, I . . .'

'I suggest you do exactly as I ask, Selina. Oh, by the way, you *will* be writing more books.'

'I won't!'

'After we've had some sexy fun, Danny will be allowed to come home. If you don't write and the money dries up, he'll disappear again – this time without trace.'

'You can't . . .'

'We *can* and *will* do as we please.'

Unbuttoning my blouse, I looked around the lounge. This was my home – our home, our sanctuary. How could something like this happen to us? A happily married, successful author one minute, and the next . . . Danny forced to have intercourse with the bitch, then he's abducted, I'm told to strip off and have sex with her. Sex with another woman? *Lesbian* sex?

'I can't do it,' I murmured as my blouse fell open, revealing my full bra.

'The choice is yours, Selina. Either you do as I ask, or you'll never see your husband again.'

'Where is he?'

'He's safe enough. Before you know it, he'll be back here with you and . . .'

'Until the next time.'

'My boss won't . . . There needn't be a next time, not if you play the game.'

Slipping my blouse off my shoulders, I unhooked my bra.

My breasts tumbling out of the white silk cups, my nipples elongating in the cool air of the lounge, I hung my head in embarrassment. I could feel her gaze burning into me, into my nipples. Swamped with humiliation as she ordered me to pull my skirt down, my hands trembling, I fumbled with the zip.

My skirt finally falling around my ankles, only my red panties veiling the most private part of my body, my sanctum, I told myself that I was doing this for Danny. Whatever I was forced to do, it was for Danny's sake. When our ordeal was over, we'd go and live abroad. I'd take the advance and we'd run off into the sunset. Run? Yes, there was no choice other than to run. Whoever these people were, whatever we'd got ourselves mixed up in, we had to run.

Stepping out of my skirt as she knelt before me, I closed my eyes as she pulled my panties down to my ankles. Although I tried, I couldn't block out the reality, deny what was happening to me. Her fingers running up and down my inner thighs, dangerously close to my secret place, the nightmare was all too real.

'You have a gorgeous cunt, Selina,' she drooled, her fingers parting my soft outer lips, exposing my most private inner folds. I felt dizzy with confusion, faint with humiliation. I'd never been a prude but, even with Danny, I'd kept myself within my moral bounds, within the limits of propriety. Never had he used crude words during our lovemaking, nor had he ever examined me intimately like this!

As her finger entered me, slipping deep into my vagina, I shuddered. She was violating my body, defiling my shrine, and there was nothing I could do about it. A second finger penetrating me, stretching my supple vaginal sheath open, I felt her hot breath against the skin of my inner thigh. Her tongue licking my fleshy outer lips, delving into my open sex crack, I jumped.

'No!' I squealed.

'You'll do exactly as I—'

'No, please!'

'Selina, you *do* want to see your husband again, don't you?'

As her tongue licked my moist sex valley, snaking around my clitoris, all I could do was think of Danny. I had to allow this defilement of my naked body for his sake, permit the bitch to perform whatever perversion she wished. As her slender fingers left the wet sheath of my vagina and her ardent tongue lapped around my open hole, I tried to look upon the lesbian act as cold and clinical.

'Mmm, you taste nice,' she breathed, her tongue entering my sex duct as she parted my pussy lips. The lapping and sucking sound of her tongue and mouth against my wet inner flesh resounding through my head, I tried to pretend it was Danny between my legs, as he'd pretended it was me when he'd fucked her. But the soft tendrils of her trailing hair tickling my inner thighs, her feminine fragrance tantalizing my nostrils, I couldn't deny that this was a girl licking inside my vagina. And, repulsed though I was, the act was far from cold and clinical.

As her tongue swept repeatedly over the nodule of my clitoris and her fingers explored deep inside my sex hole again, I was relieved that I felt no arousal – only shame. I'd read somewhere that lesbian sex was supposed to be good, that a lot of women enjoyed the intimate and experienced attention of another woman. But I felt disgusted by the vile and immoral act. My abuser was no better than a common whore and I was an unwilling participant. The distasteful act was merely a means to an end – Danny's release.

'Stand with your feet apart and bend your knees,' she instructed me. 'I want to get my fingers right up your beautiful cunt.' I did as she asked, my vaginal crack opening wide as my thighs parted. Trying to push her fist into my tight sheath, she licked and sucked on my exposed clitoris like a hungry dog. To my horror, my clitoris swelled, sending electrifying sensations through my quivering pelvis.

'No,' I murmured weakly, desperately trying to deny the sensations emanating from my pulsating clitoris. 'No, I can't . . .' Her fingers driving in and out of my moistening vagina, her tongue snaking around my sex nodule, I tried to think of anything and everything other than the rushes of arousal coursing through my naked body.

I didn't know what was happening to me, why I was deriving undeniable pleasure from this lewd lesbian act while Danny was being held hostage. I tried desperately to hold back as I felt the beginnings of my orgasm stirring within my contracting womb. I mustn't come, couldn't allow another woman to finger me and suck my clitoris to orgasm!

My vagina rhythmically contracting, my sex button throbbing beneath her sweeping tongue, I finally reached the verge of my illicit climax. My orgasm imploding within my pulsating clitoris and then exploding, sending shock waves of pleasure though my naked body, I cried out and clung to her head to steady myself.

'God!' I breathed as her fist entered me, squelching within my drenched vagina as my clitoris rhythmically pulsated within her hot mouth. 'God, *no!*' On and on the shock waves of orgasm rolled through my sated body, taking me to incredible heights of sexual satisfaction. My head tossed back, my eyes closed, I was flying like a bird, soaring through the air, rising higher and higher as my orgasm peaked.

The ripples of sex finally waning, my body trembling uncontrollably, I staggered back, her fist leaving my spasming vagina as I flopped onto the sofa. The door bell ringing, she looked at me, her blue eyes frowning as surprise and fear registered in her expression. Grabbing her coat, she fled from the room, the back door slamming shut as the bell rang again.

Saved by the bell? Had I wanted to be saved? I didn't know what I wanted, what I felt, as I staggered to my feet and dressed quickly. Dripping with guilt and confusion, I zipped my skirt and buttoned my blouse as I rushed to the door. Whoever it was who had rung the bell had gone, probably assuming that I was out. All I could do now was wait for Danny to return – *if* he returned. Of course they'd let him go, I reflected. We were dealing with money and sex, not murder!

Pacing the lounge floor, my mind riddled with guilt, I tried to comprehend what I'd done, why I'd experienced such a massive orgasm with another female. Was I discovering another side to myself? I wondered as I waited in anticipation for my husband. Was I a latent lesbian? What had happened to me, to my life? What had happened to Danny?

Chapter Three

Danny returned an hour later, dashing into the lounge and flinging his arms around me as if he'd been away for months. He looked tired, exhausted, and as I broke down and cried I wondered what they'd done to him.

'It's OK, love,' he said softly. 'Everything's OK.'

'Where have you *been*?' I sobbed. 'What did they . . .'

'Calm down, Selina. Are *you* all right? That's all that matters.'

'Yes, yes – I'm fine.'

'What did the bitch do to you?'

Averting my tearful eyes, I couldn't tell Danny the appalling truth, that I'd stood with my legs apart, the girl's mouth pushed between my gaping vaginal lips, and enjoyed one of the best orgasms ever. I didn't understand it, how the vulgar act had excited me, aroused me to the point where I'd come in her mouth – and I knew Danny would never understand.

It was like a dream, something that hadn't really happened and yet was so vivid in my mind. Her fist deep inside my vagina, stretching the drenched silken walls of my sex sheath, my clitoris sucked into her wet mouth as my amazing orgasm gripped my naked body . . . No one would ever understand.

'Nothing happened,' I finally replied softly. 'The doorbell rang and she fled, rushed out of the back door.'

'How long was she here?'

'Not long. Danny, what happened to *you*? You went for a walk and . . .'

'A car drew up alongside me and the driver asked for directions. Before I knew what was going on, he'd leaped out of the car with another man and bundled me into the back seat. Christ, I wondered what the hell they were up to as they blindfolded me. I was shit-scared, I can tell you.'

'Where did they take you?'

'I don't know. We drove for a while and then I was marched down some steps into a basement. I didn't connect them with the girl until they told me to ring you and . . . Anyway, some time later, they dropped me off at the end of the road – and here I am. So, what did the girl want? What did she do?'

'She wants me to write the second novel. She said that if I don't, you'll be taken away again. I can't understand what it is they want, Danny. Money, OK, but . . .'

'They're obviously trying to frighten us, Selina. Taking me away like that was clearly designed to let us know that they mean business.'

'But, the sex . . .'

'I reckon it's all part of the blackmail plan. The more they have on you, the more incriminating photographs, the better the position they'll be in to demand money.'

'I can't believe that this is happening to us. You were abducted, for God's sake!'

'Look, all you have to do is write the second book and . . .'

'How the hell can I write a book with all this going on?'

'You'll have to. I'll make some tea, OK?'

'OK.'

As he left the room, I tried to get my mind around the horrendous situation. I could see Danny's point. The more they had on me, the better the position they'd be in to blackmail me, but . . . My being in what appeared to be a lesbian relationship was the ultimate blackmail material!

How often would the girl call round to have sex with me?

Would she want Danny to screw her again? Would Danny be safe going for his walks or would they snatch him again? These people, whoever they were, were obviously into this sort of thing in a big way. They'd targeted me and were going all out to get me, probably intending to take me for every penny I earned. I was trying to think of too many things at once, clogging my mind with too many thoughts. I had to relax my head.

I didn't know which was more worrying, the thugs who'd abducted Danny – or the terrific orgasm I'd had with the bitch. Had she not fled the house, who knew what she'd have demanded next? Perhaps I could do a deal with them, I mused. If I said that I'd write the book if they kept away from us . . .

'Tea's up,' Danny smiled as he carried a tray into the room and placed it on the coffee table. 'I've been thinking, they won't grab me again.'

'They might. They've done it once, so why not again?'

'It's a pretty risky business, snatching someone off the street and bundling them into the back of a car. Not the sort of thing they'd want to do too often.'

'I suppose not.'

'OK, the girl came here and told you to write the second book, and they got me to ring you to make sure that you knew they meant business. They're obviously not big-time gangsters because, at the very most, they'll only get, say, half your advance.'

'*Half?* That's fifty thousand . . .'

'It's a lot of money, yes – but hardly big-time stuff. They've achieved what they'd set out to do, which was to frighten us. I reckon they'll back off once they know that you're writing the book and the advance is on the way. When the girl next contacts us, we'll tell her that you've started the book.'

'But . . .'

'There are no buts, love. You'll *have* to write the book.'

'What about the detective?'

'It's too late to ring him now. I'll call him in the morning and fill him in with the latest. You never know, he might have seen the girl leave and . . . I'll call him in the morning.'

'I'm tired and my head's aching like hell. I think I'll go to bed.'

'Don't you want some tea?'

'No, not now.'

'OK. Try not to worry, I reckon that the worst is over.'

'Apart from giving the bastards thousands and thousands of pounds.'

'It might not come to that. You go up and I'll join you later.'

Again, I barely slept. My dreams wouldn't leave me, restless monsters roaming my mind, conjuring vivid images of the girl's mouth closed over my clitoris, her fist driving deep into my pussy. But that was my secret. No one, apart from the girl, would ever know the dreadful truth. If she told Danny, I'd deny it – and he'd believe me.

I was up at six the next morning, making tea – and my plans. I hadn't told Danny about the royalty cheque, and I wasn't going to. If the girl started questioning him, he couldn't let something slip that he didn't know about. I'd open another bank account and hang onto that money if it was the last thing I did.

Oversleeping, Danny wandered downstairs at nine-thirty. I reckoned that he'd been mentally exhausted and had fallen into a deep sleep the minute his head had hit the pillow, unlike me! As he made himself a cup of coffee, he started on about the book again, how I should begin as soon as possible, how I had no choice. I couldn't take it, listening to him rambling on and on about the bloody book.

'I rang the publisher,' I finally interrupted him.

'Oh?'

'I spoke to Tammy about the book.'

'Good girl! I knew you'd . . .'

'Danny, there's a problem.'

'What do you mean?'

'After lunch with Tammy the other week I'd thought the second book was definite, but . . . Things have changed.'

'Changed?'

'The sales of the first novel peaked, and then died a sudden death.'

'But the press has been quoting *fantastic* sales figures.'

'It was hype. The publisher deliberately inflated the figures to try and boost the flagging sales.'

'So, what are you saying?'

'They don't want a second book, after all.'

'But . . .'

'They wanted to see how the first one did before they'd commit themselves and, by the look of it, it's died.'

'I can't believe it! It hit the top of the best-sellers list and . . .'

'And now it's dropped off. Tammy reckons that the false figures they've given the media might revive it, but she doesn't hold out much hope.'

I didn't like lying to Danny, but I had to put an end to his obsession with the book. He didn't understand that my head had to be clear to write, my mind free of worries and problems. I'd explained many times that to produce successful work I had to become part of the book, to dissolve into my characters. Unless I was left to become totally absorbed in my work, to concentrate wholly on my writing, I could produce nothing worthwhile.

Gazing out of the window, Danny sighed, obviously believing that I'd rung the publisher and no doubt wondering what the blackmailers would do once they found out. But, if we told them that the publisher didn't want a second book, there'd be nothing they could do about it. There'd be no point in forcing me to write a book that no one wanted, that carried no financial gain.

I reckoned that this was the only way we could win. OK, they could still go to the newspapers, but what would they gain? If I told the bitch that I had no career to destroy, that the first book had died a death and there was to be no second book, that would be the end of the matter.

'But the book was doing so well,' Danny persisted, turning on his heels to face me.

' "*Was*" being the operative word. Tammy reckons this is nothing new. They launch a new author, the book shoots to the top of the list, and then dies.'

'So there'll be no royalties?'

'How can there be? Book sales generate royalties, Danny – and if a book doesn't sell . . . Anyway, that should shut the thugs up.'

'I doubt it!'

'What do you mean?'

'As I was saying, they mean business.'

'Danny, if the publisher doesn't want another book, then . . .'

'Try telling *them* that!'

'I intend to. When the girl contacts us, I'll tell her exactly what Tammy said, and that'll be that.'

I wasn't sure whether Danny believed me as he gazed out of the window again. My story sounded feasible enough, but he seemed suspicious. I supposed he was worried, probably thinking that the thugs wouldn't believe a word of it and grab him again. As I made toast and marmalade, he paced the floor, his forehead lined, his eyes tired. We were both tired, tired of the whole damned business!

'They won't do anything, Danny,' I smiled reassuringly.

'Who won't?' he asked abstractedly.

'The thugs and the girl.'

'I've been thinking,' he murmured, his dark eyes frowning as he gazed at me. 'I reckon you should start the second book anyway.'

'Why?'

'The time might come when they want it. If the first one picks up, they might ask you for the second.'

'But . . .'

'Don't you see? Firstly, if the day comes when they want it, you'll be well underway with it – you might even have finished it. Secondly, we can show the girl that you're writing it, show her the book on your computer screen.'

'Danny . . .'

'Selina, you don't know what it's like being dragged off the bloody street by a couple of thugs! I was in that basement, tied to a bloody chair, almost pissing myself with fear. It's all very well you saying that it'll be OK, but I'm the one who's going to end up . . . Christ knows where! Six feet under, more than likely!'

'OK, OK, I'll start the bloody book.'

'Sorry, I didn't mean to get irate, it's just that I was shit-scared in that basement. Before I knew they were connected with the girl I thought of all sorts of terrible things. Political killings . . .'

'You're not into politics.'

'No, but they might have thought I was. It's happened before, where the wrong person gets murdered. Screwing some tart is one thing, but . . .'

'OK, I'll start on the book today.'

'Good. Shit, this is a bloody mess!'

'You're telling me!'

He flounced off, leaving me to have breakfast alone. He

really was frightened, and I couldn't blame him. Again, I wondered how on earth we'd got into this mess. I'd been lying my head off to Danny, he'd been abducted and tied up in a basement, I'd watched him screw the bitch, I'd had lesbian sex with her, we'd given away ten thousand pounds . . . What the hell was going to happen next?

As I sat at the table nibbling my toast, I realized that I couldn't take any more. Physically and mentally drained, I knew I had to get away, have a break from the nightmare before it swallowed me up. Ringing Chrissy, I asked her whether she felt like spending a few days in a hotel somewhere.

'I can't,' she sighed. 'We're really busy at work. I'm free today but there's no way I could get any more time off.'

'Never mind, it was just a thought.'

'Shall I come round for coffee?'

'Yes, I haven't seen you for ages.'

'Give me fifteen minutes.'

'OK, see you soon.'

Chatting to Chrissy might help, I reflected as I washed up. Unloading my problems . . . No, Danny was right, it was best not to tell anyone. As for the book, I'd try to write the first few pages, just to show willing. My thoughts turning to Tammy, I decided to ring her. I knew she'd ask how the book was coming on, and I'd have to make up some excuse or other, but I thought it best to make contact.

'Selina, how are you?' she trilled.

'Fine, fine. I thought I'd just ring and say hi.'

'I'm glad you did. The sales have gone through the roof! Look, the second book . . . We want to follow the first with another as soon as possible.'

'Yes, I know,' I sighed, rather too despondently.

'Is there a problem?'

'No, no, it's just that . . . Writer's block, that's what it is.'

'Don't worry, it happens. Just relax and don't force it. It'll come, believe me.'

'I hope so.'

'How far have you got with it?'

'I haven't.'

'You've not even started?'

'No.'

'Oh. Er . . .'

'I haven't had the contract yet, Tammy.'

'Don't worry about that, it'll be with you any day now.'

'Good. Look, I'll try and get my brain into gear.'

'OK, I'll talk to you soon. Get those fingers working, Selina.'

'I will.'

More pressure, more problems! I reflected as I replaced the receiver. I felt as if I was going mad as I wandered up to my den and sat at the desk. Switching the computer on, I pondered on the book, bringing the synopsis up on screen and wondering how the hell I was going to write.

'I rang the private dick,' Danny informed me, appearing in the doorway. 'He didn't see the girl leave last night.'

'She went the back way, probably over the wall into the alley.'

'Oh, great! Anyway, I told him about the thugs, that I'd been dragged off the bloody street.'

'What did he say?'

'He agreed with me, you should write the book. At least it'll give him time to . . .'

'I *am* writing the bloody book, or *trying* to!' I snapped.

'I'm sorry, I'll leave you in peace.'

'No, no, *I*'m sorry. What are you going to do?'

'I don't know, I'll have a coffee and then I might try to write something. See you later.'

The private detective was bloody useless, I reflected. Apart from sitting in his car, he'd done nothing. God knew how much he was going to charge us! Trying to clear my head, I read the synopsis. The idea was good, but where to start? Page one, paragraph one, sentence one.

'Hi!' Chrissy beamed as she breezed into the room with a cup of coffee. 'Danny let me in.'

'Chrissy, it's good to see you! Plonk yourself on the couch.'

'I'm not stopping you from working, am I?'

'No, no. To be honest, I haven't worked for ages.'

'Why's that?'

I told her the story – well, most of it. I couldn't bring myself to confess to having had a girl lick me to orgasm, but I did say that Danny had screwed her while I'd watched. Hooking her long raven hair behind her ears, Chrissy listened intently, her eyes widening or frowning as I mentioned the thugs and the basement, the money and the naked girl.

'I'll tell you what I think,' she pronounced when I'd finished. 'Danny's in on it.'

'No, he's not,' I replied. 'Admittedly, it did cross my mind, but he's not.'

'It fits, Selina,' she insisted, raising her eyebrows. 'It fits perfectly.'

'I know it does, but . . . What would he have to gain by dreaming up fantastic stories of abduction and being tied up in a basement?'

'Money.'

'But it's *our* money.'

'Sex.'

'If he wanted to have an affair, he wouldn't go to all this trouble. And why have me watch him screw a girl?'

'He might get a kick out of it.'

'You should write fiction, Chrissy! God, you're so cynical!'

'I can't help it. Anyway, it fits.'

I decided to tell her the rest of the story. Closing the door, I told her about the girl forcing me to strip, about her fingering and licking me to orgasm. Her expression one of disbelief, Chrissy didn't take her eyes off me until I'd finished relating the sordid details. Saying nothing, she sipped her coffee, obviously mulling over the incredible act the girl had performed on my naked body. Initially, I was so embarrassed that I wished I hadn't said anything.

'Shit!' she finally breathed. 'And you say you haven't told Danny?'

'How the hell can I?'

'Yes, I see your point. God! What are you going to do?'

'I don't know. What would *you* do?'

'I'd tell the girl where to get off. Tell her that she can go to the newspapers and . . .'

'I've thought about that. But there's more to this than simple blackmail, Chrissy.'

'How do you mean?'

'If I was rich, a millionairess, I could understand it. But going to all this trouble for a relatively small amount of money – the photographs, snatching Danny . . . Somehow, it doesn't add up.'

'It's not that much trouble for, what did you reckon, fifty grand?'

'Yes, but . . . There's something that I can't quite put my finger on. I don't know why, but I feel that there's far more to this than meets the eye.'

'You're a celebrity, Selina. You could quite easily end up a millionairess and . . .'

'That's it!'

'What is?'

'You've just hit the nail on the head. They're getting all this on me now so that, if I do strike it rich, they'll *really* have a hold on me.'

'God!'

Pacing the floor, I could see clearly what their game was. Danny screwing the same girl I was having a lesbian relationship with? Now that really *was* a juicy story! They could demand hundreds of thousands, and I'd have to pay up. Tammy had already mentioned the possibility of film rights. The more I thought about it, the more I realized that I could quite easily end up a millionairess – and sooner rather than later. Yes, that was their game, all right.

'At least it now makes sense,' I murmured, sitting at my desk.

'I'll tell you what I'd do,' Chrissy proffered, almost triumphantly.

'What?'

'End it now.'

'How?'

'Let them go to the papers now, before they get too much on you. It'll soon blow over and, you never know, it might even boost your book sales. All publicity is good publicity, as they say.'

'Is it? I'm not so sure.'

'If you allow them to carry on, they'll get so much on you that . . .'

'It's a good idea, but . . .'

'You've no choice, Selina.'

'I reckon you're right.'

'I *know* I'm right.'

There was nothing to prove that I'd allowed the girl to lick me to orgasm. So I wouldn't be branded a lesbian. OK, so they had photographs of me watching Danny screw her . . . Chrissy was right, it would probably boost my sales no end! Feeling positive, I was about to ring Tammy and tell her the story when I thought better of it. The last thing I wanted was to do anything rash. I needed time to think.

'Chrissy, I've a lot to do,' I said as she stood up.

'I could see that you were deep in thought,' she smiled. 'I'll leave you to it. Give me a ring and keep me posted.'

'I will. And thanks.'

'Any time. I'll see myself out.'

Pacing the floor again, I mulled over the idea of telling the girl where to go. The thugs might turn nasty, but that was a chance I had to take. If Danny and I went away for a holiday for a month or so, there'd be nothing they could do to us, other than go to the papers. Dashing into Danny's room and finding him at his desk, I told him the plan.

'I reckon that's the answer,' he said pensively. 'Yes, that's it. If you do strike it rich, they'll have nothing on you – it'll be old hat.'

'It's perfect!' I beamed.

'Christ, I'm feeling better already.'

'We'll go to the airport and take a flight, any old flight.'

'Right. Er . . . We'd better wait until the tart contacts us, Selina. It's no good going away until we've told them to sod off.'

'OK. I hope she rings soon because I want to get away from all this.'

'So do I, love. Christ, I could do with a break. We *both* need a break.'

I felt so awash with relief that I cried. As Danny held me close I felt that a holiday would not only do *us* good but would also help our relationship. A month in the sun, good food and plenty of wine . . . Yes, that was the answer. And when I returned to face the media, I'd have no comment. I'd say nothing at all and the whole thing would blow over before I knew it.

'I'm going back to my den,' I said, kissing his cheek.

'The book?'

'Yes, the book,' I smiled. 'See you later.'

Closing the door, I sat at my desk, contemplating the story

once it broke. The newspapers would have a field day! *Selina Goodman watches her husband bonk a naked tart* – I could already see the headlines in my mind's eye. But I didn't care what people would think: they could go to hell as far as I was concerned. Besides, as Chrissy had said, it would probably boost my book sales.

But I couldn't help thinking of the girl kneeling before me, her mouth locked to my vulva, licking me, sucking me. It was something I'd never forget for as long as I lived. Another skeleton in the cupboard! But it *had* been an experience, and that was what life was all about – experiences. 'I might even write a lesbian scene into the book!' I chuckled.

As Danny wandered into the room, his face pale and drawn, I knew that something was wrong. The phone hadn't rung, so what was it? Had he thought of a flaw in the plan? Standing beside me, he stared at me accusingly.

'What is it?' I asked. 'Danny, what's wrong?'

'This,' he said, passing me an envelope. 'It was on the doormat. I opened it.'

Taking the envelope, I pulled out a photograph of me standing in the lounge, my head back, my eyes closed, sheer sexual satisfaction depicted in my expression as the girl licked and fingered me. *My eyes closed*: my mind had been blown away with my immense orgasm – and I hadn't noticed the bloody flash. As I stared open-mouthed at the disgusting picture, I felt as if I'd been wrenched out of my body. I couldn't look at Danny, let alone speak.

'Why didn't you tell me?' he finally asked.

'Danny, I . . .'

'They've really got you over a barrel now.'

'I did it because she said that you . . .'

'You should have told me, Selina. I'm not blaming you for what you did. I know why you did it and I understand that, but you should have told me.'

As he mooched out of the room, I cried again. This time, they weren't tears of relief but of horror, shock, fear. My plan shot to pieces, I held my head, wondering what the hell to do. Got me over a barrel? Christ, they'd got me *chained* to a bloody barrel! And to top it all, Danny was in a sulk.

Finally composing myself, I dried my eyes and walked to the window, gazing at the world. A funny old world? It stank! 'How are you, Selina?' I murmured. 'I'm OK, it's the others.' As the phone rang, I turned and stared at it. I knew instinctively that it was the bitch and decided to let Danny answer it. I didn't want to speak to the cow, listen to her threats, her demands for crude lesbian sex. The front door slamming shut, I looked out of the window to see Danny walking away down the path.

'What the fuck do you want?' I screamed as I ran across the room and snatched the receiver. 'Why don't you fuck off?'

'Selina, that's not very nice,' the bitch cooed. 'After our intimate time together, I'd have thought . . .'

'You can go to hell!'

'I'd rather come in your mouth.'

'If you think . . .'

'I assume you've seen the photograph?'

'Yes, I have.'

'It's come out rather well, don't you agree?'

'No!'

'I'll be round this evening.'

'You will not!'

'What a shame, I really thought you'd see sense. No doubt my boss will invite Danny round again. Well, not "invite", exactly.'

'What good will that do?'

'It'll get you working on the book, for one thing.'

'Danny's gone away. He's . . .'

'Yes, of course he has. I'll be round at seven.'

As she hung up, I knew there was no way out of it. She'd come round and probably demand that I finger and lick her to orgasm while Danny watched. 'God!' I breathed, picturing the vile scene. I'd always put sex and love together, sex and love between Danny and me, but now? She could demand anything of us and . . . Us? Danny had said that he'd have nothing to do with her. If she didn't get her way, if he wouldn't play the game . . .

Why the hell hadn't I noticed the camera flash? I wondered. Not that it would have done me any good. I should have known there'd be a photographer lurking and drawn the curtains. I could have kicked myself for being so dopey. But there was no point in hindsight – the damage was done and that was that.

My mind hurt with thinking. They now had all the evidence they needed, so why was the girl coming round for sex? There'd be little point in taking more photographs, so why put herself at risk by returning to the house? Her boss, as she called the unknown bastard, wouldn't send her round – he wasn't stupid. Perhaps she was taking advantage of the situation and, unknown to her superior, planned to enjoy sex sessions with Danny and me.

I pondered on the notion for some time. It would have been an idea to speak to her boss but, presumably, he hadn't made contact himself because the bitch was the go-between. The thugs would have been employed by the man, also protecting his anonymity. I was determined to find out where the girl lived, discover her true identity. The private detective was useless and I decided that, if I wanted a job doing properly, then I'd have to do it myself.

I'd make sure that Danny was out of the way that evening, do whatever I had to with the bitch, and then follow her. If I was right and her boss didn't know she'd planned to come round, there'd be no photographer – and no getaway car waiting for her. Although I felt a little more positive, I knew that discovering her true identity wouldn't really help me. But it was a start.

I walked into town and opened a new bank account, depositing my royalty cheque. At least I had *some* money, I reflected as I made my way home. I felt terribly guilty for keeping it secret from Danny, but I knew it was the right thing to do as he had a habit of manipulating me and I'd end up paying the girl again. At least I had *some* money, I repeated to myself for reassurance.

'I'm sorry,' Danny smiled as I walked into the lounge.

'It's OK. The reason I didn't tell you was because . . . Well, it's not the sort of thing I'd want to tell anyone, let alone my husband.'

'I understand. Where have you been?'

'I went for a walk into town. The girl phoned while you were out.'

'What did she say?'

'She's coming round this evening.'

'Oh, God!'

'Danny, I have a plan. I want you to go out this evening, go to the pub for a beer or something.'

'What, and leave you here alone with her?'

'Yes.'

'But . . .'

'Trust me, Danny. I have an idea, trust me.'

'What are you going to do?'

'I'll tell you later, if my plan works.'

Leaving Danny in the lounge, I bounded upstairs to my den. If I discovered where the girl lived I might be able to discover the identity of her boss. Again, it would do me no good, but at least I'd know who I was dealing with. I might tell him that the girl had been taking money, money that he'd obviously know nothing about, and get her into serious trouble. If he thought she was working alone, taking money on the side . . . But that was a long way off. I had to prepare for the evening.

Under duress, Danny went out at six. I waited a good ten minutes and then stood by the front gate, looking up and down the road. I realized that I might have to wait an hour or more and, if she did come by car, she'd park well away from the house, but I had to discover which direction she came from.

I was in luck. After half an hour, I noticed a red car pull up some hundred yards away. As the girl climbed out and started walking towards me, I dashed back into the house. I should have had Danny there, I reflected. He could have nipped over the back wall into the alley and got the bitch's registration number. Perhaps we should have told the private detective? But I'd kept my plan to myself. It was too late now.

So far, so good, I ruminated, pacing the hall as I waited for the bell to ring. I reckoned that I was right – her boss knew nothing of her visit, of her continuing demands for sex. What horrendous sexual ordeal I was going to have to endure I couldn't imagine, but my plan was looking good. Whatever I was put through, it would be worth it.

'Hi,' she smiled sweetly as I answered the door. 'I've been looking forward to this.'

'Have you?' I sneered as she stepped inside.

'Of course. Where's my stud?'

'Out.'

'Oh, what a shame. Still, we can have plenty of sexy fun without him.'

Following me into the lounge she wasted no time, discarding her coat and draping it over the back of the sofa. She was naked underneath the coat, as I'd expected, and I gazed at her breasts, her long nipples, her vaginal crack clearly visible through her sparse blonde pubic hairs. I shuddered with apprehension as I imagined my tongue there, between her female lips, licking her clitoris to orgasm, but I had to play the game.

'We'll start by having you naked,' she smiled, her slender fingers unbuttoning my blouse. I said nothing as she slipped the garment off my shoulders and squeezed my full bra cups. Looking down at my deep cleavage as she encircled my nipples with her fingertips, I felt proud of my body – but sharing it with another woman? To appease my guilt, I tried to imagine Danny was with me as she unhooked my bra. He was massaging my breasts, enjoying my body – but the touch was soft, gentle, feminine.

Peeling the silk cups away from my firm breasts, gazing longingly at my erect nipples, she leaned forward and licked each areola in turn. My nipples stiffening, becoming erect in arousal, I closed my eyes as she engulfed my milk teat in her hot mouth and gently sucked. Her wet tongue teasing my nipple, expertly encircling the sensitive brown protrusion, I breathed deeply as the sensations permeated my body. She knew how to treat another woman, what another woman wanted. Was that what *I* wanted?

Opening my eyes as I wondered whether Danny would return, I glanced at her coat slung over the back of the sofa. She'd not brought a bag with her – her car keys were obviously in her coat pocket. As she sank her teeth gently into my nipple, sending electrifying sensations of sex through my quivering body, I prayed for a chance to get the keys. Her bag was probably in the car and . . .

'Now *you* can suck *my* nipples,' she declared, standing upright and squeezing her firm breasts in her hands, her brown nipples distending. Leaning forward, I took one teat into my mouth and sucked. Life was about experiences, I found myself thinking as I bit her milk bud. Did I want to experience this? 'Bite me harder,' she breathed, tossing her head back. I complied, wondering where Danny was, what he was doing while I was biting another woman's nipple. 'God, I've been looking forward to this. Finger my cunt!' she gasped, parting her feet.

My hand tentatively moving between her thighs as I bit and sucked her nipple, I hesitated. I couldn't do it, although I knew I had to. 'Come on, Selina,' she coaxed me huskily. 'I'm hot and very wet. Finger my cunt.' My hands trembling as her crude words resounded through my tormented mind, my fingertip between her fleshy sex lips, I found the drenched entrance to her vagina and pushed my finger inside.

She shuddered, her breathing deep, heavy, as I entered her. The walls of her vagina were silky, soft, hot, creamy. This wasn't so bad, I mused as she instructed me to massage her clitoris. To discover her identity, to try to halt the blackmail, as a means to an end, this wasn't so bad.

Her clitoris was solid, hard beneath my fingertip, and I recalled her licking me to orgasm. I became confused as I massaged her pleasure spot and she began whimpering in her sexual awakening. What was I *doing*? This was lesbian sex. What the hell was I doing? Her hands fumbling with my skirt, tugging it down, I again thought I couldn't go through with it and stepped back.

'Selina,' she said throatily, threateningly. 'You're not going to stop now.'

'I . . . Look, I . . .'

'My boss has your husband.'

'No, he hasn't,' I countered. 'I know where Danny is. He rang me just before you arrived.'

'I wouldn't bet on it, if I were you.'

She was bluffing, I was sure as she knelt before me and yanked my skirt down to my ankles. Danny was safe, either walking or . . . Pulling my panties down, she looked up at me, her face grinning as she ran her fingertip up and down my moist sex crack. Her boss didn't know she was with me, I was positive as her finger deftly teased my clitoris. I deliberately hadn't drawn the curtains, which would prove my theory if there was no camera flash.

'You're nice and wet,' she purred, her finger opening my tight hole and entering my slippery sex duct. 'And *very* hot.' Pushing a second finger into my vagina, she began thrusting in and out of my sheath. Involuntarily bending my knees, I gasped, quivering like a leaf as the incredible sensations transmitted deep into my contracting womb.

Danny knew what I'd be doing, which helped to eradicate my guilt. He knew what I'd be forced to do, that we were in this together, that I had no choice. *Had* I a choice? As she parted my vaginal lips and sucked on my clitoris, adding to the amazing sensations, I knew that I could put up with this. More than put up with it, I . . . Again, I tried to deny the illicit pleasure another woman's intimate attention was bringing me. I didn't want a lesbian relationship, and yet . . .

'It's my turn,' she grinned, her glazed eyes staring at me as she sat on the sofa with her legs spread, her vaginal slit gaping. 'Come and kneel between my feet.' Almost mechanically I took my position, gazing at her alluring pinken valley, the opaque droplets of sex liquid clinging to her intricate folds.

I knew what she wanted me to do as I massaged her soft inner lips – that she wanted my mouth pressed against her sex flesh, my tongue caressing her clitoris to orgasm. Experiences? It had taken me long enough to bring myself to suck Danny to orgasm and swallow his sperm, let alone licking the quim of another woman – a virtual stranger.

'Lick me,' she murmured, her eyes closed as she parted her thighs further, the portal to her sex duct opening invitingly. 'Lick my cunt.' Stroking her velveteen folds, running my fingertip up and down her moist sex valley, I circled her solid clitoris. Moving my head forward, my tongue protruding, eager, I hesitated, examining her most intimate flesh. *Could* I lick her there? Did I *want* to taste her juices of lesbian arousal? I was torn between my own unbelievable arousal and the immorality of the crude act.

'Lick my cunt,' she instructed me again. Moving closer, I tentatively licked her full outer lips, tasting her heady female juices. 'My clitoris!' she gasped, moving forward on the sofa until her buttocks were over the edge of the cushion. Again, I licked the soft hillocks of her swollen outer lips, not daring to venture into her wet valley.

Wondering at my lewd behaviour as I felt my own clitoris swell and throb, I stretched her sex lips wide apart, exposing her erect clitoris. The pink protrusion was swollen, larger than I'd imagined, and I pressed my mouth against her vulval flesh, repeatedly sweeping my tongue up and down her open valley. The exhilarating scent of her femininity arousing me beyond belief, I fervently lapped around her sex nub, mouthing and sucking as I lost myself in my wanton act. Breathing heavily, her stomach quivering, her thighs twitching, I knew she was quickly nearing her climax, and I mouthed, sucked and licked her with a passion that frightened me.

'My cunt!' she whispered urgently as the crudity of my sinful act registered in my whirling mind. 'Finger my cunt!' Driving three fingers deep into her open sex hole, I continued to lick and suck her clitoris, my mind awash with thoughts of her coming in my mouth, how I'd feel as her juices bathed my fingers and her sex button pulsated in orgasm beneath my caressing tongue.

'God, don't stop!' she screamed in her coming, gyrating her hips and forcing the open centre of her femininity hard against my wet mouth. Her juices spurting from her rhythmically contracting vagina, running down my hand, I sustained her massive orgasm with my snaking tongue. 'Yes, yes!' she cried, arching her back and gripping my head, forcing her open sex valley harder against my mouth.

Quivering uncontrollably, her climax finally beginning to wane, she let out long low moans of pleasure, slowing her rocking hips to bring out the last waves of sex from her swollen clitoris. Gently mouthing and sucking, I again pondered on my indecent behaviour, wondering what I'd done, how I could have brought myself to do such a thing to another woman – to my blackmailer.

Sitting back on my heels as she began to recover, I watched her juices issuing from her inflamed sex hole, my mind swirling as I realized that I might be a lesbian. No, the idea was crazy. I'd been *forced* to commit the obscene act. Never again would I . . . Never again?

'I'll reciprocate,' she smiled, her pink tongue provocatively licking her succulent lips as she slipped off the sofa. 'Come on, swap places.' As if in a dream I mechanically took my position, half dazed, not really in control of my actions as I sat with my thighs wide, my open vagina blatantly on offer to another woman. Yanking my fleshy sex cushions wide apart in her eagerness, she locked her hot mouth to my open hole, sucking and drinking my flowing juices.

Her honeydew lingering on my tongue, my arousal dangerously high, I desperately needed to come. Images of Danny loomed in my mind as her finger entered me and she sucked my clitoris into her hot mouth. I wanted him there, a man licking me, I wanted . . .

'God!' I cried as wonderful preorgasmic rushes flooded through my naked body. 'God, don't stop!' The sensations rapidly building as she worked expertly on my ripening clitoris, I arched my back, my thighs open to the extreme as I forced my yawning vulval valley into her thirsty mouth.

'Yes, yes!' I screamed, my orgasm coming, my body shaking violently. 'Ah, yes!'

Engulfed in the beautiful sensations of sex, my orgasm erupting within my pulsating clitoris, I gasped and panted, my head tossing from side to side as she sustained my inconceivable pleasure. Never had I known such heights of sexual ecstasy, experienced an orgasm of such strength and duration. My very being was soaring to the heavens. On and on she fingered my spasming vagina, my juices of lust spewing from my open hole as she sucked and licked on my pulsating sex button.

The beautifully agonizing sensations finally beginning to wane, I imagined Danny witnessing the crude scene. What would he think? *What's this going to do to our relationship?* His words haunted me, crawling across the webs of my mind like spiders as she slipped her wet fingers out of my burning vagina and gave my clitoris one last hard suck. Shuddering, my naked body sated, I didn't open my eyes. My mind lost, blown away on clouds of lust, I lay trembling in the aftermath of my phenomenal coming.

When I emerged from my stupefied state, she'd gone. My plan in ruins, I staggered to my feet and dressed, concealing my sex-drenched body, my dripping vaginal slit – the stark evidence of obscene lesbian lust. Climbing the stairs and flopping onto my bed, I cried. In my sobbing, I dreamed my dreams of lesbian desire.

Chapter Four

Danny woke me gently from my dreams at nine o'clock. Towering above the bed, his dark eyes frowning, he was obviously wondering what sexual acts the girl had forced me to endure. Did the thought excite him? Did the thought of me licking another woman to orgasm arouse him? Climbing off the bed, I realized that my inner thighs were sticky. The exotic taste of her orgasmic juices was on my lips. What I'd done had excited me, but Danny . . .

'Are you OK?' he asked concernedly.

'Yes, yes, I'm OK,' I smiled.

'What did she do to you?'

'She . . . The same as before,' I murmured in my embarrassment.

'Did your plan work?'

'No, no, she left before I could . . . Danny, I'd rather not talk about it.'

'I understand,' he said. 'I'll be downstairs.'

But he didn't understand. *I* didn't understand. No one could ever begin to comprehend what I'd done, the pleasure I'd derived from lesbian sex. Making my way downstairs, my vaginal lips wet and slippery, my panties damp, I found him in the kitchen filling the kettle. He looked tired. The thought of me with another woman was obviously anguishing him, worrying him, and I wondered where it would all end. Essentially, I'd committed adultery, and the terrifying notion haunted me. God only knew what it was doing to my husband!

'What was your plan?' he asked curiously.

'I was going to follow her, but she left before . . . before I was ready. She said that her boss had taken you again.'

'She lied. I went for a long walk. Selina, I want to ask you something.'

I knew what was coming next – that he was going to ask me whether I'd enjoyed the intimate sexual attention of another woman. I couldn't take much more, the blackmail, the lesbian sex. I was losing my identity, my direction in life – my morals. I didn't know who I was or what I wanted any more. I'd been a writer, a happily married successful author – but now? Now, I wondered whether I knew the difference between right and wrong.

'Selina, did you like it?' he finally asked.

'Like what?'

'The girl – did you enjoy what she did to you?'

'Danny, I . . . I don't want to discuss it.'

'I'm sorry, love. It's just that, while I was out walking, I did some thinking.'

'Oh?'

'This whole bloody business, this girl and everything – it's coming between us.'

'It needn't, not if we're strong.'

'It's not a case of being strong. I'm out walking while you're having sex with another girl!'

'What are you trying to say?'

'I don't know. I asked you whether you'd liked it because . . . This is obviously going to carry on, the blackmail and the sex.'

'We'll get her. The next time she comes here, we'll get her.'

'Get her?'

'Her car number, her name and address.'

'We've been through this before, it won't do us any good.'

I knew it wouldn't do us any good, but it was better than

doing nothing. Danny was right, the blackmail and sex would carry on. She'd demand more and more until . . . What? I couldn't begin to envisage what the future held, what fate had in store for me. Discovering her identity might lead us to her boss and then . . . Then what?

Wandering into the lounge to escape Danny's questioning, I held my hand to my head. I just wanted the whole damned thing to go away, the nightmare to come to an end. I wanted things to be as they had been, with me enjoying my writing and Danny working on his book. But I couldn't turn the clock back. Time had passed, water had run under the bridge, fingers and tongues had . . .

'Oh, no!' I breathed, my eyes wide as I noticed a pink vibrator on the sofa. Grabbing the device, I hid it beneath the cushion, thanking God that Danny hadn't seen it. The girl must have left it for me, I reflected. No, it must have fallen out of her coat pocket. She'd probably planned to use it on me and . . .

'I'm going up to work to try and take my mind off all these problems,' Danny said, popping his head round the door. 'I want to change a few things in the book before I send it off again.' I said nothing as he climbed the stairs. There was nothing to say. Nothing to say about his book, either, other than it needed more than a few changes before sending it to yet another publisher.

Hearing the door close upstairs, I took the vibrator from beneath the cushion, wondering where to hide it. The best place was the dustbin, I decided, switching it on. The vibrations running through my hand, I closed the lounge door, mesmerized by the weird sensations. What would it feel like? I wondered as I switched it off. The vibrations running through my clitoris . . . Would I come? I'd never even masturbated before, let alone used a vibrator!

Slipping my wet panties off and hiding them beneath the

cushion, I sat on the sofa and pulled my skirt up. My thighs wide, I tentatively parted my swollen sex lips and examined my sticky vaginal folds, my erect clitoris. Imagining the girl's tongue there, encircling my sex button, I was about to try the vibrator but had a change of mind. I couldn't bring myself to pleasure myself, perform yet another lewd act.

Instinctively caressing my clitoris with my fingertip, I closed my eyes, revelling in the beautiful sensations. My thoughts returning to the girl, her wet tongue, her hot mouth, I desperately tried to fight the overwhelming urge to use the vibrator. No matter what I'd done to the girl, the dreadful things she'd done to me, I couldn't masturbate and sink further into the murky pool of iniquity.

But my clitoris called, swelling beneath my caressing fingertip, beckoning me, screaming for attention. What if Danny caught me? I pondered fearfully. I listened for him as I ran my finger up and down my sex crack, lubricating my erect clitoris with my copious juices of arousal. Hearing him moving about in the room above, I gazed at the vibrator, my mind torn, my hands trembling. Switching it on, it buzzed softly, as if calling me. I was safe – I'd hear Danny if he came downstairs.

Pressing the pink plastic tip against my clitoris, my body jolting as the beautiful sensations permeated my quivering womb, I gasped. Never had I known such pleasure, such wonderful sexual feelings. But what was I doing? My husband upstairs while I masturbated with a vibrator in the lounge . . . What had happened to me? Stifling my whimpers as my clitoris swelled and pulsated, my mind blowing away, I didn't *care* what had happened to me. I was discovering the pleasures of masturbation, the amazing sensations my clitoris could bring me.

Parting my thighs further, I ran the tip of the vibrator around my throbbing sex nodule, breathing deeply as my climax neared. My arousal soaring, I recalled the girl's crude words. *Fuck. Cunt.* They excited me, floating around my mind, teasing me, goading me. 'Ah, my cunt!' I breathed as my lust juices trickled from my vaginal opening and ran down between my buttocks. 'Fuck my cunt!'

Suddenly gripped by the incredible sensations as my clitoris erupted in orgasm, my body shaking violently, I threw my head back, gasping as shock waves of pleasure permeated my very being. On and on the ecstatic waves emanated from my vibrating clitoris, transmitting through my spasming vagina and travelling deep into my quivering pelvis.

I thought my climax would never end as my vaginal muscles rhythmically contracted, squeezing out my creamy orgasmic juices. I'd do this again, I decided. I'd keep the vibrator and use it when Danny wasn't around. Slip my panties down and elicit wonderful orgasms from my clitoris whenever I felt the need to come.

Need? I'd never experienced the need for an orgasm before. I'd enjoyed sex with Danny, the climaxes he'd brought me, but never had I actually *craved* an orgasm. The girl had woken my latent desires, stirred something within me that I'd not known existed. I was changing, but into what? Crude lesbian sex, and now masturbating with a vibrator? What was I becoming?

'Oh, yes! Ah, my cunt!' I breathed as my orgasm peaked and then began to recede, my distended clitoris pulsating beneath the tip of the vibrator. 'God, it's beautiful!' The last ripples of pleasure leaving me, I switched the vibrator off and lay trembling on the sofa. My head spinning, my juices oozing from my burning vaginal sheath, I nonchalantly slipped the plastic shaft deep into my drenched sex duct, arching my back as my muscles tightened around the phallus.

'Selina!' Danny called, bounding down the stairs. Pulling my skirt down, concealing the vibrator embedded deep within my tight vagina, I looked up as he opened the lounge door. 'Selina, I . . . Are you OK?' he asked concernedly.

'Yes, I . . . I fell asleep,' I lied, forcing a smile.

'Your face is all red, love.'

'I was on the cushion, my face pressed against it. What did you want?'

'I was going to ask you to have a look at my book. I need some advice.'

'I'm not really in the mood,' I sighed, fearful for the inadequacy of my vaginal muscles.

'Come on, it'll only take a minute. And it'll take your mind off things.'

'No, Danny. Later, maybe.'

'You can't sit here brooding, love.'

'I'm not brooding, I'm thinking.'

'What about?'

'About going away for a few days, maybe a week.'

'What about your book? I thought you were going to . . .'

'I don't want to talk about the book, Danny. I don't want to talk about the book, the girl, the sex . . . I'm going up to bed.'

'Oh, all right. I'll plod on by myself.'

'I'll take a look at it tomorrow.'

Once he'd gone, I parted my thighs and slipped the glistening phallus out of my drenched vagina, pondering on the wonderful orgasm the device had brought me. I had to throw it outside in the bin, I knew as I left the room. If I kept it I'd use it every day, several times a day – and I didn't want that. I didn't want to become a nymphomaniac!

In the kitchen I hovered by the back door, but I couldn't do it. Gazing at the glinting piece of electronic eroticism in my trembling hand, my new, pink and most feminine friend, I knew I couldn't dispose of it. I had no choice – I was hooked. It would become a good companion, an intimate friend, I pondered as I climbed the stairs to the bedroom, clutching the wet phallus. It would be my secret, hidden beneath my pillow – my forever secret.

In bed, I curled up beneath the quilt, the desire to vibrate my erect clitoris to a massive orgasm overwhelming. But I needed to sleep. Tomorrow, I promised myself, my hand beneath the pillow, clutching the soft, pink shaft. Tomorrow, when Danny wasn't around, I'd masturbate again – and again, and again, and . . .

In the morning, I left Danny sleeping and took a shower. Massaging the soap into my vaginal folds, my ripening clitoris, I became highly aroused and was tempted to use the vibrator – but no. I had to remain in control of my uncharacteristic sexual desires, ration my orgasms. If I allowed my craving to masturbate to get the better of me . . . The thought frightened me.

Leaving the bathroom without bothering to dress, I crept downstairs. Another day, more blackmail, more sex . . . The events of yesterday playing on my mind as I stood in the kitchen gazing at my elongated nipples, my nakedness excited me. Picturing the girl sucking and biting my milk teats, recalling the wondrous sensations, I took a deep breath and filled the kettle.

I had to drag my thoughts away from sex, drive all thoughts of lesbian pleasure and masturbation from my racked mind. Sex? I hadn't had sex with Danny for weeks. Did I want sex with him? I thought not. I had my vibrator, I didn't need Danny. Did I need the girl?

Pouring my tea, I suddenly realized how horrendous the situation was. Like waking from a dream, the harsh reality hit me that I was being blackmailed, that I'd paid the girl ten thousand pounds, that I'd watched Danny screw her, allowed her to lick and finger me to orgasm. The sex, the tremendous orgasms, had somehow numbed my mind to the reality of my predicament. What had the useless private detective done? I wondered as I sipped my tea. What the hell was anyone doing about the girl and the thugs? Nothing!

Again, I felt desperately alone and pondered on calling the police. But with the photograph of the girl's fist embedded deep inside my vagina as she licked between my sex lips, I was in no position to do anything. I was at her mercy, at her beck and call, and it suddenly struck me that I was effectively her sex slave!

Aside from me, how was the situation affecting Danny? I wondered. Again, I recalled his words. *What's this going to do to our relationship?* In my confusion, I thought about offering the girl sex as and when she wanted it on the condition that she demanded no more money. But her boss was demanding money, not her. He had the incriminating photographs and knew nothing about the continuing sex. That was between the girl and me.

What would she do if I were to deny her more sex? I mused. She could hardly complain to her boss! There again, she might cause trouble. Besides, sex with her was . . . God knew what it was! Never in a million years would I have envisaged myself in a lesbian relationship!

'Oh, no clothes!' Danny grinned as he entered the kitchen dressed in his suit.

'I've just had a shower,' I smiled, wondering what he thought of my naked body. 'Why are you all dressed up?'

'I'm going to London to see a literary agent.'

'When did you arrange that?'

'I wasn't going to say anything, but I sent the synopsis to them and they want to see me.'

'That's great, Danny!'

'Yes, it is. They've read the first few chapters and they want to see the rest. I was up half the night printing it out. Anyway, I'm going to take the next train.'

'What about breakfast?'

'I'll find somewhere to eat in London. I don't want to be late for the meeting.'

'Oh, right. Well, good luck.'

'Thanks. If I can get this book published, I'll be able to contribute financially.'

'Contribute to paying the girl?'

'I've one or two ideas about the girl that I'll tell you about later. Unless I go now, I'll miss the train. I'll be home this afternoon.'

'OK, see you later.'

As he left the house, I felt relieved. It wasn't that I didn't want him around, I just needed time alone, time to think. Poor Danny, rushing off to an agent, clutching his manuscript! It suddenly occurred to me that, should he become published, then he'd be blackmailed too. They had photographs of him screwing the girl and . . . Success brought nothing but problems, it seemed, and I found myself hoping that they'd reject his book.

All I'd worked for, all Danny had been striving for . . . And we'd ended up in this horrendous bloody mess! Again, I wondered how on earth we'd got ourselves into this situation. We should never have paid the first five thousand, but what use was hindsight? The evil bastards had led me carefully down the path to my defilement, taken me step by step until they'd got enough on me to ruin me. I'd been stupid, incredibly naive. Answering the phone, I was pleased to hear Chrissy's cheerful voice.

'Shouldn't you be at work?' I asked.

'I'm just about to leave. Have you done anything about my idea?'

'No, I haven't.'

'Why not? I thought you were going to tell that girl where to get off.'

'Things have developed, Chrissy – things have changed. It's a long story.'

'Look, I haven't got the time to talk now. I'll ring you this evening.'

'All right.'

'You *are* OK, aren't you?'

'Yes, I'm OK. I'll talk to you this evening.'

Wandering through the hall into the lounge, I gazed at the sofa, the white stains on the cushion, wondering what Chrissy would think when I told her what I'd done. Far from being OK, I was in such a bloody mess that I didn't know which way to turn! It was all right for Danny. Off to London with his bloody manuscript, it was all right for him! I supposed it wasn't fair to say that. The nightmare was affecting him as much as it was me.

First things first, I decided – get dressed, clean the cushion, do some housework, and then try to get down to the bloody book. Before, I'd been so eager to write, so keen to get to my desk and work. Now it was *the bloody book*. Things change, I reflected. Nothing lasts.

As I was about to go upstairs to dress, the phone rang. This was my chance to tell the tart that the publisher didn't want another book! She'd tell her boss and, if he believed it . . . One step at a time.

'Hi!' she trilled. 'How are you this morning?'

'What do *you* want?' I snapped.

'Another five thousand pounds.'

'There *is* no more money, you've taken it all.'

'Of course there's more.'

'They don't want another book. The first one's died a death and . . .'

'Now, now, Selina – stop telling lies.'

'I'm not lying. They don't want another bloody book.'

'In that case, my boss will give the photographs to a

journalist he knows and . . . Well, that'll be curtains for you.'

'It's not my fault that they don't want another bloody book!'

'Maybe not, but . . . I'll tell you what, I'll have a word with my boss. He's a reasonable chap, he might . . .'

'*Reasonable?* How the hell can you say that?'

'Leave it with me, Selina. I'll get back to you.'

Perhaps it *would* work, I reflected as I hung up. Have a word with her boss? Yes, he might believe it and . . . What if he rang the publisher? I thought. What if Danny called Tammy and asked her about it? Grabbing the phone, I rang Tammy and told her that the book was coming on well, but I wanted to keep it under wraps for the moment. Readily agreeing, she suggested that we launch the second book with a bang, taking the media by surprise.

'Thank God for that!' I breathed as I replaced the receiver. At last, I might find a way out of the bloody mess. Of course, if and when the book was published, the girl would come at me with her threats again. But at least it would give me time to plan. To plan what, I had no idea, but time would be on my side.

Feeling positive, I spent the morning cleaning the house. I decided to cook a really nice meal for Danny that evening and make a start on rebuilding our marriage. The vibrator played on my mind as I cleaned the sofa cushion, but I managed to deny my yearning for an orgasm, keeping myself busy for as long as I could.

When the doorbell rang at midday, I initially thought that Danny had forgotten his key. Opening the door, dying to ask him how he'd got on, I wasn't surprised to see instead the girl – but shocked as I focused on the young man standing beside her. Her boss? I speculated as they stepped into the hall. Had he believed my story and come to do a deal with me?

A thousand thoughts flooding my mind, I prayed for my plan to work.

'This is Dave,' the girl informed me as I followed them into the lounge. Dumping a large leather bag on the sofa, she turned to face me. 'Get your husband and we'll . . .'

'He's not here,' I broke in. 'He's gone to London.'

'That's a shame because I wanted him to fuck me again.'

'Tough!' I spat.

'Not really, Selina. You see, Dave's come here to fuck *you*.'

Speechless, I stared at the good-looking young man, imagining his penis driving deep into my vagina. This wasn't happening, I thought fearfully as he grinned at me. This couldn't be happening to me! Having sex with the girl was one thing, but with another man? Male or female, which was worse? There was no difference, sex was sex, adultery was . . .

'Well?' the bitch smiled. 'Aren't you going to say hallo?' My hands trembling, my eyes locked to his, I couldn't comprehend the predicament I was in. From bad to worse, from a nightmare to a horror story. 'You don't have to speak to him,' she said, slipping her coat off and revealing her naked body. 'But you *do* have to fuck him.'

I should never have answered the door, I chastised myself. I should have known that Danny wouldn't be back by midday! Why did he have to go to London today? I wondered. Today of all bloody days! Fate moved in mysterious ways. Alone in the house with the tart and a man I'd never met before? As he began unbuttoning his shirt, I thought of rushing out into the street and running away.

'What's the problem?' he asked, taking his shirt off and throwing it over the back of the armchair. 'I take it that you *do* have a cunt?'

'She's got a cunt, all right!' the girl giggled. 'A beautiful cunt.'

'I'm pleased to hear it,' he grinned, unbuckling his belt.

'Come on, Selina – strip off and we'll have some sexy fun.'

As he pulled his trousers down, I stared in horror at his massive erect penis, his huge balls. This wasn't her boss, I knew. Was he one of the thugs? I wondered, gazing at his solid veined shaft, his purple knob, as he pulled his foreskin back. Or was he the photographer?

'I'm not going to do it!' I said firmly, eyeing his hairy bronzed chest, his rippling muscles. 'The only way you'll have sex with me is if you rape me!'

'No one's going to rape anyone!' the bitch laughed. 'There's no need to resort to that sort of thing.'

'Oh yes, there is!' I returned.

'Selina, we have the photographs.'

'I've already told you, the publisher . . .'

'I'm not interested in the publisher. My boss wants money from you, and I want sex.'

'He doesn't know about this, does he?' I blurted out.

'You're a clever girl. You're right, he knows nothing about this – and he never will because I'm the go-between.'

'I'm not having sex with anyone.'

'You are, Selina. You see, I told my boss that there'll be no more books or money, and he wasn't at all happy. I mentioned that you have a new car, a new BMW – and *that* made him very happy.'

'You can't take my car!'

'We don't want to take your car. You'll sell it and give me the money.'

'No!'

'I can make it easy for you, Selina. I get on well with my boss, he listens to me, takes my advice. If I tell him that you're being uncooperative, he'll become extremely annoyed. When he's happy, he's fine, when he's upset, he's not too bad – but when he's annoyed . . . On the other hand, if I tell him that you're doing your best to get some money together, that you're working on your next book and you'll soon have your advance, he'll be happy and probably give you time.'

Time. That was what I needed. But sex with another man? I hadn't really looked upon having sex with the girl as adultery, it was mutual masturbation – oral masturbation. But another man's penis inside my vagina? The girl's fingers, her tongue, was one thing, but . . . Only Danny had ever made love to me, only Danny had pushed his penis into my vagina and . . .

'Clothes off, Selina,' she grinned, unbuttoning my blouse.

'No!' I protested, pulling away.

'The sooner you take your clothes off, the sooner it'll be over.'

Slipping my blouse off my shoulders, she unhooked my bra and peeled the cups away from my firm breasts. The man watched eagerly, his penis pointing skyward as she tugged my skirt down, displaying my bulging panties. The sooner it'll be over? She was right, it was best to cooperate and get the vile act over with. I wouldn't tell Danny that another man had made love to me, fucked me. There'd be no incriminating photographs, he'd be none the wiser. But the young man would return for more sex, I knew. It wouldn't stop there.

As the bitch tugged my panties down to my ankles and the man moved towards me, a shudder ran up my spine. My embarrassment mounting as he gazed at the most intimate part of my body, I kept repeating the words in my mind. *A cold clinical act, a cold clinical act*. It was only sex, a man's penis sperming inside my vagina – my cunt. *A cold clinical act.*

'Kneel down and suck his knob,' the tart instructed me. There was no point in protesting, arguing. A penis, a vagina, a clitoris, a nipple . . . There was no difference, I tried to convince myself as I knelt before the young man. Sperm, vaginal juice . . . He wouldn't come in my mouth, I was sure. He'd save his sperm for my vagina, my cunt.

Gazing at his penis, his huge knob, his heavy balls, I knew I couldn't do it. I'd only ever taken Danny in my mouth, sucked his knob during our lovemaking, and I knew I couldn't betray him by sucking another man. Danny had screwed the girl, but I'd been there, a part of it, it was different. I couldn't suck another man's knob behind my husband's back, while he was away in London.

'Selina, we haven't got all day!' the bitch complained with a hint of anger, pushing my head towards the man's erect organ. His purple globe pressed against my pursed lips, they adhered defiantly. 'Selina!' she hissed impatiently. 'Unless you suck his cock . . .'

Taking his silky knob into my mouth, I gently sucked, savouring the salty taste of his organ. He gasped, thrusting his hips forward and driving his glans to the back of my throat. My lips stretched tautly around his huge shaft, his public hairs tickling my nose, I breathed in the heady scent of his sex as the girl knelt behind me and reached between my thighs, massaging my swollen vaginal lips.

Again, I tried to deny my arousal as her finger entered my wet vaginal sheath. Drag my mind away from sex, ration my orgasms . . . I couldn't deny the immense pleasure her fingers were bringing me, my soaring arousal as I ran my tongue around the man's bulbous knob. What had happened to me? I wondered as I sucked. What had I become?

'Nice?' she purred, slipping her wet fingers out of my vagina and massaging my erect clitoris. 'He'll fuck you in a minute, force his lovely cock right up your tight cunt and fuck you until you come.' Her crude words battering my aching mind, I again thought of Danny. What was he doing? How was he getting on? What if he came back and discovered me sucking another man's knob? *What's this going to do to our relationship?*

Holding my head, the young man slowly withdrew his

shaft until my lips were around his swollen knob. 'Use your tongue,' he murmured as I sucked his smooth plum. Running my tongue round and round his glans as he gasped with pleasure, I prayed that he wouldn't come. I didn't want his sperm in my mouth, down my throat.

'God!' he breathed, driving his knob to the back of my throat as the girl fervently massaged my pulsating clitoris. 'God, I'm going to come!' I tried to pull away but he gripped my head, repeatedly withdrawing his solid penis and driving into my mouth. Try desperately though I did to free myself, he held my head tighter in his hands, forcing his knob to the back of my throat.

'Coming!' he gasped as his glans swelled and his sperm gushed, flooding my tongue. I swallowed hard as I felt my clitoris pulsate beneath the girl's massaging fingertips. I too was going to come, I knew. I tried to hold back as his sperm filled my cheeks and ran down my chin as he fucked my mouth, but I couldn't.

My clitoris exploding in orgasm, I mouthed and sucked on the man's knob, swallowing his sperm as my own climax gripped my naked body. On and on the electrifying shock waves of orgasm rolled through me, taking me to unknown heights of sexual ecstasy as the huge penis glided in and out of my jismed mouth. I could hardly endure the pleasure, the sensations of raw lust as my body trembled uncontrollably. Never had I known such amazing feelings nor dreamed that such satisfaction could be derived from crude sex.

The girl's fingers driving into my vagina as my climax receded, I swallowed the last of the man's sperm, wondering at my crudity, my uncharacteristic behaviour. A cold clinical act? It was. But my arousal, the immense sexual gratification I'd derived from the threesome, frightened me. I'd been plunged into a foul pool of depravity that should have left me cold. Yet I felt satisfied beyond comprehension.

As the girl's fingers left my drenched vagina, the man gently rocked his hips, massaging his knob against my tongue. The taste of his salty sperm lingering in my mouth, I sucked as a babe at the breast as my clitoris deflated, leaving me to recover from my shuddering orgasm. I'd done it, committed the obscene act, and I thought I'd be left to dress. In my naivety, I'd thought they'd leave, returning only when they needed my naked body again.

'Stand up,' the girl instructed me as the man's wet penis slipped out of my mouth. I complied, staggering to my feet and turning to face her as she grabbed her leather bag. 'That small table,' she directed the young man. 'Put it in the middle of the room.' I didn't know what she had planned as he dragged the table across the floor. I didn't dare imagine what horrendous sexual abuse I was to endure. 'Kneel down and lean over the table,' she ordered me.

As I took my position I assumed that the man was going to kneel behind me and slip his penis into my vagina, fucking me before leaving me alone with my thoughts, my abused body. My breasts pressed against the polished tabletop, my hands gripping the wooden legs, I closed my eyes as I waited for him to enter me and fuck me.

'No!' I protested, lifting my head as the girl handcuffed my wrists to the table legs. 'Please, don't . . .'

'What's the matter?' she asked nonchalantly.

'Let me go!'

'Let you go? But you haven't been punished yet.'

'Punished?' I echoed fearfully, turning my head as she delved into her bag.

'The whip,' she grinned. 'You're going to be whipped.'

'No! Please, I'll do anything . . .'

'Selina, the more you misbehave, the more you'll be punished.'

'I've done everything you asked!'

'Yes, I know. But we must teach you to be obedient. Obedience is very important, don't you agree, Dave?'

'Very important for a sex slave,' he murmured as the girl stood behind my trembling frame.

'I *have* been obedient!' I cried as she ran the leather tails over my tensed buttocks.

'Yes, you've done well. But this is to make sure that you behave in the future. When we come round to see you, we'll expect one hundred per cent cooperation, complete and utter obedience. We don't want arguments and protests, Selina.'

'I haven't argued!'

'You've been rude to me on the phone. You said you wouldn't sell your car, you wouldn't undress when I asked you to . . . In my opinion, that's arguing. You won't argue again, Selina. The whip will correct your ways, teach you to behave in future.'

The first deafening crack of the tails landed across my quivering buttocks, the stinging pain permeating my naked flesh. I couldn't believe what was happening to me. I couldn't slide the cuffs off the table legs as they were joined by wooden bars. I was trapped. Again, the whip lashed me, the pain unbearable as my naked body shook violently. I wanted Danny to come home and rescue me as the tails again lashed my abused buttocks. I wanted him to save me from the living hell.

'A dozen should suffice,' the cow said, whipping me again.

'No, please!' I sobbed as another deafening crack resounded around the room and my buttocks burned like fire.

'You're protesting again, Selina!'

'No, I, I . . .'

'And now you're arguing. This won't do, it really won't!'

'I'd say twenty lashes are required to correct her,' the young man said.

'We'll try a dozen first. There are seven more to come, we'll see how she behaves after that.'

Again and again the whip lashed my trembling buttocks, the excruciating pain running deep into my burning flesh. Sobbing uncontrollably as the heartless bitch continued her merciless thrashing, I prayed for my freedom, wondering what I'd done to deserve such an experience. How did these people know about me, about my past? I wondered hazily as the whip lashed me again. How had I been so gullible as to allow them to lead me down the road to such humiliation and degradation?

'There's only one more to go, Selina,' she grinned, pulling my hair and yanking my head up. 'One more lash, the hardest yet – and then we'll see how well you behave.'

As she raised the whip above her head, I squeezed my eyes shut, biting my lips as I waited in trepidation. Never would I allow this to happen again, I vowed. Never would I be forced to endure sexual abuse, merciless beatings, the crude violation of my naked body. They could go to hell, no matter what the consequences. They could all go to hell.

'Argh!' I screamed as the leather tails seared my stinging flesh. My head hanging over the edge of the table, my tears streaming, I prayed that she wouldn't whip me again. Obedience? Yes, I'd be obedient – until they'd gone. And when she next phoned or called at the house, I'd tell her to go to the devil.

'Right,' she smirked, tossing the whip onto the sofa. 'Let's see whether you've learned your lesson. Dave, kneel behind her.' As she yanked my burning buttocks apart I felt the young man's penis, his knob pressing between my dripping vaginal lips. Entering me, his huge shaft stretching the silken walls of my vaginal sheath, I didn't complain or murmur one word of protest. The last thing I wanted was another gruelling thrashing. I knew I had to behave myself.

Withdrawing his penis, he drove his solid knob into me again, his lower belly slapping my stinging buttocks as he rudely fucked me. Once he'd come, shot his sperm into my vagina, I was sure they'd leave me. He wouldn't be able to come three times, it wasn't possible.

Slipping his hard penis out of my drenched vaginal sheath, I thought he was going to shoot his sperm over my back, my naked buttocks. Once he'd come, they'd leave me, I convinced myself. I'd sucked his knob and swallowed his sperm, I'd been masturbated to orgasm, I'd endured a thrashing, and he'd fucked me – there would be no more abuse, I was positive. The girl yanking my buttocks further apart, a bolt of fear rocked my quivering frame as I felt the man's hot knob pressing against my anal portal.

'No!' I screamed as his knob pushed against the delicate tissue surrounding my bottom-hole, trying to gain entry to my rectum. 'Please, not there!'

'Oh, dear!' the bitch sighed. 'The whipping didn't do you much good, did it?'

'Please, anything but . . .'

'More arguing and protesting – and I'd thought we'd corrected your ways. This really won't do.'

'No, no, I . . .'

'Dave's going to fuck your bum, Selina. I'll give you one last chance. If you don't protest or argue, you'll not be whipped again.'

Whimpering as I felt his massive organ slip past my tightening muscles and drive deep into my rectal duct, I tried desperately not to cry out and complain. I couldn't endure the whip again! I had to behave myself. His shaft entering me, opening my private passage as the girl forced her fingers into my tight vagina, I squeezed my eyes shut again.

'God, she's got a tight arsehole!' he gasped, propelling his hips forward, his penis fully entering me. His vile words desecrating my mind, I let out a little cry as he withdrew and thrust into my bottom again. Biting my lip, I had to remain silent, I had to behave myself. 'Christ, she's got a beautiful arse!' he exulted, increasing his rhythm.

Opening my eyes as the girl slipped her fingers out of my streaming vagina, I watched her kneel with her back facing my head, her feet beneath the table. Resting her weight on her hands, her buttocks projected, her small brown hole bared before my flushed face, she ordered me to lick her there.

'No, I can't!' I cried as the young man grunted behind me, obviously nearing his climax.

'Push your tongue into my arse!' she stormed.

'Please, I . . .'

'Unless you do it, you'll get twenty lashes!'

Tentatively pushing my tongue out, I licked the brown tissue surrounding her bottom-hole as my naked body jolted with the crude anal shafting. My face pressing against her buttocks as she moved back, I ran my tongue around her small aperture, praying for the man to come, for the debauchery to finish.

'I want your tongue inside me!' she hissed, resting her head on the floor and reaching behind her back. Yanking her buttocks wide apart, opening her anal portal, she again ordered me to push my tongue into her small hole. Fearful of the whip, I pushed my tongue right out, the tip finding its way into her tight duct as she gasped in her vile pleasure.

'Here it comes!' the young man breathed, his huge organ thrusting in and out of my inflamed anal sheath. I could feel his sperm lubricating the debauched union, filling my tight duct as my tongue drove deeper into the girl's bottom-hole. This was the ultimate degradation, my soul told me. This was the most vile and humiliating degradation imaginable!

As the man slowed his thrusting rhythm and the girl moved away, I again prayed for them to leave me. I knew I could take no more – the vile sex, the beatings. His shaft slipping out of my burning anal duct, I could feel his sperm oozing from my inflamed hole, running down between my swollen labia. My tears flowing as the girl stood up, I waited for her to release the handcuffs, to give me my freedom and allow me to dress.

'Was I all right?' I found myself sobbing as I heard the young man dressing.

'You were very good,' he replied.

'But not good enough,' the bitch rejoined.

'What do you mean?'

'You protested again, Selina.'

'No, I didn't!'

'And now you're arguing again. I'm sorry, but I did warn you about your behaviour. We'll try another dozen lashes.'

'No, please, I . . .'

'Twenty lashes for your insolence!'

Grabbing the whip, she stood behind me and raised it above her head. The leather tails swishing through the air, cracking loudly across my trembling buttocks, I screamed for mercy. Ignoring me, she lashed me again and again, the pain agonizing, my bottom burning like fire. I couldn't take any more, I knew, as the tails bit into my flesh again. I wanted Danny! Where was Danny?

'Please, no!' I screamed as the whip tortured my tensed bottom again.

'That'll do for now,' she conceded, placing the whip in her bag. 'But you'll have another thrashing the next time we come round.'

'No!'

'Pardon?'

'Nothing, I . . .'

'Good. Dave, release her and help her up.'

As the young man freed my wrists, I staggered to my feet

and clutched my burning buttocks. Watching the bitch slip into her coat, I vowed that this was the last of the sexual abuse, that they'd never violate me again. No matter what they threatened me with, never again would I . . .

'We'll see you tomorrow,' the bitch smiled as they left the room. Following them, I watched them open the front door and step outside. My naked body trembling, my buttocks stinging like hell, sperm oozing from my inflamed bottom-hole, I staggered to the door and watched them walk down the path.

'No!' I screamed as they neared the road. 'You're a vile, filthy, stinking bitch!'

'You'll regret that, Selina,' she mocked as she turned and started walking menacingly back to the house.

'Come on, Alison,' the man whispered, grabbing her arm.

'You'll regret that!' she yelled again.

'Fuck off!'

'The day will come, very soon, when you'll wish to God that you'd never said that.'

Closing the door, my heart pounding, my breathing heavy, I suddenly realized that the man had called her Alison. It was a small lead – but where would it get me? *The day will come, very soon, when you'll wish to God that you'd never said that.*

Chapter Five

Danny returned at four to find me curled up on the sofa. I'd taken a shower, rubbed cold cream into my burning buttocks and dressed in an effort to try and appear normal, but he knew something was wrong. I couldn't tell him what I'd been through. I couldn't even bring myself to recall the horrific sexual abuse, let alone tell my husband.

'What's happened?' he asked immediately.

'Nothing,' I smiled. 'I was just having a rest. How did you get on?'

'I gave them the manuscript and they're going to let me know within a couple of weeks. Selina, are you all right?'

'Yes, I'm fine. What else did they say?'

'Nothing much. It was a waste of time going, really. I could have posted the manuscript and saved myself a lot of time and money.'

'It's best to meet them.'

'Yes, I suppose so. Have you been working on the book?'

'Non-stop.'

'The girl . . . Has she been in touch?'

'No, not a word – thank God.'

'Good. I'm going to grab a beer from the fridge: want one?'

'No, not for me.'

Watching him leave the room, my buttocks stinging, I knew I couldn't continue the pretence. But I could hardly tell him the truth! I'd never lied to Danny, never kept anything secret, but now? If he noticed the state of my buttocks, the weals . . . If the girl came round again with the young man and Danny happened to be at home . . . I didn't know what to do, what to say to him as he wandered into the room, swigging from a can.

'I hate London,' he said as he sat next to me. 'The bloody traffic and the crowds, I hate it.'

'Danny, I want to move away,' I sighed.

'Because of the girl?'

'Of course. It's not going to stop, I know it.'

'But you said she'd not been in touch.'

'She hasn't, but it won't be long before she phones or comes round. She always withholds the number when she rings so . . .'

'As I said this morning, I have one or two ideas about this business.'

'Go on.'

'The next time she comes here, we'll kidnap her.'

'*What?* Danny, are you crazy?'

'Listen to me, Selina. The only way to sort this out is to find out who she's working for, right?'

'Yes.'

'If she disappears, her boss might come here looking for her.'

'Or the thugs!'

'I'm sure the heavies won't come barging in here, it would be too risky. She disappears – so, if I were her boss, what would I do?'

'God knows.'

'I might think she'd run off with the blackmail money. Whatever I thought had happened to her I'd have to send someone else to replace her.'

'What, another girl?'

'I don't know.'

'Danny, if her boss thinks for one minute that she's here, he'll send his thugs out to get you. It's too dangerous.'

'Yes, I suppose you're right. I'm just trying to find a way out of this bloody mess. Unless we do something, God knows what'll happen next. Christ, I've just had a thought!'

'What?'

'She's already had me screwing her while you watch, she might bring the thugs here to . . .'

'Don't, Danny. I don't want to hear it.'

'Sorry, love. I'm going upstairs, I have one or two things to do. Are you sure you're OK?'

'Yes, yes, I'm fine.'

I knew instinctively that the girl would bring the young man round and have Danny watch him screw me. It was logical – she'd forced me to watch Danny with her, so why not the other way round? Knowing her filthy mind, I was surprised that she hadn't brought several men round to fuck me!

Hearing Danny moving about upstairs, I jumped as the phone rang. It was too early for Chrissy to call – it had to be the bitch. If she told Danny what had happened . . . As it stopped ringing, I pressed the secrecy button and carefully lifted the receiver.

'It's a shame you weren't around today,' the tart giggled.

'What do you mean?' Danny asked angrily.

'Selina and I had some sexy fun. It's a shame you weren't there to join in.'

'You're lying!' he snapped.

'Am I? I thrashed her with a leather whip. Go and ask her to show you her bum, that'll prove that I'm not lying. By the way, I'm waiting for the next five thousand. You'd better get it by tomorrow evening.'

Hanging up, my hands trembling as I heard Danny bounding downstairs, I didn't know what to do. If I refused to show him my buttocks, he'd know I was lying. If I . . . Grabbing the phone as he burst into the room, I pretended to be talking to Chrissy.

'How's the job, Chrissy?' I asked, smiling at Danny as he stood before me. 'That's good. Oh, I'm still bashing away at the keyboard.' Danny paced the floor, rubbing his chin and looking decidedly anxious as I rambled on. All I was doing was delaying the inevitable, I knew, but it might give me time to think of a way out of the situation.

As Danny grouched from the room, obviously thinking I'd be on the phone for ages, I realized that the weals wouldn't fade for several days. I'd have to confess, there was no other way out of it. I'd have to tell him the shocking truth. As he returned and began pacing the floor again, I replaced the receiver, taking a deep breath as I waited for him to question me.

'Selina,' he said, gazing at me accusingly. 'The girl just rang.'

'Oh, God! I hope you told her where to go.'

'Did she come here today?'

'No, she didn't.'

'She said that she'd whipped you.'

'Whipped me? That's ridiculous!'

'Show me your bum, Selina.'

'No! Christ, if you'd rather believe her than me . . .'

'Just show me.'

'Danny, she didn't come here today – but someone else did,' I lied.

I didn't know why I'd said that. Instinctively, the words had tumbled from my mouth. Thanking God that I hadn't let slip to Danny the tart's real name, proving that I'd had contact with her, a hare-brained idea came to mind. Rising from the sofa, I walked over to the window.

'Who?' he asked. 'Who came here?'

'A woman. She . . . she wouldn't say who she was but she knows the girl,' I replied, wondering where the incredible lie was coming from.

'She *knows* her?' he gasped.

'Yes, her name's Alison.'

'Christ! Alison what?'

'She wouldn't say. She was frightened, Danny – really frightened. She wouldn't even come into the house.'

'What else did she tell you?'

'Nothing. She left before I could ask her anything.'

Pacing the floor, Danny was obviously deep in thought. At least I'd found a way of telling him the bitch's real name, *and* I'd got out of showing him my burning buttocks. But where to next? What other lies would I tell him? I wouldn't lie again, I decided. I'd got away with it this time, but there was no point in lying again.

'I'm going to see the private dick,' Danny said pensively, moving to the door.

'Why don't you ring him?'

'No, I'll go and see him.'

'Danny, we only know her Christian name – it's hardly anything to go on.'

'It's the first lead we've had.'

'From what he's done so far, it wouldn't do any good if you told him where she lives. Why bother with him?'

'It's better than doing nothing, Selina. I won't be long, I'll see you later.'

Deciding to examine my buttocks in the full-length mirror, I went up to the bedroom and pulled my panties off. I was hoping that the weals wouldn't appear too fierce, but when I lifted my skirt and bent over, I was shocked. Gazing at my reflection, the crimson weals fanning out across my burning flesh, I knew that Danny would go mad if he saw the stark evidence of the ruthless whipping.

Standing with my feet apart and leaning over further to get a better view, I observed my vaginal lips nestling between the tops of my thighs. My pink inner labia protruding from my sex valley, I realized that I'd never examined myself, never studied my intricate folds. Taking the mirror from the dressing table, I placed it on the floor and stood with my feet either side of it. Squatting, I looked in the mirror at my open vaginal valley, the wet pink flesh surrounding my sex hole.

Realizing that the sight was arousing me, I replaced the mirror and grabbed my panties. I desperately wanted to masturbate, to massage my sex spot with the vibrator and take myself to a shuddering orgasm. I could feel my clitoris swelling, my vagina contracting, my juices oozing from my love sheath. The urge, the need, was overwhelming, but I didn't understand why.

Recalling the young man's knob sperming in my mouth, his rock-hard penis driving deep into my bottom, my stomach somersaulted. What was I becoming? I wondered as I slipped my hand up my skirt and ran my fingertip up and down my wet crack. Why this incredible transformation? The blackmail had understandably turned my life upside down, but what was happening to me sexually was incomprehensible.

Massaging my solid clitoris, I was aware of a desperate need to come, to vibrate my sex button to orgasm, and I lay on the bed with my thighs wide apart. Taking the vibrator from beneath my pillow, I switched it on and pressed the tip between my dripping inner lips. Easing the plastic shaft deep into my pussy, closing my eyes as the beautiful vibrations permeated my contracting womb, I began to gasp.

The sensations were wonderful, transmitting through the silken walls of my vagina and playing around my erect clitoris. But guilt consumed me. I'd sucked a stranger's penis to orgasm and swallowed his sperm, I'd had anal intercourse with him, I'd licked the girl's bottom-hole, and I was masturbating again. I knew I couldn't carry on behind Danny's back like this. The lies and deceit were destroying me.

As the sensations built, I slipped the vibrator out of my vagina and ran the tip around my pulsating clitoris. My mind lurching between my guilt and the beautiful sensations emanating from my sex button, I finally became lost in my masturbating. My body trembling, my neglected vagina rhythmically contracting, I switched the vibrator off and grabbed a large plastic bottle from the dressing table. My thighs wide as I lay on the bed again, I eased the end of the bottle between my swollen vaginal lips, gasping as the huge phallus entered me.

Running the vibrator around my erect clitoris again, my vagina tightening, gripping the bottle, I closed my eyes and waited for my orgasm to come. Barely able to endure the amazing sensations, my back arched, my eyes rolling, I reached beneath my thigh and thrust the bottle in and out of my pussy, adding to my wondrous pleasure.

'Yes!' I cried involuntarily as my clitoris erupted in orgasm and my juices ran down between my stinging buttocks. Again and again I thrust the phallus in and out of my spasming vagina, the beautiful squelching sounds mingling with my whimpers as my clitoris pulsated beneath the vibrator. Wailing as my climax peaked, I tossed my head back, my nostrils flaring, my breasts heaving as I pistoned my vaginal canal faster with the phallus.

My clitoris solid, sending electrifying sensations deep into my contracting womb, I thought my climax would never end. Again, my euphoria peaked, and I realized that I was experiencing a multiple orgasm. Six or seven times I felt my clitoris swell and revive, the exquisite pleasure gripping my trembling body, blowing my mind away on the wind of lust.

'Yes!' I cried again as I thrust the bottle faster in and out of my squelching vaginal duct, ramming my cervix as my juices poured from my inflamed sex hole. Picturing the young man's penis, imagining his sperm pumping into my mouth, bathing my tongue, my orgasm peaked for the last time. My clitoris aching with pleasure, the vibrator driving me wild, I finally stilled my hand, leaving the bottle embedded deep within the burning sheath of my vagina.

Switching the vibrator off, I lay trembling in the aftermath of the most incredible orgasm I'd ever experienced. My mouth dry, my breasts heaving, I wallowed in the divine sensations emanating from my bloated vagina, my mind drifting on clouds of sexual satisfaction. My body finally relaxing, I lay with my legs splayed, the phallus hugged by the silken walls of my sex sheath as I fell into a deep sleep.

I woke to hear Danny moving around downstairs. Had he been up to the bedroom and seen the bottle emerging between my swollen sex lips? I wondered fearfully. Had he seen the vibrator lying on the bed next to me? Slipping the bottle out and hiding the vibrator beneath my pillow, I leaped off the bed and grabbed my panties. Praying that he'd not seen the evidence of my masturbation session, I went downstairs and found him in the kitchen.

'Oh, hi,' he smiled. 'I wondered where you were.'

'Have you just got in?' I asked, my face flushing with embarrassment as I felt my panties wetting.

'Two minutes ago. I saw the private dick.'

'What did he say?'

'He didn't have much on today so he decided to spend a couple of hours parked outside the house. He told me that as he pulled up, he saw the girl leaving with a young man.'

'No one's been here, apart from the woman I told you about.'

'He saw them walking away from the house.'

'I was listening to music while I worked on the book, I obviously didn't hear the doorbell. I wonder who the man was?'

'I don't know. Wilkins lost them, but he's got the registration number of the car they were in. He's going to get back to me.'

'Perhaps the man was her boss.'

'Maybe.'

Thanking God the detective hadn't seen them entering the house, I knew it was only a matter of time before Danny discovered the awful truth. I also realized that I was becoming distanced from him. Having anal sex with the young man, licking the girl's bottom, masturbating with the vibrator and a plastic bottle . . . I had so many secrets that I felt an increasing detachment from Danny.

Recalling my mind-blowing multiple orgasm, I wondered whether I'd ever make love with Danny again. After the girl and the young man, I didn't see how I could ever find physical love and warmth with my husband. The worrying thing was that masturbating with the vibrator and bottle was far better than . . . I shouldn't say that. Although masturbation brought me massive orgasms and immense satisfaction, the act was loveless.

Watching Danny take another beer from the fridge, I again recalled his words about our relationship. His prediction was right. The whole sordid business was affecting our marriage more than we could have imagined and I knew in my heart of hearts that we'd slipped anchors and were drifting apart. But, as I looked back, I realized that throwing myself into my work as I had over the last year or so had also caused a rift between us.

'I'm going up to take a shower.' Danny looked wan, vulnerable. I smiled at him, remembering when we'd first met, the hours of lovemaking, the desperate passion. Nothing lasts, I reflected, wandering into the lounge as he climbed the stairs. Plonking myself on the sofa, I thought about the future, whether this would all come to an end and Danny and I could rebuild our relationship. Would the blackmail ever stop? I wondered as the phone rang. Lifting the receiver, I was expecting to hear Chrissy's voice. It was the bitch.

'How's your bum?' she giggled.

'Unless you stop ringing and . . .'

'Now, now, Selina – be nice to me.'

'*Nice?*'

'My boss wants to meet you.'

'When?'

'Now, on the common by the railway bridge.'

'Why won't he come here?'

'Be there as soon as you can.'

As she hung up I was about to rush upstairs and tell Danny, but I had a change of mind. I didn't want him saying anything stupid, threatening the man or getting into a fight. At long last, I thought, my chance had come to put an end to the horror and I was determined not to ruin that chance. Calling to Danny through the bathroom door that I was going out for a walk, I left the house and made my way to the common, feeling really positive about the forthcoming meeting.

As I neared the railway bridge, I stopped and look around. The common was deserted and I felt that I was alone in the world. Wondering whether I might be walking into a trap, I edged my way cautiously towards the trees. The thugs might be lying in wait, I reflected. They might kidnap me or . . . No, they wouldn't do anything like that, there'd be no point.

'Hallo!' I called as I neared the trees. 'Are you there?' Only the birds replied as I tentatively followed a path into the woods. A train trundled through the tunnel and the canopy of leaves blocked out the sunlight as I ventured further into the woods. 'Hallo!' I called again, jumping as a rabbit dashed into the undergrowth. I knew I was making a mistake as I walked on. The girl's boss wouldn't want to meet me in such a place, I was sure.

'Ah, Selina!' the bitch grinned as I entered a clearing.

'Where is he?' I asked, looking about me.

'He'll be here shortly. Why don't you strip off and . . .'

'I'm here to meet your boss, not to . . .'

'Selina, you remember I said you'd regret what you called me?'

'He's not coming, is he?' I asked fearfully.

'I told you that you'd wish to God that you'd never said it.'

'I'm going!' I responded firmly, turning on my heels.

'Going where?' the young man asked menacingly as he emerged from the undergrowth.

'Home!' I cried.

'Home?' another young man grinned mockingly, blocking the pathway.

'Clothes off, Selina,' the bitch smirked.

I should have known that this was a trap. In my stupidity, I'd walked straight into their lair, into the lion's den – and there was no way out. I couldn't understand my naivety, how I'd been so gullible. Her boss would have rung me if he'd wanted to talk to me. I should have taken Danny with me, told him about the so-called meeting and . . .

'We're waiting, Selina,' the bitch grinned, taking the leather whip from her bag. 'I really don't understand your disobedience. You called me a vile, filthy, stinking bitch, and then you told me to fuck off. You'll be punished, Selina – severely punished!'

I said nothing as she pulled several lengths of rope from the bag. Trembling as I watched the men unbutton their shirts, I knew I was going to have to endure the most gruelling whipping imaginable. As they tugged their trousers down, their erect penises coming into view, I looked around the clearing for an escape route, but there was only the one path – blocked by the naked men.

'Unless you cooperate, my boss will send copies of these to his journalist friend,' the whore hissed, taking several photographs from the bag. I stared in horror at the lewd scenes, the man's penis embedded deep inside my anal sheath, my brown ring stretched tautly around his huge shaft. She must have had a camera, I reflected, gazing at the weals across my naked buttocks. My face wasn't in any of the shots, but my chestnut hair and the small mole on my back revealed my identity. It was obvious that the photographs had been taken in my lounge.

'Well?' the bitch leered as she slipped her coat off, revealing her naked body. 'I don't think you have any choice, Selina. We have quite a collection of photographs now. Either you do exactly as I say from now on, or you'll be exposed as a bisexual nymphomaniac. Imagine it, literary wonder Selina Goodman takes it up her bum . . .'

'There's nothing to prove that it's me,' I countered feebly.

'I think you'll find these prove it's you beyond all doubt,' she grinned, taking more photographs from her bag.

Two shots showed me sucking the man's rock-hard penis, my lips taut around his wet shaft, his sperm dribbling down my chin. Another showed me licking between the girl's parted buttocks, my tongue pushed out, teasing her brown anal flesh. Little wonder that I hadn't noticed the flash – the bastards had been careful to ensure that my eyes were closed in apparent bliss before taking the incriminating pictures.

I froze. I was done for. Apart from the newspapers, what would my friends and neighbours think? It was all very well Danny saying fuck the neighbours, but I wouldn't be able to show my face. As for my family, my mother and father . . . The bitch was right, I had no choice. But where would it all end? All I could envisage was a lifetime of sexual abuse, as a sex slave to the cow and her accomplices.

'Obedience is of paramount importance,' the girl said as she stood before me and unbuttoned my blouse. 'I will not tolerate objections, protests or any hesitation when I tell you what to do. You will comply instantly with my commands, no matter what they are.' Slipping my blouse over my shoulders, she unhooked my bra, exposing my naked breasts to the men. 'Remove your skirt and panties.'

Tugging my skirt down, I slipped my thumbs between my panties and my hips, watching the men as their eyes widened with expectation. My embarrassment rising, my fear soaring, I stepped out of my skirt and pulled my panties down, displaying my vaginal slit. I couldn't endure the whip again, the agonizing pain, the merciless thrashing – but there was no escape. Perhaps someone would come, I mused. Someone walking their dog, or children coming to the woods to climb trees. Someone had to save me! Where was the world?

'I might spare you a buttock-thrashing, Selina,' the tart grinned, painfully twisting and pinching my nipples. 'If you prove to be an obedient sex slave, completely submissive, I *might* spare you a buttock-thrashing. Right, let's get started. I want you to lie on the ground.'

Sitting on the soft grass, I reclined and looked up at the sun sparkling through the canopy of leaves high above me. As the men tied ropes around my ankles, I wondered what Danny was doing, again wishing that I'd brought him with me. This was going to be the last time I'd be subjected to sexual abuse, I vowed as the men slung the ropes over the branches of two trees. I couldn't win, I knew – but I could run.

Lifting my head, I watched my feet rise into the air as the men pulled on the ropes. My thighs parting wide as my feet rose higher, my vaginal entrance rudely bared, vulnerable, I rested my head on the soft grass and closed my eyes. They could do whatever they wished to my naked body, and I'd not complain. They could take it in turns to fuck me, to sperm in my mouth, anything – as long as they didn't whip me.

'Very nice!' the girl giggled as she settled on the grass and yanked my sex lips apart. 'OK, who wants to fuck her first? Mick, you haven't had the pleasure yet, I think you should go first.'

'I'd be delighted!' the man chuckled, running his hand up and down his solid shaft.

'Dave, get the video camera and record the fucking.'

Video camera? God, that was all I needed! The evidence of my wanton ways on videotape would be the ultimate blackmail material! Hearing movements, I opened my eyes to see the girl's vaginal crack hovering above my face. Her knees either side of my head, she lowered her naked body, pressing her wet sex folds against my mouth as I felt a man's knob running up and down my vaginal slit.

'Lick me!' she instructed me as the penis drove deep into my vagina. 'Lick my cunt!' My body jolting as the man fucked me, I pushed my tongue out, tasting the girl's copious juices as she gyrated her hips and gasped in her lesbian lust. I was nothing more than an object, a naked body to be used and abused by both male and female.

For the umpteenth time I wondered why my life had been snatched from me, what I'd done to deserve this hell. Far removed from writing, home cooking, gardening, I felt as if I'd been plunged into a dungeon where monsters roamed, where the very air I breathed was thick and heavy with the foul stench of evil. These people weren't human, but demons, feeding on crude sex, living their debased lives in thrall to the devil.

As I tongued the girl's vaginal sheath, her lesbian juices flowing from her hot sex hole and running down my face, I felt as if my soul had left my body, as if my very being had been rent from me, leaving only my physical form. A man's penis driving in and out of my once sacrosanct vagina, his heavy balls slapping my tensed buttocks as I drank from the girl's cunt, I knew I'd reached the bottom of the pit of depravity. I could fall no further.

'Tongue-fuck my cunt!' the she-devil gasped, her treacherous lust juices almost drowning me as the man grunted and thrust his solid organ deep into my burning vagina. 'Lick my cunt out, bitch!' Poking my tongue out further, licking the drenched walls of her hot sex duct, I found myself thinking back to my girlhood.

I'd been about fourteen, lagging behind on a school cross-country run, when two girls had leaped out of the bushes and grabbed me. Lifting my top and laughing at my small developing breasts, they'd forced me to pull my knickers down and show them my crack. As they'd pushed me to the ground and yanked my legs wide apart, we'd heard voices, and they'd fled. I'd never have believed that I'd find myself in the same situation again, let alone with adults as my abusers.

'Coming!' the girl cried triumphantly, rubbing her solid clitoris over my wet mouth as the man thrust his penis into my cunt with a vengeance. I could feel his sperm shooting into my burning vagina, lubricating his pistoning organ. I knew that I'd have to take the second man's penis inside my spermed pussy, and I was sure that they'd both use my bottom-hole to satisfy their debased lust before allowing me my freedom. As long as they didn't whip me, as long as they didn't thrash my naked buttocks . . .

'Suck out my cunt milk!' the girl wailed, forcing her drenched vaginal flesh harder against my face as the man spurted the last of his sperm into my inflamed sex duct. I sucked and drank, my mind awash with a thousand thoughts as my abusers satisfied their sickening craving for debauched sex. 'Tongue my cunt, bitch!' the girl screamed as she writhed and gyrated her hips.

I thought about the heroine in my first novel, the meek country girl who'd found love and happiness after enduring a terrible childhood with her cruel father and stepmother. She'd married her young man and they'd made love behind the closed bedroom door on their wedding night. There'd been no debauchery, no gratuitous description of the act. The analogy of crashing breakers on the seashore had said it all.

Had my heroine experienced a multiple orgasm? Had she sucked the sperm from her husband's penis? Had he pushed his tongue deep into her young vagina? I now wondered. Should I have let my readers wonder? I'd always thought such matters best left to the imagination. Perhaps I was wrong. Perhaps I should have written the truth, the sordid details of their sex lives. Sordid? No, their writhing and coming wasn't sordid, but beautiful, the entwining of two people in love, making love.

The man's spent penis slipping out of my drenched vagina, I continued licking and sucking on the tart's sex-flesh, wondering whether I'd ever be entwined in love with Danny again. Would I miss the sordid sex? Having experienced group sex at its lowest, tasted the forbidden fruit, would I forever crave the darker side of carnality?

The girl's sated body finally collapsing, falling to the ground as she panted and writhed in the aftermath of her coming, I opened my eyes and focused on the man with the video camera. He'd recorded the vile act. Copies would be made of the tape and used as evidence against me. The tape depicted me as a whore, a wanton bisexual nymphomaniac. I had no defence, I was guilty beyond all reasonable doubt. Innocent until proved guilty? I was guilty as charged.

'My turn to spunk up her cunt!' the man chuckled, passing his friend the video camera. As he knelt on the grass and pushed his bulbous knob between my sperm-drenched inner labia, I closed my eyes again. His huge penis penetrating me, violating my vagina, I listened to the birds singing in the trees. They were oblivious to the sordid sounds of sex, the filth taking place in the clearing below. The world was oblivious to my plight. My tethered body rocking with the second fucking, I was aware of the other young man above me, his knees either side of my head.

'Take my balls into your mouth,' he ordered me, his hairy scrotum resting on my pursed lips. Opening my mouth as wide as I could, I sucked his balls inside. Asking the girl to record the obscenity, he grinned at me as I opened my eyes and looked up at him. His stiffening penis towering above my face, sperm and vaginal juice running down his veined shaft, he instructed me to wank him. Taking his rock-hard organ in my hand, I moved his foreskin back and forth over his purple glans as the girl moved closer and focused the camera on the crude act.

Sucking on his huge bollocks, my tongue snaking over the wrinkled skin of his scrotum as he gasped, I knew he was going to shoot his sperm over my forehead, splatter my hair. When I finally returned home, Danny would notice my matted hair, my sperm-starched face. He'd question me, ask me where I'd been, why I'd been so long. All I could do was lie to him. I'd vowed never to lie again, but I had no choice.

Ordering me to wank his cock faster, the man let out long, low moans of pleasure as his penis swelled and twitched within my hand. The other man ramming his shaft in and out of my cunt, his solid knob pummelling my cervix, I knew he was about to come. They'd both come, one filling my cunt with sperm and the other splattering my face with the product of his climax.

'That's great!' the girl squealed, moving the camera closer to my hand as I wanked the young man. 'You're not going to write one more book, you're going to write several and make us rich!' Several? I could no longer write about romance, relationships, of the warmth and closeness between two people in love. Now all I could relate to was filth, debauchery, crude sex. Romance had been driven from my mind by cold lust, love banished forever.

As the man's jism shot from his knob, splattering my face, my hair, I closed my eyes. The girl was giggling as she recorded the vulgar scene, egging the man on, telling him to keep his sperm coming. The other man moaned as he released his heavy load, filling me to the brim with his ejaculate as he rammed his penis in and out of my burning vagina, fucking my tight cunt. Fuck? Cunt? The crude words were becoming commonplace in my vocabulary. *Fuck, cunt, balls, sperm, wank* . . . Like my femininity, the words had lost their mystique.

The last vestiges of his sperm dripping onto my face, the man moved away, leaving the other man to finish unloading his treacherous cargo into my cunt. What did they have in store for me next? I wondered as his penis slipped out of my sopping vagina. What crudity was I to be forced to endure next?

'OK,' the bitch declared, placing the camera on the ground. 'Tie her hands and fix the rope to that tree behind her head.' Like slaves, they did as she'd requested, pulling my hands behind my head and securing the rope to the tree. My legs high in the air, my naked body completely defenceless, I thought the men were going to take turns to pump their sperm into my anal duct, and I tensed my buttocks in readiness for the profanity.

'I'm going to enjoy this!' the tart chuckled, taking the whip from her bag.

'No, you promised!' I cried.

'I said that I might spare you a buttock-thrashing, and that's what I'm going to do.'

'But the whip . . .' I murmured fearfully.

'Don't worry, you're not going to have a buttock-thrashing. The whip is for your tits.'

'No, please!'

'Obedience, Selina!'

'Please!'

The leather tails flailing my firm breasts, my futile screams served only to send the birds fluttering from the trees. The tails catching my nipples, the stinging pain permeating my milk-white breasts as the men looked on with glee, I knew I was far from the bottom of the pit of depravity. The pit was bottomless.

'Danny!' I cried as the tails lashed my breasts again. 'Danny, help me!' My abusers laughed as I struggled and writhed, pulling on the ropes in an effort to escape the gruelling thrashing. The whip biting into the soft flesh of my breasts, I wondered how to explain the weals to Danny. I'd have to tell him the truth, I had no option. Lies would only lead to more lies – lies to lies, deceit to deceit.

'OK, that'll do for now,' the girl relented, much to my relief. 'Tighten the ropes so her bum's off the ground.' Whimpering as the men pulled on the ropes, my buttocks leaving the ground, I thought she was going to thrash my bottom. My breasts stinging, my nipples on fire, I couldn't face another buttock-thrashing, the excruciating pain of the leather tails biting into my bottom.

'Who's going to take her arse first?' the girl asked, discarding the whip.

'I will,' one of the men replied, kneeling on the grass.

'You'll enjoy this, Selina!' she giggled. 'Two cocks fucking your bum, spunking up your arse. You'll enjoy this.'

'No, please!'

'Don't argue, Selina!'

'You bitch! You dirty bitch!' I spat.

'Oh, dear. It would appear that you're still in need of correction.'

Feeling the man's bulbous knob pressing against my anal

rose, I squeezed my eyes shut, praying for the filth to come to an end. As he forcefully entered me, my bottom-hole yielding to his massive knob, I felt his huge shaft sinking deep into my rectum. Fully impaling me on his penis, his hairy balls pressing against my crimson buttocks, I could feel his organ deep inside me, bloating my pelvic cavity.

As he withdrew his hard cock and thrust into me again, my body swaying, I wondered whether Danny had ever thought about anal sex. Had he contemplated fucking my bottom-hole? Perhaps he'd been afraid to suggest such a vile act, too embarrassed to reveal his perverse male desires. But no, Danny wasn't like that. He had morals – and love for me.

'The spunk's spraying out of her cunt!' the man chuckled as he repeatedly propelled his penis deep into my bowels. 'Every time I ram my cock up her arse, spunk spurts out of her cunt! Get it on videotape!'

As the others laughed and hurled crude comments at me, I again wondered what Danny was doing while I was having anal sex in the woods with another man. Was he working? Was he pacing the floor, wondering where I'd got to? I imagined staggering into the house naked, sperm oozing from my cunt, my bottom-hole, my hair matted with spunk, my breasts and buttocks bearing the stark evidence of a thrashing.

Never had I dreamed that such debauchery existed, been even remotely aware of the vile desires of my fellow human beings. But they weren't human, I again reflected. They were grotesque fiends, ghouls risen from the reeking swamps of hell. They wouldn't entrap me again, I vowed in my enforced defilement. Never again would they entice me to enter their debased domain. Over Lucifer's cursed corpse, I'd make sure that I'd never succumb to their trickery again.

'Here it comes!' the young man breathed, ramming his cock in and out of my inflamed anal duct. I felt his sperm jetting from his knob, gushing into my bowels as his heavy balls slapped my scarlet buttocks. All I had to endure was the other man's cock fucking my bum, and then I'd be allowed to go home. I'd take a shower, wash away the sperm and vaginal juice, cleanse my abused body – but I wouldn't be able to cleanse my mind.

'God, she's bloody tight!' he cried, my body swaying as he made his last thrusts, draining his swinging balls. Finally stilling his penis, his knob embedded deep within my bowels, I waited for him to withdraw, leaving my spermed anal sheath vacant for the other man's penis. As he slipped his cock out of my once private hole, I felt the sperm oozing from my cunt, from my anal rose. My vagina, my bottom, my mouth, my hair – I was awash with sperm. I felt as if my mind was swimming in a lake of sperm. I was drowning.

'My turn!' the other man chuckled as he knelt on the grass. My anal ring well lubricated, his knob glided deep into my bottom with ease, stretching open the silken walls of my once secret duct. I had to bear one more anal fucking, one more load of sperm pumped into my bowels before I tasted freedom again. If I could endure that without complaining . . .

But I *had* complained – I'd protested and argued and called the girl a dirty bitch. As the man fucked my bottom I knew I'd be punished for my insubordination, that she'd use the whip to correct me. One last thrashing and I'd be free! At last I'd be permitted to stagger home, abused, fucked, spermed and severely whipped.

'Here's your second helping!' the young man gasped, his penile shaft swelling, his knob gliding in and out of my velveteen duct as his orgasm erupted and his sperm gushed. The girl moved in with the video camera, recording the obscene act, ensuring my face was in frame as my bowels filled with sperm.

'Beg for more!' she instructed me. 'Ask him to fuck your arse harder!'

'No, I . . .' Recalling the whip, I knew I had to comply and I gasped, begging the man to fuck me harder.

'Ask him to fill your arse with spunk.'

'Fill my arse with spunk!' I echoed as she focused on my contorting features.

They'd edit the tape, and I'd be depicted as a willing participant in the debauchery. They now had all they needed, more than enough evidence to enslave me for life. As the man fucked my bottom, pumping his sperm deep into my hot bowels, a tear ran down my cheek. I'd lost the battle, lost my identity, my femininity – my life.

'Christ, that was good!' he breathed, dragging his wet shaft out of my burning anal canal. Was that it? I pondered fearfully as the men dressed. I looked at the girl, wondering whether she'd whip me again, punish me, correct my ways. As she slipped her coat on and placed the whip in her bag, I breathed a sigh of relief. I'd done it – endured the most vile and debased sex imaginable.

'Release her,' the bitch commanded as the men finished dressing. The ropes untied, I hauled my aching body up and staggered to my feet. Sperm oozing from my inflamed holes, coursing down my inner thighs, I watched them leave the clearing. The sound of twigs cracking underfoot fading, I looked down at my breasts, the pitiful weals fanning out across my mammary globes. Running my fingers through my hair, matted with bodily fluids, wiping the sperm away, I knew I had to face Danny, tell him the appalling truth.

The birds returned to the trees as I dressed. As they began chirping, it was as if they knew the debauchery was over, that the evil had left the woods. Another train trundled through the tunnel, taking people home from work, families home from a day out. The world had returned too late.

Chapter Six

I found Danny working at his desk when I finally managed to stagger home. Popping my head round the door, I didn't go in. In my sordid state of disarray, I dared not! 'I've been for a nice long walk and now I'm going to take a shower,' I smiled perfunctorily as he began questioning me, quizzing me about where'd I'd been. Hurriedly crossing the landing and slipping into the bathroom, I breathed a sigh of relief as I heard him chase after me.

'Selina!' he called, knocking on the locked door. 'Selina, are you OK?'

'I'm fine!' I replied, surveying my matted hair and sperm-starched face in the mirror before slipping my sex-stained clothes off.

'I was worried about you.'

'You shouldn't have been. I'm fine.'

Stepping into the shower, the hot water bathing my naked body, stinging my whipped breasts, I lathered my sullied hair with shampoo. When I was clean, when I'd washed away the last remnants of the obscene abuse, I'd tell Danny the truth, I decided. Then he could take me away, we could rent a flat somewhere, another town, another county. Several hundred miles away we'd be safe – free.

Massaging soap into my vaginal folds, I took the shower nozzle from the hook and pressed it between my swollen outer labia. The hot water gushing into my cunt, inflating my sex sheath, I gasped. Sperm and water spraying from my bloated vaginal cavern, the sensations sending electrifying ripples of pleasure through my pelvis, I tried desperately to push all thoughts of orgasm from my tortured mind.

My clitoris swelling, pulsating, I couldn't allow myself to masturbate – succumb to my base desires. I'd had so much sex, I had to fight the overwhelming temptation to massage my clitoris to orgasm. Moving the shower head away, my cunt draining, I pressed the nozzle between my stinging buttocks to cleanse my inflamed bowels. Pressing the nozzle hard against my sore hole, the water gushing into my rectal duct, I gasped again as the wonderful sensations rippled through my naked body.

'Selina!' Danny called again as my fingers moved between my sex lips and massaged my throbbing clitoris. 'Selina, are you sure you're OK?'

'I told you, I'm fine!' I panted, hanging the shower head on the hook, water and sperm gushing down my thighs as my bowels drained. 'I'll be out in a minute!'

Resisting the temptation to appease my yearning clitoris, I stepped out of the shower and wrapped a bath towel around my naked body. The time had come to show Danny the weals, to put an end to the lies and deceit. Taking a deep breath as I left the bathroom, I tentatively crossed the landing.

'Ah, there you are,' he smiled as I wandered into his room.

'Danny, I was only having a shower. There was no need to keep calling through the door.'

'I've been worried, love. You went out for a walk ages ago. Where have you been?'

'Doing exactly that – walking. Danny, I have something to tell you.'

'And I have something to tell you. The private dick rang while you were out.'

'Oh?'

'He reckons he's getting somewhere at last. You remember the girl used a hire car?'

'Yes.'

'Well, he went to the company and made a few enquiries. It was hired by a man called David Holmes, and he had a girl with him – a girl fitting the description of . . .'

'The address – what's this man's address?'

'Wilkins has his address and he's been to see him. Holmes hired the car to go away for a couple of days with his girlfriend.'

'Didn't Wilkins ask him about me?'

'He could hardly ask him whether he was blackmailing you, love.'

'No, but . . .'

'Listen, the dick's going to keep an eye on this bloke's place. The next time the girl rings, I'm to phone him and let him know. In the meantime, he's trying to find out as much as he can about this man. This is a real breakthrough, Selina. Whether this Holmes character is the tart's boss or one of the thugs, I don't know, but he's involved. One thing we must do is hand over another five grand.'

'I haven't got five grand.'

'I know you haven't. We'll have to get it from somewhere, borrow it or . . .'

'There might be a royalty cheque due,' I said, wishing I hadn't.

'Good, that's good. We've got to play the game to give the dick a chance to find out who's involved in this. Anyway, what was it you wanted to tell me?'

'Nothing, nothing. I'm going to get dressed.'

Walking into the bedroom, I slipped the towel off and surveyed my naked body in the mirror. The weals across my breasts had developed, like pink ferns fanning out across my pale flesh. I couldn't show Danny, he'd go mad. Besides, if the private detective discovered who these people were and put an end to the horror, my husband could be spared the truth.

As I dressed, veiling my abused body, I suddenly remembered the video camera. If Danny were to see the tape all hell would be let loose! The tape, the photographs . . . Even if the sleuth were to find these people and threaten them, have them sorted out, the evidence would still exist. I doubted very much that he'd be able to get his hands on the tape and photos. Undoubtedly there'd be copies too, hidden God knew where.

Feeling hungry, I made some toasted sandwiches and called Danny down to the kitchen. I was tired, physically and mentally exhausted after my ordeal in the woods, and decided to have an early night. What tomorrow would bring, I dreaded to think. If I stayed locked in the house, I'd be safe enough, I reflected.

'I'm going to work on the book tomorrow,' I said as Danny munched his sandwiches.

'The money,' he murmured anxiously, gazing into my eyes. 'We've got to get our hands on five grand.'

'God knows how.'

'The girl rang, just after you'd gone out. She wants the cash tomorrow afternoon.'

'Danny, this is ridiculous!'

'We've no choice, love. I wasn't going to tell you yet, but . . . As I said, she wants the cash tomorrow.'

'OK, I'll go to the bank and see what they can do,' I sighed.

'With your next advance due, I'm sure they'll lend it to you.'

'God, it's crazy! I have to take out a loan to pay a blackmailer!'

'I know, I know. Anyway, the private dick will get us out of this mess.'

'I hope so, Danny – God, I hope so. I'm tired, I'm going to bed.'

'OK, I'll do some more work.'

'Try not to wake me when you come to bed, I'm exhausted.'

'I won't. Sleep well.'

Pigs might fly! Tossing and turning as usual, nightmares haunting me, monsters chasing me through dank, stone-walled corridors, I finally crawled out of bed and dressed. Again I found myself in the garden, watching the sun rise above the trees, wondering what life was all about. The hell I'd been through had changed my way of thinking, my perception of the human race.

'What's it all about?' I whispered to the still morning air, to the birds in their dawn twittering, as I sat on the bench beneath the beech tree. 'What the hell's it all about?' I'd tried so hard to become a successful writer, and succeeded beyond my wildest dreams. Yet all my success had done was plunge me into the stenching abyss of evil and debasement.

Checking my watch as the front doorbell rang, I wondered who on earth it could be. Surely the girl wouldn't call at seven-thirty in the morning? I thought as I dashed into the house. We didn't have a milkman and it was too early for the post. Spying through the letterbox, I was surprised to see Chrissy standing on the step.

'Hi!' I smiled, opening the door. 'You're an early bird.'

She looked uneasy. 'I'm on my way to work,' she said, stepping into the hall and following me to the kitchen. 'I rang last night but Danny said you were out.'

'I went for a long walk to do some thinking.'

'Selina, *I*'ve been doing some thinking.'

'What about?'

'This mess you're in.'

'Want some coffee?'

'Please. It's Danny, I'm sure of it.'

'What is?'

'He's involved.'

'Chrissy! God, we've been through this before.'

'I know but . . . Look at it logically. The insurance fiddle, the thing you had with Barry . . .'

'Chrissy, Danny's been doing all he can to help me. He's hired a private detective and . . .'

'Have you met the detective?'

'No, Danny's been dealing with him.'

'Have you spoken to him on the phone?'

'Well, no.'

'He doesn't exist, Selina.'

'Of course he exists, I've heard Danny talking to him on the phone. Anyway, he's discovered the name and address of one of the men involved.'

'What is the address?'

'I don't know. Look, I know you've never really liked Danny, but he's doing all he can to help me. He's come up with plans and ideas, he's tried to follow the girl . . .'

'It's not that I don't like him, it's just that I have a nagging feeling about this whole business. I mean, it's like something out of a movie. Your husband grabbed from the street, bundled into the back of a car and tied up in a basement . . . Call it intuition, call me cynical, but I'm sure he's involved.'

Pouring the coffee, I pondered on her words. Danny had handed the money over to the girl on both occasions, he'd been dealing with the detective, he'd been on at me to take the advance and write the second book, it was down to me to take out a loan to pay her . . . No, the evidence was circumstantial – it wasn't evidence at all. He wasn't involved, I was certain. He couldn't be.

'Test him,' Chrissy suggested as I passed her a cup of coffee.

'What do you mean?'

'Tell him that the girl's been round and you gave her more money.'

'What good will that do?'

'If I'm right, and I hope I'm not, he'll ask the girl about the money and, obviously, she'll deny it. If he's in this with her, he'll believe that she's taking your money and not telling him.'

'Chrissy, this is my husband you're talking about.'

'I realize that. As I said before, it fits.'

'It might fit, but Christ!'

'Look, I'd better get going. Think about it, Selina.'

'Yes, I will. But I really don't believe that Danny's involved.'

'You can't trust anyone – not even your nearest and dearest.'

Finishing her coffee, she saw herself out, leaving me with horrendous thoughts about my husband. To test him would be tantamount to betraying him. My mind aching, I pondered on the recent events. My suspicion rising, I wondered where Danny went to on his long walks, what he got up to. When the girl had first come to the house he'd got an erection, fucked her and come. The sight of her naked body, her cunt, had obviously aroused him and . . . No, I was sure Danny wasn't involved with her. If he was, then I didn't know him at all! Only a monster would do such a thing to his wife, a man so evil that . . . Danny was kind, loving, trustworthy and loyal.

'Hi!' he smiled as he wandered into the kitchen. 'I thought I heard the front door shut.'

'Yes, the . . . the private detective called,' I lied.

'What?'

'He . . . he called round to see you but I didn't want to wake you. He's going to ring you later.'

'Oh, right. It's odd that he should come here.'

'Why?'

'Well, he . . . I don't know, I'd have thought he'd have phoned rather than come round. In fact, he said to me that he'd never call at the house in case the girl saw him, which would blow his cover.'

'Well, he did come round.'

'What did you think of him?'

'He seems OK.'

'Yes, yes, he is.'

As Danny poured a cup of coffee, I scrutinized him, wondering whether there really was a private detective. If there was, Danny would soon find out that he'd not been to the house, and I'd have to dream up some lie or other. If there wasn't, he'd be wondering who the hell had called.

My mind riddled with confusion, I couldn't deny that Chrissy was right. It all fitted. Test him? I pondered. If he was working with the tart, he'd know what I'd been forced to endure, he'd know about the sexual abuse in the woods, he'd know everything. I couldn't imagine my husband putting me through all that for money.

'It's best that you go to the bank as soon as you can,' he said thoughtfully.

'Why?'

'I never know when the girl's coming round, she changes the times to protect herself. We'd better have the money ready as soon as possible.'

'I have things to do, I'll go later.'

'Don't leave it too long, we don't want her . . .'

'I'll go when I'm ready, Danny. What are your plans for today?'

'I was going to have a look around the second-hand

bookshop and do one or two things in town, but I'll have to wait until the girl's been.'

'I'll pay her, you don't have to wait.'

'Oh, er . . . All right.'

If I gave her a couple of thousand and told Danny that I'd given her five thousand . . . I didn't want to have to test him but, because of Chrissy, I now had a nagging doubt at the back of my mind. If he *was* involved, the tart would tell him that I'd only given her two thousand, and it would be her word against mine. Danny would question me and . . .

No, I couldn't bring myself to do it. I couldn't believe that Danny, my husband, would put me through hell just to get his hands on a few thousand pounds. Besides, he didn't have the imagination to dream up such a scam. Bundled into a car, tied to a chair in a basement . . . Never in a million years could he come up with such an idea. That was the problem with his books – apart from the fact that he couldn't write, his imagination was as fertile as the desert.

'I'm going upstairs to ring Wilkins,' he said. 'If he came here to see me, he must have discovered something important.'

'He'd have told me if he had.'

'I'll ring him anyway.'

Creeping into the lounge as Danny climbed the stairs, I pressed the secrecy button and carefully lifted the phone. The dialling tone purring in my ear, I replaced the receiver, wondering why I was checking up on him like this. Again, I lifted the phone only to hear the dialling tone. Perhaps he was doing something else – switching his computer on or tidying his desk? Tired and confused, I returned to the kitchen and sat at the table, my head resting in my hands.

'There was no reply,' Danny imparted, appearing in the doorway. 'I'll try again later.'

'Did the detective tell you this man's address?'

'No, he didn't.'

'Why not?'

'He doesn't want me going round to see him, interfering. He likes to work on his own.'

'Well, I might as well walk into town and get the money. I can't get into the book knowing that I have to go out.'

'OK, love. I'll see you later.'

As I grabbed my bag and left the house, I tried to imagine what I'd do if I discovered that Danny was involved with the girl. I'd have to divorce him and . . . Divorce? God, what was I thinking? I wished Chrissy had never put the ludicrous notion into my head. The very idea was crazy.

Drawing five thousand pounds from the bank, I decided to go along with my plan, only giving the bitch two thousand. She'd tell her boss and, hopefully, he'd believe that the money had dried up. If Danny questioned me about it, then I'd be sure that he'd been in contact with her, although it wouldn't prove that he was in league.

Danny'd gone out by the time I returned home with the money. I could hardly start writing with my mind in turmoil! All I could do was wait for the girl to turn up. As I paced the lounge floor, I couldn't drag my thoughts away from Danny. Why was he always out when the girl came round? How come I'd never spoken to the detective?

Wilkins, I mused, deciding to ring the detective as I bounded upstairs to my den. Grabbing the phone book, I ran my fingertip down the numerous rows of Wilkins . . . it was no good, I didn't even have his initials. There was no Wilkins listed under private detectives in the Yellow Pages and I wondered how Danny had got onto the man in the first place.

Answering the phone, I cringed as the bitch asked me how I'd enjoyed my time in the woods. 'I've got some money here for you,' I said, ignoring her crude comments. 'Two thousand.'

'I want five thousand, Selina!' she hissed.

'Sorry, that's all there was in the bank – I'm broke.'

'My boss won't be at all happy.'

'I don't care whether he's happy or not, *Alison.*' She said nothing, obviously wondering how I knew her name. 'How's David Holmes?' I asked.

'David who?'

'Holmes, one of the men who's working with you.'

'I've never heard of him. How do you know my name?'

'I've been digging around, doing some detective work.'

'Well, it won't help you. Even if you discover my address, it won't help you.'

'Won't it?'

'No, it'll only make matters worse. My boss will become extremely upset and probably grab your husband again and . . . God only knows what he'd do to him.'

'Are you going to collect this money or not?'

'Yes, I'll come round now.'

I reckoned I'd worried her. Although she'd denied knowing David Holmes, I'd worried her. I had to clear the cobwebs from my mind and sort my thinking out, make my plans. If she arrived with the men, I wouldn't let them in: I'd pass the cash through the letterbox. If she came alone . . . Why was Danny out yet again? The very time she was due to turn up, he was out. But I'd told him not to wait: it had been my idea. I had to stop thinking that he was implicated.

Pacing my den, I finally looked out of the window. I'd see the girl clearly when she arrived, making sure that she was alone before opening the door. In my confusion, I began to wonder whether I could tie her up, whip the truth out of her. The last thing I wanted was a fight, but if I could manage to tie her hands behind her back . . .

Bounding downstairs as I saw her walking up the path, I opened the door, a devious plan coming to mind. She had her bag with her, no doubt containing her whip and, hopefully, some rope. As I opened the door wider, I donned a sweet smile, making out that I was pleased to see her.

'Come in,' I trilled. 'I'm glad you've called while my husband's out.'

'Why?' she asked, following me into the lounge.

'Because . . . because I *did* enjoy my time in the woods. I've been looking forward to seeing you again, Alison.'

'What is this? What's your game?'

'Game? I'm not playing games. To be honest, I didn't really like what those men did to me but . . . but I enjoyed what *we* did together.'

'You're bluffing,' she frowned, dumping her bag on the floor.

'I've never told anyone this but, when I was in my teens, I had a lesbian relationship. Neither of us could come to terms with it and, in the end, we split up.'

'What's that got to do with me?'

'Alison, after the things we did together, I realized that I'm a lesbian.'

'Whatever you are, it won't help you.'

'I know that. What I thought was . . . Well, I enjoy sex with you. I've run out of money but at least we can enjoy sex together.'

'My boss isn't interested in me having sex with you. All he wants is five thousand.'

Having sex with her? I was entering a domain, a dangerous domain that I might never return from. It was like walking deeper and deeper into a forest until the towering pines obliterated the sun, all sense of direction gone as darkness engulfed me. There'd be no way out, no escape, only trees and the dank smell of decaying leaves whichever way I turned. But I had to enter that forest, venture into the unknown.

'This is about money, Selina,' she said, her eyes focused on my firm breasts billowing my blouse.

'There's two thousand, on top of the piano.'

'When will you have the rest?'

'I don't know. The publisher doesn't want another book so . . . I don't know.'

'You'll have to sell your car. My boss will be very upset if . . .'

'Yes, so you keep saying. Are you naked beneath your coat?'

'Yes.'

Undoing the buttons, I leaned forward and sucked her nipple into my mouth – the first step into the forest. She gasped, squeezing her breast to distend her milk teat as I gently sank my teeth into the sensitive brown protrusion. *So far, so good*, I reflected, running my fingers down over her smooth stomach and parting her fleshy vaginal lips. If I could turn her on and grab the ropes from the bag . . .

'Why don't you kneel down and lean over the table?' I asked, encircling her wet vaginal entrance with my fingertip. Moving away, she pulled the table into the centre of the room. Slipping her coat off, she knelt down, projecting her buttocks, exposing her small brown hole. I knelt behind her, stroking her rounded buttocks, teasing her delicate anal tissue with my fingertip as I reached for her bag. She began whimpering in her lesbian arousal, losing control as my fingertip encircled her anal portal.

'You'd like me to lick you there, wouldn't you?' I breathed, rummaging in the bag.

'Yes, yes – I would,' she murmured.

'You'd like my tongue inside your bottom, wouldn't you?'

'God, yes!'

Running my fingertip up and down her anal crease, I couldn't find the ropes, but pulled out two pairs of handcuffs.

If I could manage to cuff her wrists to the table legs, she'd be mine! God only knew what I thought I was doing as I opened the handcuffs. I'd have to release her, eventually, and she'd . . . I didn't know what she'd do. But she might break under torture, I found myself thinking. Break under torture? What the hell was I doing?

Sheer madness though I knew it was, I had to execute my plan. Licking her smooth buttocks, my tongue venturing dangerously close to her small hole, I reached beneath the table and cuffed her right wrist to the wooden leg. She began to struggle, kicking and shouting as I cuffed her other wrist and managed to secure the cuffs to the table leg. Spitting expletives, cursing and threatening me, she tried to lift the table off the floor to stand up.

'You can't escape!' I hissed, taking the whip from the bag.

'You bitch! Christ, you'll pay for this!'

'OK, who are you working for?'

'I'm not telling you anything!'

'Then I'll whip the truth out of you.'

'No! You just dare to . . .'

'Who are you working for?'

'Go to hell!'

Like a woman possessed, I lashed the tart's naked buttocks again and again with the leather tails. She screamed and yelled vile expletives, but still she wouldn't tell me who her boss was. Twenty, thirty lashes – I lost count. My arm aching, I finally discarded the whip. Sobbing, she begged for mercy as I threatened to thrash her again, but even then she wouldn't tell me what I wanted to know.

'You've got a thing about your bum, haven't you?' I asked her.

'What . . . what do you mean?' she sobbed.

'You like having your bum licked, it turns you on. Let's see how you like what I'm going to do to your bum.'

'What are you going to do?'

'You'll see.'

Taking a cucumber from the fridge, I cut it in half and returned to the lounge. I'd show her what sexual abuse was about, I mused, kneeling behind her weal-lined buttocks. I'd really show the bitch what it was about! Parting her tensed buttocks, I pressed the cut end of the cucumber against her anal rose, pushing and twisting the green shaft. Ignoring her threats, I watched as her delicate brown tissue yielded, the fruit slipping effortlessly into her rectal duct.

'Who are you working for?' I demanded again, forcing the green shaft deep into her bowels.

'I'll never tell you!'

'You will! I'll keep you here all day and night if I have to. I'll thrash you until you tell me everything.'

'Never!'

Leaving the end of the cucumber emerging between her crimson buttocks, I grabbed the whip and jumped up. Revenge was sweet, I reflected as the tails cracked loudly across her twitching orbs and she cried out for mercy. After all she'd put me through it was now time to retaliate, and I thrashed her and thrashed her until my head was spinning and my arm was numb.

'*Now* will you tell me?' I yelled, running the tails over her fire-red flesh.

'No, I can't!' she sobbed pathetically. 'If I tell you, my boss won't only punish me, he'll come after you and . . . Selina, you must understand, I'm only the go-between.'

'Don't shoot the messenger?'

'Something like that.'

'But you're more than a bloody messenger, Alison. You're as good as the perpetrator in all this. Anyway, I know who you're working for.'

She remained silent, obviously waiting for me to enlighten

her. Did I dare suggest Danny? I pondered. No, he couldn't be working with her! I again wondered at my reaction if I were to discover that he was her boss. After the hysterics, the ranting and raving, the hurling of saucepans and plates, I supposed that I'd eventually calm down. But what would life hold for me after that? The terrible psychological scars would remain forever, haunting me, taunting me.

'It's my husband, isn't it?' I finally asked her.

'Your husband?' she gasped. 'No, of course it's not!'

Was her astonishment genuine or was she feigning it, simply shocked to discover that I knew the terrible truth? About to thrash her again, I decided to release her. I didn't want her in the house, especially as Danny might come back at any time. She yanked the cucumber out of her bottom-hole and slipped into her coat, scowling at me as she stuffed the whip and handcuffs back into her bag. I thought for a minute that she was going to attack me, but she probably realized that she'd met her match.

'You'll be hearing from me!' she yelled, grabbing the money from the piano and walking into the hall. 'You'll pay dearly for what you've done, believe me!'

I *did* believe her. As the front door slammed shut, I knew only too well that I'd made a fatal mistake. But I'd never be so stupid as to be lured into the woods again, never again fall prey to her lies and trickery. She'd retaliate, but at least I'd had the pleasure of whipping the bitch. I'd tell Danny that I hadn't even let her into the house, passing her the five grand through the letterbox. The outcome would be interesting, I reflected – especially if she were to tell him not only that I'd paid her two thousand instead of five, but whipped her to boot!

I managed to work on the book, miraculously writing several thousand words. I suppose, having tasted revenge, that I'd somehow found a renewed strength, inspiration. I surprised myself by bashing away at the keyboard, completely unaware of the time, just like the old days. When I finally glanced at my watch, I couldn't believe it was the middle of the afternoon. Where was Danny? I wondered, gazing out of the window at the world. He'd been gone so long.

He finally returned at six, obviously the worse for drink, and flopped onto the sofa. Chuckling, he rambled on about meeting some old friend in town and spending hours in a bar. I supposed it was an escape, an outlet for the anxiety and worry he'd endured. But where was *my* escape – my own solace from the nightmare?

'How have you been getting on?' he slurred.

'Fine,' I smiled. 'I've been writing.'

'That's great! God, do I feel pissed! I'm sorry I've been so long, love. We got talking and, well, you know how it is.'

'Yes, I know how it is. Are you hungry?'

'No, no, just pissed.'

As he dozed off, I went into the kitchen and made a ham sandwich. I'd not been eating properly, munching on toast and nibbling biscuits instead of having decent meals. My renewed strength waning as I pondered on the situation, I began to feel as if I was in a void, floundering in the dark. I didn't know what to do that evening. With Danny drunk, I didn't know how to pass the time. I didn't feel like writing anymore – I'd had enough for one day – and I pondered on going into town. Ringing Chrissy, I suggested that we go to a bar.

'Yes, why not?' she enthused. 'It's about time we went out.'

'That's just what I was thinking. It's about time we got drunk.'

'Great! Actually, there's something I want to talk to you about.'

'Oh?'

'I was going to ring you . . . I'll tell you later. Shall I meet you in the Hen and Chickens?'

'OK, give me half an hour.'

'Right, see you there.'

I needed to get out, I reflected as I bounded upstairs and changed into a miniskirt and blue satin blouse. Brushing my hair and applying my make up, I knew it would do me good to get away from the house for a while. Away from the bitch, the phone and the doorbell, I'd relax with Chrissy for the evening and, for once, enjoy myself.

Leaving Danny snoring on the sofa, I walked down the road and passed the common, uncomfortable memories flooding my mind as I heard a train rattling through the tunnel. Never again would I wander into the trees, I vowed, quickening my step as I recalled the men abusing my naked body. Wondering where the tart was, whether she'd told her boss that I'd thrashed her, I hurried into town. I had to forget about her, I told myself as I walked into the pub. This was *my* evening. I had to push all thoughts of the bitch to the back of my mind.

'Hi!' I beamed, joining Chrissy at a corner table.

'I've got you a vodka and coke,' she said, pushing the glass towards me as I sat down.

'That'll do for starters. Cheers!'

'We should do this more often. I can't abide being stuck alone in my flat night after night.'

'No sign of Mr Right, then?'

'None whatsoever. Anyway, let's not talk about me – how are you?'

'Wading on through the shit life keeps throwing at me.'

'What's the latest on the blackmail front?'

'She wants more money. I gave her another five thousand this morning which just about wiped me out, but she'll be back for more and more.'

I decided that if I was going to lie to Danny about the money, then it was best to lie to Chrissy as well. Although it had been her idea to test Danny, I didn't want her inadvertently letting it slip that I'd only given the bitch two thousand.

'What about the sex?' she asked.

'I'd rather not talk about it, Chrissy.'

'It's still going on, then?'

'Yes, yes, it is.'

'I still reckon Danny's behind the whole thing. Have you tested him yet?'

'Yes, and he has nothing to do with it. What was it you wanted to talk to me about?'

'About Danny. Selina, I know you don't think he's involved, but . . .'

'But what?'

'I saw him with a girl.'

'A girl? When? Where?'

'Today, by the common. I didn't think anything of it when I drove past but . . . They were holding hands and then he kissed her.'

'What did she look like?'

'Blonde hair, quite attractive. I only caught a glimpse of her as I drove past.'

My stomach churning, I knew it was the tart. So he *was* involved with her! My eyes filling with tears, I leaped up and went to the loo. I couldn't believe it: Danny, my husband! *It all fits*, I mused, recalling Chrissy's words – *it all bloody well fits!* Looking in the mirror at the tears running in rivers down my cheeks, I tried to work out why he'd done it. Money? Jealousy? I was the one bringing in the money while he'd been struggling to write, I was the best-selling author, the celebrity . . .

The money was one thing, I reflected – but the sexual abuse? How *could* he have put me through all that? More importantly, where to go from here? I didn't know what to think, what to do. Confront him? He'd only deny it. I should have realized from the start that something wasn't right. A girl coming to the house demanding five thousand pounds because I'd ripped off an insurance company and been conned by Barry? That was hardly blackmail material! Danny saying that we shouldn't involve the police, that I had to write the second book and pay the bitch . . . I reckoned that he knew I'd be listening on the lounge phone when she'd rung. What an act he'd put on! The sex, the photographs . . . All cleverly designed to get as much evidence against me as possible.

The bastard must have met the tart after she'd left my place, I thought incredulously. They'd obviously got pissed together, on *my* money! An old friend, my foot! The lying, two-timing, cheating bastard! *Calm down*, I told myself. OK, they'd had twelve thousand pounds from me, but they'd not have a penny more. Drying my eyes, I returned to the table and sat down, wondering what to say to Chrissy.

'Are you OK?' she asked worriedly.

'Yes, I suppose so,' I snivelled. 'I should have guessed, shouldn't I?'

'How could you have guessed? I mean, there was nothing to implicate Danny.'

'He'd seemed so concerned, so helpful and supportive. I still can't believe it!'

'Look, don't tell him that I saw him with the girl. I don't want to get dragged into this, Selina.'

'Don't worry, I'm not going to say anything to him. I shall carry on as if I know nothing. How he dreamed up such a scam, I'll never know. He's got no imagination whatsoever.'

'Bear in mind that Danny might not be the only one involved.'

'What do you mean?'

'You're obviously in no fit state to think properly, but I

am. I reckon that he joined forces with the girl some time after the blackmailing started.'

'If that's the case, then she *is* working for someone – her boss, as she calls him.'

'It's unlikely that Danny thought this up. As you said, he has no imagination. From what you've told me, I reckon, after he'd screwed the girl, he started seeing her behind your back.'

'Yes, that fits because she's only been to the house once and had sex with him. Every time I've seen her, Danny's not been around. When he'd had a go at her on the phone, that must have been for real, and he probably did go to a private detective. At some stage, he must have met her . . . Perhaps she came to the house while I was out and . . .'

'And he screwed her again. That's when it began, Selina. He arranged to meet her, started seeing her, having sex with her and, like all men who put their cocks before their brains, he couldn't stop.'

I was sure that the bitch hadn't told Danny about the men on the common, and he couldn't put a stop to the blackmailing because her boss was in control. He was just screwing her behind my back, meeting her for sex. There was nothing he could do to help me, so he'd taken advantage of the situation and fucked her. He wasn't getting a share of the cash, he wasn't in league with the tart – he was just using her for crude sex.

'Chrissy, I'm going home,' I sighed.

'Don't go yet. Stay and have another drink, it'll calm you down.'

'Funnily enough, I do feel calm. God knows why I'm not in hysterics!'

'I'll get you another vodka.'

'OK, thanks.'

Perhaps the private detective was still on the case, I mused.

OK, so Danny was fucking the bitch, but he was probably still doing his best to end the blackmail. She'd hardly tell her boss what she was up to with my husband, and Danny certainly wouldn't tell anyone. When the horror ended – if it ended – he'd appear to be completely innocent. His cock before his brain? We'd not had sex for ages – he was obviously getting it from somewhere.

'There you go,' Chrissy smiled, placing my glass on the table. 'I'll tell you what I'd do if I were you.'

'What's that?'

'Follow Danny the next time he goes out.'

'What good will that do?'

'Well, for starters, it'll prove my theory. Don't say anything to him, just carry on as usual, if you can. Follow him the next time he goes out.'

'It's the last thing I want to do, but I will.'

Finishing my drink, I told Chrissy that I was tired and needed to sleep. She insisted that I stay but, with my mind a swirling ocean of anger, I left the pub. Finally reaching home, tears streaming down my face, I was pleased to find Danny still asleep on the sofa. I couldn't have faced him that evening, I was in no mood to talk to him. Climbing the stairs, I stripped naked and crawled beneath the quilt. Completely exhausted, I fell into a deep sleep.

Chapter Seven

Danny came down in his new jeans and a clean white shirt the following morning. Reeking of aftershave, he'd had a shower and combed his hair, as if he planned to go out. I was quietly fuming, aching to have a go at him, but composed myself as best I could, I forced a smile.

'Got a hangover?' I asked, hoping he had.

'No, I feel fine.'

'You should have a pounding headache, you were completely pissed.'

'Selina, the girl rang while you were out last night. She said that you only gave her two grand.'

'*Two* grand?' I echoed surprisedly. 'I gave her five thousand. What the hell's she playing at now?'

'God knows. Hang on, if she's told her boss that you only gave her two grand and she's pocketed the rest . . . Christ, this is getting worse!'

'I've just about had enough of this, Danny. I'm going away.'

'Away? Where to?'

'Anywhere. I can't take any more, I've had it.'

'OK, we'll have a break somewhere. Er . . . Look, I've got to go into town again.'

'What for? You went yesterday.'

'Yes, but I ended up in a pub, didn't I? I won't be long, only an hour or so. Why don't you get on with the book while I'm out?'

'Yes, I will.'

'OK, see you soon.'

Surely he wouldn't be meeting the tart for sex so early in the morning? I pondered as he left the house. There again, why not? He was probably screwing her at every opportunity, while I was out, when he went for his walks . . . He'd probably fucked her dozens of times. But this might be my chance to prove it once and for all, I contemplated as I grabbed my bag and left.

I saw him walking some hundred yards or so ahead of me. Keeping my distance, I followed him, slipping into driveways every now and then in case he looked round. As he reached the common, I was sure he was going to meet the bitch there, but he walked on. Knowing my luck, the very first time I was following him he was probably going to do nothing more than stroll into town!

He spent some time in the second-hand bookshop before going into a stationer's and emerging with a carrier bag. As I followed him home, I began to wonder about Chrissy's theory, as she'd called it. It did fit, all added up, but I still couldn't believe it. If the girl's boss had sent her round to blackmail me, and then Danny had taken a fancy to the tart, become involved with her . . . It was feasible, but I couldn't imagine Danny doing a thing like that. Screwing her on the side when he knew she was blackmailing me? Time would tell, I mused as he entered the house – time would tell.

'Oh, you're back,' I smiled, finding him in the lounge.

'You've been out?' he asked.

'Only to post a letter. Did you get what you wanted?'

'Yes, paper and ink for my printer. There was nothing of interest in the bookshop. Selina, I've been thinking about this break. I have a lot of work to do, so would you mind if I didn't go with you?'

'I suppose not. I was only thinking of spending a couple of

days in a hotel somewhere, just to get away from it all – relax my mind.'

'OK, that'll leave me to get on with my next book. I've had this great idea . . . I won't tell you about it yet.'

'I'm going up to my den to book a hotel. I want to leave as soon as possible.'

'I'll miss you, love.'

'Yes, I know you will. I'm going upstairs.'

Sitting at my desk, I deliberated on going away for a couple of days. I didn't want to go, but I knew I needed some time and space. Looking through the phone book, I found a hotel in a town about twenty miles away, far enough from the horror. As I was about to lift the phone and book a room, it occurred to me that Danny might have the tart round while I was away. Intuition or whatever, I felt that going away would be a mistake.

Walking to the window, I gazed at the front garden, making my plans. I'd tell Danny that I was leaving and then hide in the house. The more I thought about it, the better the idea seemed. I had to be sure that he was screwing the bitch, and I might even discover . . . Dreadful though the thought was, I might even discover that Danny was her boss.

Taking a suitcase from the top of the wardrobe, I went downstairs. I didn't know where I was going to hide, what I'd do for food, but that didn't matter – the plan had grabbed me. Finding Danny sitting in the garden, I told him I was leaving, just going away for a couple of nights.

'*Now?*' he asked surprisedly, gazing at the suitcase.

'Yes, why not?'

'Well, I . . .'

'I'll walk to the station.'

'Where are you going?'

'I've a choice of two hotels, I'll ring you when I get there.'

'I don't see why you have to go this minute.'

'I'm only going for a couple of nights, Danny. The sooner I get there, the sooner I can relax.'

'OK, I'll come to the door with you.'

'No, it's OK.'

'All right, I'll see you the day after tomorrow.'

I went back into the house, opened the front door and slammed it shut, and then crept up to my den. I felt guilty, angry, morose . . . Having to lie to Danny like this, trick him, hide in the house . . . This wasn't what my marriage was supposed to be about! Marriage? What marriage?

Locking the door, I sat at my desk, wondering what to do. My plan was ridiculous. There I was, locked in my den . . . Hearing the front door shut, I dashed to the window to see Danny walking down the path. Now where was he off to? I wondered. How come, the minute he'd thought I was out of the way, he'd gone out?

I paced the floor, gazed out of the window, sat at the desk, and ignored the phone five or six times when it rang. Checking my watch, I realized that Danny had been gone for three hours. He was probably with the bitch, fucking her dirty cunt. 'Shit!' I breathed, finally unlocking the door and going downstairs. 'He's a bastard!'

The afternoon dragging on, I drank far too much wine, wondering when he was going to come home. I'd make some excuse or other, tell him that I'd changed my mind about going away. No doubt he'd make his own excuses, lie to me about going for a walk or bumping into an old friend. Lies and deceit were enveloping me, crushing my mind.

By eight o'clock that evening, the wine had worked well. After falling into a deep sleep on the sofa, I awoke two hours later. Danny still hadn't returned, I perceived through my alcoholic haze. Looking out of the window, sure that he was with the bitch, I wondered why he'd not taken the car. She must have lived within walking distance, maybe twenty or thirty minutes away. The radius would take in thousands of houses and flats. Even if she lived only ten minutes away, I'd never find her.

By midnight, it was pretty obvious that he intended to stay with the slag, so I staggered upstairs to bed. I doubted very much that he'd be home early: he was probably planning to spend the next morning as well as the night fucking the slut. He'd probably pretend that he'd been out walking or had been asleep when I told him I'd phoned from the hotel. He'd come up with some lie or other, I knew!

Saturated with alcohol, I slept well, waking at ten o'clock to the sun streaming in through the window. Venturing downstairs, I went into the kitchen to make some black coffee. There was still no sign of Danny, the bastard! Pacing the lounge floor, wandering out into the garden, drinking more and more coffee, I became increasingly angry as the morning wore on.

When the phone ran at midday, I grabbed the receiver, thinking that it would be Danny. He'd probably ask me when I'd got back, say that he'd popped out for a while and wouldn't be long. As the bitch started giggling in my ear, asking me whether I missed my husband, I told her to fuck off.

'Now, now, Selina – don't be rude.'

'You can go to hell!' I screamed.

'I want three thousand pounds by tomorrow morning, or else!'

'I'm not going to give you three pence, let alone . . .'

'My boss has your husband, Selina. I told you that he'd get upset and . . .'

Slamming the receiver down, I reckoned that Danny had been sitting next to the bitch when she'd phoned me – either that or actually in bed with her. How the hell could he do this to me? I wondered as the phone rang again. Ignoring it, I had a shower and changed into some clean clothes. The phone continuing to ring intermittently, I was determined not to let them rile me. Danny could play his games for all I cared – pretend to be tied up in a bloody basement or whatever. He could play his stupid games!

He didn't come home that night, and by the following morning I began to worry. I might have been so very wrong, I reflected. Chrissy could be barking completely up the wrong tree. But she'd seen Danny with the tart, holding hands and kissing her. Was it the tart? Perhaps he was having an affair with some other blonde bitch. My thinking becoming muddled, I finally decided to ring Chrissy for advice.

'You're lucky to find me at home,' she exclaimed. 'I've managed to get a day off because . . .'

'Chrissy, Danny's gone missing,' I interrupted her.

'Missing?'

'He went out two days ago and I haven't seen him since. The bitch rang and said that her boss has him.'

'God! OK, er . . . Look, I'll come round.'

'Yes, yes – come round.'

Waiting for Chrissy to arrive, I imagined Danny with the bitch, the two of them counting out my money, scheming their schemes. Had he enjoyed anal sex with her? I pondered. He'd have seen her weal-lined buttocks and she'd have told him what I'd done to her. But it didn't matter – nothing mattered any more. At last, the bell rang and I dashed through the hall.

'Why didn't you ring me yesterday?' Chrissy asked as I opened the door.

'I . . . I've been away for a couple of nights, staying at a hotel.'

'How do you know Danny's missing, then? He might have gone out somewhere.'

'I've been phoning on the hour, every hour, Chrissy. He's not been back since he left two days ago and I don't know what to do.'

'What did the girl say?'

'She reckons that her boss has Danny and they want another three thousand pounds. If Danny's not involved . . .'

'Hang on, let's think about this. I still reckon he's involved, and he's doing this to make you pay up.'

'I don't know, I really don't!' I sighed as we walked into the lounge. 'I've thought of everything, every combination.'

'The other night in the pub, my conclusion was that Danny became involved with this girl some time after she'd started blackmailing you. But there are at least two possibilities. Firstly, my original idea might be right. She's working for her boss and Danny's just screwing her for the hell of it. Secondly, Danny's in this with her.'

'So, where do I go from here?'

'If you pay up, whether Danny's in with her or not, he'll come home, right?'

'Yes, if he has been kidnapped, they'll release him, and if he's with the tart . . .'

'OK, so the first thing to do is get him back here, which means paying the girl.'

'How will I know whether Danny's lying or not? If he's been with the girl, he'll lie. If he really has been tied up in a basement . . . No, I'm not going to pay her.'

'It's up to you, but you'd be taking a risk.'

'I realize that. On the one hand, I can't believe that he'd do this to me, on the other . . . Kidnapped and dragged into a basement?'

'If I were you, I'd pay up this time and take it from there.'

'Wait a minute. If the girl *is* working for some man or other and Danny's screwing her . . . If he'd been dragged into the back of a car, he's not likely to go off and screw the tart, is he?

He said that he was shit-scared the first time it happened. He's hardly going to . . .'

'You never know with men, Selina. From what you've said, this girl is a bloody nymphomaniac. What normal man wouldn't . . .'

'Yes, I see what you mean. OK, I'll give her the three grand, get Danny back, and take it from there.'

'When's she coming round for the money?'

'This morning.'

'You'd better go to the bank.'

'No, no, I've got it hidden upstairs. What about you following her, Chrissy?'

'Do you know what time she's coming?'

'No, she didn't say.'

'Well, I can't hang around all morning. I've got a dental appointment, for one thing. When you've paid her and Danny gets back, take it from there.'

'OK.'

'I won't stay, Selina. She might turn up at any minute and I don't want to be hanging around. Ring me later.'

'Yes, I will.'

Seeing her to the door, I didn't feel any better. I still had no idea whether Danny was innocent or not. But at least I'd had someone to talk to, to discuss the horrendous situation with. All I could do was wait for the bitch, and then wait for Danny to come home. If I told him that I was going to the police, and he tried to stop me, that might suggest that he was working with the tart. If he really had been abducted a second time I was sure he'd agree to call the police in – no matter what might happen to my career.

When the bitch finally arrived, I showed her into the lounge, not a word passing between us as she stood by the mantelpiece in her gabardine coat. *Another three thousand pounds*,

I thought bitterly as she grinned at me. But that would definitely be the last of the money!

'Your husband's quite safe,' she reassured me. 'But if you're going to carry on mucking me about like this, I can't say what my boss will do. And if I were to tell him what you did to me . . .'

'I don't want to talk about it,' I interrupted her. 'The money's on the piano. Take it and get out.'

'I'm not ready to leave yet.'

'I've been doing some more digging around. I know my husband's involved in this and . . .'

'Of course he's not!' she laughed.

'You were seen with him, by the common.'

'That's rubbish. He's a good fuck, and I might come round and get him to fuck me again, but . . .'

'Take the money and get out!'

'By the way, the videotape came out really well. My boss is delighted with it: he's made several copies.'

'There's no more money, so you can do what you like. There'll be no more books, and no more money.'

'Selina, you don't seem to understand,' she began, sitting in the armchair. 'Your husband is tied up, being held hostage, and you're saying that there'll be no more money or books.'

'I don't believe that he's been taken hostage, it's rubbish.'

'You really think that he's in this with me, don't you?'

'Damned right I do!'

'OK, I'll leave the money here, and you'll see what happens.'

'Yes, that's a good idea – let's see what happens.'

'Right, the choice is yours,' she taunted, leaping to her feet. 'I'll tell my boss that you wouldn't pay up and you'll see what happens. I'll be in touch.'

Recalling Chrissy's words as the tart left, I knew I was taking a risk, but I felt that it was the right thing to do. The ball was in their court now, it was their move. Speculating on the outcome if Danny really had been taken hostage, I knew they wouldn't kill him – and they couldn't keep him prisoner forever. Eventually, they'd have to release him and . . . *They might come for me*, I thought. If the thugs came to the house . . . All I could do was wait.

Spending several hours working on the book, I was surprised how much I'd written. Considering my husband might be in real danger, I'd worked extremely well. I'd at least expected a phone call from the girl, more threats and demands – but there'd been nothing. Perhaps they were wondering what to do, planning their next move. When the phone finally rang, I took a deep breath and lifted the receiver.

'Selina, it's me,' Danny said urgently.

'Where are you?' I asked angrily.

'You know where I am! Why didn't you give her the money?'

'I haven't *got* any more money, Danny. She took five thousand the other day, that was all the bank would give me.'

'You sound so cold and callous, Selina.'

'Of course I'm not, I'm worried sick. But what can I do?'

'Get some money and get me out of this place, for Christ's sake!'

As the phone went dead, I hung up, wondering what would happen next. I knew Danny would call again, or possibly the girl, and I was right. Within ten minutes the phone rang. I ignored it for a while, stupidly thinking that I'd let them sweat. Finally, I lifted the receiver.

'Meet me in the woods,' the bitch ordered me.

'No way!' I returned.

'If you want proof that we've got Danny, meet me in the woods in fifteen minutes.'

'I know you and your bloody tricks!' I spat.

'Fifteen minutes. And bring the money with you!'

The situation was getting worse by the minute. What proof could she give me? I wondered. Would they take Danny there? No, of course they wouldn't. Stuffing the cash into my bag and leaving the house, I decided not to go into the woods, but stay on the common. They'd hardly grab me in broad daylight, not with people about. At some stage, they'd have to come out of the woods to speak to me.

Unfortunately, there weren't many people on the common – only a man with his dog and a couple walking hand in hand. Standing close to the trees, my anxiety rising, I called the bitch, but there was no reply. I was going to have to play the waiting game, I knew, as I sat on the grass. Whoever was under cover of the trees with the girl would have to come out eventually.

After a while, I heard the girl calling me and rose to my feet. Turning round, I couldn't see her as she called me again. Was Danny with her? I wondered as I ventured a little closer to the pathway. Whoever was with her, whatever her threats, there was no way she'd lure me into the woods.

'Selina, we haven't got all day!' she shouted.

'Come out into the open!' I yelled. 'I'm not coming in!'

'Danny's here with us!'

Certain it was a trap, I resisted the temptation to enter the woods. If they did have Danny tied up and gagged . . . I didn't know what to do. Perhaps I should get help? I pondered, but the man with his dog had long since gone and there was no one else on the common.

'God,' I murmured, cautiously following the path. 'What the hell am I doing?' Walking deeper into the dark woods, I finally came to the clearing and stared at the bitch. Standing either side of her were the two young men, grinning as they looked me up and down. But there was no sign of Danny.

'Well, where is he?' I asked. 'If this is another one of your tricks . . .'

'Where's the money?'

'Here,' I said, passing her my bag.

'So far, so good. You'd better take a look at this Polaroid,' she smiled, passing me the photograph.

Gazing at the picture of Danny tied to a chair, a bolt of fear shot through me. With a dirty brick wall behind him, he could well have been in a basement. I had to accept that I'd been wrong. If only I'd . . . If only, if only. Looking up at the girl, her dishevelled blonde tresses, I knew what was going to happen as she slipped her coat off, revealing her curvaceous, naked body.

'Clothes off, Selina,' she grinned, snatching the photograph and dropping it into her bag. 'Hurry up, you've kept us waiting long enough as it is.'

'No, no more sex,' I returned, gazing at her pink inner lips protruding from her vaginal crack. 'You can have the money, but no more sex.'

'Here we go again,' she sighed, taking the whip from her bag. 'I'll teach you to be obedient if it's the last thing I do. Now, take your clothes off!'

As the men blocked the pathway and unbuttoned their shirts, I couldn't believe that I had walked straight into their lair again. I'd vowed never to be lured into the clearing by the cow but, in my stupidity, there I was! Watching the young men tug their trousers down, their erect penises catapulting into view, my stomach somersaulted. A pang of arousal sending a quiver through my pelvis as they pulled their foreskins back, I imagined sucking their swollen knobs into my mouth.

My thoughts lurching between Danny's predicament and my soaring arousal, I was horrified as my clitoris swelled and pulsated. How could I be thinking of enjoying sex with two strange men at a time like this? What had happened to me to make me put crude sex before my husband's safety? My cunt, my insatiable clitoris, was beginning to rule my life.

Unbuttoning my blouse as the bitch again ordered me to strip, I recalled whipping her naked buttocks, forcing the cucumber deep into her tight bottom-hole. She'd have her revenge, I knew, as I slipped my blouse off and tugged my skirt down. I couldn't endure another thrashing and yet, to my horror, the thought excited me, juiced my pussy.

Pulling my panties down, I kicked them aside and unhooked my bra. My nipples becoming erect in the cool air of the woods, my outer labia swelling, I felt my juices of arousal oozing from my tightening cunt, trickling in little streams over my inner petals. Recalling the girl's tongue between my love lips, licking my clitoris to orgasm, the shocking truth registered. From a faithful, loving wife I'd changed into a bisexual . . . A nymphomaniac?

'Kneel down, slave!' she ordered me as the naked men stood before me. 'Kneel down and suck their cocks.' Dropping to my knees, I gazed at their huge organs, their purple knobs. Slave? Quietly submissive, completely obedient, I didn't protest as they projected their hips, their swollen plums pressing against my moistening lips.

Both at once? I pondered, opening my mouth as wide as I could and taking their glandes inside. Cupping their heavy balls in each hand, I sucked and ran my tongue over their silky-smooth knobs, wondering what it would be like to have two cocks sperming in my mouth. Although aware of my crude and immoral behaviour, I couldn't deny the immense pleasure I was deriving from the obscene act. Sucking off two men at the same time? Impatient for two knobs to spunk in my mouth? I'd changed beyond all recognition!

For some reason, I forgot about Danny, his predicament. I didn't know why, but it was as if I didn't care about him as I sucked the men's twitching knobs deeper into my thirsty mouth. In a way, I blamed him for my transformation. If he'd allowed me to go to the police, if he'd not paid the girl in the first place, if . . . It was his fault that I was naked in the clearing, desperate for the strange men to spunk in my mouth.

'Do you like being mouth-fucked by two stiff cocks?' the girl giggled, moving in with the video camera. *More incriminating evidence*, I mused, wanking the men's solid shafts as I mouthed and tongued their knobs. But I was beyond caring – nothing mattered any more. I'd been wrenched from a life of normality and plunged into a world of insanity where sexual abuse reigned. Frighteningly metamorphosed into a sex-ravenous creature.

Where to from here? I wondered as the men began gasping, their orgasms dangerously close as their knobs swelled within my gobbling mouth. What would my relationship with Danny become now? Where would my creative writing take me? I could no longer write about romance, about love. The swamp of my mind bubbling with thoughts of crude sex, I could no longer comprehend love.

'Coming!' one of the men breathed. Wanking their shafts faster, I moved my head back until their swollen knobs were enveloped by my lips, my tongue snaking around their salty plums. Sperm suddenly jetting from one cock, I sucked and drank as the other man reached his climax and pumped his spunk into my mouth. Fervently gobbling, swallowing the gushing liquid, I felt my clitoris pulsate, my vaginal muscles tighten, squeezing out my sex juices. Lost in my debauchery, I took the orgasming knobs to the back of my throat, my lips stretched tautly around the twitching shafts as I drank their jetting lust milk.

'That's good,' the girl murmured, moving the camera closer to my face, capturing the jism dribbling down my chin as the men mouth-fucked me. 'We've really got you now.' I didn't care what they'd got, photographs, videotapes . . . Had I found my domain? I wondered, sucking out the last of the men's sperm as their cocks began to deflate. Was this my kingdom?

As the penises withdrew from my wet mouth, I lapped up the sperm coursing down my chin, wondering what crude act I was to perform next. *Lick the girl to orgasm?* I pondered, gazing at the opaque liquid dripping from her inner sex lips as she stood before me. Handing the camera to one of the men, she peeled her fleshy outer lips apart, exposing her wet, pink folds to my wide eyes.

Gazing at her sexual centre, the pink flesh forming a funnel around her open vaginal portal, I wondered how many cocks she'd had spunking inside her cunt. Focusing on her ripening clitoris emerging from beneath its pinken hood, I imagined her masturbating with a vibrator, her clitoris pulsating in orgasm, her juices of arousal spurting from her gaping sex hole.

Ordering me to lap up her cunt milk, she moved closer, her open vulva only inches from my face. Pushing my tongue out, I breathed in her female scent, realizing that neither of the men had touched her. Why hadn't they fucked her? Why hadn't she sucked their cocks to orgasm? Only Danny had fucked her, and again, I began to wonder whether he was in league with her. Was she remaining faithful to him? Apart from my tongue entering her vagina, was she saving her cunt for his cock? As I began licking the wet flesh surrounding her open hole, my lesbian arousal mounting, all thoughts of Danny faded.

'Lick me until I come!' she gasped, parting her pussy lips further, fully exposing the swollen nodule of her erect clitoris. Moving up her yawning sex valley, I snaked my tongue around her pleasure spot as the men knelt either side of me. A finger delving between my swollen sex lips, penetrating my cunt, I gasped as another finger slipped between my buttocks and massaged my anal rose.

Sucking the girl's clitoris into my mouth as the finger entered my rectal duct, massaging the velveteen walls of my secret sheath, I closed my eyes as another finger caressed my pulsating clitoris. Swamped in sex, my mind drifting upon a sea of lust, I sensed the beginnings of my orgasm stirring within my trembling womb. The girl gasping above me as her clitoris swelled beneath my sweeping tongue, I knew we were going to come together as she clung to my head to steady her sagging body.

'God, yes!' she cried, forcing her vulval flesh hard against my mouth as my own orgasm erupted. A second finger entering my anal duct, stretching my brown ring wide open, I fervently sucked and mouthed the girl's sex button as my orgasm completely engulfed my very being. On and on the waves of pleasure emanated from my throbbing clitoris and rolled through my naked body, touching every nerve ending, tightening every muscle.

'Finger my cunt!' she gasped, her vaginal juices spurting from her open hole as I slipped a finger into her tight sex duct. Locating her anal portal, I pushed another finger deep into her hot bottom-hole and began thrusting, pistoning her two sheaths. Writhing, she gripped my head harder, gyrating her hips as I sustained her climax. My own orgasm peaking as fingers thrust in and out of my lust holes, my cunt milk flowing in rivers down my inner thighs, I thought I'd pass out from the immense pleasure.

'I'll do her bum afterwards,' one of the men said, his crude words drifting around my blown mind. 'Give her a bloody good arse-spunking.'

'And I'll take her cunt,' the other rejoined. 'We'll give her a double fucking.'

Picturing the obscene act, wondering what it would be like to have two penises bloating both my sex sheaths simultaneously, my clitoris swelled again, pulsating in its second coming. I'd never have thought that such crude thoughts would excite me, send my arousal soaring. Two cocks fucking my sex holes? What would Danny think if he knew of my uncharacteristic thoughts? Where *was* Danny?

As the girl staggered back, my fingers slipping out of her hot holes, she collapsed to the ground and lay with her legs parted, her dripping cunt gaping. She *was* a tart, I reflected as my orgasm began to recede – nothing more than a filthy whore. But what was I? Two men fingering me, spunking in my mouth, using and abusing my naked body – what was I?

The men's fingers leaving my inflamed ducts, I shuddered as the last ripples of orgasm rolled through my shaking body. One young man ordering me to position myself on all fours over his naked body, he lay on the ground with his solid penis pointing skyward. *A double fucking?* I speculated as I crawled over his body and the other man knelt behind me, his bulbous knob delving between my naked buttocks.

'Get your cock up her arse and then I'll shove mine up her cunt,' the man beneath me breathed, running his swollen glans around my gaping vaginal entrance. The solid knob pressing against my brown hole as my buttocks were crudely yanked apart, I recalled the last time I'd been forced to endure anal sex. Was I being forced this time? I wondered as the massive knob slipped past my anal ring, stretching my secret hole wide open. Was this extortion or my own desire?

The solid shaft gliding deep into my anal canal, I shuddered as my delicate brown tissue stretched tightly around the intruding organ. Completely impaled, I grimaced as the man beneath me forced his solid penis deep into my cunt, my pelvic cavity bloating as the two cocks swelled within my tightening sex sheaths. Slowly withdrawing, they thrust into my tight holes, finding their rhythm as they double-fucked me.

'That's great!' the girl cried, moving behind me with the video camera. My naked body rocking as the double pistoning continued, the men gasping in their crudity, I wondered at my wanton behaviour, the exquisite pleasure pervading my being. The very whorishness of the illicit act was enthralling, plunging me ever deeper into a lake of decadence where lust ruled. I knew then that I'd never find love again. My femininity crudely stripped, I'd become nothing more than a tart, a sex object to gratify the lust of my abusers.

But who was abusing whom? I wondered as the men's heavy balls smacked between my open thighs, beautiful squelching sounds emanating from my inflamed cunt as my juices decanted. I was the abused, but the exquisite satisfaction the abuse brought me was frightening. Had I wandered into Lucifer's kingdom? Had he snatched my soul?

'God, I'm coming!' the man behind me gasped as he quickened his fucking motion, ramming his solid cock in and out of my inflamed bottom-hole. Both cocks swelling, stretching my ducts to capacity, I felt the sperm jetting, gushing simultaneously deep into my arse and into my hot cunt. The squelching sounds growing louder as my sheaths filled with the products of their orgasms, I cried out as my own climax erupted within my pulsating clitoris.

My body shaking violently, I rocked back and forth, meeting the penile thrusts, the swollen knobs repeatedly withdrawing and ramming into me as the spunk flowed in torrents. The man beneath me pinching and twisting my nipples, heightening my pleasure, I raised my head and looked up at the trees. This haven of nature had become my secret place, my unnatural domain, where I'd derive illicit pleasure from my sexual abusers.

As my orgasm receded, leaving me quivering and gasping,

the realization that I was being blackmailed hit me. Sperm coursing down my inner thighs as the men made their final thrusts into my inflamed holes, I looked at the girl as she focused the camera on my sex-flushed face. My domain? The domain was hers: she was my mistress and I her slave. Lowering the camera, she grinned at me as the men slipped their spent cocks out of my spunked ducts.

'You enjoyed that, didn't you?' she asked.

'Yes, yes, I did,' I murmured as I clambered off the stud beneath me.

'OK, tie her up and we'll see whether she enjoys what I have in store for her.'

Rolling me onto my back and tying ropes around my ankles as the girl delved into her bag, their penises stiffening afresh, the men said nothing as they slung the ropes over the branches of a tree. As they pulled on the ropes, my feet rising, my legs parting, I stared wide-eyed at the girl as she grabbed the whip. My buttocks leaving the ground as my legs rose higher into the air, I knew she was going to have her revenge for my earlier merciless thrashing of her.

'I don't think you'll enjoy this,' she taunted, standing between my legs and raising the whip above her head. The leather tails lashing my swollen vaginal lips, I screamed and begged for mercy. Ignoring my pleas, she lashed my vulval flesh again, the tails biting into my protruding inner lips. 'I've been looking forward to this!' she cried in her wickedness, thrashing my sex lips with a vengeance.

Standing either side of my head, their knobs above my face, the men wanked their erect cocks as the ruthless thrashing continued. My sex lips stinging like hell, my upper body writhed on the ground, screaming and struggling to break free, but there was no escape. On and on she lashed my cunt, the burning pain transmitting deep into my vulval flesh as the men neared their orgasms.

Sperm jetting from their swollen knobs, splattering my face as my cunt burned like fire, this was degradation in the extreme. The white liquid raining over my hair as the crack of the whip resounded throughout the woods, I prayed for the bitch to halt the abuse, but she continued like a woman possessed. Lash after lash flailing my cunt lips, my gaping vaginal valley, she finally discarded the whip and knelt on the ground between my open thighs.

The last of the men's spunk splattering my face, the lesbian licked between my inflamed cunt lips, sucking out the sperm, drinking my juices. Moving down, her mouth pressing between my parted buttocks, she licked my bottom-hole, lapping up the oozing spunk as I licked the sperm running over my mouth, my chin.

'You'll have another cunt-thrashing tomorrow,' the tart stated, rising to her feet.

'You're not going to do that to me again, you bitch!' I returned.

'What insolence! What bloody insolence!' she stormed, grabbing the whip.

The leather tails swinging through the air, cracking loudly across my vaginal flesh again, I yelped, wishing I'd kept my mouth shut. Again and again she lashed my cunt lips, the stinging pain permeating my protruding inner folds as she laughed uncontrollably in her devilry. After a dozen or more lashes, she tossed the whip to the ground and snapped a branch off a bush. Thrashing my naked buttocks, the leaves biting into my tensed flesh, I squeezed my eyes shut as her laughter resounded throughout the clearing.

'Let that be a lesson to you!' she hissed, standing by my side. 'Obedience, Selina – you'll . . .'

'Go to hell!' I screamed, immediately wishing I hadn't.

'Right, hold her arms behind her head!' she instructed the men.

The branch swishing through the air as the men held my arms, she thrashed my breasts, my sensitive nipples. The pain coursing through my mammary spheres, I felt my cunt milk oozing from my inflamed vagina, my clitoris swelling as my arousal heightened. Why was I deriving pleasure from such a debased act? I wondered fearfully as my nipples stiffened painfully. What dark transformation had I undergone to experience such arousal from such abuse of my naked body?

Again and again the branch lashed my burning breasts, the leaves flailing my sore milk teats as my naked body shook uncontrollably. My clitoris pulsating, I thought I was going to come as the beating continued. But instructing her accomplices to release my arms, she finally discarded her instrument of torturous pleasure.

'I didn't think I'd have to do this,' she grinned, delving into her bag. 'But your disobedience leaves me no choice.' Lifting my head, I watched her pull a large metal band from the bag, wondering what horrendous ordeal I was to be forced to endure now. Untying the ropes, she hauled me to my feet and spun me round, gazing at my weal-lined breasts.

'This will ensure that you behave yourself in future,' she declared, opening the hinged band and placing it around my body. My nipples protruding through holes in the band, my breasts squashed, she fastened the device behind my back, locking the band around me. 'There's no way you'll be able to remove it,' she grinned, running two chains over my shoulders and fixing the ends to the device. 'It's rather like a steel bra.'

As my abusers dressed, I gazed at my sore nipples protruding through the holes in the cold steel. Dreading to think what Danny would say were he to see the terrible device, I wondered when he'd be released. Was he part of the scam? I again wondered as I dressed, veiling my abused body. Being tied to a chair and having his photograph taken was easy enough, I reflected – it proved nothing. If he did return home, I'd question him and . . .

'I'll ring you tomorrow,' the bitch leered. 'If you cooperate, I'll remove the band.' Frowning at me as I stared at her, she moved closer. 'You'll do *what* you're told, *when* you're told. Do you understand?'

'Yes,' I murmured.

'Good, because I have other devices. You wouldn't want clamps attached to your cunt lips, would you?'

'No.'

'Or a metal clip locked to your clitoris?'

'No.'

'Right, I'll be in touch. Oh, there's one more thing. Shave your cunt.'

'No, I . . .'

'You *will* shave your cunt, Selina – and that's an order!'

As they left the clearing, I finished dressing and grabbed my bag. My sore nipples brushing against my blouse as I followed the path through the trees, my stinging breasts squashed by the metal band, I crossed the common. The first thing I'd do when I reached home was have a shower and wash away the sperm, then shave my . . . No, I *couldn't* shave my pubic hairs off! There again, if I didn't, who knew what the bitch would do to me?

Rain began to fall as I walked home, wetting my sperm-starched hair, running down my face. The sky becoming darker with heavy black clouds, the rain torrential, I cried as I arrived home. Cried for myself, for my marriage, for Danny. But he wasn't there.

Chapter Eight

I didn't dress after my shower, repairing to the lounge naked apart from the metal band. When Danny returned, *if* he returned, I'd show him my abused body, the band, the weals across my buttocks, my cunt, my breasts. Hopefully, by his reaction I'd be able to determine his innocence – or his treachery.

Was I innocent? I wondered, gazing at my distended nipples protruding through the holes in the metal band. Teasing my milk teats with my fingertips, I felt my clitoris swell, my vaginal muscles contract. Running my hand down over my stomach, I slipped my finger between my crimson pussy lips and massaged my sex spot, pondering on using the vibrator. Jumping as I heard the front door open, I took a deep breath.

'Selina!' Danny gasped, dashing into the lounge and gazing in horror at my spoiled body. 'What the hell have they done to you?'

'You can see what they've done. What I want to know is, what happened to *you*?'

'Didn't you see the photograph they took?'

'Yes.'

'Then you know what happened.'

'No, I don't.'

'What do you mean?'

'Danny, you were seen standing by the common – kissing the tart.'

'*What?* Who told you that?'

'It doesn't matter who told me, you were seen.'

'It wasn't me, for Christ's sake! I've been . . .'

'It was before you were abducted.'

'Selina, whoever said that is trying to cause trouble. Fucking hell, as if we haven't got enough trouble as it is!'

'There are a lot of things that don't add up, Danny.'

'If you're going to start going on about this girl and me . . . Why don't you take that awful metal thing off?'

'It won't come off, it's locked.'

'Here, let me have a look.'

'Don't worry about that now, I want some answers.'

'Answers?'

'What's the private detective's phone number?'

'It's upstairs, on my desk.'

'Go and get it.'

'I will in a minute. Selina, look at the state of your body. What the hell . . .'

'Don't worry about me. As I was saying, a lot of things don't add up.'

'Such as?'

'For a start, you look fine. I would have thought that, after spending all that time locked in a basement, you'd need a shave.'

'I was allowed to wash and shave, Selina – and I was given food.'

'How accommodating of them.'

'Where do you think I've been?'

'Not tied up in a basement.'

'Where, then?'

'With the bitch, more than likely.'

'Fucking hell! Do you think I'd put you through all this for that tart?'

'No, for the money.'

'What money?'

'The money she's been taking from me.'

'I don't fucking believe this! I've been dragged off the street again, tied up and . . .'

'Danny, put yourself in my shoes. *I'm* the one being blackmailed, *I'm* the one who's been sexually abused, who's had to pay thousands of pounds . . . You're never around when she comes to the house for sex, you were seen kissing a blonde girl by the common, you disappear for several days . . .'

'I was dragged off the bloody . . .'

'Hear me out, Danny. You're the one who's been dealing with the detective, you don't know the address of that man allegedly involved, it's pouring with rain and you come home completely dry . . .'

'They dropped me off. Selina, what are you getting at?'

'It doesn't add up.'

'Basically, you're saying that I'm blackmailing you?'

'I suppose so.'

'There's no fucking "suppose" about it! I'm not going to listen to this fucking rubbish, I'm going upstairs.'

Watching him storm from the room, I wondered whether I'd made a huge mistake. There was no way I'd discover the truth, no way to determine whether Danny was lying or not. Perhaps Chrissy had been mistaken? Perhaps it was someone resembling Danny she'd seen by the common? Perhaps this, perhaps that . . . The situation was worsening by the minute!

The metal band hurting my scarlet breasts, my distended nipples sore, I went up to the bedroom to dress. Gazing at my naked body in the full-length mirror, I recalled the massive orgasms I'd enjoyed, and again wondered why I'd derived so much pleasure from having my breasts thrashed. My once secret holes fucked by two men? Two knobs spunking in my mouth?

It was as if some sex fiend had been lurking in my subconscious, waiting to be roused from a deep sleep – and now it was wide awake. I had to stop picturing the men's huge knobs in my mouth, my hands wanking their penises to orgasm. But the obscene image wouldn't leave my tormented mind.

'I'm going out,' Danny growled, breaking my reverie as he appeared in the doorway. Gazing into his dark eyes, I wondered where he was going but didn't ask. I supposed I didn't want to know where he was going, who he was meeting. We were drifting further apart, I knew.

'You'd better try and take that metal thing off,' he said, gazing at my protruding nipples.

'I like it,' I replied. 'I liked the sex, the things they did to me.'

'They?'

'The girl and two men.'

'Two men . . . Have you gone crazy?'

'Probably.'

As he bounded downstairs and slammed the front door shut, I wandered into his room to find the detective's phone number. Finding nothing on his desk, I rummaged through the drawers, half expecting to find some incriminating evidence. There were no phone numbers, no photographs of a blonde tart, no love letters . . . I found nothing to implicate Danny.

As I was about to return to the bedroom, the filing cabinet caught my eye. Opening the top drawer, I went through the files, not knowing what I was looking for. Discovering a wad of money, I frowned. 'Eight hundred pounds,' I murmured, counting the notes. 'Where the hell did he . . .' Dashing to the desk as the phone rang, I grabbed the receiver.

'Mrs Goodman?' a man asked.

'Yes, speaking.'

'My name's Wilkins. I'm working for your husband.'

'Oh, yes. He's not here at the moment.'

'Actually, it's you I want to speak to.'

'Oh?'

'I've phoned several times but there's been no reply.'

'My husband was abducted again and I . . . I've been away for a couple of days.'

'Abducted *again?*'

'Yes, he . . .'

'Has the girl been in touch with you?'

'Yes, she has. I gave her another three thousand, that's fifteen thousand altogether.'

'OK, I'll give you my mobile phone number. The next time she calls, let me know.'

'Yes, yes, I will.'

'When she next goes to your house, I'll . . .'

'I've met her on the common twice.'

'The common?'

'Yes, in the woods by the railway bridge.'

'What was the idea of that?'

'She . . . I was sexually abused by the girl and two men.'

'Fucking hell! Er . . . I'm sorry. Why didn't your husband tell me?'

'He didn't know.'

'Christ, this is getting pretty serious. OK, grab a pen and I'll give you my number.'

Scribbling down the number of Wilkins's mobile, I thanked him for his help and promised to call him the next time the girl rang. Replacing the receiver, my mind racked with guilt, I returned to the bedroom. What a fool I'd been! It didn't bear thinking about how Danny must have felt when I'd accused him of blackmailing me. I should never have listened to Chrissy's daft theory. The sleuth was obviously all too genuine.

Feeling more alone than ever before now that I'd virtually exiled Danny, I pondered on the money hidden in the filing cabinet – and the unknown blonde girl. Again thinking that Chrissy must have been mistaken, I slipped into a summer dress, veiling my thrashed body, hiding the horrendous metal contraption.

I was pleased to see Chrissy standing on the step when I answered the door. For one thing, I wanted to tell her that I'd spoken to the detective, blowing her theory, and for another, I wanted to question her about the girl she'd supposedly seen Danny kissing.

'The detective rang me,' I said smugly as we walked into the lounge.

'Danny could have got a friend to phone and pretend to be a detective,' she returned.

'Chrissy! How far are you going to take this? You're so negative and cynical! As I said before, you should write fiction.'

'Maybe I should. Anyway, he was kissing a girl.'

'You might be mistaken. After all, you were driving past, not walking, you might have . . .'

'It was Danny, all right. So, what's the latest?'

I told her what had happened on the common, wishing I hadn't mentioned the metal band when she asked to see it. My embarrassment disallowing her a view, she had to be satisfied with a description of the device. Sitting wide-eyed on the sofa as I related my story, I wondered what her reaction would be, what she'd think. Brushing her long black hair away from her face as I finished, she stood up and walked to the window.

'She hasn't got a boss,' she declared, turning on her heels to face me.

'But Danny was abducted.'

'*She*'s the boss. She's employing these men, Selina – *she*'s the boss.'

'This is just another theory,' I sighed. 'Danny's involved, there is no detective, she's the boss . . . All theories, Chrissy.'

'We have nothing factual to go on so all we *can* do is theorize. If this was a simple case of blackmail, you handing over cash to shut someone up, OK – but it's not. It's this sexual stuff that's confusing things. OK, so they wanted something on you to blackmail you, and they got it – so why carry on with the sex?'

'I don't know.'

'This girl might be taking money from the men, selling you for sex.'

'That's a thought.'

'It's another theory, Selina. Why not send Danny away for a week or two? If he goes off on holiday, they can't kidnap him, right?'

'Right.'

'The worrying thing, apart from the sex . . .'

'Whether Danny's here or not the sex will continue.'

'Yes, but you could tell this girl that Danny's left you.'

'What good will that do?'

'It'll change everything. You can't be lured to the woods because you'll know that Danny's safe. She'll have to come here and . . .'

'But she has so much evidence, Chrissy. I *have* to do as she asks otherwise she'll ruin me.'

'Then let her. It'll put an end to the whole affair.'

Pacing the floor, I contemplated the idea. It was good, very good. There'd be nothing the girl could do if she believed that Danny had left me, and if he *was* in league with her . . . Danny would have to pretend to be on holiday, and she could hardly make out that her boss had grabbed him again.

'Where's Danny now?' Chrissy asked.

'We had a bit of a row and he went out.'

'When he gets back, tell him about the idea. If he agrees, get him away as soon as you can.'

'OK.'

'I'd better be going, I only called in as I was passing.'

'Well, thanks for your help,' I smiled, seeing her to the door.

'Any time. Keep me posted.'

'Yes, yes – I will.'

My breasts aching, I went out into the garden and waited for Danny to return, wondering where he could go for a couple of weeks. A holiday would do him good. A holiday would have done *me* good! But I had to put an end to the horror before relaxing in the sun on a sandy beach. The end was nearing, I knew. The end of the nightmare wasn't far off.

'Danny!' I called running into the house as I heard the front door shut. 'Danny, I've had an idea.'

'Have you?' he snapped. 'I suppose you're now going to suggest that I . . .'

'No, listen to me. I'm sorry for what I said earlier. Look, that doesn't matter. Go away on holiday for a week or two.'

'What, on my own?'

'Yes, that way they won't be able to kidnap you.'

'What will you do? You can't stay here alone with that girl . . .'

'I've got it all worked out.'

'*Did* you enjoy the sex?'

'No, no, of course I didn't. I said that because I was angry. Come and sit in the lounge and I'll tell you my plan.'

Danny thought it was a good idea, although he didn't relish going abroad alone. He was also worried about leaving me – but, as I reassured him, there'd be no point in the thugs taking *me* to the basement. Besides, if I had a problem I had Chrissy to call on. Finally deciding to stay in a hotel somewhere – as he'd thought I'd done – he went up to pack a case while I cooked the evening meal. I didn't ask him about the money, or mention that Wilkins had called. For his own safety, I just wanted him to go as soon as possible.

After the meal, he suggested that he try cutting the metal band off, but I declined. I wanted the bitch to believe that he'd left me because he thought I'd enjoyed the perverted sex and loved wearing the kinky contraption.

'Are you going to be OK?' he asked as we walked to the front door.

'Yes, of course. You go off and have a break and, hopefully, when you get back all this will be over. Are you all right for money?'

'Yes, I've got my credit card.'

'Good. Phone me as soon as you can.'

Feeling positive as he left the house and drove off, I climbed the stairs to bed. At least Danny was safe, I reflected, trying to make myself comfortable beneath the quilt as the metal band crushed my stinging breasts. At least I didn't have him to worry about.

Waking at nine, I pushed the quilt back and gazed at my aching nipples popping through the metal band, the weals fanning out across my crimson breasts. While my bum no longer hurt, my vaginal lips were still sore, and I decided not to wear panties as I climbed out of bed. After a shower, I slipped into my summer dress and bounded downstairs, wondering where Danny had stayed and when he'd ring.

The morning passed uneventfully, allowing me to work on the book for several hours. It puzzled me that Danny hadn't phoned, but I was sure he was OK. When the phone finally rang, I hoped it was the bitch so I could impart the good news to her that Danny had left me. Her reaction would be more than interesting! Lifting the receiver, I grinned as she asked me how my tits were.

'Aching,' I replied. 'But I like the sensation of my erect nipples brushing against my dress.'

'Are you pleased to have your husband back?'

'I haven't got him back.'

'What do you mean? He should have been there . . .'

'He's left me.'

'What? You're lying.'

'I wish I was, Alison. Whether or not he has another woman, I don't know, but he seemed to think that I enjoyed the abuse in the woods and that the metal band was my idea. He said that he doesn't want a wife who has sex with other men and women.'

'I don't believe a word of it.'

'I don't really care what you believe. Danny's gone, and that's that.'

'You'd better get yourself down to the common.'

'No, thanks, I'm busy.'

Hanging up, I wondered what she'd do. Come round to the house, more than likely! Initially I decided not to let her in, but I changed my mind. I wanted to hear what she had to say, find out what her next move would be. Going along with Chrissy's theory that she might not have a boss, I made my plans. Firstly, I'd not call the detective, secondly, I'd only let her in if she was alone, and thirdly, I'd tell her once and for all that there was no more money and that she could go to the newspapers with her evidence of my debauchery if she so pleased.

She arrived, alone, within twenty minutes. Standing haughtily on the step with her bag slung over her shoulder, her long blonde hair dishevelled, she followed me into the lounge. I was sure that she was flummoxed now that she believed Danny had left me. There'd be no more threats of kidnapping him or . . .

'If your husband really has left you, it changes things,' she said.

'I know it does!'

'But not in the way you think. Anyway, I won't talk about that now. Remove your dress, Selina.'

'No, I won't!'

'I have a contingency plan,' she said gruffly. 'And I'll set it in motion unless you strip off.'

'I'm not going to do anything of the sort!' I returned.

'Right, one phone call is all I have to make to ruin you.'

'I'm not bothered about the newspapers.'

'It's not only the newspapers I have in mind,' she grinned, impishly cocking her head to one side.

'Oh?'

'Copies of certain videotapes will also be sent to your family, your publisher, your friends and neighbours . . .'

'Look, we're going to have to come to some kind of arrangement,' I said, imagining the neighbours watching my debauchery on their VCRs. 'There's no more money and my husband has left me. The publisher doesn't want another book . . .'

'Arrangement?' she frowned. 'What sort of arrangement?'

'I don't know. This boss of yours, if there's no more money . . .'

'If there's no more money, he'll become extremely upset. Sex – what about sex?' she asked.

'What about it?'

'I don't know how you'll keep my boss happy, but you can keep *me* happy by doing what I ask, when I ask.'

'There *is* no boss, is there?'

'There is, Selina – believe me!'

'Then, in effect, you're both blackmailing me.'

'Yes, you could say that. He'll go to the papers unless you pay up, but I do have *some* influence over him. If you keep me happy, I might, just might, be able to keep him happy. Now, take your dress off.'

I knew I was in for a thrashing as I slipped my dress off, but I felt that I was getting somewhere at last. She'd seemed to accept that Danny had gone, and that there was no more money, and I was sure that all she could get from me now was my body.

Dragging the small table across the room, she placed it in front of the sofa, the hard edge against the cushion. Wondering what she had in mind as she took my arm and ordered me to sit on the table, I complied with the obedience of a trained sex slave.

'Lie back and rest your head on the sofa, keeping your feet on the floor,' she instructed me.

Reclining as she rummaged in her bag, I allowed her to part my feet and cuff my ankles to the table legs. I was complying to substantiate my claim that Danny had gone and the money had dried up, that all I now had to offer was my body, I told myself. But I couldn't deny my building arousal, and, frightening though it was, my eagerness to have her attend my cunt with her wet tongue, her slender fingers.

Binding each wrist with lengths of rope, she stretched my arms out, tying the ends of the ropes together behind the sofa. My thighs wide, my cunt gaping, I was completely defenceless, vulnerable to her every lesbian whim. I was in the wrong position for a buttock-whipping, and wondered whether I was to endure a vulval thrashing as she delved into her bag. The thought sending a lascivious quiver up my spine, I lifted my head, gazing in horror as she pulled a razor and a can of shaving foam from the bag.

'No!' I protested as she knelt between my feet and squirted the foam over my vaginal lips, my mons.

'I like my girls shaved,' she smiled. 'Schoolgirl-lookalike cunts turn me on.'

'No, please don't shave me!'

'I'll do exactly as I wish.'

My head flopping back onto the sofa cushion, the foam cooling my sensitive outer lips, I cringed as she dragged the razor over the rise of my mons. I dared not look as she worked between my splayed thighs, carefully unveiling my most private place. Pulling my pussy lips up and apart, removing every curl, she shaved the soft skin between my thighs and my sex cushions.

I felt ravaged, pillaged. My pubes would take weeks to grow back, and I dreaded to think what I'd look like with the most intimate part of my body so brazenly displayed. A schoolgirl-lookalike cunt? What would Danny say? Why hadn't he phoned?

'You're looking *much* better!' the bitch giggled. 'I'm going to have to get you a gymslip and a pair of white ankle socks!' I said nothing as she finished her work of depravity, wiping away the foam and pubic-thatch hairs with a towel. 'There, take a look,' she grinned, stroking my smooth vaginal lips. 'Just like a schoolgirl!'

Lifting my head, I gazed at the hairless skin of my sex cushions, my naked mons. The pink weals fully visible, fanning out over my intimate flesh, I couldn't believe what she'd done to me She'd stripped years off my cunt, and I recalled my schooldays when I used to examine my soft girlish lips in the bath, wondering when my pubic hairs would sprout. Focusing on my pink inner folds protruding from my naked sex valley, I recalled the days before my petals had developed, my neat crack tightly closed.

'Right, you're ready for my first customer,' she leered, rising to her feet and leaving the room. First customer? She *was* selling me for sex! I thought fearfully, recalling Chrissy's words. *First* customer? How many were there? I knew it was futile to struggle – there was no way I could escape. How bitterly I regretted allowing the cow into the house and thus making yet another fatal mistake!

'Here she is,' she grinned, showing a young man into the room.

'Nice, very nice!' he beamed, focusing his lustful eyes on my shaved cunt. 'I like her metal bra! And her cunt . . . God, it's beautiful!'

'So, what's it to be?' she asked him.

'Just a quick fuck.'

'OK, fifty pounds.'

As he handed her the money, I felt swamped with humiliation, degradation. I was no better than a common prostitute. Worse, I wasn't getting a penny myself for my services! Watching the man kneel between my feet and unzip his trousers, I couldn't believe the predicament I was in. Just a quick fuck? I was nothing more than a lump of flesh to be used and abused, to satisfy men's sexual cravings!

'Don't take too long,' the bitch said, kneeling beside the man and watching him run his swollen knob up and down my naked sex valley. 'I have several other clients waiting.'

Where had she found the clients? I wondered as his knob slipped between my inner lips and glided deep into my wet cunt. Had she advertised me, my naked body? Jolting as he repeatedly withdrew his huge penis and thrust back into me, I shuddered as I imagined man after man entering me, fucking me and spunking up my tight cunt. How many could I take?

'God, she's nice and tight,' he murmured, his heavy balls slapping my naked buttocks. 'Worth every penny.'

'You can have her whenever you like,' the bitch volunteered as my juices squelched with the pistoning. 'Fuck her every day, if you want to.'

'I'd love to, but I can't afford it,' the panting man replied, parting my hairless lips and exposing my erect clitoris.

'I can do you a special price, but we won't discuss it now. You carry on and enjoy yourself.'

A special price? What did she think I was, a blow-up doll?

Perhaps I shouldn't have told her that Danny had left me, I reflected, recalling her chilling words. *It changes things.* It certainly did change things, leaving me wide open for commercial sex! Again, I'd been so naive, so stupid.

'Here it comes!' the man groaned, his penis swelling as he increased his rhythm. 'God, I'm coming!' I felt his sperm jetting from his solid knob, gushing deep into my cunt as his swinging balls slapped my naked buttocks. How many cocks were going to penetrate me? How much sperm was going to be pumped deep into my burning cunt?

Making his last thrusts, his dark eyes glazed, he leaned on the sofa and rested his weight on his hands. Gasping, his knob embedded deep within my vaginal sheath, he gazed longingly at my open sex valley, my exposed clitoris. *Number one*, I mused as he finally slipped his spent cock out of my brimming cunt. *Number one of how many?*

As he rose to his feet and followed the girl to the front door, I renewed my attempts to break free from my bonds. Sperm oozing from my open sex hole and running down between my buttocks as I struggled, I knew there was no escaping my fate.

'Put some effort into the next one,' the girl rebuked me as she came back into the room. 'Make out you're enjoying it.'

'No, I won't!' I spat.

'You certainly will! Unless, that is, you want the cunt-thrashing of your life.'

Answering the front door, she returned with another man. In his sixties, his grey hair markedly receding, he gazed in delighted disbelief at my naked body, my drenched cunt-slit. Closing my eyes as the tart asked him what he'd like, I shuddered as he told her that he wanted to fuck my mouth and then my cunt.

'That'll cost you eighty,' she pronounced.

'As much as that?'

'I'd have thought that's a pretty good price, considering you'll be fucking her twice.'

'OK, eighty it is. I like my whores shaved.'

'So do I!' she giggled.

Looking through my lowered eyelashes as he passed her the money and slipped his trousers off, I gazed in horror at his semi-erect cock. By far the biggest I'd seen yet, my eyes widened in shock as his member stiffened to its full extent, reminding me of a horse's shaft. His huge purple globe swollen, glistening in the light as he knelt on the sofa, his parted thighs either side of my head, I shuddered as he positioned himself with his glans inches from my mouth.

'Suck him off,' the girl instructed me crudely as I focused on his sperm-slit. Opening my mouth, I took his glans inside and gently sucked. I had no choice, I knew, as he drove his knob to the back of my throat and began gasping. He'd paid up front, and I was to satisfy his perverted needs or bear the consequences.

'Don't forget what I told you, Selina,' she murmured as the man's heavy balls pressed against my chin, his pubic hairs tickling my face. Breathing in the heady scent of his dark curls, I sucked harder, moaning through my nose as if I was enjoying the crude coupling. Was I enjoying it? To my horror, I found myself craving his spunk, longing for him to come in my mouth, to bathe my tongue with his white jism.

As he withdrew his solid shaft, my taut lips engulfing his purple plum, I snaked my tongue over its silky surface. His body becoming rigid, he rocked his hips, gently fucking my hot mouth as his sperm jetted from his glans. Moaning, his balls slapping my chin, he clutched my head as he pumped his salty liquid into my thirsty mouth, filling my cheeks. Swallowing hard, I continued to drink from his orgasming knob, draining his heavy balls as his huge penis twitched in its coming.

Could he manage to fuck me and shoot more spunk deep into my cunt? I wondered as he shuddered and slipped his wet cock out of my mouth. Clambering off the sofa as I slurped his lust-fruits from my chin, he knelt between my feet. Surely he couldn't achieve a second erection so quickly? Feeling his knob stabbing between my inner sex petals, I prayed that he could.

I was not to be disappointed. 'Christ, she's wet!' he breathed as his shaft entered me, stretching the silken walls of my vagina. Didn't he know that I'd just been fucked? I wondered as he withdrew and rammed his knob into me again. Obviously not, I concluded as he quickened his rhythm, his huge balls smacking my buttocks.

Moaning, initially merely pretending to enjoy the enforced fucking, I realized to my amazement that my gasps were becoming for real as he thrust his huge wet cock in and out of my tightening vaginal duct. My clitoris erect, pulsating as his shaft massaged the sensitive tip, I knew I was going to come. My craving for crude sex was heightening and, in a moment of madness, I imagined selling my body to men myself to satisfy their lust.

But *was* it a moment of madness? I enjoyed being fucked, having men's huge cocks driving in and out of my burning cunt, their spunk jetting over my cervix – so why not get paid for it? I loved having my clitoris licked and sucked to orgasm, my bottom fucked, my . . . No, I couldn't do it. Selling my body for sex wasn't . . . But I *was* doing it! I was a prostitute and the girl was my pimp!

The balding man's jism jetting from his swollen knob, bathing my cervix as he fucked me, I reached my own mind-blowing climax, wondering what had happened to the old Selina Goodman. Happily married housewife, best-selling author . . . What was I now? I wondered as my orgasm peaked, sending electrifying ripples of sex through my shaking body. Selina Goodman, the whore.

Lifting my head, I gazed at the man's wet shaft as it repeatedly sank into my cunt and emerged. My hairless love lips stretched tautly around his massive organ, my clitoris completely exposed, I imagined two cocks fucking me, both forced up my cunt, spunking me. My orgasm peaking again as I watched the beautiful sight, I whimpered in my incredible coming, my entire body alive with sex. Again and again he drove his swollen knob deep into my lust sheath, battering my cervix as his spunk flowed and spilled from my bloated cavern.

Finally collapsing over my sated body, he breathed heavily as his glans absorbed the heat of my inflamed duct. Twice today already I'd had my cunt filled with sperm and I wondered how many more clients the bitch had lined up as I lay quivering in the aftermath of my beautiful multiple orgasm. Three, four, five . . .

'I'll have to come again,' the man grinned as he climbed to his feet, his flaccid penis slipping out of my inflamed vagina, dripping with a blend of sperm and cunt-milk. 'Excuse the pun!'

'Indeed you will!' the tart chuckled as he tugged his trousers up his legs. 'Ring me any time and I'll arrange it.'

Sperm pouring from my burning cunt, I closed my eyes as she showed the old boy out, wondering how many more men I could take. If Danny stayed away for two weeks and she brought half a dozen men round every day . . . Over eighty men! Over eighty penises sperming my cervix!

'Lessons in love,' the bitch grinned, leading a very young man into the room. 'As it's your first time, I'll only change you twenty pounds.' He gazed in wonderment at my bared sex valley, my inner folds, the sperm trickling from my open sex sheath. 'You've never seen a naked woman before?' she asked him.

'No, never,' he replied sheepishly. 'She's beautiful!'

'Take a good look at her, examine her cunt, and then fuck her.'

He knelt between my legs and stretched my pussy lips wide apart, scrutinizing my inner flesh as I watched his eyes grow wide. Tentatively slipping a finger into my open hole, he explored inside my duct, massaging the silken walls of my vagina, not once taking his eyes off my most intimate place.

'That's her clitoris,' the girl said, kneeling beside him and massaging my erect sex spot. 'Rub it like this, as fast as you can, and she'll come.' Following her instructions, he massaged my solid pleasure button with his free hand, his finger still inside my tightening cunt as he watched my flushed face for a reaction. Closing my eyes, I thought I'd have to fake an orgasm, but I couldn't deny the immense pleasure I was deriving from the inexperienced young man.

'Push as many fingers into her cunt as you can,' the tart directed as I began to quiver. 'A girl likes her cunt stretched wide open.' Slipping more fingers into my drenched vaginal canal, he rubbed my clitoris faster, the electrifying sensations transmitting deep into my contracting womb. 'You'll soon enjoy your first fuck,' the bitch murmured. 'You can fuck her and spunk up her cunt.'

His first fuck? The thought of his virginal penis penetrating me sent quivers of excitement running up my spine. My clitoris pulsating in the beginnings of my climax, I pictured his fresh cock driving into my lust hole, fucking me, sperming inside me. 'God!' I breathed as my clitoris exploded in orgasm, the agonizing pleasure rippling through my naked body. 'Don't stop!'

On and on the waves of pure sexual ecstasy rolled through my trembling flesh as he finger-fucked me and massaged my solid clitoris. I could hear him talking to the girl, but his words drifted through the haze of my mind, floating on a sea of pure sexual bliss. The open centre of my femininity crudely displayed to the young man, my vulval flesh shaved, the crudity of my wanton act thrilled me.

'Don't stop!' I sang again in my ecstasy as my clitoris palpitated, sending exquisite ripples of sex through my trembling pelvis. My cunt gripping his thrusting fingers, the mixture of sperm and my orgasmic juices gushing from my open hole and running down between my buttocks, I thought I'd pass out with the immense pleasure surging through my debased body. My sensitive nipples erect, peeping like small penises through the holes in the steel band, my entire body was awash with sex.

At last my orgasm waned, leaving me shaking violently, my cunt spasming, my sex button receding. As the young man's fingers left my love duct, I waited in anticipation for him to push his fresh, uninitiated cock into my yearning vagina and sperm my creamy cervix. I listened to the girl instructing him as he pulled his zip down. *Lessons in love? Lessons in lust!* I mused, opening my eyes and gazing at his beautiful prick.

His purple globe glistening in the light as the girl pulled his foreskin back, she instructed him to run his swollen knob up and down my wet crack to lubricate his virginal organ. His glans between my inner petals, he gasped as he slowly entered me, stretching me open with his solid penis.

'Nice?' she asked as his shaft impaled me completely, his young balls pressing against my buttocks.

'She's so hot and wet!' he exclaimed excitedly.

'Better than wanking?'

'God, yes! The real thing!'

In his sexual frenzy, he thrust his cock in and out of my tightening cunt, gasping as his virginity slipped away. His young balls buffeting my naked buttocks, I closed my eyes, wondering where my life was taking me. A young man fucking me? An old man fucking my mouth? What was I doing?

'Ah, I'm . . . I'm coming!' he cried, thrusting his young tool in and out of my cunt with a vengeance. I felt his spunk gushing into my sex sheath, filling me, overflowing and running down between my buttocks. The table would be stained, a stark reminder of my debauchery. 'Ah, it's incredible!' he breathed, ramming into me, his spunk jetting as his swinging balls drained.

He halted the fucking before I reached my climax, resting his weight on his hands as his cock deflated inside my drenched vagina. Watching him through my eyelashes, his young flushed face, I smiled. I'd never been fucked by a young virgin before and the notion sent erotic quivers through my womb. For as long as he lived, he'd never forget me, his first fuck.

'Well?' the bitch smiled as he pulled his newly baptized cock out of my sex duct. 'How was it for you?'

'Amazing!' he beamed, clambering to his feet and zipping his jeans. 'Absolutely incredible!'

'You're a man now.'

'Yes, yes, I am.'

As they left the room, I lifted my head and gazed at my hairless vaginal lips, the blend of sperm and cunt milk glistening in the open groove of my sex valley. Were there any more men? I wondered as I heard the front door close. Where was Danny? He still hadn't phoned and I began to worry about him. Was he worried about me?

'Well, that's all for the time being,' the bitch grinned as she stood before me. 'I'll take the metal band off in a minute.'

'You needn't think that you're going to use me like this again!' I hissed.

'Right, as you seem to have forgotten that I call the shots, I'll whip your cunt.'

Delving into her bag of tricks, she pulled out a small plastic paddle with a long handle. Lifting my head as she knelt between my feet, I grimaced in anticipation as she gently patted my swollen vaginal lips with the flat paddle. The slapping sound growing louder as she smacked my jismed sex-flesh harder, I bit my lip as the pain began to permeate my sensitive outer labia. Striking my protruding inner lips, she lost control and thrashed my stinging flesh for all her worth.

'This'll teach you!' she stormed, beating my cunt. 'You're going to earn me a lot of money! If you dare to argue with me again, I'll keep you chained up like an animal!'

My fleshy vaginal cushions stinging like hell, she repeatedly thrashed me with the paddle, turning my cunt a fire-red. My fists clenched, my head tossing from side to side as the smacking sounds resounded around the room, I squeezed my eyes shut, determined to endure the beautifully agonizing pain. Was I a masochist? I wondered as the pain intensified and my clitoris throbbed.

'More!' I cried involuntarily, shocking myself as she continued to thrash my burning cunt. To my horror, I climaxed, my clitoris pulsating in orgasm, my rhythmically contracting vagina pumping out its exotic blend of sperm and cunt juice. On and on the pleasure coursed through my rigid body, taking me to incredible heights of sexual gratification as she crudely abused the most private part of my naked body.

'That'll do for now,' she finally said as she tossed the paddle to the floor and examined her handiwork. 'For your insolence, I'm going to leave you tied up there for a few hours. I'll be back this evening with some more clients.'

'You can't leave me here!' I protested, pulling on my bonds.

'No, you're right,' she smiled, releasing my ankles and untying my wrists.

Helping me to stand on my trembling legs, she cuffed my hands behind my back and packed her instruments of sexual torture into her bag. Sperm coursing down my inner thighs, I couldn't believe that she was going to leave me like that. I couldn't dress, answer the phone . . . I couldn't do anything!

'See you later,' she smiled sweetly, leaving the room.

'Please!' I called. 'Please, Alison!'

The front door slamming shut, I wondered what to do as I walked around the room. Try as I might, I couldn't slip my hands out of the cuffs. When Danny phoned – if he phoned – I might be able to answer by knocking the receiver off and . . . No, it was useless, I thought anxiously. The bitch had me right where she wanted me.

Flopping into the armchair, I gazed at my nipples seeking air from their monstrous confinement, at my hairless cunt lips glowing scarlet. I was a prisoner in my own home and all I could do was wait for the tart to return with more clients. Sperm oozing between my abused pussy lips, I made myself as comfortable as I could, wondering at my latest horrendous predicament. Would the horror ever end?

Chapter Nine

The evening nearing, my apprehension rose as I paced the floor, my hands cuffed behind my back. When would the girl return? Who would she bring with her? More men, more cocks, more spunk. My vaginal lips sticky with a sordid cocktail of sperm and sex milk, I desperately wanted to have a shower, to dress and escape from the house. But with my hands secured behind me, I couldn't even make myself something to eat or enjoy a cup of coffee.

Danny still hadn't phoned, and again I began to wonder whether he was in league with the tart. My only contact with the outside world now being with the bitch and her clients, I felt so isolated. It seemed that everyone was ganging up against me, scheming their schemes, planning my life.

As I passed through the hall to the kitchen, it suddenly occurred to me that the bitch couldn't get in. I couldn't open the door, and she didn't have a key. Panicking as I thought I'd be imprisoned in the house forever, I tried to unlock the back door, but the key fell to the floor. Tears streaming down my face as I knelt to try and retrieve it, I jumped as I heard the front door open. *Danny?* I wondered, dashing into the hall. Had he changed his mind and . . .

'Ah, there you are,' the bitch grinned.

'How did you get in?' I gasped as three men followed her into the house and gazed at my shaved pussy lips, my naked mons.

'I have a key, Selina. Not only a key to the door, but a key to your life.'

'You can't just walk in here and . . .'

'I *have* just walked in.'

Staring at her in shocked amazement as she opened the dining-room door, a bolt of fear shook my naked body as she grabbed my arm and marched me into the room. Numb, I couldn't speak as she dumped her bag on the floor and ordered me to lie on the table. My chest tight with anxiety as she released the handcuffs, I knew I had no choice – my fate was sealed.

'That's it, on your back,' she said as I climbed onto the table. 'Legs wide apart, Selina,' she instructed me, dragging me along the polished top until my buttocks were over the edge of the table. 'We want your cunt open,' she giggled, placing my feet on two chairs. '*Wide* open!'

Pulling my arms behind my head, she bound each wrist with rope and secured the other ends to the table legs. Tying my feet to the chairs, she placed another chair at the foot of the table and sat down between my parted thighs as the men tugged their trousers down. Her tongue lapping between my pussy lips, cleansing me, she pressed her mouth against my open sex hole and sucked out the cocktail of juices and sperm. Her tongue entering me, exploring deep inside my slippery vaginal duct, she peeled my fleshy sex cushions wide apart, exposing my inner folds.

Looking up at the ceiling as she lapped between my pink petals, teasing my clitoris, exploring inside my vaginal duct, I wondered where this would all end. In hell, I supposed. This *was* hell! But the illicit coupling excited me. The men watching the crude lesbian licking, I felt a quiver run up my spine. A battle of morals raging in my mind, I knew I should stop fighting. After all, who was I fighting? Myself?

'Mmm, you taste nice,' she breathed. 'I love drinking spunk and cunny milk, it turns me on.' Rising to her feet, she took her coat off, revealing her naked body, her pert breasts topped with beautifully elongated nipples. Clambering onto the table, she placed her knees either side of my head, her open vaginal entrance hovering above my face as she buried her head between my thighs and lapped between my sex lips.

As one of the naked men knelt behind her, his heavy balls brushing my forehead as his huge knob drove deep into her cunt, I looked on in amazement. The sex coupling only inches from my wide eyes, the girl's cunt lips stretched tautly around the base of the huge penis: I had never before seen anything like it, even in a blue movie. The man's erect organ withdrawing, dripping with her sex milk, I watched her pink inner lips clinging to the veined shaft. Driving into her again as she continued to lick and suck my clitoris, the man's heavy balls rolling over my forehead, I closed my eyes as she lowered her body, her hot cunt flesh pressed against my face, his wet shaft gliding over my nose.

'I'll take her cunt,' another man enthused, moving to the foot of the table. The penis squelching within her slippery vagina, my face wet with her flowing juices, I felt a knob stabbing between my own sex lips. Driving into my cunt, the huge shaft stretching me open, never had I known such obscenity, such debauchery. The tart obviously wasn't saving her sex sheath for Danny, I reflected, watching the man's massive cock fucking her wet cunt as another cock shafted my spasming vagina.

'Lick me, bitch!' she gasped, forcing her wet flesh harder against my mouth, the man's dripping cock rubbing my nose. Pushing my tongue out, I tasted her sex milk, licked the pistoning shaft, lapped at her crimsoning flesh. The man gasping, I knew he was about to come, and I waited in anticipation for his spunk to drip from his shaft, to pour from her bloated cunt and baptize my mouth.

Aware that the dark hand of debauchery had gripped me,

I wondered whether I'd ever again find normality again. But it was already too late, I feared. I'd travelled too far down the path of corruption, crossed the threshold of iniquity to a realm of perverted sex.

'Coming!' the man towering above my head gasped, his cock swelling as he fucked the bitch. His lower belly slapping her naked buttocks as he rammed his knob in and out of her drenched cunt, I lapped up the spunk dripping from his shaft, gushing from her bloated vagina. On and on the opaque liquid flowed, bathing my face, running down my chin as I savoured the products of their orgasms.

The other man gasping as he drove his knob deep into my inflamed vagina, fucking me in his sexual frenzy, I felt his sperm jetting over my cervix, filling my spasming lust sheath. My own climax erupting as his pistoning shaft massaged my exposed clitoris, I licked the girl's pink flesh, stretched tautly around the shafting cock. Lapping up their sex juices as my cunt contracted, hugging the thrusting penis, I delighted in my obscenity.

My orgasm gripping me, sending exquisite ripples of sex through my shaking body, I wondered whether I was the devil's daughter. I felt strangely comfortable in a domain where perverted sex ruled, at home with my immorality. Nothing else mattered – the outside world didn't exist. My life was born of crude sex, my cunt the centre of my very being. Had Lucifer taken my soul?

'Don't stop!' the girl cried, rocking her hips to meet the man's thrust as he drained his swinging balls. Sucking on her swollen outer lips, swallowing the flowing spunk as my own orgasm peaked, I tossed my head back and took his bulbous knob into my mouth as his cock slipped out of her juiced cunt. Mouthing, licking as my climax rolled on, I sucked out the last of his sperm as he gasped with pleasure.

'Drink from my cunt!' the girl breathed as the salty knob

left my mouth. 'Suck the spunk out of my cunt!' Staring at her open hole, the sperm trickling over her distended inner folds, I pressed my lips hard against the flesh surrounding the portal to her vagina and sucked.

'Yes!' she breathed, rocking her hips, her yawning sex valley gliding back and forth over my wet mouth, my protruding tongue. 'Ah, yes!' The man between my thighs making his last thrusts as my orgasm receded, I wondered what would be served next on the menu of depravity. A cunt-thrashing? An arse-fucking? In my debasement, I recalled the two cocks fucking the tight holes between my legs, using and abusing my naked body. Was that what I wanted?

The spent penis leaving the drenched sheath of my vagina as I sucked the last of the spunk from the girl's hot cunt, I felt the third man's knob stabbing between my pussy lips. Another crude fucking, another spunking, another massive orgasm . . . How much could I take in one day? I wondered as the girl climbed off the table.

Lifting my naked body, she released the steel band, allowing my aching breasts to assume their natural form. Tweaking my sore nipples, she clipped two metal clamps to my brown teats, the pain permeating my breasts as she grinned at me. Reaching into her bag as the man thrust his swollen cock in and out of my burning sex duct, she placed two steel rings over my breasts.

'Christ, she's hot!' the man gasped as he fucked me and the girl turned the screws, my breasts ballooning as the rings tightened.

'Don't spunk up her yet,' she decreed, moving to her bag again. 'Take your cock out and I'll shove this up her arse.'

As the man slipped his massive penis out of my inflamed vagina, I lifted my head, watching the girl force a huge vibrator deep into my aching pussy. Slipping the dripping device out, she parted my buttocks and drove the shaft deep into my bowels. My delicate brown tissue stretching to capacity, I gasped as she switched the formidable phallus on. The vibrations running through my quivering pelvis, the man thrust his cock deep into my cunt again, my holes bloating as he impaled me on his giant weapon.

'Now you can fuck her!' the tart chuckled as she tightened the rings, my breasts swelling, my aching nipples distending. 'Ah, welcome to the orgy!' she grinned, turning as two more men and a naked teenage girl entered the room. Wide-eyed, I gazed at their bodies, their erect penises, the girl's shaved vulval flesh. My house had become a den of iniquity, nothing more than a brothel! 'Start by having her lick your cunt out,' the bitch said, taking the pretty girl's hand.

'Coming!' the man between my thighs gasped, his sperm shooting into my aching lust sheath as the girl climbed onto the table. Her gaping vaginal crack hovering over my face, I automatically opened my mouth as she peeled her youthful sex lips apart. Pressing her wet inner flesh to my mouth, she slowly gyrated her hips, massaging her sensitive folds against my protruding tongue as the man rammed his solid knob in and out of my sated vagina.

Drowning in a sea of perverted sex, I licked and mouthed the girl's open sex valley, swallowing her decanting juices, breathing in the aphrodisiacal scent of her femininity. My body jolting as the man shot the last of his sperm over my cervix, amazing vibrations tantalizing my anal canal, the lesbian gasping above my tethered body, I imagined that I could hear the devil coaxing me. *Give your body to me, to your Satanic Majesty!*

The smell of sex hanging heavy in the air, the room seemed to darken as the girl reached her climax, her naked body writhing as she ground her hot vulval flesh into my hungry mouth. I felt I was being swallowed up by sex itself, engulfed in the darkness of perversion, sinking into a pool of depravity. Deeper and deeper I was drawn into the very core of carnality.

My solid clitoris erupting in orgasm again, my rectal duct bloated by the huge vibrator as the man fucked my contracting cunt, I swallowed the girl's juices of lust. Swinging her hips, bringing out the last waves of her orgasm, her clitoris pulsating beneath my wet tongue, she cried out in her lesbian coming. On and on my orgasm rolled as I sucked out the girl's sex milk, rocking my naked body, gripping my very being.

As someone tightened the nipple clamps, my milk teats painfully squeezed, the spent cock slipped out of my fiery vaginal sheath. Fingers exploring inside my abused cunt, massaging the fleshy walls, I knew another penis would enter me, fuck me and sperm my cervix. The degeneracy was far from over!

As the trembling girl clambered off the table, I licked my cunny-wet lips, wondering what the others were going to do to me as my wrists were released and my feet untied. Two men hauling my quivering body upright as the girl pulled the vibrator out of my bottom-hole, sperm draining from my sex duct as I was dragged off the table, I was ordered to get on all fours on the floor. Obediently taking my position, one of the men crawled beneath me. I was to have my bottom and my cunt fucked simultaneously!

As his penis glided deep into my hot vagina, another man knelt behind me, his bulbous glans pressing against my sensitive brown ring. Two more men knelt before me, offering their swollen knobs to my mouth as the girl pulled my head up. Taking their purple globes into my mouth as the cock between my buttocks drove deep into my anal sheath, I shuddered in my perversity.

Four penises entering my orifices? Four knobs jetting jism into my body? This was perverted sex in the extreme! Again, the room seemed to darken as I sensed the devil close to me, coaxing me. My eyes closed, I thought I saw faces peering at me – angelic faces. *Angels?* I wondered. *The devil's angels?*

My breasts swollen, my nipples sore, I sucked on the swollen knobs as the penises within my tightening lust ducts began thrusting, fucking me. Never in a million years would I have dreamed that I'd be involved in such corrupt sex, or that such profane acts existed. Worse, I was deriving immense pleasure from the debased five-way coupling.

The coarse words of lust drifted through my tormented mind. *Her cunt's hot and wet! Her arse is tight! She's a good cock-sucker!* I jumped as the bitch slapped my naked buttocks with the palm of her hand. Spanking me to a crescendo as the cocks within my lust sheaths synchronized their pistoning, the other girl reached beneath my abused body and pressed the tip of the buzzing vibrator against my swollen clitoris.

The sensations transmitting deep into my trembling womb, I quickly reached my mind-blowing orgasm. Moaning through my nose as I fervently sucked on the beautiful cocks, the silken walls of my sex sheaths massaged by two more swollen knobs, I thought I'd die from the exquisite pleasure. The angel of carnality had touched me, I knew.

'All spunk at the same time!' the bitch giggled as the young girl ran the tip of the vibrator round my pulsating clitoris. My juices decanting as my orgasm peaked again, enveloping my trembling body, my mouth suddenly filled with sperm. Swallowing hard as I felt spunk jetting into my contracting cunt, gushing deep into my bowels, I had never experienced an orgasm of such force and duration. The gasping sounds of sex resounding around the room, squelching noises emanating from my bloated sex ducts as I was filled with jism, I felt as if I was drowning in a sea of sperm.

'God, her cunt's tight!'

'Her arse is beautiful!'

'Gobble, baby, gobble!'

'Swallow my spunk, bitch!'

The obscenities drifting through the sexual haze of my mind, I shuddered as my orgasm peaked yet again. The vibrator playing on my throbbing clitoris, sustaining my incredible pleasure, I drank from the engorged knobs like a babe at the breast, thirsty for their sex liquid. The flow of sperm finally stemming, the spent cocks leaving my mouth, I whimpered as the vibrator took me again to my sexual heaven. My inflamed sex sheaths receiving the last penile thrusts, my mouth swallowing the last dribbles of sperm, I finally collapsed on the man beneath me, my panting, glistening body sated.

'Pull your cocks out,' the bitch ordered. They complied, their huge shafts vacating my drenched ducts with loud sucking sounds, allowing my abused orifices to close. Grabbing my arms, two men loosed my bonds, hauled me to my feet and steadied my sagging body. *What now?* I wondered as sperm coursed down my inner thighs like rivers of milk. Lifting me, they laid me face down on the table, my pinched breasts pressed against the polished top as my wrists and ankles were once more tied with rope.

Someone rudely parted my buttocks, examining my private hole, massaging the oozing sperm into my brown tissue. Fingers played between my thighs, kneading my hairless cunt lips, delving into my sex crack. Looking through my eyelashes, I saw the bitch rummaging in her bag, her long blonde hair cascading over her face. *The whip?* I speculated apprehensively. Not one minute of respite from their debased games would they allow me, the perverse sex rolling on unabated.

As she passed a cucumber to the younger girl, I shuddered. Never had I seen such a large specimen, and I was sure my tight vagina couldn't accommodate it. The girl forcing the green shaft deep into my pussy, the sheath of my vagina stretching open to the extreme, I grimaced. I felt as if I was going to split open as she pushed it deeper into my tight cunt, my inner labia painfully distended around the giant phallus.

'Please!' I cried as she drove the cucumber fully home. 'I can't . . .'

'Of course you can!' she laughed, lifting my head by my hair. 'It's going deep into your arse in a minute.'

'No, please!'

'Don't you dare to complain!'

The cucumber slipping out of my bloated vagina, I jolted as the girl eased my buttocks wide apart and pressed the end against the tight portal to my inner core. Trembling as the phallus slowly entered me, my inflamed hole progressively opening with the widening shaft, I screamed as a leather strap landed squarely across my tensed buttocks. Again and again the strap lashed my naked globes as the young girl forced the massive fruit deeper into my bloating bowels. The merciless thrashing sending my naked body into convulsions, I knew I couldn't take much more as a man sat on the table and lifted my head.

Gazing at his erect penis, his purple knob, as the gruelling buttock-whipping continued, I knew what I had to do. Sucking his solid cock deep into my mouth, his dark curls tickling my nose, I ran my tongue over his wet shaft. My vagina decanting a blend of sperm and cunny balm, my buttocks stinging, I breathed heavily through my nose as someone pistoned my anal canal with the cucumber, the gnarled shaft massaging the velveteen walls of my rectal duct.

Clutching my hair, the man moved my head up and down, his knob repeatedly driving to the back of my throat and emerging between my taut lips. As he gasped, his swollen glans gliding over my wet tongue, I wondered how much more sperm was going to be pumped into my abused body, how many more buttock-lashings I could endure.

'Suck it, bitch!' the man cried, ramming his purple knob deep into my mouth as the strap lashed me harder. Sucking and licking his glans, my mouth suddenly filling with sperm as the cucumber was twisted and thrust in and out of my inflamed anal duct, I swallowed hard. The strap lashing my burning buttocks, my naked body jolting as the man crudely mouth-fucked me, I prayed for my ordeal to come to an end.

I could hear the phone ringing as spunk jetted from the orgasming knob, and I guessed it might be Danny. Loud cracks from the leather strap resounding around the room, I swallowed the last of the sperm. Where *was* Danny? I wondered in my sexual fog. What was he doing while my every orifice was being fucked and spunked by several men? Was he in league with the bitch? The devil? Did he know of the sexual abuse I was enduring?

'Right, let's turn her over,' the tart said as the spent cock left my mouth. The cucumber embedded deep within my bloated bowels, the ropes untied, I was rolled onto my back again like a rag doll. My buttocks over the edge of the table, my shaved cunt gaping, I gasped as the bitch tightened the steel rings gripping my swollen breasts and removed the nipple clamps. The young girl bending over my naked body and sucking my sore milk teat into her hot mouth, one of the men yanked my hairless vaginal lips apart.

'I haven't had her cunt yet,' he complained, pressing his bulbous glans between my inner petals. His solid shaft entering me, stretching my inflamed vaginal sheath open, he began his fucking motions. Again, I wondered when the debauchery would end, when they'd leave me to recover. Ramming the cucumber in and out of my rectal duct in time with his pistoning cock, he gasped expletives as my vagina tightened around his huge penis. Could I take any more?

I pondered, my pelvic cavity rhythmically inflating and deflating as the bitch climbed onto the table and placed her knees either side of my head.

'Lick my cunt out,' she ordered me, pressing her dripping vaginal folds hard against my mouth. My tongue entering her wet duct, tasting her flowing juices, I closed my eyes, wishing Danny hadn't gone away. He wasn't involved with the tart, I was sure. Even if he *had* wanted money, blackmailed me, there was no way he'd consent to several men fucking my orifices, two women bringing themselves off in my mouth. No man would put his wife through that!

Grimacing as the young girl tightened the steel rings again, my breasts painfully ballooning, I continued to suck the bitch's juices out of her hot cunt. I was sure that my ordeal would soon be over. Studs though they were, the men couldn't keep on forever fucking me, sperming my lust ducts.

'Bite me!' the bitch cried, her creamy juices decanting in torrents as her arousal soared. 'Bite my cunt lips!' Obediently complying, sinking my teeth into her fleshy cushions, I felt the man's sperm pumping into my quivering vagina. My body shaking violently as my clitoris exploded in orgasm again, sending exhilarating palpitations through my contracting womb, I knew the devil had snatched my soul.

The girl's juices of lust streaming down my face as I bit and nibbled her sex flesh, the gasping man's spunking cock thrusting in and out of my burning pussy, I rode the crest of my orgasm, climbing higher to my sexual ecstasy, sinking deeper into my debauchery. How many more times could I come? I pondered, gasping through a mouthful of drenched vaginal flesh. How many more orgasms would rock my naked body?

'My clitty!' the tart wailed as the phone continued ringing. 'Bite my clitty!' Nibbling her swollen sex button as she gasped and quivered above me, my pleasure was heightened as two hot mouths closed over my nipples and sucked my sore teats. Never had I known such carnal pleasure – every nerve ending tingling, every muscle tightening as the cock shafted my cunt and the cucumber pistoned my arse.

The girl finally clambering off the table, I lifted my head and watched the two men sucking on my nipples. The huge penis slipping out of my brimming vaginal duct, the men rose from their orgy as the bitch ordered them to dress. Resting my head on the table, my body sated but strangely serene, I closed my eyes, sure, as the breast rings were removed, that they were finally leaving.

'I'll be back tomorrow with a surprise for you,' the bitch grinned, donning her coat as the others dressed. Helping me off the table, she pinched my nipples. 'Don't do anything silly, like running away,' she warned menacingly. 'You're my sex slave, Selina – remember that.'

As they filed out of the room, I waited until the front door closed before staggering into the lounge. The small table was still by the sofa, the polished top glistening with sperm and cunny milk. A length of rope lay on the sofa, a stark reminder of my debauchery.

Looking down at my weal-lined breasts, my swollen nipples, I leaned over and gazed at my hairless vaginal lips, wondering what had become of my femininity. I was no longer a woman – stripped of my morals, crudely used and abused, I had no claim to femininity.

Answering the phone, I was pleased to hear Danny, but also suspicious. Where had he got eight hundred pounds from? Had he been with a blonde by the common? Did he know what I'd endured in the dining room?

'Hi!' I said as cheerily as possible.

'I've phoned several times, Selina – where have you been?'

'I went out. Where are you?'

'Knightsdale, in a call box. I'm looking for another hotel –

the one I stayed in last night was dreadful. Any word from the girl?'

'No, nothing.'

'Are you OK? You sound . . . I don't know, you sound different.'

'I'm fine, just a little tired.'

'I'd have thought the girl would have been in touch by now.'

'So would I.'

'Selina, are you sure you're all right?'

'Yes, of course I am. Don't worry, things are OK. By the way, the detective called me.'

'Oh?'

'He wants me to ring him the next time the girl is due to come here. I don't know what his plans are.'

'I hope he does something soon. Look, my money's running out. I'll call you tomorrow.'

'OK, and don't worry.'

Replacing the receiver, I thought about the detective. Should I call him the next time the bitch rang? No, she wouldn't ring, she had a key. She could arrive at any time and let herself in. At least I wasn't handcuffed, and I wondered whether to go away, stay with Chrissy for a while. Danny was safe, and if I went away . . . But they had photographs, videotapes – all the evidence they needed to ensure that I remained forever obedient.

My weals stinging, I took a shower, cleansing my naked body, my spermed holes. I'd go out for a walk, I decided, washing the spunk from my face, my hair. Go for a long walk and contemplate my life, where it was taking me. What was life? I asked myself, lathering my hair. I'd followed a path, a flower-lined path, seeking love and happiness. But I'd been led astray, coaxed off the path to follow another into the darkness of a forest where Lucifer waited. His horns were erect phalluses, his penis ever-solid above his heavy balls, his face grinning as he offered me his hand. Had I taken it? Had I reached out and taken his hand in mine? *I proffer immortality in return for your soul.* Where was my soul?

Leaving the shower, I dried my whipped body with a soft towel, but didn't dress. I felt I should always be naked, my body unveiled and ready for my abusers. In the kitchen, I made ham sandwiches, drank tea and pondered on the darker aspects of my world. Darkness engulfed me again, as if the sun had slipped behind a black cloud. Were there ghosts about me, watching me? Were there ghouls scrutinizing my nakedness?

I was too exhausted to go for a walk, I decided. Climbing the stairs, I went to bed, crawling beneath the quilt to conceal my nudity. Lucifer was waiting to meet me in my dreams, I knew. He and his disciples of sex were waiting to receive me. Would I ever wake?

With no dreams, no nightmares, the morning came quickly. The sun rising, pushing the night away, I rose from my bed and pondered on the new day. More cocks, more fucking, more sperm . . . No, I had to make changes. I couldn't allow the girl to rule my life, dictate to me – own my body!

Naked, I bounded downstairs and went out into the garden where the sun greeted me with its warmth. I felt different without Danny around – free, uninhibited in my nakedness. Wandering across the lawn, I sat on the bench beneath the beech tree, gazing at the fullness of my breasts, my erect nipples, wondering what life would be like without Danny.

We had no sex life any more, no physical contact. I had my vibrator – did I need Danny? Our relationship could hardly be called a marriage, I decided. What difference would it make if he stayed away permanently? My fingers toying between the soft swelling of my outer lips as I imagined living alone, I felt my clitoris inflate and pulsate. The urge to masturbate was overwhelming, my vibrator calling me. I needed to come, to appease my yearning clitoris with the buzzing phallus, to bring myself off. But no, I couldn't centre my life around sex.

Leaping to my feet, I returned to the kitchen and filled the kettle. There was a strange air about the house, like a presence, lurking but unseen. Had the debauchery seeped into the walls of the building? Perhaps the illicit acts had stirred something from the underworld, roused the interest of a supernatural sex fiend. My imagination was working overtime, I was sure, as I poured a cup of tea.

Taking my tea up to my den, I sat at the word processor and worked like a Trojan for several hours. No phone calls, no visitors – at last I had some peace! But my clitoris called, constantly begging me for my intimate attention. As I worked, I rubbed my sex spot now and then, appeasing it, taking myself to the verge of orgasm and then forbidding myself the pleasure. Delighting in my naked body, I allowed the warm sensations of sex to gently bathe me, long and languorously.

When the phone rang at four in the afternoon, I was sure it was the bitch. My cunt wetting, I wanted her to attend me, to lick and suck my clitoris to orgasm, drink my juices. *No!* my mind screamed. *No! Yes!*

'Mrs Goodman, it's Mr Wilkins,' the detective announced as I lifted the receiver. 'You've obviously not heard from the girl?'

'No, nothing,' I lied, massaging my pleasure button.

'That's strange. I hope you don't mind my saying so, but there's something very odd about this case.'

'How do you mean?'

'I don't know, I can't put my finger on it. I'm fully au fait with blackmail, taking money in return for keeping quiet, but this sex business worries me.'

'It worries me, too!'

'Yes, of course. Have you had any thoughts about it?'

'The girl's selling me to men for sex. Apart from her boss demanding money, she's . . .'

'Why didn't you tell me? I can't work in the dark, Mrs Goodman.'

'I did say that two men had abused me in the woods on the common.'

'Yes, but I didn't realize that the girl was taking money from them. I think it's high time we met and had a good chat. Are you busy right now?'

'Er . . . No, no.'

'I'm on my mobile, not far from your place. How does ten minutes suit you?'

'Yes, yes, that's fine.'

'Right, see you shortly.'

Rushing upstairs, I slipped my silk shift dress over my head and pulled it over my naked body. I'd have to tell him everything, I decided. There was no point in keeping secrets when he was trying to help me. I'd have to tell him that the bitch had brought several men and a young girl to the house, and give him details of the sexual abuse. They'd whipped me, fucked me, brought me massive orgasms . . . My clitoris needed me.

Should I tell him my thoughts about Danny? I pondered as I descended the stairs, my erect nipples caressed by the sensual silk of my dress. No, he'd think it odd that Danny had hired him if he was in league with the tart. Danny wouldn't have hired a detective if he was working for her – the notion was crazy! Unless, as Chrissy had said, a friend of Danny's was posing as the detective. Would the detective abuse me?

'We meet at last,' he smiled as I answered the door to him.

'Indeed we do, Mr Wilkins,' I replied.

'John, call me John.'

'Right, I'm Selina. I was beginning to think that you didn't exist.'

'What do you mean?'

'Nothing. Come through to the lounge.'

He was younger than I'd imagined, in his early thirties, and very good-looking. As he plonked himself in the armchair, I sat on the sofa, wondering why he was wearing jeans and a T-shirt rather than a suit. He wasn't a policeman, I reminded myself as he leaned forward and clasped his hands. Did he fancy me? Did he want to fuck me?

'OK,' he began, his dark eyes locked to mine. 'Is there anything else you haven't told me?'

'I've often wondered whether my husband's involved with the girl,' I blurted out.

'Your *husband*? Forgive me, but why would he hire me if he was involved?'

'I don't know. I suppose certain things fit, things that have happened that might implicate my husband.'

'I really don't think he'd get onto me if he was working with this girl.'

'You never know.'

'I suppose not. OK, tell me everything that's happened, every detail.'

Watching me intently as I began my story, he was obviously very interested in the details of the abuse that I'd been subjected to. I told him everything: the shaving, bondage, vaginal whipping, the men and the younger girl coming to the house – every detail from day one. Did my words of sex excite him? I wondered. Was he stiff? Shaking his head as I finished my story, he rubbed his chin.

'I'm not at all happy about this,' he frowned. 'If the girl's boss is into digging up dirt on celebrities and then black-mailing them, he wouldn't bother with prostitution.'

'Why not?' I asked. 'It's all money.'

'He's had fifteen grand from you, so why bother with the odd fifty or eighty pounds? Pimping would be too risky. Why risk advertising for clients when he's making real money by blackmailing you? And having the girl bring men here to . . . No, he wouldn't do that.'

'I reckon she's working alone, earning extra money on the side.'

'Possibly. There again, if this man's into having thugs dragging people off the streets and tying them up in basements, he's obviously not a very savoury character. If he found out what she was up to, God knows what he'd do to her. No, she'd be too frightened to work on the side.'

'John, if her boss isn't into prostitution and she's not working on the side, then what's happening?'

'I don't know, yet.'

'I did wonder whether she really has a boss.'

'That's just what I'm thinking. OK, if there is no boss, she's richer by fifteen grand. But we're back to square one – why bother with prostitution? Initially, she needed the photographs to get some real blackmail material, but to bring clients here? And as for taking clients to the woods on the common . . . It doesn't make sense, Selina.'

'Where do we go from here?' I sighed, my clitoris swelling as I stared at his bulging jeans.

'Let's assume that your husband *is* in alliance with the girl.'

'He wouldn't have called you in, would he?'

'He might, to make you believe that he's doing everything possible to help you. Right, let me give that some thought for a minute.'

'Would you like tea or coffee?'

'Coffee, please – no sugar.'

Leaving him contemplating the idea, I went to the kitchen and switched the kettle on. Danny *might* have called him in to cover himself, I mused, taking a cup from the cupboard. If he misled the detective, gave him false information . . . No, I couldn't see Danny going to all that trouble. He and the bitch had fifteen thousand pounds, so why bother with prostitution? Again, it didn't make sense. Taking my money was one thing, but the sexual abuse?

My cunt moistening, I lifted my dress and massaged my solid clitoris. Did I want the detective to come in my mouth? I didn't know what I wanted as I took the cup and ran the rim up and down my sex crack. His lips would press against it, my juices wetting his mouth. Would he taste me? Pouring the coffee, I wondered what I was doing, why I couldn't stop thinking about perverted sex.

'I don't think my husband's involved,' I said, taking a tray of coffee and biscuits into the lounge.

'If he is, it would explain how the girl knows about the insurance fiddle, and about the married man you went out with. It would also explain how she has a key to your house.'

'Yes, but . . .'

'It wouldn't be the first time I've ended up investigating the person who hired me.'

'But we're back to the same question – why bother with prostitution?'

'I don't know,' he frowned, sipping his coffee – tasting my sex juices.

'What about the man who hired the car?'

'He's married with kids. He picked the girl up in a pub and hired a car to spend a dirty weekend with her. He says that he knows nothing about her, other than that she's a prostitute.'

'You believe him?'

'Yes, I do. Selina, your husband has been urging you to write another book, he didn't want the police called in, there are several things that he didn't tell me, you say he has eight hundred pounds stashed away, he was seen kissing a blonde girl, he's now gone away and you don't know where he is . . .'

'It's not looking good, is it?'

'No, it's not. As far as the sexual abuse is concerned, I can only come up with one answer. They're both putting you through hell for the fun of it, for kicks.'

It was looking *far* from good! Everything pointed to Danny – but why put me through hell? Did he intend to leave me for the bitch? If so, why sell me for sex? My mind swirling as I stared at the handsome detective, I didn't know what to think. Where was Danny? Why hadn't he phoned again?

'Right,' John said, finishing his coffee and rising to his feet. 'As from now, I'm investigating your husband.'

'God, this is a mess,' I sighed, seeing him to the door. 'What am I supposed to do?'

'Don't say anything to your husband, and let me know the minute you find out where he's staying. And try not to worry, Selina – we'll get to the bottom of this.'

As he left, I returned to the lounge and flopped onto the sofa. Tears running down my cheeks, I couldn't believe that Danny might be involved. The breast-whipping, buttock-thrashing, cunt-lashing, shaving my pubic hairs, four men fucking and spunking me, two girls coming in my mouth . . . If Danny knew what I was going through, then he was the devil incarnate!

Chapter Ten

Danny still hadn't phoned by the following morning, and the girl hadn't been round with more clients. I seriously believed that they were together somewhere, scheming, drawing their plans against me. It fitted like a jigsaw puzzle. Danny couldn't write, he was jealous of my success, he was having an affair with the girl, they wanted money and had hatched the idea of blackmailing me . . . But I couldn't believe that the abuse they'd put me through was for kicks. That was the only piece of the puzzle that didn't fit.

It was all so sad, I thought tearfully – angrily. I'd thought I'd known Danny. But can you really know anyone – any human being? Their reactions in certain situations, what evil lurks within the canyons of their minds? I'd thought I'd known Barry! Did I really know myself? I pondered, recalling my terrific orgasms, the men's knobs spunking in my mouth. *What prowls in the recesses of our minds, waiting to surface? Evil?*

Answering the phone, I was annoyed to hear Danny's deep voice, but tried to suppress my anger and come across as normal. I didn't like him or want him any more. His cock had been up the girl's cunt, and probably up her arse. My anger rising, I knew I should remain calm, but failed miserably.

'How are you?' he asked.

'More to the point, *where* are *you*?' I demanded.

'Sorry I haven't phoned, I've been trying to find a half-decent hotel.' 'Have you found one?'

'No, I'm thinking of coming home.'

'Oh, are you?'

'What's wrong, Selina? Has the girl . . .'

'Danny, what's eight hundred pounds doing in your filing cabinet?'

'Eight hundred . . . Oh, that. It's for a rainy day.'

'Where did you get it from?'

'A couple of short stories. You remember, don't you?'

'No, I don't.'

'It was for the two stories I wrote for . . .'

'Are you coming home or not?'

'I don't know what to do. I don't fancy being dragged into that basement again, but . . . Have you given the girl any more money?'

'There *is* no more money.'

'You'll have to agree to the second book and take the advance, Selina.'

'Will I?'

'I don't see that there's a choice, do you?'

'Danny, will you get it into your head that the publishers don't *want* another book?'

'They will, once the first one picks up.'

'Look, let's not go through all that again. Where are you?'

'Knightsdale, in a call box. I'll give it one more try, see if I can book into a decent hotel.'

'The minute you do, ring me.'

'Yes, of course. The money's running out, I'll ring . . .'

Quietly fuming as I replaced the receiver, I paced the lounge floor. I felt frustrated, impotent to deal with the situation. I couldn't check up on Danny, the detective couldn't start investigating him until he knew where he was, I didn't know when the bitch would be round with her clients, I was in no mood for writing . . . For the moment, there was nothing I could do, no way to turn. I felt utterly helpless.

Finally calming down, I had some breakfast and went out

into the garden. Black clouds greeted me in place of the sun, reflecting my mood. Plonking myself on the bench, I pulled my dress up and gazed at the weals fanning out over the swell of my hairless cunny lips. Sighing, I yanked my dress back down, veiling the evidence of my debauchery, desperately trying to suppress the desire to use my vibrator.

My debauchery? I'd been forced to commit the obscene acts, and yet . . . Yes, it was *my* debauchery. Forced or not, I'd enjoyed playing the slave, revelled in the perverted sex. Whatever happened now, whatever life threw at me, I was a bisexual nymphomaniac – and I couldn't deny it. Neither could I deny my rising need for an orgasm, and I didn't see why I should refuse myself the pleasure of the vibrator. I'd fought with myself for too long, trying to convince myself that I didn't enjoy the darker pleasures, that the whipping hadn't aroused me. No longer would I deny the new me, my sexual desires.

Returning to the kitchen, I pulled my dress over my head and opened the fridge. The cool shaft of the cucumber beckoning me, my cunt tightening and juicing in anticipation, my clitoris swelling expectantly, I grabbed the fruit and went up to my bedroom. Naked on the bed, my thighs wide, I pushed the end of the cucumber between my gaping inner lips and gently drove it into my drenched vagina. Sighing as the huge shaft cooled my vaginal cavern, stretching the silken walls of my sex sheath, I tossed my head back and closed my eyes.

Never again would I go for one day without masturbating, I vowed as my cunt tightened around the beautiful green shaft. Never would I neglect my feminine needs, my craving for orgasms. Repeatedly sliding the wet shaft out of my pussy and pushing it back deep into my sex cavern, the gnarled surface teasing my taut inner lips, I vowed to pleasure myself every day. As I was about to reach for my vibrator and appease my throbbing clitoris, I heard a door close. I sat bolt upright.

'The bitch,' I breathed, hearing someone moving about in the hall. Slipping the fruit out of my yearning pussy, I leaped off the bed and crossed the landing. As I leaned over the banister and peered down the stairs, to my surprise I saw the pretty young girl standing in the hallway. The bitch must have been with her, I reflected as she looked up at me and smiled. She was probably in the lounge with her clients, and her bag.

'I hope you don't mind,' the girl began as she climbed the stairs. 'The back door was open so I . . .'

'Are you alone?' I asked as she stood before me on the landing, her blue eyes gazing longingly at my pert breasts, my elongated brown nipples.

'Yes, I'm alone.'

'What do you want?'

'I . . . I thought I'd come and see you.'

Leading her into the bedroom, I turned and faced her, wondering whether I could glean any information from her. Unbuttoning her blouse and tugging her miniskirt down her long legs, it was pretty obvious that she'd come to me for lesbian sex and I decided to use that as a weapon. My clitoris called again as I gazed at her long blonde hair framing her angelic face. She was feminine in the extreme, radiating an air of female sex that I'd never before known. But, sadly, sex wasn't foremost on my agenda.

'If you want me, then you'll answer some questions first,' I said huskily, sitting on the bed with my thighs wide apart, my open vaginal valley clearly displayed.

'Anything,' she smiled, tugging her red panties down, unveiling her hairless pussy lips, her tightly closed sex crack.

'Where does Alison live?'

'I don't know.'

'Where did you meet her?'

'In the pub. We got talking and she said that she had a friend who was into anything and everything.'

'Meaning me?'

'Yes. She said that you like to play the submissive role, pretend that you're being forced into having sex. That is right, isn't it?'

'Yes, yes, it is. Do you have her phone number?'

'No, but she has mine. If you're her friend, why don't you know her phone number and where she lives?'

'Don't worry about that. The men she brought here – where did she meet them?'

'In the pub.'

'Which pub?'

'Why all these questions?'

'Which pub?'

'The Thieves' Tavern.'

'Yes, I know it. What's your name?'

'Crystal.'

'Well, Crystal, seeing as you're here . . . I take it that Alison doesn't know you've come to see me?'

'She told us never to come here without her, but . . . I like you and I thought we could get to know each other. You won't tell her, will you?'

'No, of course I won't. You'd better take your bra off and join me on the bed,' I smiled, reclining with my legs wide apart.

As she unveiled her fresh young breasts and settled beside me, I knew that I was getting somewhere at last. The Thieves' Tavern was about three miles away. If that was where the bitch found her clients, she most likely lived nearby. Slowly but surely, I was homing in on her.

'What have you been doing with this?' Crystal asked curiously, clutching the wet cucumber.

'Guess,' I smiled.

'I think *this* is what you've been doing,' she grinned mischievously, leaning over my naked body and parting my swollen outer lips.

Closing my eyes as she eased the cucumber deep into my tight vagina, I gasped with pleasure. Now what was I doing? I wondered as she sucked my nipple into her hot mouth and ran her tongue around my sensitive areola. This wasn't blackmail, enforced lesbian sex – it was what I wanted. But where would it take me? Enjoying sex with a naked teenage girl, allowing her to piston my cunt with a cucumber and suck my nipples . . . Which alley was I stumbling down now?

'I'll show you something I've learned to do with a cucumber,' she proffered with girlish enthusiasm, her blue eyes sparkling as she sat with her buttocks between my splayed thighs. Lifting my head and resting on my elbows, I watched as she placed her feet either side of my body, her open vaginal entrance nearing the end of the green shaft protruding from my gaping sex valley. Holding the fruit, she aligned the rounded end with her open hole and pushed the phallus deep into her young pussy, gasping as her eyes rolled and she tossed her head back.

Gyrating her hips, the cucumber massaging our vaginal sheaths, she leaned back and rested on her hands, her swollen cunt lips stretched tautly around the massive phallus. Rocking her naked body back and forth, our wet pussy lips kissing, I gazed in awe at the wonderful sight.

'Nice?' she murmured, her lower stomach swelling and deflating as the fruit repeatedly bloated her vaginal duct.

'Very,' I breathed, unable to take my eyes off her swollen love lips, her exposed clitoris.

'Meet my thrusts, rock your hips so our pussy lips smack together.'

Following her instructions, our fleshy cunt lips slapping together, I felt my clitoris pulsate, longing for the girl's hot, wet mouth, her snaking tongue. As we fucked in our lesbian lust, I pictured our naked bodies entwined, our tongues lapping at each other's cunts, our mouths sucking each other's clitorises to orgasm. The notion sending my arousal soaring, I gazed in wonder at our sex juices glistening on the cucumber, lubricating our female fucking.

There was something about Crystal, something I didn't understand. It wasn't the sex, the immense pleasure we were sharing. Was it her femininity? I pondered. Her angelic face was rouged with sex, her small, rounded breasts firm in youth, her young nipples perfectly formed, her curvaceous body unblemished . . . But there was something deeper about her, almost spiritual. Her long blonde hair cascading over her shoulders like a golden curtain, she was a cherub. Did she have wings?

'I've been dreaming about you,' she breathed, rocking her hips, her vaginal juices squelching as we fucked. 'We made love in my dreams.'

'We're making love now,' I replied, my eyes transfixed on her hairless outer lips, swollen around the green phallus.

'In my dreams, we flew high in the sky and floated on the clouds. You loved me in my desiring.'

Smiling at me, she stilled her body and grabbed the cucumber, moving it back and forth, the fruit entering my tight cunt and then hers. Unlike the bitch, she was soft and gentle in her femininity, delicate and graceful. Lucifer hadn't touched her, I knew. An ethereal sparkle in her blue eyes told me that he hadn't taken her soul. Her rare beauty, her charisma, enchanted me. Had I found love?

'You're beautiful, Selina,' she murmured, her small hand easing the cucumber in and out of our vaginal sheaths. 'My searching for love has come to an end.' Her softly spoken words sent a quiver up my spine, and I gazed into her wide blue eyes. Love? I could no longer comprehend the word, it held no meaning for me. Where was she from, this angel? She was enigmatic, surreal in her beauty.

'And now we come,' she smiled, licking her succulent lips.

'I have a vibrator,' I whispered, reaching beneath the pillow.

'I'll show you what I've learned to do with a vibrator,' she murmured softly, moving away, the dripping cucumber slipping out of our love sheaths.

Taking the pink device, she lay her naked body on mine, the warmth of her firm breasts permeating my mammary globes, her naked mons lovingly rubbing my own. Switching the vibrator on, she lifted her body and slipped the phallus between my vaginal lips, the beautiful sensations rippling through my solid clitoris. Resting her weight on me, the vibrator nestling in our sex valleys, our pussy lips rubbing, she locked her pretty mouth to mine. Our love lips kissing, our mouths kissing, I felt a fiery passion engulf me, bathing my very being.

Her tongue tasting mine as our naked bodies trembled in our loving, she parted my legs with her feet, pressing the firmness of her mons hard against my own pubic swelling. Our arms entwined, her long hair forming a gold curtain around my face, we breathed heavily through our noses as our mutual pleasure soared. My cunt spasmed, my clitoris pulsating as the vibrator buzzed softly between the wetness of our fleshy labia. The fullness of her breasts heaved against mine, our nipples kissing, our orgasms nearing.

Her body quivering, she mouthed my neck, fervently sucking and love-biting me. Tossing my head back, my eyes closed as my clitoris pulsated in the beginnings of my orgasm, I gasped with pleasure. Nibbling my ear, licking me, she began her moaning, her orgasmic trembling. I could feel her juices of love trickling over my splayed inner petals, mingling with my own liquid desire, running in rivers between my buttocks.

'Now!' she gasped, her beautiful body becoming rigid. 'Now, come now!' Our wailing reverberating around the bedroom, together we reached our sexual heavens, the vibrator transmitting its pleasure deep into our quivering pelvises. 'Ah, ah!' she breathed, nuzzling her face into my neck, her hot breath against my skin. 'Ah, Selina! Selina, we're there!'

On and on our orgasms rolled, our naked bodies entwined in desire, quivering in our lovemaking. My vaginal milk flooding from my open sex hole, her love juices coursing over my vulval flesh, we locked our mouths together again, moaning through our noses as our pleasure heightened. Breathing in her female scent as my clitoris swelled and throbbed, I'd flown far away from the cold crudity of the bitch and her orgies, far away from the realms of lust to love's domain. *What of my future now?* I wondered as another series of shock waves rocked my glowing body. What would life bring me now that I'd experienced the ultimate in lesbian loving?

As our orgasms receded, we lay panting on the bed, our love juices flowing, mingling as we recovered. Smiling at me, Crystal switched the vibrator off and turned round, her open vaginal crack hovering above my flushed face as she mouthed and sucked the juices from my burning cunt. Her tongue entering me, I reciprocated, pushing my tongue deep into her drenched vagina.

'You taste of love, Selina,' she murmured, lapping between my swollen labia. 'The heady wine of sex flows from your pussy in rivers of love.'

'You're beautiful,' I breathed, sucking her cunny milk out. 'I've never known anyone like you.'

'Now I will unleash the ultimate pleasures your body holds. I shall reveal the secrets concealed within your clitoris.'

Sucking my swollen clitoris into her hot mouth, her tongue sweeping over its sensitive tip, she took me to the edge of orgasm. Swaying on the verge of my climax, I whimpered as she licked my inner lips, avoiding my throbbing sex spot, holding me on the brink of my coming. Again and again she sucked and licked my clitoris, pausing when the explosion of orgasm threatened. I could hardly endure the exquisite pleasure rippling through my quivering body as she repeatedly took me to the shore of ecstasy, holding me back as waves of pleasure lapped at me.

'Please!' I cried. 'Please, let me come!' Again, she took me to the outskirts of erotic utopia, but didn't allow me to enter. Her fingers massaging the silken walls of my sex sheath, her tongue repeatedly taking my clitoris to the border of paradise, I was drunk with sexual pleasure. Again, I begged her to allow me to come, but she held me back, expertly teasing my clitoris, fingering the pleasure from my sopping vagina.

'Now,' she finally conceded as I quivered and writhed on the bed. 'Now I will take you to your sexual heaven.' My clitoris sucked into her wet mouth, her fist bloating my vaginal cavern, she allowed me my release. Gasping, my back arched, my breasts heaving, I dug my fingernails into the quilt as my very being floated through clouds of elation. My face buried between her gaping vaginal lips, my tongue darting in and out of her flooding love duct, higher and higher I flew on the winds of paradise until I slipped into the enigmatic realms of semi-consciousness.

I returned to my quivering body to find Crystal gazing into my eyes, her pretty face smiling, wet with the juices of my orgasm. I couldn't speak. My senses numbed, all I could do was gaze at her as one would gaze in awe at an angel. She kissed me, her succulent lips glued to mine with our sticky vaginal juices. I felt her finger between my burning pussy lips, gently caressing my clitoris, sending little ripples of sex through my quivering womb.

'Are you all right?' she breathed, her finger dragging my sex milk up my valley and lubricating my sex spot. Still unable to speak in the aftermath of my coming, I smiled. 'I must go now,' she said softly, kissing my mouth, her long golden hair caressing my burning face. 'But I shall return.'

As she climbed off the bed, I gazed at the violin curves of her naked body, her swollen sex lips rising either side of her valley of desire. I wanted her to stay and love me again, but she dressed quickly and drifted out of the room like a dandelion seed on the breeze. Was she real? I wondered. Had I been dreaming? *We made love in my dreams.*

The phone ringing, I clambered off the bed and staggered downstairs, my head dazed, my juices of arousal streaming down my inner thighs. I didn't want to speak to Danny, I had nothing to say to him. If it was the bitch . . . She wouldn't phone, she'd come round.

'Hi,' Chrissy greeted me as I pressed the receiver to my ear. 'How are things?'

'Things are . . . OK,' I replied hesitantly, licking Crystal's pussy milk off my lips.

'Update me, then. What's been happening?'

'Nothing. Danny's staying at a hotel and I'm . . . I'm getting on with my work.'

'Oh, is that it?' she asked, a little disappointedly.

'The detective came to see me. He's really nice, younger than I'd expected.'

'You sound as if you fancy him!' she giggled.

'No, of course I don't.'

'So, what did he have to say?'

'He's as baffled as I am. We went through every connotation: the girl has no boss, Danny's involved, he's not involved . . . We went round in circles, getting nowhere.'

'You've not heard any more from the girl, then?'

'No, nothing. The phone has rung a few times but I've either been in the bath or the garden and missed the calls. Anyway, how are you?'

'I'm OK, still plodding on through life's drudgery.'

'Things aren't that bad, are they?'

'It's my job, I hate it. So, you're alone in the house.'

'Yes. Why don't you come round for coffee?'

'I will, on my way home from work. God, here comes the boss – I'll see you later.'

'OK, bye.'

My mind in turmoil, I gazed at my naked breasts, picturing Crystal sucking my erect nipples in turn, her full lips locked to my areola. I didn't know what to do, what to think. My stomach somersaulting, I wanted her to come back and share my bed with me. 'God!' I sighed, recalling the cucumber driving into our vaginas. 'What the hell shall I do?'

Love. The word haunted me like a ghost from the past, and I recalled when I'd first met Danny. We'd loved, made love, writhed in our passion. Now? Now there was nothing between us. Even if he was innocent, my love for him had melted in the seething cauldron of my debauchery, dissipated with my vanishing morals. I felt as if there was a void inside me as I wandered out into the garden and lay on the lawn beneath the overcast sky. There was emptiness, nothingness – apart from my memories of Crystal.

She'd taken me to the epicentre of sexual passion, and then left me adrift on a lake of carnal love. I couldn't stop thinking about her, her naked body, her pretty face. Was I in love? I pondered. In love with a young girl? I hardly knew her, I consoled myself – there was no way I could be in love with her. No, it had been sex and nothing more. But the way she'd held me so expertly on the verge of orgasm, the way she'd kissed me . . .

The clouds darkened, their shadows engulfing me like a huge black hand, I closed my eyes. The summer would soon be over, I reflected as drops of rain fell upon my naked body. Autumn would arrive, the leaves turning golden brown, and then winter . . . Cold and barren, as my heart.

The rain teeming down, stinging my flesh, I spread my legs wide and parted my pussy lips. Like a thousand fingertips, the droplets of water played on my inner flesh, my clitoris. The sky dark and heavy, I wondered whether Lucifer had returned. Had he seen me loving Crystal, worshipping a false idol? Had my act of love with the angel roused his wrath?

The rain falling harder, lightning streaking across the black sky, I parted my vaginal lips further. Was I offering my naked body to the devil – my open cunt to Lucifer? The rain streaming down my face, coursing over my firm breasts, I felt alive with sex, as if I was floating on a sea of lust. My clitoris swelling as the raindrops played on its sensitive tip, I began gasping, writhing on the wet grass.

My nipples erect, the rain stinging my delicate teats, I tossed my head back, wallowing in the pleasure the elements were bringing me. 'Make me come!' I cried, looking up at the heavy black clouds. 'Make me come!' Without my fingertips massaging my solid clitoris, I climaxed, shuddering as the lashing rain took me to my sexual heaven.

Parting my vaginal lips to the extremity, exposing the full bud of my pulsating clitoris as my orgasm rolled on, I imagined penises driving in and out of my orifices, sperming my naked body as I writhed on the wet grass in my wanton pleasure. Was it male or female I craved? I wondered as my cunt spasmed, yearning for attention. A penis or a vagina?

'Crystal,' I whispered, my sex button lashed by the rain, sending electrifying waves of desire through my sated body. Tears mingled with the rain streaming down my face as my orgasm finally began to wane. Was I crying for love or for sex? Whimpering, I released my pussy lips, my fleshy cushions closing, concealing my drenched hole, my receding clitoris. I was crying for love *and* for sex.

Returning to the kitchen, my naked body dripping, my arousal dangerously high, I wondered what to do. Take a shower? Try to work? Use my vibrator? No, I couldn't allow my yearning cunt to rule my life. Walking into the lounge,

I looked out of the window at the rain. What had I done? I reflected guiltily. Stretched out on the wet grass, the rain lashing my clitoris to orgasm . . .

Did Chrissy masturbate? I found myself pondering. Did she use cucumbers, bring herself off with a vibrator, shave her vaginal hair, lick other girls to orgasm? I had to stop feeling guilty. My sexual desires were excessive, I knew, but I shouldn't feel guilty for deriving pleasure from my naked body. Should I feel guilty for deriving pleasure from another girl's body?

Pacing the floor, my hair dripping, my craving for another orgasm was overwhelming. Finally bounding upstairs and drying myself, I slipped my dress over my head and thought about working. If I threw myself into the book I might be able to suppress my desires, forget about my swollen clitoris, I told myself.

I worked for several hours, bashing away at the keyboard without interruption from the phone or the doorbell – or my clitoris. The book was taking shape at last, the words flowing. Wondering why the bitch hadn't come round with her clients, I finally switched the computer off. Chrissy would arrive soon, I mused, looking at the clock. Did she masturbate?

Naked beneath my dress, the temptation to massage my sex spot was overwhelming. Covering my cunt with silk might suppress my craving to come, I mused, crossing the landing to the bedroom. I had to stop thinking about sex, wondering whether Chrissy masturbated, imagining knobs spunking in my mouth, cocks driving into my bottom-hole. Grabbing a pair of panties from the drawer, I slipped them on and went downstairs.

It had stopped raining by the time Chrissy arrived. Dressed in a white silk blouse and blue miniskirt, her long black hair shinning, her succulent lips smiled as I led her through to the kitchen. I saw her in a different light now. A lesbian light? I pondered, gazing at her shapely thighs, her nipples pressing against the tight material of her blouse as she sat at the table.

'Where's Danny staying?' she asked.

'Knightsdale,' I replied, not really wanting to talk about him. 'Would you like some wine?'

'Thanks. At least he'll be safe there. I'm surprised the girl hasn't bothered you again.'

'Yes, so am I.'

'It'll be interesting to see how she reacts when you tell her that Danny's left you.'

'Actually, I did tell her,' I confessed, pouring two glasses of wine.

'But you said . . .'

'She rang me. I told her that Danny had left me and she's not been in touch since.'

'If he's involved with her . . .'

'Let's not go through all that again, Chrissy. To be honest, I've had enough of the whole thing.'

'I'm not surprised. So, what's the detective going to do?'

'What *can* he do? There's nothing to go on, no leads – nothing.'

'He's off the case, then?'

'Not exactly. Chrissy, do you masturbate?'

'Do I . . . Selina!'

'Sorry, I just thought I'd ask.'

'Doesn't everyone masturbate?'

'I don't know, that's why I asked.'

'Do *you*?'

'Yes.'

'You do ask some weird questions, Selina. Actually, I do masturbate. Not having a partner, I don't have any choice.'

'How? How do you do it?'

'With my fingers, I suppose.'

'There's your wine.'

'Thanks. Didn't it rain earlier! Thank God I wasn't out in it.'

Joining her at the table, I imagined her masturbating, gasping and writhing in her bed as her fingertips massaged her swollen clitoris to orgasm. My thoughts turning to Crystal, I thought about telling Chrissy but decided against it. No one knew that she'd been to the house alone, and that was the way I wanted it. I didn't tell her about the Thieves' Tavern, or the men screwing me in the dining room. I wanted to keep the whole episode secret, not have to discuss the sordid details.

Gazing at her nipples pressing through her blouse as she sipped her wine, I felt an overwhelming urge to ask her to strip naked. I wanted to see her breasts, examine her nipples. Did I want to love her? I wondered, gulping my wine. If I got her drunk . . . No! What the hell was I thinking?

'I was in the garden in the rain,' I said, wishing I hadn't.

'What were you doing out there?'

'Nothing, just enjoying the rain.'

'You're mad!' she giggled.

'Maybe. Want some more wine?'

'Yes, I might as well. There's no one waiting for me at home and you're all alone, so why not?'

I poured her glass after glass of wine, my clitoris swelling as she became tipsy, giggling uncontrollably. I behaved as though I didn't know what I was doing, although I knew only too well. In my confusion, my sexual craving, I took two more bottles from the fridge and opened them, suggesting that we go upstairs and relax on the bed. Laughing and joking, Chrissy worse for wear than I, we staggered up the stairs.

Pretending to drink as much wine as she was as we sat on the bed, my hands trembling as I imagined slipping her panties down, I plied her with more and more alcohol. As we laughed and bounced around on the bed, I poured a glass of wine down the front of her blouse, apologizing profusely as she leaped to her feet.

'Selina!' she laughed. 'I'm soaked!'

'Sorry, I was laughing so much that I . . . You'd better take your blouse off.'

'God, my head's spinning,' she slurred, unbuttoning her blouse. 'I'd better not drink any more.'

'Go on, have another one,' I grinned, refilling her glass and placing it on the bedside cabinet. 'We might as well get drunk.'

Slipping her blouse over her shoulders, she gulped down her wine and flopped onto the bed. Lying on her back, her bra straining to contain her full breasts, I gazed at her nipples clearly defined by the white material. I knew that what I was doing was wrong as I moved to the end of the bed and gazed at her full red panties beneath her short skirt. Her legs parting as she laughed and joked, I focused on her black curls sprouting either side of her tight panties.

My cunt moistening, contracting, the craving to slip my fingers beneath her panties was overpowering. But this was Chrissy, my friend, not some lesbian nympho. I had to restrain myself, to suppress my sexual desires. Plying her with more wine, I imagined tying her to the bed and ripping her panties off, licking between the swell of her pussy lips, sucking her clitoris into my wet mouth.

'I'm going to watch TV,' I said, rising to my feet, desperately trying to turn my thoughts away from her curvaceous body.

'Stay here!' she laughed. 'Let's have another drink.'

'All right, one more. At this rate, you'll have to spend the night here.'

'So what? Let's get pissed out of our heads!'

My panties creaming as she drank several more glasses of wine, my hands trembling, I sat beside her as she finally rolled onto her back and fell into a deep sleep. Tentatively lifting her skirt up over her stomach, my heart racing, adrenalin coursing through my veins, I pulled her panties to one side and gazed at her fleshy outer labia.

'No,' I breathed, running my fingertip up and down her moist sex valley. 'This is wrong.' But I couldn't help myself. Her mouth hanging open, Chrissy fell deeper into her alcoholic coma, completely unaware of me, of my wickedness. Tugging her panties down her shapely thighs, I slipped them over her feet and parted her legs as wide as I could. Her sex crack gaping, her pink inner lips protruding from her valley of desire, I lay on the bed with my head between her thighs.

She stirred as I kissed the gentle rise of her mons, but didn't wake. I had plenty of time, I knew, breathing in the heady fragrance of her sex – plenty of time to abuse her. Parting her delectable lips with my quivering fingers, I examined her inner folds, the moist entrance to her vagina. I lay there for several minutes gazing at her feminine intimacy, wondering whether to lick her, to suck out her slippery juices.

Was Lucifer watching, goading me? I wondered as I pushed my tongue out and tentatively tasted her liquid desire. Something was coaxing me, driving me on to commit this illicit act. I felt powerless to resist the temptation to push my tongue deep into her wet cunt and lap up her sex juices. What if she woke? How would she react to find me tongue-fucking her cunt?

In a sexual haze, I parted her swollen lips further and licked her clitoris, savouring the aphrodisiacal taste of her secret place. Her pubic curls tickling my nose, I moved down her yawning valley and licked the pink flesh surrounding her vaginal portal. My cunt contracting, my juices flowing, I slipped my tongue deep into her wet hole.

I was sex-crazed, I knew, as I lapped up her copious juices. Transformed into a bisexual nymphomaniac, I was unable to control my desires. What had become of me? I wondered as I licked her reddening inner flesh. I'd enjoyed Chrissy's company as a friend, but now . . . She'd never know, I consoled myself. She'd be sweetly oblivious that I'd violated her secret duct with my wet tongue.

The phone ringing, I leaped off the bed as she stirred and mumbled incoherent words. 'Damn,' I whispered as she rolled onto her side, her cunt concealed, snug between her closed thighs. Running downstairs, I dashed into the lounge and grabbed the receiver, praying that it wasn't Danny.

'Selina, it's John,' the detective said.

'Oh, hi. Er . . . How are you?'

'Fine. I'm just calling to let you know that I happened to see the girl walking along the street.'

'Really?'

'I'm pretty sure it was her – long blonde hair, very attractive, short skirt . . . And she had a largish leather bag with her.'

'Yes, that sounds like the bitch. Did you follow her?'

'Yes, she went into a block of flats in Woodlands Road. The problem is that there are eighty or so flats in the block.'

'But it's a start.'

'Yes, it is. I couldn't sit outside the place and wait. She might have been hours and I didn't have the time.'

'What are you going to do?'

'Tomorrow I'll check the electoral register. I'm assuming she lives there and wasn't visiting someone.'

'If she lives alone, she should be on the register.'

'Exactly. Anyway, I'll be in touch.'

'Right.'

'Bye for now.'

That was a turn-up for the books, I mused, wondering whether to go to the flats and knock on every door. But it was getting dark and that particular action was probably best left to John. Besides, I had Chrissy upstairs, and I hadn't finished with her. Returning to the bedroom, I found her on her back, her legs spread and her vaginal valley gaping once more. Grinning as she breathed heavily in her sleep, I settled between her splayed thighs again.

As I was about to part her pussy lips and lick her inner flesh, she stirred, rolling onto her side as I leaped off the bed. 'God, my head!' she moaned, hauling herself upright. 'I drank far too much.'

'You'd better . . . you'd better get under the quilt,' I said shakily, slipping my dress over my head and tugging my wet panties down.

'Yes, I think I will,' she murmured, pulling her skirt down and tossing it on the floor.

Joining her as she crawled beneath the quilt, my naked body longing for her feminine caress, I lay on my back praying for her to fall asleep again. She'd not noticed that I'd taken her panties off, and I wondered whether I could remove her bra as she lay with her back to me. Carefully unhooking the garment, hoping she'd turn over and display her full breasts to my wide eyes, I waited for what seemed like hours. Finally, in a deep sleep, she rolled onto her back, her breasts tumbling out of her bra cups, her elongated nipples inviting my mouth.

Leaning over her, resting on my elbow, I took her milk teat into my mouth and gently sucked. My finger exploring her wet sex valley, slipping into the dank heat of her vaginal canal, I shuddered as my clitoris swelled and throbbed. Massaging the silken walls of her sex duct, inducing her juices to flow, I suckled her breast, finally falling into a deep sleep as the night came and darkness engulfed us.

Chapter Eleven

Chrissy had gone by the time I'd woken in the morning. My legs spread beneath the quilt, my fingers toying between my fleshy sex hillocks, I was still fighting my desires but didn't know why. I supposed I'd wanted someone to share my body with, rather than masturbate alone. Perhaps the bitch would arrive with several men and . . . No, I didn't want that any more.

As was becoming my wont, I didn't dress, wandering downstairs in my nakedness and filling the kettle for tea. The sun was bright, welcoming me as I stepped into the garden and looked up at the blue skies. *No more Lucifer, no more darkness*, I mused, dashing into the house as the phone rang.

'Hi.' It was Danny. 'I've booked into the Mayflower Hotel.'

'The Mayflower,' I echoed, making a mental note. 'What's it like?'

'Great, and not expensive. How are things with you?'

'Not bad. Chrissy stayed last night: we got drunk so she slept here.'

'At least you've had some company. I've been pretty lonely. By the way, I rang the private dick last night and he seemed to clam up when I asked him how things were going.'

'I wonder why? Did you tell him where you're staying?'

'Yes, I did. It's odd, he rang back ten minutes later to ask me how long I'd be away.'

'What's odd about that?'

'It was as if he was checking up on me. I'd already told him that I'd be here for a week or two.'

'He must have forgotten. Anyway, there's been no word from the bitch. Perhaps she's given up at long last.'

'I hope so! I was thinking last night that I'm stuck here in a bloody hotel room, you're alone in the house . . . It's a right mess!'

'It'll soon be over, Danny, I know it.'

'Let's hope you're right. Well, the money's going again. I won't put any more in as I'm about to go in for breakfast.'

'OK, ring again.'

'Yes, I will. Bye, love.'

So he *was* staying at a hotel. There was no need for me to ring him back as John had established that he was there. It suddenly occurred to me that the bitch might not have been in touch because she was staying with Danny. Had they been fucking in his hotel room? I wondered. Shaking my head, I didn't know what to think as I returned to the kitchen and poured a cup of tea. Whether they'd been fucking or not, I didn't really care as I took my tea up to my den. All I wanted was to be free of everyone and to get on with my life. Free of Crystal? I didn't know.

Sitting at my desk, I switched the computer on. Although my clitoris continually called for my intimate attention, I wrote for several hours and was more than pleased with myself. As the day wore on there was no word from the bitch, strengthening my belief that she was with Danny. After lunch, I had a shower, shaving the stubble from my vulval flesh, the urge to masturbate soaring as I dragged the razor over my sensitive skin. I wanted Crystal to shave me.

Drying my naked body, I slipped into my dress – no bra or panties. My nipples brushing against the exquisite silk, my cunt naked, I went for a walk, contemplating my book, which way the story would turn. I also thought about Crystal, wondering why she'd not been to see me.

Walking across the common, the sun warming me, the breeze wafting up my short dress, swirling around my hairless pussy, I knew I'd have to appease my clitoris at some stage. Wandering into the woods, I entered the clearing and looked about me, recalling the debauchery, the massive orgasms, the spunking knobs. The branch the bitch had lashed my breasts with lay on the grass, as if beckoning me. I felt cold surrounded by the trees, the sun blocked out by the canopy of leaves high above me. The woods were eerie, the clearing heavy with an uncanny air of vile sex. It was no place to be alone, I reflected, following the path back to the common.

Walking, thinking, my clitoris perpetually begging for my caressing fingertips, I followed the path round the lake and came across a secluded spot surrounded by bushes. Sitting in the sun, I contemplated the meaning of life. Childhood, growing up, marrying, old age – death. What was the plan? What was the point? Dreams, aspirations, failures . . . No, I'd found success. I'd been through hell recently, but I was successful.

'Oh, sorry.' I looked up from my meditation to see a young man emerging from the bushes. 'I usually come here to think, but . . .'

'No, it's OK,' I smiled. 'I was just going.'

'I've disturbed you, haven't I?'

'I was doing some thinking, but if this is your thinking place . . .'

'Don't go,' he said, sitting beside me. 'Let's think together.'

'We can't think together!' I laughed. 'I know, let's think aloud. What are your thoughts?'

'My thoughts? God, do you really want to know?'

'Yes, I do. I'm Selina.'

'Hi, I'm Barry.'

'I used to know someone called Barry. Anyway, that was years ago. Tell me your thoughts.'

'Well, my marriage is in ruins, I'm broke . . . You don't really want to know.'

Gazing into his deep-set eyes, I felt comfortable with him. In his early twenties, good-looking, I wondered how he could be in such a mess. His life had barely begun, and he was having marital and financial problems? What had he done to deserve it? What have any of us done to deserve the shit that life throws at us?

'I do want to know,' I smiled. 'Tell me all about it.'

'I married too young, for starters. Kay's a lovely girl, but . . . I don't know, we just don't hit it off any more. So, what are your thoughts?'

'I'm not broke, but my marriage is just about over. It's funny, you never know what's around the next corner. One minute I'm celebrating my first novel, and the next . . .'

'I thought I recognized you. I've seen you on TV, and in the papers.'

'Selina Goodman, prestigious authoress. Or I was.'

'What went wrong?'

'Everything! Still, let's not dwell on the past. Not that the past is over yet.'

'What do you mean?'

'I'm still having horrendous problems with . . . I'd rather not talk about it. Let's just sit quietly and contemplate.'

Reclining on the soft grass, I looked up at a small cotton-wool cloud drifting across the blue sky. That's what I was doing, drifting aimlessly, going nowhere. *Barry: what a coincidence!* I reflected, gazing at his dark swept-back hair. If only I hadn't ripped the insurance company off, if only I'd never got involved with the other Barry, the lying, two-timing bastard. If only, if only . . .

I could have the young man fuck me, I mused, imagining

his solid penis driving in and out of my aching vagina. His balls would be heavy with sperm, his shaft smooth in its youth, erect as he slipped his swollen knob deep into my lubricating cunt. I'd suck him after he'd fucked me, lick the sperm and cunny juice from his beautiful glans, nibble his hairy balls.

Male or female? I pondered in my rising confusion, recalling my time with Crystal, her hairless love lips, her wet tongue. I didn't know what I wanted. *Sperm or pussy juice?* A pulsating clitoris in my mouth or an orgasming knob? The rugged hardness of the male body, or the soft femininity of a young girl's naked form? One thing was certain as I gazed at Barry – I wanted sex!

But no, it would ruin our friendship. We'd become friends, I decided – there'd be no sex, no debauchery. But my mind was again battling with my physical needs, my swollen clitoris, my moistening vaginal sheath. I couldn't allow sex to rule my life, but my overwhelming desires were winning. Sex was like a drug, the withdrawal symptoms unbearable.

Nymphomaniac. The word swirled within my tortured mind, hurting me, taunting me. Cocks sperming my orifices, a girl's clitoris exploding in orgasm within my wet mouth, whips, ropes, handcuffs, cucumbers, the vibrator . . . I desperately needed to come! I looked at Barry again, my stomach somersaulting. He was a stranger, and I was imagining him fucking me! What had I become in my sexual cravings?

'Your thinking place!' I giggled, trying to force all thoughts of sex to the back of my mind. 'It's funny, isn't it?'

'Yes, I suppose it is,' he smiled, looking down at me. 'We all need somewhere to go in times of trouble. Some people try to drink their worries away, others sit in churches and pray, and I sit here.'

'What do you do for a living?'

'God, that's another problem! I used to work for a travel agent, but they made me redundant.'

'You *have* got problems!' I sighed. 'Still, try and look on the bright side.'

Did I dare invite him back to the house? I wondered, my vaginal juices seeping between my swelling labia. We could drink wine, forget our problems and . . . No, I didn't trust myself. I knew that, the minute I'd lured him into the house, I'd offer him my naked body, part my hairless pussy lips and present my vaginal mouth to his erect penis.

Should I appease my inner desires and fuck him on the common? I wondered. Amongst the bushes we were secluded, hidden from the prying eyes of the world. No one would know, and I'd be safe in my debauchery. I should have been at home, writing, cooking, pottering in the garden as I used to, I chastised myself. Housewife, homemaker, writer . . .

But the more I thought about his beautiful cock, his purple knob, the more I wanted to suck him to orgasm. Fight myself as I did in the battlefield of my mind, my clitoris pulsated as I pictured sperm jetting from his twitching penis, and I thought I was about to come.

'Barry,' I said softly. 'Barry, I . . .'

'You what?' he smiled, lying beside me.

'Nothing.'

'It's nice here, away from the crowds, the world. I could sit here beneath the sun forever.'

Resting on my elbow, I gazed at the crotch of his jeans where it bulged with his penis, his balls. Did he masturbate? I wondered. With his marital problems, did he wank and waste his spunk? My hand trembling, I almost reached out and squeezed him, stroked the swelling denim. Friends? I pondered as my mouth watered at the thought of drinking his gushing sperm. What was the matter with me? Why couldn't I control myself? He'd think me a tart if I unzipped his jeans and pulled his penis out!

As I unbuckled his belt, he closed his eyes as if he'd been expecting me to make a sexual advance. Perhaps he'd glimpsed my knickerless pussy. Had he sensed my desire? I wondered as I tugged his zip down. Raising his buttocks as I pulled his jeans and boxer shorts down, he remained silent. What was he thinking? I wondered, taking his stiffening penis in my hand. What were his male thoughts?

Pulling his foreskin back, I ran my fingertip over his purple plum, wondering whether to suck his glans into my thirsty mouth or sit astride him and impale my spasming cunt on his solid shaft. Gasping as I kneaded his heavy balls, his penis twitching, he was obviously enjoying my intimate attention and I wondered how long it had been since he'd last had sex.

Leaning over, I sucked on his ballooning knob, pulling his foreskin right back, exposing his silky-smooth globe to my sweeping tongue. Lowering my head, I took as much of his solid cock into my mouth as was possible, my lips stretched tautly around his veined shaft, his knob at the back of my throat. His balls rolled and heaved as I gently tickled his hairy bag with my fingernails. If he came in my mouth, would he be able to fuck me? Since he was just a youth, he'd probably be able to come at least twice, I decided, bobbing my head up and down, fucking him with my wet mouth. Even the balding old man had come twice.

Emitting long, low moans as I hugged his glans between my full lips, he arched his back as I ran my tongue round his salty globe. Desperate for his sperm, I licked and sucked his purple crown, kneaded his rolling balls, wanked his hard shaft until his body became rigid in the beginnings of his coming. His sperm suddenly jetting into my mouth, bathing my sweeping tongue, he thrust his hips, mouth-fucking me as his orgasm rolled on.

I didn't swallow, allowing his spunk to pour from my mouth and run down his cock, flowing over his heaving balls in rivers of milk. Gasping and moaning, his body shaking uncontrollably, he continued to pump out his white liquid as I expertly caressed his throbbing knob with my wet tongue. Repeatedly sucking his cock-plum and then opening my mouth, I made his sex milk gush down his shaft and over his hairy ball bag until the flow finally stemmed, leaving him gasping in the aftermath of his obvious release.

Slipping his cock out of my mouth, I licked his twitching shaft, lapping up the white liquid as he writhed on the grass. Did I want to whip his cock? In my crudity, I wanted to thrash his veined member, watch the weals fan out over his brown skin. But he wouldn't allow me such pleasure, I knew. If only I had a pair of handcuffs, I reflected, imagining him at my mercy, his naked body writhing beneath the whip.

As I lifted my dress and sat astride him, settling my gaping vaginal crack over his flaccid penis, I rocked my hips, the sperm squelching, mingling with my own juices of desire. I felt my clitoris throb in expectation against the silky-smooth wetness of his knob, my cunt tightening, my womb rhythmically contracting.

His shaft quickly hardening, I grabbed the base of his cock and sank his glans deep into my burning cunt, my pelvis bloating with his magnificent organ as my swollen outer lips hugged the base of his young penis. Bouncing up and down as his shaft fully stiffened, I whimpered in my debauchery, the sensations of crude sex sending quivers up my spine.

My clitoris massaged by his dripping cock, I came quickly, crying out as my orgasm gripped me, shook me to the core. My vulval flesh sticky with his spunk and my own juices of lust, I prayed for him to come again as his knob battered my cervix. My orgasm rolling on as I bounced my trembling body up and down faster, my breasts heaving, my nipples brushing against the sensual silkiness of my dress, I sustained my multiple orgasm.

At last, I felt his second flow of spunk jetting deep into my cunt, pouring from my inflamed duct, squishing between us as my fiery sex flesh repeatedly slapped his balls. Riding him to my sexual heaven, sustaining our illicit climaxes, I shuddered, tossing my head back as the last ripples of carnality surged through my pelvis and touched my womb. I'd done it, seduced a stranger on the common, sucked out his spunk, fucked him, appeased my thirst for crude sex. The nymphomaniac within me had found gratification – for the time being.

Finally rolling off his trembling body, I licked his balls, lapping up the copious blend of sperm and cunny juice. Sinking my teeth into his flaccid shaft, I was desperate for his cock to restiffen, to enter me and fuck me again. Sucking his wet knob into my hot mouth, tonguing his plum, I closed my eyes as my cunt tightened again. My insatiable thirst for crude sex would never wane, and I knew I'd meet him at our thinking place again – our secret fucking place.

Cleansing his balls, lapping up our orgasmic juices, I finally sat upright and looked into his dark eyes. What did he think of me now? I wondered as he tugged his shorts and jeans up. Selina Goodman, the best-selling author – the common whore, the tart. The possibility of friendship between us had been blown away, tossed on the winds of lust.

'OK?' I asked as he buckled his belt. Smiling, he said nothing. There were no words, only thoughts and emotions drifting between us. As I climbed to my feet and tugged my dress down, he glimpsed my hairless sex crack, his lips furling into a grin. Had he noticed the fading weals?

'We'll meet again,' I said at last.

'I hope so,' he replied pensively.

'Here, in our thinking place.'

'Our loving place.'

Walking through the bushes and out onto the common, I left him to his thoughts of sex and love. His sperm ran down my inner thighs as I made my way home, trickling, seeking, cooling my soft skin. Sex and love? They were miles apart, only bridged briefly during fleeting moments of passion. Had I found love with Crystal? She had no sperm.

Nearing my house, I became aware of the world, as if waking from a dream. People walked, cars passed, the distant laughter of children from a nearby school drifted through the still air, a dog barked in the distance. I was different, living my life like a dream, living my life through sex. Sex was my life.

Opening the front door, I decided to get back to work, carry on with the book while Danny wasn't around to disturb me. I'd ring Tammy at some stage to reassure her, tell her that I was doing well with my writing. I should have taken Crystal's phone number. I wanted to call her, invite her round for the evening.

'At last!' the bitch grinned as I walked into the lounge to answer the phone.

'Get out of my house!' I spat, my stomach churning as I glared at her. 'How dare you . . .'

'Calm down, Selina. Remember what I said about obedience?'

'Sod obedience! I don't care what you . . .'

'You will obey me at all times! I'll discipline you if it's the last thing I do!'

'No, it's over, finished. Do what you want with your videotapes and dirty photographs, I'm not going to . . .'

'My boss has discovered something very interesting, Selina. Does Knightsdale ring any bells? It should, seeing as your husband's staying at a hotel there.'

'Your boss didn't discover anything. You know about Knightsdale because *you*'ve been there – with my husband.'

'Of course I haven't!'

'There's no other way you could know where he is.'

'Enough talking, let's get down to business. I want another five thousand by tomorrow afternoon.'

'There is no more . . .'

'Selina, I don't want to hear that – and neither will my boss.'

'I haven't got a bottomless pit of money!'

'Just get it by tomorrow afternoon. Now, if you'd care to go through to the dining room, you'll see that we've made a few changes.'

We? I registered fearfully as I followed her into the hall. Entering the dining room, I froze with horror. The furniture had gone, chains hung from steel rings set in the ceiling while a horrendous wooden contraption resembling a chair with leather straps fixed to the arms adorned the centre of the room. As I turned to face the bitch, six naked men filed through the door, their huge penises stiff, their heavy balls swinging menacingly.

'You . . . you can't do this to my house!' I cried as the bitch grinned at me.

'I've done it, Selina. This is your sex den, the room where you'll entertain my clients every day. OK, take your dress off.'

'No, I . . .'

'Either you take it off, or we will!'

Tugging my dress over my head, I stood naked before my audience, wishing I'd gone away somewhere – run away. But I knew there was no escaping my fate as two men lifted my arms and cuffed my wrists to the chains dangling from the ceiling. My feet pulled wide apart, I hung my head as my abusers scrutinized my naked body, examined my gaping vaginal crack.

'Sperm,' the girl murmured, frowning as she stared at my

bubbling pussy slit, my sticky inner thighs. 'You've been a naughty girl, Selina. You've been fucking behind my back, and I don't like that.' Gazing at a thin bamboo cane propped in the corner of the room as she knelt before me and opened my vaginal entrance, I shuddered. There were huge wooden dildos on the floor, handcuffs and vibrators strewn over the carpet. My dining room had been transformed into a den of iniquity.

'We'll start with a good thrashing,' she decreed, turning to one of the men as she rose to her feet. 'Pass me the cane.' Watching as the young man grabbed the instrument of torture, I tensed my buttocks in readiness for the gruelling lashing. I had been a naughty girl and I wanted to be thrashed – and yet I didn't. 'Clamp her nipples,' the bitch growled as she took the cane.

Fixing metal clamps to my milk teats, the young man took two thin chains from a box and fixed heavy weights to the ends. Clipping the chains to the clamps, he grinned as my nipples distended, my breasts stretched into taut cones. He stood back and admired his handiwork as I grimaced with the pain.

'And her inner lips,' the bitch ordered him. 'I'll teach her to be obedient!' Taking two similar clamps with weights attached to the chains, he clipped them to my protruding inner petals. My sex flesh stretching as the weights swung between my thighs, I knew instinctively that I was to endure the most horrendous sexual abuse yet. My body trembling as the pain and pleasure mingled, I waited in silent anticipation for the thrashing of my life to commence.

How could I ever find the road back to normality? I wondered as the men gazed lustfully at my abused body and the bitch stood behind me. I'd been sucked into the mire of decadence, swallowed by a swamp of foul slime, never to resurface. As the cane struck my buttocks with a loud crack, the stinging pain permeating my tensed globes, I could have sworn I heard the devil calling me again. I'd entered my own hell.

'This is for fucking without my permission!' the bitch stormed, whacking my quivering buttocks as I hung helplessly from my chains of bondage. The weights swinging between my thighs, painfully distending my inner lips as the thrashing continued, I gazed at my violated breasts. My areolae stretched, the brown tissue indistinguishable from my nipples as the weights swayed with my rocking body, this was the ultimate degradation.

Finally halting the beating, the tart examined my distended breasts and ordered heavier weights to be attached to the chains. There was no stopping her, I knew, as a man rummaged through the equipment box and pulled out two large metal weights. Her mind a bottomless pit of corruption, there was no end to her perversity! The weights attached to the chains hanging from my sore nipples, I grimaced as my milk buds painfully stretched.

'And now her outer lips,' the she-devil ordered the man. Taking another set of clamps and weights from the box, he knelt before me, attaching the clips to my swollen outer labia. My vulval flesh painfully deforming as the heavy weights swung between my thighs, I remained silent in my abuse, wondering what macabre perversions she'd force upon me next.

Her evil eyes locked to mine as she lifted my head by my hair, she grinned. 'I have another device that I think you'll enjoy,' she said threateningly. 'You *are* going to get what I want by tomorrow afternoon, aren't you?' I said nothing as she scowled at me. 'Because, if you don't, there'll be terrible consequences for you to pay.'

Releasing my head, she bent down and took something from the box. Gazing at the long rubber hose connected to a large rubber bulb, I didn't know what the device was until she pressed the end of the hose over my exposed clitoris. Repeatedly squeezing and releasing the bulb, my clitoris distending and being sucked into the pipe, she giggled as I gasped.

'Please, no more,' I murmured, the vacuum building, sucking hard on my erectile protrusion. Ignoring me, she squeezed the bulb several more times before rising to her feet. The hose hanging between my legs, she moved behind me and ordered one of the men to spunk my bowels as she crudely yanked my buttocks apart and exposed my secret hole.

'Discipline, Selina,' she intoned as the man's knob pressed against my anal rose. 'You will do what I say, when I say – without question. Do you understand?'

'Yes,' I murmured as the huge penile shaft sank deep into my anal duct, bloating my pelvic cavity.

'You are my sex slave and I will not tolerate disobedience, I will not tolerate lies, I . . .'

'I haven't lied,' I whispered, my face grimacing as the man impaled me completely on his erect penis.

'You told me that your husband had left you. That's a lie.'

'No, he . . .'

'Admit that you lied to me!'

'Yes, I lied.'

'Who fucked you?'

'No one, I . . .'

'Who fucked you?'

'A man.'

'Obviously! Who was he?'

'I don't know, I met him on the common.'

'You owe me fifty pounds. You belong to me, Selina, remember that. You are only to be fucked in exchange for money, do you understand?'

'You can't . . .'

'Remove the nipple clamps!' she stormed, turning to the men.

My nipples were now twice their original length. As the clamps were removed, I bit my lip while she grabbed the cane. The man behind me grunting in his anal fucking, my chained body rocking, I yelped as the cane struck my left breast. Swishing through the air, the thin bamboo again whipped my areola, sending shock waves of pain and pleasure through my mammary globe. Again and again she whipped my breast, the thin weals fanning out like a pink fern over my milk-white skin.

'And now the other one,' she grinned, moving over and whipping my right breast. The cane catching my sore nipple, I winced and bit my lip again, determined not to cry out as the merciless caning continued. After a dozen or so lashes, she held the cane by her side and looked into my tearful eyes.

'The men are going to fuck your arse,' she declared, an evil glint in her eyes. 'One after the other, they'll fuck your arse.'

'Please, I . . .'

'You're not going to argue, are you?'

'No.'

'Good.'

My body swaying as the man repeatedly drove his huge organ in and out of my inflamed anal sheath, the weights swinging between my thighs, painfully stretching my labia, I closed my eyes and hung my head. I felt his sperm jetting deep into my bowels as he moaned in his coming. His lower belly slapping my burning buttocks, he rammed his knob into me, pumping his sex liquid deep into my stretched duct as I whimpered in my abuse.

Who was I? I wondered as the chains clanked above me. *What* was I? Six men queuing to fuck my arse, my vulval flesh stretched to the extreme, my breasts cruelly caned, my clitoris painfully sucked into the rubber hose . . . I didn't know what

I was, what I'd become. The sexual abuse had obliterated the real me, elicited something that lurked within – but it wasn't me. I was a nymphomaniac, a bisexual, sex-crazed whore – but it wasn't me.

As the spent penis left my anal duct with a loud sucking sound, another bulbous knob pressed against my sated hole and drove deep into my bowels. I was an object of carnal desire, my chained body nothing more than a commodity. Sold for obscene sex, I belonged to the bitch.

If only, I reflected, my clitoris swelling within the rubber hose, sending exquisite sensations of sex through my contracting womb. *If only, if only* . . . If only what? It was no good looking back, wondering how I could have avoided the abuse. Had Danny told the girl where to go the first time she'd called at the house, things might have been different.

Was Danny involved? I asked myself for the umpteenth time. Of course he was – there was no way the bitch could have known that he was in a hotel. They'd planned the whole thing, probably laughed at me as they lay in bed after their crude fucking. As the detective had said, it explained how the girl knew about the insurance scam, about the first Barry, where she'd got the key to my house . . .

'Coming!' the man behind me breathed, his penis swelling within my abused anal canal as his sperm pumped deep into my bowels. Grabbing my hips, he fucked me with a vengeance, his belly slapping my stinging buttocks as his shaft repeatedly impaled me. Could I endure six men fucking me every day? I was constantly desperate for sex, but six or more different men daily?

Hanging the heavy weights from my distended nipples as the man finished his crude fucking, the girl lifted my head and grinned. 'Five thousand, Selina,' she whispered. 'Don't let me down.' I knew I had to run away as she squeezed the rubber bulb, painfully sucking my distended clitoris into the hose.

What other horrendous devices had she in store for me? Gazing at the wooden chair-like contraption as the man's penis slipped out of my brimming anal duct, I knew that I'd be subjected to far worse than this. Where would it end? It would never end if I stayed.

'Next!' the bitch giggled. 'Only four more to go, Selina.' Another swollen glans pressing against my inflamed bottom-hole, I grimaced as the huge penis entered me, gliding into my well-spermed rectal duct until my stretched anal ring gripped the root of the invading cock. The weights swinging from my aching nipples as my naked body swayed with the anal fucking, I felt my clitoris pulsate within the rubber hose. Was I going to come? I wondered apprehensively as my juices of desire bathed my inner thighs.

As sperm shot into my anal tube, I decided to spin a web of lies, tell Danny that I'd followed the girl. I'd say that I'd gone to the Thieves' Tavern and followed her, discovered where she lived. He'd obviously know about the pub and believe me. He'd tell the bitch and she'd worry, wondering what I'd do.

Confusion was the name of the game, I decided. If I told Danny dozens of lies, I'd create a rift between him and the tart. If I was clever enough, their plans would begin to crumble, fall apart at the seams as they questioned each other, became suspicious of each other. As she knew that Danny hadn't left me, I'd tell her that I was leaving him. I'd also tell her that her clients had come to the house behind her back and fucked me. I'd create such confusion that she wouldn't know fact from fiction. I wouldn't tell her about Crystal.

'She's a good fuck!' the man pumping my arse gasped, unloading the last of his spunk into my saturated duct. 'Well worth the money.'

'Tell your friends,' the bitch smirked. 'She's available for anything and everything.'

His cock slipping out of my inflamed rectal tube, the girl grabbed the cane and stood behind me. 'I'll give you another thrashing to ensure your continued obedience,' she hissed, the thin bamboo lashing my tensed buttocks. Yelping, my chained body jolting with every gruelling whip of the cane, I knew I couldn't suffer the punishment for much longer.

'Obedience!' the crazed girl cried, the bamboo biting into my burning flesh. 'Discipline! Submissiveness!' On and on she thrashed my stinging buttocks as the men looked on. Hanging from the chains, tears flooding my cheeks, I squeezed my eyes shut, trying to block out her demonic shrieks of laughter and the cracking of the cane.

My cunt milk coursing down my inner thighs, my arousal suddenly soaring, I couldn't believe the immense pleasure I was deriving from the gruelling beating. The pain numbing my twitching buttocks, my womb rhythmically contracting, I screamed as my clitoris pulsated in orgasm within the rubber hose. On and on the lashing continued, sustaining my climax as I hung from the chains. My vulval lips painfully stretched, my nipples elongating as the weights oscillated, my juices of lust flooding from my gaping hole, my very being was tossed on the winds of lust.

Finally halting the punishment as my climax waned, she ordered the next man to fuck my arse. The fourth penis crudely entering me, sinking deep into my burning anal sheath, I only had to endure two more men and then . . . And then what? Another breast-thrashing? More abuse?

Grabbing a huge vibrator, the bitch switched it on and rammed it deep into my drenched cunt as the penis embedded within my bloated bowels began its thrusting, its anal violation. The sensations permeating my pelvis as the double pistoning rocked my chained body, I heard the phone ringing through the haze of my racked mind. Danny? I pondered. Or the detective? It was someone from the outside world, a world far removed from what had been my dining room and was now my sex den. How was I supposed to let John know when the bitch was coming round when she had a key to the house? If I had the lock changed . . . But that would incite another buttock-thrashing, another breast-caning.

'God, I'm there already!' the man breathed, his spunk issuing, bubbling within my anal cylinder as the girl pistoned my tightening vagina with the vibrator. My mouth and cunt spermed by Barry on the common, my bottom-hole fucked and spunked by the fourth man in succession, my body was a sperm-bath, awash with male come. Were all men like this? I pondered. Queuing up to fuck a prostitute, were they all sex-crazed?

My arms high above my head, aching as I hung from my chains, spunk jetted from my anal hole, spraying my inner thighs as the crude fucking persisted. Again and again the veined penile shaft thrust in and out of my inflamed duct, my delicate brown ring pulled from my bottom crease to be dragged inside my anal lust-sheath. The spent cock finally leaving my ravaged tube, I cringed as the bitch ordered the fifth man to fuck my bottom.

Only one more to go, I reflected thankfully as yet another huge member forcefully impaled me, the massive knob driving deep into the very core of my quivering body as the girl pummelled my cervix with the vibrator. Would my love holes ever recover? I wondered. Would my nipples ever return to their normal form?

The squishing sounds of sex echoing around the room as the massive organ repeatedly withdrew and drove deep into my bubbling anal shaft, I could only hang from my bondage chains and pray that my abuser would come quickly. His heavy balls slapping between the tops of my parted thighs, he began moaning in his illicit pleasure as he grabbed my hips and swung my body to meet his anal thrusts.

'I can't hold back!' he breathed as his spunk flowed, filling my bowels as he repeatedly withdrew his solid shaft and propelled his orgasming knob into my inflamed sheath. More spunk spraying my inner thighs as the squelching sounds of sperm grew louder, I reached another orbital orgasm. My clitoris pulsating within the rubber hose as the vibrations transmitted through the walls of my cunt, playing around my sex nodule, I breathed heavily in my coming.

'Spunk's pouring out of you!' the bitch giggled wickedly as I felt rivers of male milk meander down my sticky inner thighs. Riding the crest of my orgasm, I clung to the chains, my entire body shaking violently as my clitoris throbbed, sending ecstatic shock waves of sex though my naked flesh. My womb rhythmically contracting, my pelvis inflating and deflating with the indecent double pistoning, I breathed a sigh of relief as the man stilled his huge cock and my orgasm began to subside.

His penis withdrawing, the last one suddenly entered me, barely allowing my stretched hole to close before the huge shaft drove in to the hilt. The sixth anal fucking, and my body swayed as another mind-blowing orgasm erupted within my swollen clitoris. This was the last violation of my rectal duct, I consoled myself. All I wanted was to rest, to allow my exhausted body to recover. I couldn't endure another orgasm, I reflected, as my pleasure spot pulsated within the rubber hose and the vibrator continued pistoning my burning cunt. One last sperming, and I'd be allowed my freedom.

'I'm going to fill your arse!' the man gasped in his crudity as his cock swelled and his spunk jetted. Praying that the bitch wouldn't thrash me again, I gazed at my weal-lined breasts, my distended nipples pathetically distorted by the swinging weights. My buttocks stinging as the man's lower belly slapped my burning flesh, I thanked God as he slowed his rhythm and my orgasm receded.

In my exhaustion, I knew I couldn't come again. Another torrent of sperm jetting from my sore hole and coursing down my thighs as he withdrew his spent cock, I knew I'd done it – I'd been fucked and spunked by six men. But I couldn't take any more. My lust holes inflamed, burning, I couldn't endure one more cock, one more orgasm.

My eyes closing as my male abusers left the room, I listened to the sounds of laughter and joking. Had they no compassion? I wondered. Had they wives or girlfriends waiting at home? They'd all fucked me, used and abused me in their quest for sexual gratification – and all I wanted was my freedom, to go to bed and sleep. Once they'd left the house . . .

'I like my girls to have long nipples,' the bitch gloated, sliding the vibrator out of my aching cunt and rising to her feet. 'I'll leave you like this for an hour or two before releasing you.'

'No,' I pleaded. 'Please, I . . .'

'I'll leave the weights in place. Your cunt lips need enlarging, as well as your nipples.'

As she left the room, I looked up at the ceiling. The chains securely fixed to the steel rings, my wrists cuffed, there was no way I could escape. As the front door slammed shut, the phone rang again. Danny? John? Chrissy? 'If only someone would save me!' I breathed fearfully as sperm flowed from my abused anal canal. Was Lucifer laughing at me?

Chapter Twelve

After what seemed like hours of aching for my freedom, I heard someone moving about. Could Danny be home? Did I dare call out? If the bitch had returned with more men . . . . Someone was in the hall, creeping, lurking. My eyes wide as the door slowly opened, my heart racing, I waited in fear and trepidation.

'Selina,' Crystal whispered, her blue eyes sparkling as she gazed at my abused body.

'Let me go,' I whimpered. 'Please, take the clamps off and release me.'

'I didn't think Alison would go this far,' she said surprisedly, carefully removing the heavy weights and clamps from my distended nipples. 'There's something wrong with her.'

'You can say that again,' I replied tearfully as she unclipped my inflamed vaginal lips and released the handcuffs. 'How did you get in?'

'The back door – it wasn't locked.'

Lowering my aching arms, I staggered across the room and leaned against the wall. Sperm oozing from my bottom-hole, running down my legs, I massaged my crimson breasts as Crystal gazed longingly at my naked body. Thanking God that she'd come round, I wondered when the bitch would return to abuse me again. We had to leave the house. If Crystal was caught with me, she'd be put through hell, I knew. But where to go? Where to run?

'We must get out of here,' I murmured. 'She's coming back.'

'If she finds me here . . .'

'Yes, yes, I know. What about your place?'

'She knows where I live – she might put two and two together.'

'God, what a mess! I need a shower and something to eat, but she might arrive at any minute. I know, I'll ring the detective.'

'The detective?' she frowned.

'I'll explain later.'

Staggering up to Danny's room, I grabbed the piece of paper bearing the number of John's mobile and lifted the receiver. Punching the buttons, I prayed for him to answer. I didn't know what I was going to say but if he came to the house, he might be able . . .

'John, it's Selina,' I said as he answered.

'I've been ringing you. Where have you been?'

'Tied up and abused by the bitch and six men. John, she's coming back and I don't know what to do.'

'OK, I'll be there as soon as I can. I have some news, I'll tell you when I see you.'

'Please, be quick.'

'I will, just stay put.'

Turning to see Crystal standing in the doorway, I thought it best that she went home. I didn't want to have to explain to John that she was . . . What was she? I pondered as she gazed at me with her big blue eyes. A friend? A girlfriend? An angel? Her pink tongue peeping between her succulent lips, she smiled. Did she want to lick my clitoris? She was my partner in lesbian lust.

'Crystal, you'd better go,' I said wistfully, grabbing a pen. 'Give me your phone number and I'll call you.'

'I'd like to stay,' she whispered huskily, tossing her angelic tresses over her shoulders. 'I'll stay upstairs and wait until the detective has gone.'

'All right, wait in my bedroom.'

Jotting her number down, I followed her into the bedroom and grabbed a dress from the wardrobe. 'Don't make a sound,' I warned, pulling the dress over my head and veiling my abused body. 'I'll be up later, when he's gone.'

Leaving her to settle on the bed, I bounded downstairs and closed the dining-room door – the sex-room door. I'd have to clear the room of the bitch's equipment, I reflected, walking into the lounge. I'd drag the chair-like contraption out into the garden and burn it, and remove the chains from the ceiling. I'd keep the vibrators, for Crystal.

Gazing out of the window, I wondered where the bitch had put my dining-room table and chairs. Sold them, more than likely – the thieving cow. Her audacity riled me. Walking into my house, destroying my dining room and stealing my furniture was beyond belief! But I couldn't stop her. With all the evidence of my debauchery, the photographs and videotapes, I was at her mercy. Would I ever be free?

A black car pulling up in the drive, I breathed a sigh of relief as John climbed out and walked towards the house. Hopefully, the bitch would see the car, realize that I had a visitor, and back off. But for how long? John couldn't stay all night. Dashing through the hall as the bell rang out, I opened the door, wondering whether John would like to see me naked. I wanted to show him my shaved cunt.

'Come in!' I beamed, waves of relief rolling through my aching body. 'Come through to the lounge.'

'Are you OK?' he asked concernedly, closing the door.

'I am now that you're here.'

As he sat in the armchair and brushed his black hair away from his forehead, I stood with my back to the mantelpiece, eyeing his bulging jeans as he reclined. Why I was thinking about sex at a time like that, I had no idea. My clitoris swelling, I tried not to imagine sucking him to orgasm, but failed miserably. I wanted his knob spunking in my gobbling mouth.

'Selina, I have some news,' he began, focusing on my shapely thighs.

'You saw the girl at the hotel where Danny's staying?' I asked expectantly. I wanted to pull my skirt up a little, expose my pussy crack.

'No, I'm afraid not. I gave the hotel porter some cash and he's going to ring me if your husband has any visitors.'

'The girl said that her boss knows where Danny is – she knows about the hotel.'

'There's only one way she could know where your husband is. By the way, I checked the electoral register and there's no one listed in the Woodlands Road flats with the Christian name of Alison.'

'So what's the news?'

'I drove past the flats on the off chance of seeing the girl, and happened to notice your red BMW parked round the corner.'

'But Danny's in Knightsdale – *he* has the car.'

'Yes, I know. It doesn't prove anything, of course, but it's rather odd that he should be parked there.'

'I'll ask him about it.'

'No, don't say anything – I don't want him to know that we're on to him.'

'Obviously, he was visiting the girl.'

'Or a mutual friend. I don't suppose you know of anyone living in that area?'

'No, I don't. Perhaps her boss lives there.'

'I've asked a few villains I'm acquainted with, and no one knows anything about a man digging up dirt on celebrities. If there *is* a boss, and he's employing local thugs, someone would know something about it.'

'All this points to Danny being in league with the bitch.'

'Yes, but it's only circumstantial. I want you to lie to your husband, Selina.'

'I've already decided to do that.'

'Have you?'

'I thought I'd say that I've discovered where the girl lives and . . .'

'No, don't say that. Tell him that the police are involved. Say that the police turned up, asking you about prostitution. It's quite feasible that one of the girl's clients thought something odd was going on, that you might have been forced into having sex, and told the cops.'

'So Danny will tell the girl and . . .'

'And she'll not come anywhere near your place. Look, I don't have a great deal of time. Is there anyone you can stay with for a couple of days?'

'Well, there's my friend Chrissy, but . . .'

'Give her a call.'

'Yes, I'll do that. Can't you stay a little longer?'

'Unfortunately, I have an appointment. I'll call in on my way back.'

'If I'm chained up . . .'

'Why not go out for a walk, or go to a pub?'

'No, I'll be all right.'

'OK, I'll be in touch.'

Seeing him out, I debated whether or not to tell Danny that the police had been to see me. If the girl thought that they were watching the house, she'd keep well away. Returning to the lounge as John drove off, I rang the hotel, praying that Danny was there.

'Hallo,' he finally replied.

'Danny, it's me.'

'Hi, how are things?'

'The police have been here asking me about prostitution.'

'*What?*'

'The girl brought several men here to . . . Anyway, I reckon one of them realized that I was being forced into having sex, and told the police.'

'What are they going to do?'

'I said that there must have been some mistake. Either that, or someone was having a laugh. I don't think they believed me – they're going to keep an eye on the house.'

'Christ, if the girl . . .'

'She said she'll be back later. If she comes here again with several men, the police will nab her.'

'And you'll be ruined.'

'If her boss thinks that I called the police, God knows what will happen.'

'OK, let me think about it. Several men? Christ, Selina! Look, it might be best if I come home.'

'But the thugs . . .'

'I'll work something out and call you back later.'

Replacing the receiver, I thought the plan was an excellent idea. Danny would tell the bitch about the police and . . . But it wouldn't prove conclusively that he was involved if she kept away from the house. If she really thought the policc were involved, she might send the tapes and photographs to the papers or to my publisher. All I could do was wait for the outcome.

'I saw him leave,' Crystal said as she drifted into the room like an angel.

'Oh, I was just about to come upstairs,' I smiled, eyeing her neat cleavage through her partially open blouse. 'Crystal, it's nice to see you, but . . . Well, I think it best that you go home.'

'Can't I stay the night?' she asked, provocatively licking her succulent lips. 'I thought we might go to bed and make love.'

Gazing at her shapely thighs revealed by her red micro-skirt, a bolt of arousal shot through my aching body as I pictured her young pussy, her hairless lips, her tightly closed love crack. But I'd had more than enough sex for one day: there was no way I could endure another orgasm. Recalling her licking my sex slit, sucking my clitoris as I'd sucked hers, my cunt tightened and my juices flowed. I had no control over my sexual desires, I reflected as my womb quivered expectantly.

'I really think you should go,' I said, offering her a smile. 'The detective will be back later and . . . and my brother's coming to see me.'

'Oh,' she sighed, hanging her head, her curtain of golden hair cascading over the swell of her breasts billowing her white blouse. I wanted to suck her pert nipples.

'Call round tomorrow, Crystal.'

'All right, in the morning.'

'Yes, tomorrow morning.'

Sadness engulfed me as she wandered out of the room. She was so feminine, radiating an air of innocence, and yet sexual in the extreme. Again, I recalled her wet vaginal opening hovering above my face as she'd tongued my sex duct. Because of her youth, her sweet honeydew flowed in torrents, and I wanted to drink from her fresh vagina. As the front door closed I was about to chase after her, but decided to go up to bed. I was too tired for sex, physically and mentally exhausted.

After a good night's sleep, I slipped out of bed and took a shower. Washing the dried sperm and vaginal juice from my inner thighs, I stood with my feet wide apart, bending my knees and parting my pussy lips. Pressing the shower nozzle hard against my open sex hole, the hot water gushing deep into my vaginal cavern, I gasped as my lust sheath inflated and overflowed. Water streaming down my legs, my clitoris solid, I desperately needed to come as the sensations sent electrifying quivers through my contracting womb.

Dazed with sex, I bent over and pressed the nozzle between my buttocks, the hot water gushing into my bowels, the incredible sensations rippling through my pelvis. My naked body shuddering as the water coursed down my inner thighs, I needed Crystal to attend my pulsating clitoris, and wished I'd allowed her to stay. Massaging my erect clitoris as I imagined her tongue there, I heard the phone ringing. 'Damn!' I breathed, leaping out of the shower and dashing into my den. I had to answer it in case it was John with some more news. My orgasm would have to wait.

'Hallo,' I panted, water running over the floor as my lust holes drained.

'Hi,' Danny drawled, disappointing me. 'Have the police been back?'

'They're watching the house.'

'The girl's not bothered you, then?'

'There's been no sign of her, which I find odd.'

'Why?'

'She doesn't know about the police, so why not come back as she said she would?'

'Perhaps she had other plans. Has she demanded any more money?'

'Yes, five thousand.'

'You'll have to pay her, love.'

'I can't, I haven't got it. Anyway, what have you been up to?'

'Up to?'

'What have you been doing?'

'Oh, I see. Lounging around, making notes for my book and watching TV.'

'Haven't you been out at all?'

'I went for a drive. Selina, I might as well come home.'

'No, not yet. Let's wait and see what the girl does. In a way, I'm rather looking forward to her coming here. I know she'll ruin me, but it'll be nice to see her arrested.'

'Arrested for what? She hasn't done anything, has she? I mean, you can hardly tell the police what's been going on.'

'No, but . . . Oh, I don't know. Perhaps it'll put the wind up her and she'll give up.'

'Yes, after she's been to the newspapers. So, what are your plans for today?'

'I'm . . . I'm going to London to have lunch with Tammy.'

'That'll be nice.'

'Yes, I'm looking forward to it. Danny, I'd better go – I want to catch the next train.'

'OK, I'll ring this evening.'

'Yes, ring this evening. Bye.'

If Danny thought I was in London, he might come home to take a look at the dining room. The girl would obviously have told him about the sex equipment, and I was sure he'd return. He'd also look out for the police, just to confirm my story. If I hid in the house . . . No, I'd been through all that before.

My clitoris calling me, I went to the kitchen and made some tea, pondering on my vibrator. The orgasms I'd experienced the day before had increased my desire to masturbate, but I had to have *some* control over my insatiable thirst for sex. Walking into the garden, the sun bathing my naked body, drying me, I sat on the lawn and sipped my tea. I should have been working on the book, I thought guiltily as I examined my nipples. They were still elongated and very sensitive, sore from the clamps and weights. Cupping my breasts in my hands, I lowered my head and licked each milk teat in turn, the sensations sending a delicious quiver through my womb.

Again, my clitoris called for my intimate attention, and I

brought my knees up to my chest and parted my feet, my vaginal crack opening. Gazing at my fleshy inner petals, I pulled my love lips apart and examined my erect clitoris. She needed me, my caressing fingers, my massaging fingers. If only I could lick between my swollen lips, I reflected, pulling my pussy lips further apart and examining the wet entrance to my love sheath. If only I could suck my own clitoris to orgasm.

Finishing my tea, I returned to the kitchen. I had things to do: my clitoris would have to wait. Entering the dining room, I looked at the sex equipment, examined the wooden contraption. As far as I could make out, the victim sat on the wooden base, her thighs held wide apart by the leather straps, her cunt open, defenceless. Moving a lever, I watched as the back of the chair lowered, positioning the victim on her back. As I was about to move another lever, I heard a key in the lock of the front door.

'The bitch!' I whispered, slipping through the French doors into the garden. Leaping behind the conifers by the fence, my heart racing, I waited and watched. She walked into the dining room and looked about, obviously wondering where I was. Would she wait? I wondered anxiously as she left the room. I might have to hide in the garden for hours!

She returned after a few minutes, obviously having searched the house. If Danny had been in touch with her he'd have told her that I'd gone to London. So what was she doing there? He couldn't have spoken to her, I decided. He'd have told her about the police and she'd have kept well away. As she walked into the hall, I emerged from my hide and slipped into the dining room, praying that she was going to leave.

Hearing her in the lounge as I stood by the dining room door, I wondered who she was talking to. The men? I pondered. No, she was using my phone. 'She's not here,' I heard her say. 'OK, I'll come back later this afternoon. Yes, I'll bring the cash round. Right, see you later.'

As she left the house, slamming the front door shut behind her, I rushed into the lounge and grabbed the phone. Pressing the redial button, I gazed in disbelief at the zero showing on the display. The bitch must have deliberately erased the number she'd dialled. Though she was many evil things, she obviously wasn't stupid, I thought in my disappointment.

I decided that she must have been talking to her boss. Bring the cash round? There again, she might have phoned Danny, told him that she'd take the cash to him. But no, she couldn't have been speaking to him – he thought I was in London. Perhaps she'd tried to catch me before I left for London, to remind me to get the money?

Pacing the floor, I didn't know what to think. If only she'd mentioned the name of the person she'd been talking to! All my eavesdropping had done was deepen the mystery and I was now more confused than ever. I needed to get out of the house for a while, I thought, deciding to take a walk on the common. Surprisingly, I didn't want to meet the 'new' Barry. I just wanted to contemplate the puzzle.

Wearing only my skimpy summer dress, I walked down the street, wondering when Crystal would come round. I might miss her, I reflected as I neared the common. But she'd call again. Walking across the grass, I became aware of someone following me and stopped. Turning, I saw a man approaching. *One of the thugs?* I speculated fearfully. In his mid-thirties, dressed in jeans and a T-shirt, his hair long and unkempt, he certainly looked the part.

'Mrs Goodman?' he asked, standing before me.

'Yes,' I replied softly.

'I have a message for you.'

'Oh?'

'The money or the basement.'

'Who . . . who sent you?'

As he sloped away, I felt dizzy with shock. I guessed my intuition had been right – he *was* one of the thugs. As he faded into the distance I felt sure. But now my aching mind weighed even heavier with intrigue – questions. Had he been waiting outside the house to follow me, the girl would have told him that I wasn't there. How had he known I was at home? And that I was going to take a stroll? Nothing made sense. Danny thought I was in London, the girl knew I wasn't at home . . . Unless she'd heard me in the dining room.

Sitting on the grass, my heart racing, I tried to work the puzzle out. The bitch must have known that I was at home. Unless her boss had sent the thug with the message and he'd happened to see me leave the house. In that case, who had the bitch been talking to on the phone? Not her boss, that was for sure. My mind swirling, I held my aching head, trying to decide what to do.

The man might *not* have been one of the thugs, I reflected. The bitch might have sent a friend along with the message, someone who had no involvement in the affair whatsoever. But that still didn't answer the question as to how he knew I was at home, or that I'd go out. Finally climbing to my feet, I walked towards the edge of the common, dazed with confusion.

'Selina!' John called from his car as I neared the road. 'Come on, I'll give you a lift.'

'What are you doing here?' I asked, not disguising my relief as I climbed into the car.

'I was coming to see you when I noticed the girl leaving your house. I was in two minds as to whether to follow her or check up on you when I saw a man lurking in the street, continually looking at your house. Then you came out and walked down the street, and he followed you.'

'Did the girl speak to him?' I asked as he drove me home.

'No, he turned up on the scene just after she'd walked off. What did he say to you on the common?'

'The money or the basement, that was the message.'

'Let's go in and have a coffee,' he smiled, parking in my drive.

Following me into the kitchen, he sat at the table as I filled the kettle. Unable to think straight, I let him do the talking. I didn't understand what was going on, or who was involved. All I wanted to do was run away.

'I called round last night on my way home but you must have gone to bed,' he said.

'Yes, I did,' I replied, wondering whether to show him the dining room.

'I walked round the back of the house in case the girl was with you, but it was in darkness. Anyway, the plot would appear to be thickening.'

'You can say that again,' I smiled, passing him a cup of coffee.

'I don't mean the incident on the common. I'm talking about your husband pulling up at your house as I drove off to follow you and the man.'

'*What?* He came here?'

'Yes, he did.'

'He rang earlier and I said that I was going to London for the day.'

'He might have come back to collect something, clothes or whatever.'

'No, I don't think so. I also said that the police were watching the house.'

'If he'd told the girl that, she wouldn't have been round. We must bear in mind that they might not have been in touch since you spoke to him.'

'I hid in the garden when she came here. Then I crept into the house and heard her talking on the phone, saying that she'd bring the cash round later. I don't know who she was speaking to, and she dialled zero to clear the number she'd called.'

'She's a clever bitch. By the way, your husband's not had any visitors.'

'We're not really getting anywhere, are we?'

'I wouldn't be too sure about that,' he smiled mysteriously.

'What do you mean?'

'The appointment I had last night, it was with a local pimp.'

'Oh?'

'Apparently, some of his regular punters have been going elsewhere for sex. His girls have been telling him that there's someone new on the scene, namely you.'

'He knows me?'

'No, don't worry. I explained my interest and . . . It's not you he's bothered about but the girl who's blackmailing you. He doesn't like the idea of her taking his clients.'

'What's he going to do?'

'He knows who she is and where she lives.'

'Where?'

'He wouldn't say. He doesn't know me and he wants to check me out, make sure I'm kosher. He's going to give me a ring.'

'When?'

'When he's happy that I'm OK. I've also been snooping around the Thieves' Tavern. The landlord knows the girl, but only that she's been in several times and that her name's Alison. Making out that I was a would-be client, I asked him where I could contact her. He said that he knew nothing about prostitution, which he would say, seeing as he's the landlord. Anyway, he did point out a group of men standing at the end of the bar. I approached them and they said they'd give the girl the number of my mobile when they next saw her.

It seems that she calls the clients regularly, no one has *her* number.'

'That's great! If the pimp tells you where she lives and . . .'

'Don't get your hopes up, Selina. Firstly, the pimp might decide not to trust me and, secondly, the girl might not ring me. I'd better get going, I'll call you later.'

'OK. And thanks for all you're doing.'

'Anytime. I'll see myself out.'

As he left, I sipped my coffee, thinking about Danny. Why get involved with a prostitute? He'd hardly leave me for a whore who fucked men for cash, unless he was just using her to get his hands on my money. It still didn't make sense. Danny's primary interest would be taking my money, so why get involved with a tart? He could quite easily blackmail me without having the bitch ruin our dining room and run the risk of bringing men to the house.

Wondering why Danny had come home, I rang the hotel but he was out. Perhaps he'd arranged to meet the bitch at the house? I dialled Chrissy's number. Perhaps this, perhaps that . . . I was only guessing, stabbing in the dark.

'Hi, Chrissy,' I said as she replied.

'Selina, how are you?'

'OK. I thought I'd call on the off chance that you had the day off.'

'I've got more than the day off, I've been made redundant.'

'Oh, no.'

'I don't know what I'm going to do. Still, that's not your problem. Any news?'

'The plot thickens, as the detective put it.'

'What's happened?'

'I don't know, anything and everything. I'm still not sure whether Danny's involved or . . . A man stopped me on the common a while ago. He had a message for me – *the money or the basement*.'

'God!'

'I'm supposed to be handing over another five thousand today.'

'Are you going to?'

'I don't know. Things are such a bloody mess, I don't know what to do. My dining room's been wrecked and . . .'

'Wrecked?'

'Come round and take a look.'

'What do you mean, *wrecked*?'

'You'll see if you come round.'

'OK, I'll leave now.'

Meeting that man on the common had really frightened me, and I began to feel the effects of shock as I waited for Chrissy to arrive. My heart palpitating, my breathing unsteady, I sat in the garden beneath the beech tree trying to calm myself. Perhaps I needed an orgasm? I pondered as my clitoris swelled. But I couldn't masturbate with Chrissy due to arrive. Recalling licking her sex valley, I wished I'd not allowed my insatiable thirst for sex to get the better of me. I wouldn't do that again – or would I?

The front doorbell ringing as I finally walked dazedly back into the house, I again wondered why Danny had bothered to drive all the way home. Had he arranged to meet the bitch? Perhaps, believing me to be in London, they'd planned to use the sex equipment in the dining room.

'Hi,' Chrissy smiled as I opened the door. 'Let's have a look at your dining room, then.'

'You're eager,' I remarked, trying not to gaze at her breasts ballooning her tight blouse.

'Telling me that your dining room's been wrecked, and not explaining what happened, has intrigued me.'

'Well, here it is,' I announced, leading her through the hall and opening the door with a flourish.

'God!' she breathed, gazing at the chains and vibrators. 'Who did this?'

'The bitch, who else?'

'Did she make you . . . I mean, have you tried this stuff?'

'I was forced into crude sex by the bitch and six men.'

'*Six* men? God!'

'Let's go into the kitchen and have a coffee.'

'If I were you, I'd go straight to the police, Selina. You can't have people doing this to your home, let alone . . .'

'How *can* I go to the police?' I asked as we entered the kitchen. 'The bitch has got so much evidence against me, she'll ruin me.'

'She's ruined your dining room, ruined you sexually . . . You *must* put a stop to it. Does Danny know about this?'

'No. Well, yes – sort of.'

'Sort of?'

'I . . . I told him about it when he phoned.'

'You'll have to call the police. You can't have her bringing six men here to . . . Did they all, you know?'

'Yes, they did.'

'I'd have gone straight to the police. If I was forced to have sex with . . . Well, I wouldn't have done it in the first place.'

'It wasn't even straight sex – it was anal.'

'God!'

'It's all very well saying that you wouldn't have done it in the first place, but I had no choice.'

'Of course you did. When she first came here and demanded sex with you, you should have told her to piss off. Of course you had a choice.'

She was right, I'd had every choice – but it was no good looking back. Now, even if I was able to put an end to the nightmare, I'd changed: I'd still want crude sex. If the bitch never came back and things were OK with Danny and me, it would still never be the same. I'd go to the common looking for sex, I'd want to lick Chrissy to orgasm, I'd want more and more perverted sex with both men and women.

'You obviously enjoy it,' Chrissy murmured pensively.

'Hardly!' I returned.

'You wouldn't let her into the house unless you . . .'

'She has a key.'

'A key? Why haven't you changed the lock?'

'I have thought about that but . . . She'd probably break in. Besides, if I rile her, I'll be punished.'

'It's ridiculous, Selina! Some girl brings six men here to screw you, and you have to accept it? There's no way I'd allow anyone to do that to me.'

'You don't understand, it was a gradual thing. First, she wanted money, then she demanded sex with Danny . . .'

'That's when you should have done something.'

'She had photographs of her kissing Danny, holding his crotch, taking money. . . By that stage, she'd already got enough evidence to cause me problems. She now has videotapes of me in the woods on the common, doing things with several men.'

'Obviously I feel sorry for you, but I have to say that you've brought all this on yourself. You should have chucked Danny out the minute you realized that he was involved.'

'I *don't* know that he's involved, Chrissy.'

'Of *course* he is! From what you've told me, it's obvious that he's in this with the girl. Where do you think she got a front door key from?'

'That's what the detective said. I know it all adds up, it all points to Danny, but there's no conclusive proof.'

'God, how much proof do you need? He was kissing a blonde girl by the common, the girl has a key to your house, and it explains how she knew about the kitchen-ceiling fiddle and your affair with Barry.'

'Sometimes I'm positive that Danny's involved, and other times I'm not so sure.'

'There's no doubt whatsoever in *my* mind. What sort of man is he? He knows what you're going through, and he's doing nothing about it.'

'He's been . . .'

'Selina, no husband would allow the continued abuse of his wife. Can you imagine any other man allowing his wife to be screwed by six men, to be used and abused like that? Think about it – if Danny wasn't involved, he'd have taken you away somewhere, made sure you were safe.'

Her words were convincing, and I was sure that Danny *was* working with the bitch. But what could I do? Throwing him out wouldn't solve anything. The only way to solve all my problems was to get my hands on the photographs and videotapes, but that was impossible. Even if it was possible to get the originals, no doubt there'd be copies.

'What would you do?' I asked.

'Try and come to an agreement with the girl. Obviously, this will never end. She'll go on and on taking your money and using you for sex. I'd offer her a lump sum.'

'A lump sum?'

'If you offered her, say, fifty grand, she just might agree. Fifty grand in exchange for the evidence.'

'Fifty thousand pounds? How would I know that she'd keep her side of the bargain? She might hang on to copies and . . .'

'It's worth a try, Selina. It's either that, or call the police.'

'Yes, but . . .'

'If Danny's involved, and I know he is, they'll grab the money and run. They're taking a risk all the time this is going on. I reckon they'll take the money and you'll never hear from them again.'

'I haven't got fifty thousand pounds. The advance for the next book . . . Well, I suppose I could raise the cash.'

'Given the choice, I'd go to the police.'

A lump sum? I mused. Would the girl, or her boss if she had one, agree to a settlement? Even if she did agree, I'd never know whether they had copies of the sordid evidence and I'd be forever waiting for the bitch to demand more money. The only other option was to go to the police and tell them everything. No, I reflected, there was one more option – to wait and see what John came up with.

I decided not to tell Chrissy about the pimp John had met, or about Danny parking near to the flats. If I mentioned that he thought I was in London and had been home, she'd start going on about it all adding up and I didn't want that. It was best to have an open mind – to wait until John contacted me with something positive. Speculation would get me nowhere.

'How's your writing going?' Chrissy asked.

'Between the sessions of sexual abuse, I'm getting on pretty well.'

'Are you going to tell me what it's about?'

'No, you'll have to wait until it's published. Talking of work, I suppose you're going job-hunting?'

'I'm up to date with the rent and I can survive for a few weeks, but I'll have to find another job. I suppose I'd better go, I'm taking my car in for a service. Now I'm out of work, I'll call round more often.'

'Yes, I'd like that. We'll have to get drunk again.'

'I woke in the morning and found myself naked. I don't remember anything about the night before.'

'No, neither do I!' I giggled.

'As I don't have to get up for work, let's do it again tonight.'

'OK.'

'I'll bring a bottle round,' she smiled, rising to her feet.

'Right, I'll see you later.'

Seeing her out, my clitoris swelling expectantly, I knew I was making a mistake. If I plied her with alcohol and got her on the bed again, I wouldn't be able to restrain myself. I'd have liked to chain her in the dining room and abuse her naked body, use vibrators on her and whip her naked buttocks. 'God!' I breathed, closing the front door as I imagined shaving her pubic curls and licking her smooth vulval flesh. 'I must stop it!'

Recalling my early teens when I'd first taken an interest in the opposite sex, I'd never have dreamed that one day I'd want sex with Chrissy, my best friend. I had no morals, no preference – all I wanted was crude sex. Where was Crystal? I pondered, wandering up to my den. I should have sex with her and leave Chrissy alone – use Crystal and Barry to satisfy my lust.

Working at my computer for several hours, I rewrote the synopsis for my second book and faxed it to Tammy. Wondering what she'd think as I fed the sheets of paper into the machine, I decided not to take any more money out of the bank. If the bitch came round demanding cash, whether Danny had told her to or not, I'd tell her that the police were watching the house. Whether or not she'd believe me, hopefully she'd play it safe and keep away. The story was feasible enough, I reflected – one of the men had thought I was being forced into crude sex and had gone to the police. What her boss would do, if he existed, I had no idea. Time would tell, I told myself, answering the phone.

'Selina, it's John.'

'Hi,' I replied, pleased to hear a friendly voice.

'I'm parked fifty yards away from your BMW.'

'Where?'

'The same place, round the corner from the flats. You're not going to like this.'

'Go on.'

'Your husband locked the car and went into the flats.'

'That's it, then – he's working with the girl.'

'It looks that way. I watched him through my binoculars.'

'And?'

'He let himself in – he has a front-door key.'

'Oh, God. So, where do we go from here?'

'I don't know yet. I'll hang around for a while and see what happens. Are you going to be OK, Selina?'

'Yes, I suppose so.'

'I'll look in on you later.'

'Thanks.'

So that was that, I mused, holding my head as my mind began to hurt. Danny and the girl, screwing each other, screwing me, screwing my life. Wandering downstairs to the lounge, I flopped onto the sofa, my mind swirling with a thousand thoughts. My husband screwing a common tart, blackmailing me, taking my money, consenting to the sexual abuse of his wife . . . I screamed inside.

Chapter Thirteen

Clutching a bottle of wine, Chrissy arrived at seven, wearing a red leather miniskirt and a loose white blouse. Her long black hair shining in the light, her dark eyes sparkling, her succulent red lips glossed, she was eminently seducible. Following her into the lounge, I couldn't stop my gaze from falling on her rounded buttocks, her shapely thighs. My naked pussy lips swelling, I tried desperately to deny my lesbian desires as she sat on the sofa with her legs slightly parted.

I didn't tell her the latest news. I didn't want to think about it, let alone discuss it. As Chrissy sipped her wine, happily chatting, my arousal turned into an overwhelming feeling of spite. It was all right for her – apart from losing her job, she had no worries, no problems. My predicament wasn't her fault but, strangely, I felt like taking it out on her. Perhaps it was because she was the only one there.

As she reclined on the sofa, her dangerous red miniskirt riding up her firm thighs, I imagined her naked body hanging from the chains. The thin bamboo cane calling me, I wanted to thrash her full buttocks, vent my anger by lashing her until she sobbed for mercy. The notion was ridiculous, I knew, but I couldn't help my thoughts.

'Aren't you going to have a drink?' she asked.

'Yes, yes, I am,' I smiled, pouring myself a large glass of Chablis, wondering why John hadn't called in to see me. Where had Crystal got to?

'I've been looking forward to this evening. Stuck at home with nothing to do is so boring – I've been watching TV, pacing the floor, drinking coffee . . .'

As she rambled on, I gazed at her deep cleavage, the swell of her firm breasts revealed by her open blouse. I wanted to whip her mammary globes, lash her brown nipples until she screamed. My desire to punish her soaring, I felt my clitoris swell, my vagina tighten. As I was about to suggest that we go into the dining room, the sex room, the phone rang.

'Hallo,' I answered.

It was John. 'Just a quick call to check up on you. Is everything OK?' he asked.

'Yes, fine. You've got no more news, I suppose?'

'No, not yet. I'll let you know the minute I discover anything. I'll probably call in tomorrow morning, just to see how you are.'

'Thanks, I'd like that.'

'No word from your husband?'

'No, nothing.'

'I rang the hotel porter, there haven't been any visitors.'

'I suppose there's no need for the girl to go there, seeing as Danny visits her.'

'Good point. Anyway, I'll see you tomorrow.'

As I hung up, Chrissy looked at me, her head cocked to one side as if she was waiting for news. At least John's call had temporarily dissuaded me from luring her into the dining room and caning her naked breasts. Now I just wanted to suck her clitoris to orgasm.

'Well?' she finally asked. 'I assume that was the detective?'

'Yes, it was.'

'And?'

'Nothing, no more news.'

'Are you all right, Selina? You seem distant.'

'I'm OK. I suppose I'm just thinking about Danny and everything.'

'It must be a hell of a weight on your mind. Why don't you go away for a while? It's all very well Danny staying in a hotel, but you're the one who needs to get away.'

'I've thought about it before but . . . I don't know. If I disappear for a week or two, God knows what the bitch will do. I've even thought of moving to another town, or going abroad. I've thought of a hundred different ways of trying to get out of this mess, but I've never come up with anything positive. The detective suggested that I stay with a friend for a while. Would you mind me staying with you for a few days?'

'Well, I . . . You know what my place is like, so small that I can hardly move.'

'Sorry, I shouldn't have asked.'

'If I had a bigger place, you'd be only too welcome to stay.'

'No, no, I understand.'

'Look, I think I'll go. I don't feel like drinking and, understandably, you're not in the mood.'

'I'm sorry, it's just that I can't get all these worries out of my head.'

'No, don't apologize. I'll give you a ring tomorrow.'

'OK, Chrissy. You never know, I might have some more news by then.'

'I hope so.'

Finishing her wine, she smiled sweetly and rose to her feet, her skirt still high up her thighs. Eyeing her long, shapely legs, my ravenous clitoris pulsating, I imagined her yawning sex crack, her pink inner petals inviting my wet tongue. I desperately needed sex – it had become as important to me as food: I couldn't go without orgasms, without vaginal milk and sperm. Was Chrissy's sex sheath wet? Was her clitoris ripe? I wanted to lick her gaping valley of desire, to drink from her hot hole. I'd phone Crystal, I decided as I showed Chrissy out. Invite her to stay for the night.

Closing the front door, I was about to call Crystal when the phone rang. Dashing into the lounge and grabbing the receiver, I wasn't surprised to hear the bitch's voice, threatening me and demanding the five thousand pounds. Danny must have told her about the police, and she'd decided to ring rather than call. Telling her to bugger off as she threatened to thrash my naked buttocks, I felt smug. My plan was working.

'My boss isn't at all happy,' she said menacingly.

'So you keep saying,' I returned. 'That's all you ever say to me.'

'I mean it, Selina – he's not at all happy. He's instructed me to . . .'

'I know about the flat in Woodlands Road,' I broke in.

'What?'

'I said, I know about the flat in Woodlands Road.'

'What flat?'

'That's shaken you, hasn't it?'

'I don't know what you're talking about.'

'Don't you? That's odd, seeing as you go there often enough.'

'Don't play games with me, Selina. I want the money first thing in the morning.'

'There is no more money. And talking of games, your game will soon be over. I'm closing in, Alison – closing in fast.'

As she hung up, I knew I'd frightened the life out of her. *She*'d be pacing the floor now, wondering, floundering in her anxiety. A taste of her own medicine, I mused, pondering on her likely next move. If I never saw her again, that would be the end of the crude sex, I reflected. I had Crystal and Barry, but they weren't into bondage and whipping – something I'd become addicted to. I'd also miss anal sex, and four men spunking my orifices. But I could always find willing punters.

Not surprisingly, Danny called half an hour after the bitch had rung. She'd obviously phoned him, saying that I knew about the Woodlands Road flat and that I wasn't giving her any more money. I hated the sound of his voice.

'Any news?' he whined.

'No, nothing,' I replied, wondering how he was going to question me about the flat.

'I rang the private dick and, again, he seemed to clam up. All he'd say was that he had nothing to go on and that he was still working on the case.'

'I told you he was a waste of time, Danny. By the way, the police are still parked down the road.'

'Are they? You'd think they'd have better things to do.'

'They're not wasting their time checking tax discs, they're watching the house because they believe it's a brothel.'

'This is a bloody nightmare! I'll come home in the morning, it's pointless staying here.'

'All right, if you think it's best.'

'Yes, I do. Apart from anything else, look at the money we're wasting.'

'The hotel bill is nothing in comparison with what I've given that tart.'

'No, but . . . Christ, this bloody payphone eats money. I'll see you tomorrow, about ten.'

'OK, bye.'

Now Danny would be pacing the floor, wondering what to do. I really felt that I was winning, at long last. If I told Danny that the police had been to see me again, asking about a prostitute named Alison who hung around the Thieves' Tavern, I'd really put the wind up them. Pleased with myself, I decided to have an early night and climbed the stairs to bed. I wanted to call Crystal, to hold her naked body close to mine, but with Danny due home at ten . . . I'd call her in the morning.

* * *

The first thing I did when I leaped out of bed the next day was to call John and tell him that Danny was due home. 'In that case, I won't come round,' he said pensively. 'Your husband rang me last night and . . .'

'Yes, he told me. I could meet you by the common,' I said, rather too eagerly.

'I haven't any news, so . . .'

'It'd be nice to see you, John.'

'OK, what time?'

'Say, eleven?'

'Fine, I'll be there.'

Another mistake, I thought, imagining seducing him on the common, sucking the sperm from his orgasming knob. John was becoming a friend, and I didn't want to spoil that friendship with my nymphomaniacal desires. I'd just sit in his car and talk – if my clitoris would let me!

Slipping into my dress, I began to clear out the dining room. Lugging the wooden contraption through the French doors, I dragged it down the garden and hid it behind the bushes. Unhooking the chains, I bundled them into the shed along with the vibrators and the cane. Managing to unscrew the hooks from the ceiling, I looked around the bare room, again wondering where my furniture was. The bitch had probably called a house-clearance firm – I was surprised that she'd not sold my new three-piece suite! Danny would no doubt feign astonishment when he discovered the furniture gone. Just to confuse him further, I'd tell him that I'd sold it.

When he finally arrived, he kissed me, making out that he was really pleased to see me. Knowing that he'd been screwing the slag, probably fucking her arse, I could have wrung his neck. But I had to remain calm, at least until John had conclusive evidence. Then I'd really let rip!

'It's odd that the girl hasn't even phoned you,' he remarked, making himself a cup of coffee.

'I reckon that she knows about the police,' I replied, seething with anger.

'How could she know?'

'You tell me.'

'What do you mean?'

'Nothing. So, what are your plans for today?'

'I don't know yet. I might try and get back into writing.'

'I'm going out soon, so you'll have some peace.'

'Where are you going?'

'Just for a walk. By the way, I've sold the dining-room furniture.'

'Sold it?'

'I want to buy a new table and chairs, and a Welsh dresser. Oh, I forgot to tell you – the police came round last night.'

'What did they want?'

'They asked me about a prostitute who hangs around the Thieves' Tavern. Her name's Alison.'

'Christ, that's . . .'

'Yes, I know. They're closing in on her: she's wanted for things other than prostitution.'

'Did they say what?'

'No, they didn't. But, at long last, I'm going to get to the bottom of this. Whoever's involved, it won't be long now before they're exposed.'

Watching for his reaction, I was surprised that he didn't look shocked. Sipping his coffee, he seemed to be deep in thought, and I wondered whether he'd go up to his den and ring the tart, warn her about the police and the pub. As I wandered out into the garden, my clitoris yearning for my intimate attention, Danny followed and started talking about the grass, how it needed cutting.

'You don't seem very pleased,' I said, feeling my juices seeping from my sex sheath.

'Pleased?'

'That we might get to the bottom of things.'

'Of course I'm pleased! I suppose it's difficult to imagine the nightmare coming to an end. I'm also worried about you, Selina – what they'll do to you.'

'They won't do anything.'

'With the evidence they have, I'm sure they'll . . .'

'I intend to get my hands on the evidence. Once we discover where the bitch lives, and who she's working with . . .'

'*With*? Don't you mean *for*?'

'No, I mean *with*. She hasn't got a boss, Danny. She's in this with someone, a partner.'

'How do you work that out?'

'While you've been away I've been doing some digging around. I've discovered quite a lot.'

'Such as?'

'Until the mystery's solved, I'm not going to say anything.'

'You can tell *me*, surely?'

'I'd rather not. Anyway, I'm going for a walk.'

'Will you be long?'

'No, I just need some fresh air. See you later.'

Slipping upstairs and taking my vibrator from beneath the pillow, I bent my knees and drove it deep into my yearning vagina. Grabbing a pair of panties from the drawer, I tugged them up my legs, the tight material keeping the vibrator in place. I'd switch it on later, I decided, descending the stairs, my cunt tightening around the pink phallus. Perhaps enjoy an orgasm as I walked along the street.

Leaving the house, I pondered on Danny, his involvement with the girl. No doubt he'd phoned her the minute I'd gone and they'd both be worrying, sweating. But what could they do? Believing the police to be watching the house, and asking after a prostitute named Alison, there wasn't much they could do other than play it cool for a while. Whatever happened, I prayed for John to come up with some answers.

'Hi!' he called as I approached his car.

'You're early,' I smiled, climbing into the passenger seat, all too aware of the vibrator massaging my inner flesh.

'I have an hour or so before my next appointment. So, he's come home?'

'Yes, he has. I told him that I was going for a walk and . . .'

'Get down! Here comes your red BMW!'

'Are you sure?' I quavered, ducking beneath the dashboard.

'Sure as hell! Right, let's follow him.'

Turning the car round, John kept his distance as he cruised past the common. This was what I'd been waiting for, I reflected as we turned a corner. To catch Danny going into the flats or, better still, talking to the bitch, would be all the proof I needed to throw him out.

'There he goes!' John said animatedly, parking some distance away from my car. 'Straight into the flats.'

'Let's go in after him,' I whispered, grabbing his arm.

'No, that's not the way to do it. We'll wait here for a while and see what happens.'

'I told him I'd be an hour or so he won't stay in there for long.'

'He certainly is a regular visitor to this place.'

'We'll never find out which flat it is by sitting here.'

'Usually, whoever I'm following doesn't know me. Normally I would go in, making out that I'm visiting someone, but in this case . . . Hang on, he's coming out! Keep your head down.'

'He won't see me from here.'

'No, but we don't want to take any risks. He wasn't long, perhaps the girl's out. OK, he's driving off.'

'There *must* be a way of finding out which flat she's in.'

'As I said, she's not on the electoral register. Mind you, most people who rent aren't. I'll go in and have a snoop round. You stay here.'

'OK.'

I instinctively knew that we were almost there, that we'd almost got the bitch – and Danny. Gazing at the flats as John rang one of the bells, I also knew that the photographs and video tapes were in there. So near and yet so far, I mused, watching as someone opened the door. I grinned as John went inside – so far, so good! He was obviously used to this sort of thing and had come up with some reason or other to go in. But what would he do next?

'Well,' he said forlornly on returning some ten minutes later. 'I knocked on a few doors making out that I was looking for my long-lost sister, a girl with long blonde hair, but everyone reckons there's no one of that description living there.'

'She *must* live there!' I returned, almost angrily.

'OK, calm down. What I'll do is drop you back at the common and then have a word with the caretaker. If I can get a list of names . . .'

'Can't I wait here?'

'No, it's best that you go home. I'll ring you if I come up with anything.'

As we headed for the common, I didn't want to go home and have to wait for news, or face Danny and his lies. Perhaps I'd go to the 'thinking place' to see whether Barry was there, I thought as John parked the car. I'd get him to vibrate my solid clitoris to orgasm, I'd suck his sperm, and then kneel astride him and ride him, bouncing up and down on his solid cock as I fucked him.

'OK, I'll call you,' John said, obviously eager to get back to the flats.

'Don't make me wait too long,' I smiled, climbing out of the car.

'I'll ring you, no matter what.'

As he roared off, I wandered across the common, my cunt

moistening, my pleasure spot swelling as I pictured Barry's erect penis, his rolling balls, his sperm jetting from his purple knob. The chances of him being there were pretty remote, but I had to look. Wandering through the bushes I came to our thinking place, our fucking place, but he wasn't there. Desperate for sex, I wondered what to do as I looked about. No Barry, no Crystal . . . All I could do was masturbate.

Pulling my dress over my head, I slipped my wet panties off and laid my naked body on the soft grass, parting my legs as wide as I could. Running my finger up and down my hairless sex crack, lubricating my swollen clitoris with my juices of arousal, I closed my eyes as the beautiful sensations rippled through my body. Never in my life had I needed to come so much, and I parted my vaginal lips with my free hand and slipped the vibrator out of my hot cunt. Switching the device on, I ran the tip around my pulsating pleasure spot.

'Yes!' I cried jubilantly as pre-orgasmic waves of pleasure rolled though my naked body. Lost in my arousal, oblivious to my surroundings, I took myself to a shuddering climax. My clitoris pulsating, my lust juices flowing from my open sex hole, I trembled uncontrollably as my pleasure peaked. Whimpering, crying out as I sustained my incredible climax, I arched my back, my head tossing from side to side as I masturbated with the vibrator beneath the hot sun.

My first orgasm beginning to subside, I lay quivering on the grass, desperate to come again. Lifting my leg, reaching beneath my thigh, I slipped two fingers deep into my sopping cunt and massaged the silken walls of my sex sheath. My creamy duct hugged my caressing fingers lovingly, but I needed a penis driving in and out of my cunt, a huge knob spunking my cervix. I needed Crystal's darting tongue.

As I was about to take myself to another mind-blowing climax, I heard a rustling in the bushes and froze. A rabbit? A bird? I wasn't sure as I lay motionless on the grass, my fingers embedded deep within my yearning cunt. Slowly turning my head, gazing through my eyelashes, I saw a face peering through the bushes. It looked like a young man but, staring through my half-closed eyes, I couldn't be sure. Had he seen me walking through the bushes and followed me? I pondered, my stomach somersaulting as a lascivious quiver ran up my spine.

Slipping my fingers out of my hot vagina, I sat up and gazed at my breasts, my elongated nipples. Whoever he was, he was obviously delighting in my nakedness, my masturbating, and I nonchalantly turned round to face him. Reclining on the grass again, my legs open wide, my cunt fully displayed, I parted my love lips and exposed my open sex hole to my voyeur.

What was he thinking? I wondered as I caressed my clitoris with the tip of the buzzing phallus. Was his cock stiff? Would he wank in the bushes as he watched me masturbate? Reaching beneath my thigh again, I parted my love lips, opening my lust hole as wide as I could. Knowing that he was there magnified the erotic quivers coursing through my contracting womb as I vibrated my solid clitoris and gasped in my wickedness.

'Oh, my cunt!' I cried for the benefit of my unknown voyeur as I massaged the soft, wet flesh surrounding my vaginal entrance. Did he want to push his penis deep into my cunt and fuck me? Perhaps, in his wanking, he was imagining fucking me, spunking up my hot cunt. I wanted to suck his knob and swallow his gushing sperm.

Reaching another shuddering orgasm, I arched my back and opened my legs as wide as I could, delighting in my wanton act as I heard muffled groans coming from the bushes. He was splattering his seed over the ground, I knew, as I fingered my tightening cunt. Perhaps he'd return another day to watch me masturbate, keeping an eye out for me on the common and wanking in the bushes as he watched me finger-fuck my wet cunt.

My second orgasm gripping me as I pressed the vibrator hard against my pulsating clitoris, I heard another rustling in the bushes and faint breathing sounds. *What a waste of sperm*, I reflected, caressing the waves of sex from my ever-ripening cherry with the softly buzzing phallus. I could have sucked him to orgasm or had him sperm my cervix. But I knew that he'd be back as I heard him creeping away – and *then* I'd fuck him.

Bringing out the last ecstatic pulsations of my orgasm, my vibrating sex spot throbbing, I finally switched the device off. Hauling my quivering body up, I sat and gazed longingly at the vibrator – my intimate friend. The blades of grass tickling my hairless vaginal lips, caressing my protruding inner petals, I shuddered in my satisfaction as I slipped the pink shaft deep into my drenched vaginal sheath.

Wondering who my voyeur had been, I grabbed my dress and stood up. Glowing with sex, and an exhibitionist's pride, I felt smug, potent. He'd never forget the sight of my open cunt as I'd brought myself off. For the rest of his days, he'd picture me masturbating with my vibrator. Tugging my panties up, the wet material disappearing between my swollen love lips, I quivered as the pink phallus pressed against my cervix.

Pulling my dress on over my head, I slipped through the bushes and walked out onto the common, looking for the man. There he was, sitting on a bench, watching me out of the corner of his eye as I made my way towards him. There was no one else around – it had to be him, I reflected as I stood before him.

'Mind if I join you?' I smiled unashamedly.

'No, no, of course not,' he replied.

'I love it here,' I said, deciding that he must be in his teens. 'I come here every day.'

'I'm here most days around this time. I go to the college and come here during my lunch break.'

'I'm Selina.'

'Oh, right. Er . . . Dave.'

'Pleased to meet you, Dave. Do you always come here alone?'

'Yes, I do. I noticed that you came out of the bushes over there.'

'Yes, there's a small clearing where I sit and . . . and think. It's secluded, away from the prying eyes of the world. I call it my . . . my thinking place.'

'Are you always alone?' he asked, eyeing my thighs as I parted my legs slightly.

'Why do you ask?'

'I . . . I just wondered whether I could meet you here again.'

'I'd like that, Dave.'

'Really?'

'Yes, really. Have you got a girlfriend?'

'No, I haven't.'

'Have you ever had one?'

'No. There's this girl at college, but . . .'

'But what?'

'I've never had the courage to ask her out.'

'That's a shame. Listen, if I meet you here tomorrow, will you do something for me?'

'Yes, anything. What is it?'

'You'll see. Be here tomorrow at the same time, OK?'

'OK.'

Rising to my feet, I discreetly tugged my dress up and stood before him with my vaginal lips on display, my panties running deep within my crack. His eyes wide, he gazed at my shaved cunt, probably thinking me a tart. I *was* a tart, I mused – only a whore would behave in the way I was. But it excited me, how the young man's eyes focused on my cunt lips. Did he want to touch me? I pondered as I turned to leave, exposing my rounded buttocks. Did he want to fuck me?

'See you tomorrow,' I smiled, turning my head and looking over my shoulder as I walked away.

'Yes, yes – I'll be here!' he called eagerly. 'The same time.'

I could feel his gaze on my naked buttocks as I pulled my dress up a little higher, my panties working their way deep into my anal crease as I walked across the common. Would he wank again? I mused, heading for the road. Would he tell his friends what he'd seen? Elated, I tugged my dress down and made my way home, wondering whether Danny was there.

As if waking from a dream as I neared the house, I pondered on the situation as reality hit me – Danny visiting the tart, the lies, the deceit . . . I wanted to hurt him. I brooded on the matter as I walked round the back of the house and went into the kitchen. I wanted him to know what I'd done with Crystal, with Barry on the common, what I planned to do with the college boy.

'Oh, there you are,' Danny smiled as he joined me in the kitchen. 'Have a nice walk?'

'Yes, very nice. What have you been up to?'

'Er . . . Nothing, nothing.'

'Any phone calls?'

'No. I wonder why the girl hasn't rung?'

'Maybe the police have spoken to her and she's backed off.'

'Maybe. Selina, I've been thinking.'

'Oh?'

'You didn't really miss me while I was away, did you?'

'I missed you being here, yes.'

'I mean, *really* miss me. You seem to have changed, you're cold and . . .'

'Danny, any woman who's been through what I've been through would change! I've been forced to hand over thousands of pounds, to have crude sex with men and women . . . What I'd like to know is how you could allow this to happen to me.'

'*Allow*? I didn't *allow* anything to happen.'

'All right, stand by and do nothing.'

'Selina, I've hired a private detective, I've . . .'

'That's true, but what else have you done?'

'Well . . .'

'Basically, nothing. You could have put a bolt on the front door, which reminds me – the bitch has a key.'

'*What?*'

'A front-door key, Danny.'

'How the hell . . .'

'You tell me! You tell me how she knew about the insurance fiddle, how she knew about Barry, why she's not been here since the police have been watching the place and . . .'

'She must have seen them.'

'Hardly, they're plain-clothes officers in an unmarked car.'

'It sounds as if you're accusing *me*.'

'Does it?'

'Yes, it does. I didn't want to leave you alone here, it was your idea that I should stay at a hotel. I've done my best with the private dick, I've suggested that you get on with the second book in case the publishers decide they want another . . . All along I've felt that you've blamed me for this. In fact, you asked me whether I was working with the girl.'

'Are you?'

'Christ, Selina, not again!'

'Where did you go while I was out?'

'What?'

'I asked where you went while I was out. I saw you drive past the common.'

'Oh, I . . . I was going to go into town but changed my mind.'

'Really?'

'Where do you think I went?'

'To . . . It doesn't matter.'

'If you're accusing me of something, then tell me what it is.'

'Danny, I . . . There's the phone, I'll get it.'

Pursued by Danny into the lounge, I felt like telling him about the flats, but knew it would be a mistake. Besides, he'd only come out with some lie or other. Lifting the phone, I prayed that it wasn't John. I could hardly speak to him with Danny hovering behind me!

It *was* John. 'Hi, Selina,' he said cheerily. 'Are you alone?'

'No, not really,' I replied as Danny walked across the room and looked out of the window. He didn't know I had a vibrator forced up my wet cunt.

'OK, I'll do the talking. I've spoken to the caretaker. He's been there for years, knows everyone. After paying the old git, I've got a list of names of all the people in the flats.'

'That's good.'

'There's no one by the name of Alison, so I don't know where we go from here.'

'Neither do I.'

'There's been no word from the pimp, which is disappointing.'

'Yes, it is.'

'I can't understand why your husband would meet her at the flats. I mean, if it's not her flat they're meeting in, then whose is it? And why doesn't he go to her place, wherever it is?'

'Perhaps he does.'

'Perhaps. Anyway, I'll show you the list of names on the off chance that you might recognize one of them.'

'OK, when?'

'I don't think we should meet by the common, your husband might follow you. How about ringing me when he's not around?'

'Yes, I'll do that.'

'All right, I'll wait to hear from you.'

'Right.'

'And don't worry, we're getting there.'

'I won't.'

Replacing the receiver, I knew Danny would ask who it had been. What could I say? He'd know it wasn't Chrissy by the way I'd spoken. Thinking quickly as I returned to the kitchen, I turned to face him as he stood in the doorway.

'That was Tammy's assistant,' I imparted. 'The book's not doing at all well.'

'I thought you sounded odd,' he replied.

'It's depressing, to say the least.'

'Selina, I have nothing to do with this girl. I'm not working with her, love.'

'I know that. It's just that . . . Oh, I don't know. I'm fed up with the whole business.'

'It's no good us arguing, and we won't get anywhere if you're suspicious of me. And going back to my *allowing* this to happen to you, I . . . I just didn't know what to do. We couldn't go to the police, I tried following the girl . . .'

'Danny, I need to think. Why don't you go into town, as you intended?'

'OK, I suppose I need to think, too. I'll go and have a look around the second-hand bookshop.'

'All right, I'll see you later.'

Dashing into the lounge to watch him drive off, I didn't hold out much hope for the list of names. But I bounded upstairs to my den and dialled the number of John's mobile. I didn't know the bitch's surname, and I didn't know anyone who lived in that area, let alone the flats. But anything was worth trying.

'I'll be there in ten minutes,' John said enthusiastically as I told him that Danny had gone out.

'He should be at least an hour, so we'll have plenty of time to go through the list.'

'Good, put the kettle on – I could do with a cup of coffee.'

'OK, I will. Bye.'

Ambling into the kitchen, I made two cups of coffee, deciding to photocopy the list of names and peruse them at my leisure. I doubted that they'd ring any bells, but you never knew your luck. Taking the tray into the lounge, I placed it on the small table and waited for John. Danny had probably gone back to the flats, I mused. Probably desperate to fuck the dirty bitch, he'd gone there looking for her – for her cunt.

'Come in!' I beamed, answering the door to John.

'One list of names,' he smiled, following me into the lounge. 'That bloody caretaker demanded fifty quid, the thieving old git! But he knows everyone in the flats, keeps a record of them.'

'Let's have a look,' I said, taking the sheets of paper. 'R. Alexander, A. Bousoulengas, A. and L. Salamone, G. and S. Windsor, R. Snodgrass, B. Heffer, N. Hobson . . . There are several misses, but they could be nineteen or ninety.'

'Yes, I realize that. Just have a look through them all.'

'Right. Oh, there's your coffee.'

Sitting on the sofa, I scanned the names, not recognizing one of them. Despondency setting in, I tossed the papers onto the cushion beside me and sighed. Eighty-odd flats, eighty-odd names . . . I thought we'd never discover which flat Danny was visiting.

'There are no Christian names,' I complained, looking up at John as he sat in the armchair sipping his coffee.

'You don't recognize a surname?'

'There are several Smiths and Joneses, a few Davises . . . I knew a girl called Samantha Jones, another called Rebecca Smith . . . Without first names, it's hopeless. I'll go up to my den and photocopy the list.'

'It's OK, you can keep it.'

'Thanks, I'll go through it again later.'

'How's your husband?'

'He's all right.'

'I mean, has he come across as guilty or anxious?'

'No, not really. He got annoyed when I asked him whether he was working with the girl.'

'I suppose he would!'

'John, how much is this going to cost me?'

'What, my fee?'

'Yes.'

'I haven't worked it out. Look, don't worry about that now.'

'I have to. As it is I've lost my dining-room furniture and . . .'

'Lost it?'

'She sold it. She must have called in a house-clearance firm when I was out.'

'Why didn't you tell me?'

'I don't know. It's not important, is it?'

'I don't suppose there are many house-clearance firms around here. She might have given her surname.'

'Sorry, I should have . . .'

'It's OK, I'll be in touch.'

'You're going?' I asked as he leaped to his feet and placed his cup on the tray.

'Yes, to find out which firm she used. I'll ring you.'

As the front door closed, I felt stupid. I should have thought about the house-clearance firm, not that she'd give her real name. But it was worth trying, I reflected – the slightest lead was worth following up. Grabbing the list of names, I went up to my den and sat at the desk. Running my finger down the list, the vibrator moving within my tightening vaginal sheath, I realized that she might have rented a flat using another name. But no one recognized her description, and I began to wonder whether Danny had rented a flat under a pseudonym.

'Barlow, Watson, Godfrey,' I breathed, shaking my head despairingly as I hid the list in my desk drawer. I'd thought I was getting somewhere at last, but it seemed not. Staring at the ringing phone, I wasn't going to answer it, but changed my mind when I thought it might be Crystal.

'Hallo,' I sighed.

'Right!' the bitch snapped. 'I've had a word with my boss and . . .'

'Don't tell me, he's not at all happy.'

'We know your husband's back, but he won't be for long.'

'The basement again?' I asked sarcastically.

'Worse. Unless you come up with the cash by midday tomorrow . . . Well, you'll see.'

'Will you get it into your thick skull that there is no more bloody money!'

'You'd better borrow some, or sell your car. I mean it, Selina – you play the game, or else! Meet me on the common tomorrow with the cash.'

'No, I don't think I'll bother. You can do what you like to my husband, I don't want him any more.'

'The man who approached you on the common will approach you again unless you pay up – and it won't be to give you a message! It's up to you – meet me in the woods on the common at midday with the cash, or both you and your husband will be in real trouble.'

As she hung up, I wondered whether to ring John with the latest news. But he'd be busy chasing house-clearance firms, I decided – I'd call him later. Gazing out of the window, I wondered what to do. I didn't feel like working and, with Danny back, I couldn't invite Crystal round. Wishing he'd stayed away for longer, I pressed my forehead to the glass and gazed at the front garden, recalling the times when I'd enjoyed weeding and planting flowers. Long gone were the days of cooking, gardening, homemaking! Pondering on my future, I went downstairs as I saw Danny pull up in the drive.

'Hi, love,' he smiled innocently as we met in the hall. 'Everything OK?'

'Everything's fine,' I told him, feeling depression setting in. 'Been anywhere nice?'

'Only the bookshop.'

'The bitch rang while you were out.'

'Oh, God. What did she say?'

'She wants more money.'

'Christ! We'll have to pay her, Selina. If the newspapers get hold of . . .'

'No, I'm not giving her another penny.'

'But think about the consequences.'

'I have, and I'm not handing over any more money.'

'Well, it's up to you – it's your career that'll be in ruins.'

'Yes, it is.'

'Before deciding not to pay her, give it some thought. The private dick might come up with something. If you pay her, it'll give him more time.'

'He's had time enough as it is. Obviously, he's getting nowhere. You said yourself that he seemed to clam up, which is probably because he's failing miserably and doesn't know what to say.'

'Yes, I'd thought of that. Perhaps I could find someone else, another detective and . . .'

'And I carry on paying the bitch. Anyway, I have no more money – even if I wanted to pay her, I can't.'

Following me into the lounge, Danny held his head and gazed out of the window. He was putting on a bloody good act, I mused as he slouched his shoulders and sighed. But he didn't fool me. Not wanting to be near to him, I went up to my den and locked the door. Pulling my soaked panties off, I slipped the hot vibrator out of my vagina and placed it in the desk drawer.

It was early afternoon and I decided to write, to work through the evening and the night if I could. I'd ignore Danny if he knocked on the door, and the phone when it rang. I didn't want to acknowledge the world – it didn't exist. Throwing myself into my work, I'd write like I'd never written before.

Chapter Fourteen

Waking at seven in the morning to find myself on the sofa in my den, I clambered to my feet, wondering what the day would bring. At least I hadn't had to sleep with Danny. Had he slept alone in our bed or gone to screw the tart? I'd loved Crystal in the so-called marital bed, entwined in lust, our naked bodies shuddering as our tongues brought out our orgasms. Where was she?

Checking the bedroom, I took a shower before wandering downstairs and filling the kettle. I couldn't face Danny, his lies, his adultery, his treachery. Calling him, praying for him to be out, I went into the garden to look for him. Thankfully, there was no sign of him, only the rising sun greeting me as I wandered across the lawn to the beech tree. Sitting on the bench, my mind drifting, I pondered on John, wondering whether he'd discovered which house-clearance firm had taken my furniture.

The bitch's phone call surfacing from the depths of my mind, I recalled the man who'd accosted me on the common. If I didn't take the cash to the woods at midday, he'd approach me again – and not with a message! Would Danny really see me abducted, taken to a basement, tied up and used for crude sex? Yes, I decided – he'd do anything to get his hands on another five grand.

Returning to the kitchen, I poured myself a cup of tea, wondering whether it was too early to call John. Left in the dark, I had to discover what was happening, what he'd learned. More importantly, I had to find out what my adversaries had in store for me. *Should I go to the woods?* I asked myself. *Should I wade those dangerous waters again?* I didn't know what to do as I drifted into the lounge to answer the phone.

'Sorry to call you so early,' John apologized.

'That's OK, I was thinking of calling you,' I replied. 'Have you discovered anything?'

'I found the house-clearance firm, but the girl gave your surname. Have you been through the list of names again?'

'Yes, and come up with nothing. The girl rang me – she wants me to take five thousand to the woods on the common at midday.'

'If she's not going to your house to collect the money, it looks as if your story about the police has worked.'

'The minute I told Danny, he obviously went running to her.'

'Don't do anything until I get back to you. I have one or two things up my sleeve, so be patient.'

'OK. By the way, Danny went out early. Either that, or he didn't sleep here last night.'

'He might have stayed with the girl. OK, you stay put.'

'All right. Bye.'

Stay put? I would have stayed put if I'd had Crystal with me, her naked body, but I became lonely and agitated as time passed. I had to get out of the house, go for a walk and relax my mind. I didn't want to see Danny, listen to his whining. He hadn't bothered to call me to tell me where he was, reinforcing my suspicion that he'd slept with the bitch. I wouldn't have minded if I never saw him again. Perhaps he'd left me, I mused as I was about to leave the house. No, I very much doubted that I was that lucky!

'We meet again,' the bitch grinned, emerging from the kitchen.

'How did you get in?' I gasped, turning to face her.

'A change of plan, Selina. Instead of meeting on the common, I thought I'd come here – just in case you'd decided to trick me.'

'I haven't got the money,' I returned. 'There is no more money.'

'Of course there is.'

'Ask Danny, he knows that I'm broke. I'm surprised he didn't tell you last night, when he was in your bed – fucking you.'

'In my bed? You're dreaming again.'

'The police have been here asking me about a prostitute called Alison who hangs around the Thieves' Tavern.'

'The police?'

'Yes, the police, Alison.'

'My boss won't be at all happy when I tell him that you've called the police.'

'I didn't call them. One of your so-called clients . . .'

'I'm not bothered about the police, they've got nothing on me.'

'Haven't they? The Woodlands Avenue flat, the Thieves' Tavern, the client who's told them that you're a prostitute forcing me to endure crude sex . . .'

'Forcing you? How are they going to prove that? With all the evidence I have, it's pretty obvious that you're a most willing participant.'

'I'm not going to tell you who, but one of your clients has been coming round to see me. We're friends.'

Her face turning pale, I knew I'd shaken her. But what was my plan? My lies had frightened her, but I had to back them up, give her some proof. But I had nothing to substantiate my claim. Brushing her long blonde hair away from her face, her blue eyes locked to mine, she was obviously wondering what to say.

'You'd better go,' I smiled. 'Go the back way, unless you want the police to pick you up.'

'My boss might be willing to do a deal,' she murmured pensively.

'A deal?'

'He might . . . I can't speak for him, but I might be able to get him to meet you.'

'Where?'

'The woods.'

'No, I'm not going there again.'

'It's up to you, Selina. If you want to speak to him and maybe come to an arrangement, then you'll meet him in the woods.'

'When?'

'I'll ring you.'

As she left by the back door, I bit my lip, my anxiety rising. I knew that meeting her in the clearing would be dangerous, but I had to find out whether her boss really existed. Believing the police to be on to her, I doubted that she'd trick me, force me to endure more perverted sex. There again, if she thought the police might follow me to the common, she might not turn up. She'd probably arrive at the house with her so-called boss. All I could do was wait for her to call.

Checking my watch, I thought about meeting Dave, the college boy. Ten-thirty: he'd be watching the clock, eager to fuck me, to lick me to orgasm. I was eager to suck his young cock, swallow his sperm, but . . . No, before I planned anything, I had to wait for the bitch to phone – I could fuck Dave whenever I liked. Should I tell John about meeting the bitch and her boss? I wondered, walking into the kitchen. I'd ring him later, after I'd heard from the girl.

'Hallo, love.' Danny smiled as he appeared in the doorway. 'I went for a walk, it's a lovely day.'

'You've been gone a long time,' I frowned.

'I was up early and, as you'd locked yourself in your den, I went out. Any news?'

'No, nothing.'

'I don't understand it, there's been no word from the girl, the detective's come up with nothing . . . I wish I knew what was going on.'

'So do I. Danny, I have to go out. What are you doing today?'

'Writing, I suppose. Where are you going?'

'To see someone in Woodlands Road.'

His face blanched with shock, his dark eyes frowning, he moved across the room and looked out of the window. I didn't know why I'd mentioned Woodlands Road. I suppose it was because, deep down, I'd wanted to tell him that I knew he was involved with the tart.

'See you later, then,' he said nonchalantly, turning towards me. 'I'll go up and try to get some work done.' Smiling at him as he left the room, I knew he was going to ring the girl. He hadn't asked me who I was going to visit as he'd obviously wanted to appear innocent, but I knew he'd be worried sick and would contact the bitch as soon as I was out of the way.

Leaving the house, I walked down the street, not really sure where I was going. I'd miss the girl's phone call, and John's, but I couldn't stay at home with Danny – I just wanted to escape. Walking across the common, I thought it might be best if I wasn't around when the girl rang. She'd be worried, desperate to contact me, and I'd leave her to sweat.

Following the path through the trees, I entered the clearing and looked about me. The air still heavy with the smell of sex, my clitoris swelled and pulsated, my cunt moistened, and I imagined that the devil was near. Had the reverberations of perverted sex permeated the trees? I wondered. Had the vile debauchery summoned some sex fiend from an unseen world? The idea was crazy, but I sensed a presence, something prowling, watching me.

Noticing a carrier bag hidden beneath a bush, I pulled it out, wondering whether the bitch had stashed her equipment in readiness to use on me the next time she lured me to the clearing. Opening the bag, I peered inside. The whip, handcuffs, lengths of rope, a vibrator . . . I was right, she obviously intended to abuse me again.

'I thought it was you wandering into the woods,' Dave smiled, emerging from the bushes. 'I haven't got college today, so I thought I'd hang around the common and wait for you.'

'You shouldn't be here,' I said, fearful of the bitch catching us.

'Why not?'

'This place is . . . It's not good.'

'Not good?'

'It's evil, Dave.'

'Evil? What are you talking about?'

'I'll show you,' I grinned, unbuttoning his shirt as a powerful desire to whip his penis gripped me.

Saying nothing as I slipped his shirt over his shoulders and unbuckled his belt, he looked down at me as I knelt before him and pulled his trousers down. I'd lost control, I knew, as his stiffening penis came into view. I couldn't help myself, my craving for debased sex possessing me.

Recalling the dining room darkening as I'd been forced to endure crude sex with the girl and her clients, I began to wonder whether there really was something evil lurking, following me, goading me. My insatiable thirst for perverted sex had been running wild, continually soaring. Was it simply my sexual awakening? Or was it something more sinister?

Gazing at Dave's swinging balls as he slipped his shoes off and stepped out of his trousers, I grabbed his solid organ and yanked his foreskin back, exposing his virginal glans to my wide eyes. Gasping as I took his plum into my mouth and sucked, he held my head, obviously revelling in his first experience of oral sex. It was wrong for us to be together there, I knew, as I wanked his young shaft and ran my tongue over his swollen knob. I should have initiated him into the art of oral sex in my thinking place, not in the sinister woods.

Taking his swollen knob to the back of my throat, my lips stretched around his hard shaft, I wondered what I was doing to the innocent teenager. His first time should have been with a girl of his own age, discovering sex together – not with a perverted tart like me. But I'd traded my soul for sex, exchanged my femininity for the pleasures of the flesh. This was my domain, and anyone who entered would be sexually violated. As I sank my teeth into his twitching cock, I realized that I could no longer tell the difference between right and wrong.

'You'd better go,' I murmured, slipping his knob out of my mouth and standing up, a glimmer of my old self flickering in the dark.

'Go?' he frowned.

'I'm not good for you, Dave.'

'What do you mean?'

'I mean . . . I mean that I'm not good. Go now, before I . . . before I destroy you.'

'Destroy me?'

'Can you tell love from lust?'

'What?'

'Can you tell the scent of flowers from the stench of sex?'

'Yes, of course.'

'You won't, if you stay.'

'I *want* to stay.'

'You're young and innocent. You've not yet found love and, if you stay, you never will.'

'Of course I will.'

'All right, but you'll remember this day forever. Recall my words to the end of your days.'

'I don't understand.'

'No, you don't. But you will, one day. Lie on the ground.'

As he lay down, I grabbed several lengths of rope from the bag and knelt by his feet. Tying each ankle, I stood up and slung the ropes over the branches of a tree and pulled. His legs parting, rising, his buttocks clear of the ground, he said nothing as I secured the ropes. Binding his wrists, I pulled his arms behind his head and tied the rope to a bush. He was mine now, his naked body mine to do with as I wished. Standing with my feet either side of his head and lifting my dress over my head, exposing my hairless pussy to his wide eyes, I looked down at him and smiled.

'Are you sure you want to stay?' I breathed, tossing my dress to the ground as I squatted, my cunt close to his face, my vaginal lips gaping.

'Yes, of course!' he replied eagerly.

'Have you ever seen a cunt before?'

'No, no, only in magazines.'

'Well, what do you think?'

'I think it's . . .'

Pressing my inner sex flesh over his mouth, I slowly rocked my hips, juicing his face as I gasped in my wanton debauchery. His penis solid, pointing skywards, his heavy balls rolling as he pushed his tongue into my hot pussy, I wondered what he was thinking, what he thought of his first taste of cunt milk. As he licked the silken walls of my sex sheath, explored inside my wet cunt, I felt an overwhelming desire to corrupt him. In his innocence, he probably believed he was in love with me, that we'd go out together, hand in hand in love. But I'd show him the difference between love and cold, crude lust.

'I like your cock,' I smiled, moving aside and focusing on

his young organ, erect between his splayed thighs. 'I suppose you want me to push it up my cunt.'

'Yes,' he murmured as I eyed his naked buttocks, perfectly positioned to receive the leather tails.

'Before I fuck you, I'm going to have a little fun.'

Tightening the ropes, his buttocks rising, his feet wide apart, high above his naked body, I took the whip discreetly from the bag. The first lash of the tails across his fresh young buttocks jolting his body, he looked up at me with fear mirrored in his wide eyes. Again, I lashed his tensed anal orbs, watching his penis twitch, his balls roll as he cried out for mercy. His pleas only serving to drive me on, I thrashed him as hard as I could, venting something I didn't understand. Was it anger? Was I seeking retaliation for all I'd been put through? I didn't know or care as I flailed his beautiful virginal buttocks.

'Please, no more!' he grimaced as the tails bit into his crimson flesh with deafening cracks. Again and again I lashed his twitching buttocks, delighting in my wickedness as he writhed on the ground. Finally discarding the whip, I settled on the grass and grabbed his solid penis, kneaded his young balls.

'Did you enjoy that?' I asked huskily, pulling his foreskin back and exposing his young glans.

'No, for God's sake!' he returned. 'What the hell . . .'

'You're mine, Dave – you belong to me now.'

'What the hell are you?' he demanded as I squeezed his balls and dug my fingernails into his rock-hard shaft. 'Who are you?'

'What am I? I'm a nymphomaniac. Who am I? I'm the devil's daughter!' I cackled wickedly, grabbing the vibrator from the bag.

'No!' he protested as I slipped the pink shaft between his parted buttocks and drove it deep into his anal duct.

'Until I decide to release you, you belong to me. I'll do anything I wish to your naked body – anything!'

The devil must have me in his grip, I realized as I switched the vibrator on and pushed it fully home. Kneeling with my gaping cunt close to Dave's weal-lined buttocks, I pulled his penis over his balls, bending his shaft and positioning his knob between my swollen pussy lips. Driving his ballooning glans deep into my vaginal sheath, completely impaling my cunt on his cock, I knew Lucifer had taken me.

His shaft at ninety degrees to his stomach, pressing my inner flesh hard against my pubic bone, I leaned forward and gyrated my hips. Gasping, he closed his eyes as I rocked my body, his bulbous knob massaging the silky walls of my wet cunt. The vibrator buzzing within his anal sheath, I wondered what he thought of his introduction to crude sex as I bounced up and down, his cock driving in and out of my tight roost. Perhaps he thought this was love.

'Spunk me!' I cried as pre-orgasmic waves surged through my quaking womb. 'Spunk up my cunt!' Breathing heavily, he tossed his head from side to side as his shaft swelled, inflating my sex duct. 'I want your sperm!' I gasped, my orgasm erupting within my solid clitoris, my juices of desire streaming from my vagina. On and on I bounced up and down, sustaining my incredible climax, his penis squelching my bubbling sex liquid as we fucked.

'Coming!' Dave finally cried, his spunk jetting into my lust hole as I screwed him in my crudity. His body rigid, the ropes taut, his eyes rolled as his virginity surrendered to manhood – to debauchery. Surveying my hairless pussy lips gripping his glistening shaft, I decided to have him drink his sperm from my cunt before thrashing him again. Then I'd thrash his penis, treat him as a sex slave and lash his young penis with the leather tails.

He'd be forever mine, I mused, my clitoris massaged by his

wet cock as I bounced up and down. Again and again he'd return to the clearing to offer me his body, his erect penis, his spunk. I'd defile him, corrupt him, use and abuse him to satisfy my craving for perverted sex as I'd been used and abused. My clitoris swelling, my orgasm nearing as his sperm jetted over my cervix, I knew I'd found myself a sex slave.

'God!' I breathed as my clitoris exploded in orgasm, my naked body shaking violently as his cock pistoned my spasming cunt. Gyrating my hips, bouncing up and down, I sustained my pleasure as Dave emitted long, low moans. His balls draining, the last of his sperm pumping deep into my hot cunt, his penis began to deflate. Grinding my sex flesh into his cock as it slipped out of my juiced vaginal duct, my clitoris rubbing against his wet shaft, I brought out the last of my orgasm. The squelching sounds of sex resounding throughout the clearing, I finally fell back, collapsing on the soft grass.

'Please, let me go now,' he murmured as I lay on the ground massaging my insatiable clitoris.

'Let you go?' I echoed.

'It's not supposed to be like this, whipping me and . . .'

'Of course it is,' I grinned, climbing to my feet. 'This is sex, Dave.'

'But . . .'

'And now you'll cleanse me,' I asserted, standing with my feet either side of his head and, squatting, I forced my drenched inner flesh over his mouth. 'Lick my cunt out: drink your sperm and my juices of desire.'

His tongue entering my wet hole, delving deep into my hot cunt, I realized that time was passing quickly. Wondering whether the bitch would come to the clearing and discover my debauchery, I tightened my vaginal muscles, squeezing my sex milk into Dave's mouth as he drank from my hot hole. I had to release him and go home, but I'd meet him again to use and abuse him.

'Enough,' I breathed, standing and looking down at his wet face. 'One last thing, and then you may go.' Grabbing the whip, I raised it above my head and brought it down, the leather tails lashing his erect penis. Screaming, he pulled on his bonds, desperately trying to halt the beating as the tails lashed his young cock.

'Please, stop!' he cried. 'What do you think you're doing?'

'Initiating you,' I grinned, placing the whip in the bag and pulling the vibrator out of his anal duct. 'You now belong to me.'

'I don't belong . . .'

'Silence! You will meet me here tomorrow for your next lesson in sexual corruption.'

Untying the ropes, I helped Dave clamber to his feet, his flaccid penis hanging over his heavy balls, bearing the weals of the cruel thrashing. As he dressed, I cleared away the evidence of my perverted behaviour and pushed the bag beneath the bush, wondering whether he'd return. He'd be back, I knew, as I pulled my dress on over my head. He couldn't resist the debauchery now he'd had a taste of lust.

'I'll see you tomorrow,' I smiled as I left the clearing. Following the path, my cunt wet with desire, I pondered on my depravity, my wicked corruption of the teenager. He'd never find love now, I reflected as I emerged from the woods and walked across the common. He'd never be able to make love – only cold lust.

Hurriedly walking home, I opened the front door and staggered into the hall, sperm oozing from my inflamed cunt and coursing down my inner thighs. *Another fuck, another conquest*, I reflected, wondering how many more men I'd seduce.

'Hi!' John called, walking up the drive as I was about to close the door. 'I've been waiting in my car.'

'Oh, John, er . . . Come in,' I smiled, my face flushing.

'Your husband went out about half an hour ago.'

'Again? He's always going out.'

'Selina, you'd better come and sit down,' he said mysteriously, leading me into the lounge.

'That sounds ominous.'

'The flats in Woodlands Road . . . I've discovered which one your husband's been visiting.'

'You have? John, that's great!'

'The girl, Alison – she doesn't live there.'

'Then who does?'

'Another girl, a Miss Johnson.'

'Who's she?'

'I'm not sure what her part is in all this, but I do know that your husband's been visiting her regularly. I can't figure out the connection between the three of them. Your husband's probably having an affair with this Johnson girl, Alison has been there to see her . . . I can't work it out.'

'I thought Danny was screwing the bitch.'

'So did I.'

'Perhaps the bastard's screwing both of them. The girl who lives in the flat, has she got long blonde hair?'

'No, why?'

'I was just wondering whether Crystal . . .'

'Who's Crystal?'

'No one, it doesn't matter.'

'The caretaker reckons that Johnson only moved in a couple of weeks ago. He knows nothing about her.'

'What does she look like?'

'About your age, very attractive, long black hair – her name's Christine Johnson.'

'Christine?' I gasped.

'Yes, ring any bells?'

'No, it can't be! Chrissy, she's my best friend!'

'*What?*'

'But she lives in Milton Road. No, it can't be Chrissy.'

'Hang on, hang on. This best friend of yours – have you told her what's been going on?'

'Yes, everything from Day One.'

'When did you last go to her place?'

'I haven't been there for months. It's a very small flat, she always comes here.'

'The three of them in it together,' he breathed pensively. 'Give me a moment to think.'

Pacing the floor, I stared dazedly at John as he held his hand to his forehead. I couldn't believe that Chrissy and Danny had hired the bitch to destroy me! There had to be some mistake. My best friend? Never in a million years! She'd have told me if she'd moved to another flat.

'It all fits, Selina.'

'God, the times Chrissy's said that!'

'Listen to me. I reckon that your husband was having an affair with your best friend, you came into some money, and he decided not to leave you. Together, they came up with the idea of blackmailing you.'

'Danny wouldn't put me through all that. And as for Chrissy . . .'

'Alison has visited Chrissy, your husband has visited Chrissy – they must be in this together.'

'I rang Chrissy, the number's the same.'

'It's easy enough to keep your old phone number when you move. Look, there might be another Christine Johnson.'

'With long black hair, about my age . . . Hardly!'

'OK, so where do we go from here?'

'I'll kill her!'

'That won't do any good. We can now assume that there is no big, bad gangland boss, which is something to be grateful for.'

'John, we can go to the police now and . . .'

'No, we don't want to involve the police. The blackmail's over, and the sex – all we have to do now is get the tapes and photographs back.'

'What, and let them off the hook? They've got my money!'

'I might be able to get it back. If I threaten them with the police . . . Look, leave it to me. Don't go doing anything silly, wait until I get back to you.'

'OK.'

'Promise me you won't do anything.'

'I promise.'

Seeing him out, my mind numb, I couldn't come to terms with the shocking truth. Everything I'd told Danny had got straight back to the bitch. Everything I'd told Chrissy had got back to her. What was it that had driven them to destroy me? I wondered. Jealousy over my success? I wanted to ring Chrissy and tell her that I knew, but managed to restrain myself.

Wandering out into the garden and sitting beneath the beech tree, tears flooding down my face, I tried to compose myself. It was no good getting het up. Now, of all times, I had to think straight. Chrissy had been so convincing, suggesting that I call the police, that Danny go away for his own safety. There was no basement, no villainous boss . . . Who was the man who'd approached me on the common? A friend of the bitch, no doubt. There were no thugs, only Danny, Chrissy and the cow.

But why had Chrissy continually tried to implicate Danny? I pondered. To throw me off the scent? I didn't know, I couldn't work it out. There were so many unanswered questions, all I could do was wait for John to contact me again. Wondering what Chrissy had said when Danny had told her that I was going to visit someone in Woodlands Road, I couldn't restrain myself from ringing her.

Bounding into the lounge, I dialled her number, wondering

what I was going to say. 'Hi, Chrissy,' I trilled when she answered.

'Selina, how are things?'

'Coming to a close, at long last.'

'Oh, er . . . What's happened?' she asked hesitantly, obviously terrified.

'The private detective's been great. He reckons that he's got to the bottom of everything.'

'So, who . . . What I mean is . . .'

'He hasn't told me yet. He has one or two loose ends to tie up, and then he's going to reveal all – names, addresses, the lot.'

'Right, well . . . That *is* good news, Selina.'

'Isn't it just? And he reckons that he can get my money back. Anyway, I have to go – I'll keep you posted.'

'Yes, please do.'

'Talk to you soon. Bye.'

'Bye.'

That put the wind up the slag's cunt! She'd tell Danny and the bitch and then . . . And then what? I hadn't got a clue what to do, what to say to Danny. Wondering where he was, I poured a glass of wine. No doubt he'd come home and spin his lies once Chrissy had told him what I'd said. How the hell he could lie his way out of it, I had no idea, jumping as the phone rang.

'I've spoken to my boss,' the bitch said as I answered. Had Chrissy told her that I'd called?

'And?'

'He's agreed to meet you. He says he might settle for a lump sum.'

'How much?'

'Thirty thousand.'

'No, tell him to sod off.'

'Selina, unless . . .'

'What I should say is, tell *her* to sod off.'

'*Her?*'

'Chrissy, your boss.'

As she hung up, I grinned smugly. At long last, the puzzle had been solved. All I had to do now was confront Danny and . . . Recalling John's words, I realized that I shouldn't have spoken to Chrissy or told the bitch what I knew. Gulping down another glass of wine, I paced the floor, wondering what would happen next. When Danny came home I'd remain calm, say nothing until John had got back to me.

My mind awash with confusion, I wondered why Chrissy had said that she'd seen Danny kissing a blonde girl. Why would she try to implicate him when they were working together? As the phone rang again, I guessed that it was Danny. Grabbing the receiver, wondering what lies he'd come out with, my heart raced as he asked me whether I'd heard anything from the girl.

'No, nothing,' I replied, barely unable to stop myself from letting rip. 'Where are you?'

'I'm in the call box by . . .'

'You're at Chrissy's, aren't you?' I blurted out.

'Chrissy's?' he echoed.

'At her new flat in Woodlands Road.'

'No, no, I'm . . .'

'It's over, Danny – I know everything.'

'Look, I'd better come home.'

'Yes, I think you had.'

As I hung up, my hands trembling, adrenalin coursing through my veins, I pulled my dress over my head and tossed it onto the sofa. Naked, I looked out of the window, waiting for the bastard to return and spin his web of lies. But I'd got him now – nothing could convince me of his innocence. I'd show him my shaved cunt, tell him that I'd seduced two young men on the common, that I was now a nymphomaniacal whore. Would he be jealous?

When he arrived, he wandered into the lounge, his dark eyes frowning as he stared at my naked body, my shaved cunt. Standing before me, his expression pained, he forced a smile and asked me what I'd meant about him being at Chrissy's new flat.

'I know everything, Danny,' I said, my eyes locked to his. 'You, Chrissy and Alison have been in this together, blackmailing me and . . .'

'*What?*' he gasped surprisedly. 'When I rang, I thought you meant . . .'

'What did you think?'

'I thought you'd found out that I've been having an affair with Chrissy.'

'Yes, I have found out. I also know that you've been blackmailing me.'

'I've *not* been blackmailing you! Admittedly, I've been seeing Chrissy behind your back, but . . .'

'Stop lying, Danny. The detective has told me everything – Alison visiting Chrissy, you going there to see her.'

'Hang on, Chrissy doesn't know this Alison girl – she isn't blackmailing you!'

'She is, the detective has discovered everything.'

'I've been seeing Chrissy, but I swear I know nothing about her blackmailing you.'

'Everything I've told you got back to the bitch, everything I've told Chrissy got back to her. You're all in this together, there's no point in denying it now.'

'Selina, you've got it all wrong. OK, so I've been seeing Chrissy, going to her new flat – but I've never seen the girl there. Had I known that they were blackmailing you . . .'

'I don't believe you, Danny. Anyway, I don't want to talk about it. You know the truth, and I know the truth.'

'No, you don't!'

'Stop shouting at me. I just want you to go.'

'Go?'

'Get out of my life. Go to your bit on the side.'

'But I want to stay with you.'

'Don't talk rubbish. You've been screwing my so-called best friend, but that wasn't enough, was it? You wanted my money, you blackmailed me, you had me sexually abused . . .'

'No, I fucking didn't! I know nothing about this!'

'Just go, Danny – get out of my life.'

As he left, the front door slamming shut, I began to wonder whether he *was* involved. Perhaps Chrissy had blackmailed me, hoping to cause so many problems that my marriage would break up and she could get her man. But Danny must have known what she was up to. She could hardly keep it secret, with Alison going to her flat. My mind torn, I looked down at my naked breasts, my erect nipples, recalling the crude sex, the bondage and whipping. Had Danny known what I was being subjected to?

Answering the front door, I smiled at John as he gazed open-mouthed at my naked body. 'Come in,' I invited, opening the door wider.

'I'll call back if . . .'

'No, I want you to come in.'

'I've . . . Er . . .'

'Come into the lounge and tell me,' I said, closing the door and leading the way.

'I've got your money back. Well, most of it.'

'How did you manage that?'

'I went to the flat and told the girl that she'd end up in Holloway. I also have the videotapes and photographs,' he smiled, placing a carrier bag on the piano.

'You've done well, John – very well. Danny's been here and I told him everything.'

'What did he say?'

'He denied blackmailing me but admitted that he'd been screwing Chrissy. I told him to get out.'

'Selina, why are you naked?'

'I like my body. So, where to from here?'

'Well, it's over – my job's done.'

'Excuse me,' I smiled, answering the phone.

It was Tammy, ranting and raving about my synopsis. She loved the idea and wanted to discuss it, but I couldn't, not with John there. When she mentioned the advance, I almost keeled over. At last, my problems were solved – financially, anyway. Arranging to meet her for lunch the following day, I replaced the receiver, my face beaming as I turned to face John.

'Good news?' he asked.

'Very good!' I grinned. 'So, how much do I owe you?'

'God knows, I'll have to work it out. Selina, are you expecting someone?'

'Why do you ask?'

'Well, you're naked.'

'I told you, I like my body.'

'I have to go, I'm afraid.'

'I don't want you to go,' I smiled, licking my lips provocatively.

'I have an appointment, but I can come back later if . . .'

'Yes, I'd like that.'

Seeing him to the door, my cunt moistening, I knew I'd seduce him when he returned – as he knew. Imagining sucking his knob to orgasm, swallowing his gushing sperm, I went up to my den and found Crystal's phone number. Ringing her, I invited her round for a celebration drink.

'I'd like that,' she said in her cherubic tone.

'This evening, about eight.'

'OK, I'll be there. I've not been in touch because I was

worried about Alison, what she might do. If she finds out that . . .'

'She won't bother you now, it's all over. I'll tell you about it tonight.'

'See you later, then.'

Replacing the receiver, my clitoris swelling, I wondered whether to call Chrissy. She'd be in her new flat, pacing the floor in her anxiety. No job, stone broke, all she had was Danny. I'd lost my supposed best friend and my husband, but I'd found myself, my sexuality. I had Crystal, Dave, Barry, John – and an offer of an advance that would set me up for life. I had to ring her and tell her my good news.

'Chrissy, it's Selina,' I said brightly as she answered.

'Oh, er . . .'

'Don't worry, I'm not ringing to have a go at you. I just thought I'd let you know that, in some respects, I'm grateful for all you've done.'

'Grateful?'

'Is Danny there?'

'No, he . . .'

'I'd like to talk to him.'

'Hallo, Selina,' Danny said timidly.

'I've been offered an advance for my next book,' I enlightened him.

'Oh?'

'Half a million pounds.'

'*What?*'

'It's my autobiography. I've been working on it since the day the girl came here demanding money. It's about you, Chrissy, Alison, the crude sex, blackmail . . . Don't worry, I've changed the names to protect the guilty.'

'You can't put me in the book, Selina! Ask Chrissy, she'll tell you that I had nothing to do with it.'

'I don't want to ask Chrissy anything.'

'She's told me all about it and I'm not staying with her. After all she's done, I don't want to know her.'

'That makes two of us. Anyway, now I have the end to the book I'd better get working.'

'Selina, can't we work something out?'

'No, Danny – we can't.'

'What about the house – our house?'

'*My* house – you'll sign your half over to me.'

'Selina, I'm innocent!'

'Are you? We are gathered here today . . . Let no man put asunder. Goodbye, Danny.'

Returning to the lounge, I took the money and the incriminating evidence from the carrier bag. Gazing at the photographs, my arousal soaring as I focused on a huge penis embedded deep within my distended bottom-hole, I smiled. I'd won, if it could be called winning. The battle was over, my transformation complete. I now had nights of lesbian sex with Crystal to look forward to, sessions of crude sex with Barry, Dave . . . and John? Good and bad, love and hate, sex with lust, sex with love – who knew? Perhaps, with John, the coin might turn again.

I never saw the bitch again, or Chrissy. And I never discovered if Danny had been involved in the plot or not. But it didn't matter. The nightmare had ended and, whether the richer or the poorer for my debacle, I had my life to resume.

I now have money, power, sex – possibly love. But, as I put the finishing touches to my story, I wonder. Have I lost myself or found myself? Perhaps a bitter-sweet intermingling of the two. My fingers poised over the keyboard, I await the next chapter with trepidation.